Brothers of the Milky Way

Tim Adams

WWW.BLUETOWERPRESS.COM

This is a work of fiction that includes some real-life people and events, and several chapters set in a real-life contest. Detailed information can be found in Fact and Fiction, on page 396.

First printing 2013

Book cover art by Larry Welz

ISBN 978-0-9896203-1-4

Table of Contents

PART I

CHAPTER ONE

The only reason a joker like me got a lead on the big famous Cuauhtémoc cup that Saturday is that I drove my 'Cuda out to Fiesta Speedway for the weekly drag races they used to run back there in the seventies. And the only reason I did *that* was that I was an Asphalt Monarch. I'd got the Monarchs flier announcing the Vulcan of Speed cylinder head giveaway, and figured out the clue on KBXC, and thought I stood as good a chance of walking away with those heads as anyone in NorCal.

Well, I didn't get the heads. My hated foe Earl Howser got them, and I met up with an unnatural human spawn of Bigfoot and a Kodiak bear, and that monster clobbered me so bad I can sometimes still feel the spot on my jaw where he slugged me. As you'll see shortly. I lost that hand, in life's big poker game. I admit it.

But what I drew instead was the missing card for a king high straight flush in one of the biggest hands ever played on earth. Because I never would have got the lead on the Cuauhtémoc cup if I hadn't gone chasing after those heads, and next to the cup the heads and the Hope Diamond and the Star of India and the damn Koh-I-Noor put together wasn't worth four plastic toys out of a Cracker Jack box. It was bare minimum the single most important object ever to come out of the ancient Americas, just like Logos said, with rumors and myths and legends swirling about it clear back to the Civil War, and at least half the rumors claimed it had mysterioso psychic and supernatural powers.

Which no one could prove or disprove one way or the other. Because no one had any idea where it was.

No one, that was, except me. Thanks to what I saw at Fiesta. I was the sport who got the big lead on it.

But I'm getting ahead of myself. I better back up.

•   •   •

The cylinder head kit in the giveaway was the Vulcan of Speed model, only one notch below the full race Empyrean of Speed model in the Mr. C. Engineering catalog. You didn't get the roller rocker arms or the titanium intake valves. Everything else was in there. One piece stainless valves, double springs, titanium retainers, and the main course: the C Engineering limited edition modification of the Sebring casting, with the relocated exhaust and the custom porting. It said in the catalog that a personally designated apprentice of legendary chief C team engineer Boss Maryland inspected every head in the Vulcan series.

Exclusively for the B and RB series Mopar big block. If you wanted free heads for your 'Stang or your rat motor Chevelle, you got to wait for another contest.

"Stay tuned to KBXC for more information." That was the only clue. That, and that the giveaway would be within one week.

I got the Asphalt Monarchs flier announcing the giveaway on Tuesday afternoon, right before my swing shift at Hardy's. Right away I told myself not to pull a cardiac, because I knew instantaneously what a major rod I had for those Vulcans and what a dim shot I had at actually getting them.

But by mid-shift at Hardy's I was so hot and bothered that I was putting go-backs on the wrong shelves and mixing up all my cash register codes. The Mopar B series was *my engine*. At least half the Mr. C giveaways was for Chevy parts. What was the odds that he'd have a giveaway practically in my back yard, and it would be for top of the line heads that would bolt right onto my block?

I hunted up KBXC on the FM band and zeroed in the Alpine in my 'Cuda on it, and the clock alarm in my bedroom, too, and even hauled an old Magnavox into the crapper, so I could listen in while I sudsed up my chiseled Grecian physique. It was a country station. My skin practically turned green from listening to old Merle and Tammy and George moan and slobber on their banjos, but I kept the volume up, just in case the DJ dropped the bomb in mid-song.

By Wednesday I'd almost forgot that the giveaway was in a contest. Those heads was *mine*. You show me one Mopar rodder who wouldn't have sold nudie pix of Pat Nixon to Chairman Mao for those heads. Even if my block wasn't ready. I didn't even have a start on a second engine like I'd planned, 'cause the block I'd got from that communist Logos had a crack in it. But still. If I got those Vulcans, I'd do something. Work triple shifts at Hardy's. Sell Mom into slavery.

Just the *look* of those Vulcans. With all Vulcan of Speed class and Empyrean of Speed class heads, you got a special gold rocker arm cover imprinted with the Mr. C Professional Class logo, real tasteful and high class, with Security Torx fasteners and a monogrammed wrench for your keychain. I could just see myself lining up for a bacon double cheese at Pilgrim's, and in the next line there's my ex main squeeze Cindy with her barfy new boyfriend Milt, who's got a neck like a Pez dispenser and never washes his underwear, so there's always a yellow ring around the collar, and I glance at them like I can hardly be bothered, and then accidentally on purpose drop the keychain on the counter while I fish out the change. So they can't miss the Mr. C Professional Class monogram. Whoops. Oh, hi there, Cindy. Didn't see you come in. Almost dropped my keys. Heh heh.

Or it would happen in the parking lot. That was better. There'd Cindy be yakking with Milt, and maybe disgusting Earl Howser, who I'd hated since he'd pantsed me in seventh grade P.E., and I rumble in in my 'Cuda, and Cindy kind of sneers, but they all notice how strong my 'Cuda sounds, 'cause I've got the new engine in there that I'd build around the Vulcans. With my hood off. Why not? Just leave the hood in the garage. And I don't even look at Cindy when I pull in. Like I can hardly be bothered, like my life is so different now that I'm a Vulcans owner, but I can feel their eyes on me, 'cause my 'Cuda sounds like a damn C Team Kydra, practically, and I rev the engine a little before I shut it down. Just a little blip rev, like an accident. Then walk in without looking at them. And, Jack, I know, I *know*, that they're all going to walk over to my 'Cuda and check out those gleaming gold rocker arm covers while I'm inside getting my bacon double cheese, and reading the logo. Mr. C Professional Class. Vulcan of Speed. Maybe then Cindy would think twice about telling her girlfriends that I wanted to be intimate without cleaning the engine crud out from my fingernails first, and that I didn't stay up on my elbows.

•   •   •

The D.J. dropped the bomb on Saturday at 2:00 a.m., two hours into my graveyard shift at Hardy's. I was restocking the pet care section on aisle 12, right under one of the store speakers. I'd talked Dirk into letting me dial in KBXC on the intercom. Of course he would have said no if he possibly could have, being Dirk, but nobody cared what you listened to in there after midnight. It was all restocking.

"And now, a special news item," the D.J. said. "As many of you know, the great Mr. C, the legendary Mr. C is offering another giveaway this week. Our station is honored that he's chosen KBXC to convey news of the giveaway to Bay Area car buffs."

I froze. I stood there with a can of dog food in my hand and my ear cocked up at the ceiling speaker, like a SWAT team had a twelve gauge leveled at my back.

Dirk was about five feet away, tallying up inventory. He was listening too.

"Today," said the DJ, "is the one year anniversary of the death of Concord drag racer Chet Siegel. Many of you motor race fans will remember the cherry red '62 Dart that Chet campaigned in Super Stock here in the late sixties."

The DJ was Farmer Fred Dayton. I'd gotten to know every one of the syrupy country-western SOBs from listening to KBXC all week. He'd posed for his DJ photo in suspenders and a corn cob.

This had to be the big clue. They'd have to feed me intravenous if I had to listen to one more C&W singer blubber for his cider and grits. I couldn't take it anymore.

"Today Chet Siegel's death will be commemorated by the living legend of motor sports himself, Mr. C. A matching pair of modified, race ready C Enterprises 'Vulcan of Speed' cylinder heads will be given away in Chet's honor. The Vulcans will fit all Dodge and Plymouth B and RB series big blocks. Many of you know that Chet campaigned a 413 wedge in his DART.

"Again, race fans: the giveaway is *today*. Today.

"And now, for your listening pleasure ..."

And then he intro'd *Jolene*, or some other gut-churning C&W number that hicks moan along with while they're pulling on milky cow tits in Bakersfield. I looked down at the spazzy Great Dane slobbering up at me from the labels of the dog food cans and tried to straightjacket my brain. That was *it?*! What kind of clue was that?! He hadn't even give one hint about where they was hid.

"He bought it at Fiesta," Dirk said.

I looked at him. He had a faraway glint in his icy blue eyes, like he was Himmler watching a fresh load of Jews getting hauled out of the ovens at Dachau. I'll fill you in on my charming boss Dirk in a few more chapters.

"I saw it," Dirk said. "That Dart bounced down the track like a tumbleweed. They had to pull him out through the windshield. Like a bloody limp rag. Blood all over the air vents."

Dirk grinned and nodded a couple of times, like he was smacking his lips on the memory. It was the first real smile I'd seen on him since before Christmas, when the Hardy's big wheels had said he couldn't bring a gun to work anymore.

Then he looked at me, and my expression must have told him he'd accidentally told me something valuable. He gave me a dirty look and went off to do inventory on another aisle.

I was so amped I could hardly work. Of course. Fiesta. That the heads was being given in honor of Chet Siegel. *That* was the clue. Why hadn't I figured it out right away? Everybody knew how Mr. C felt about honoring fallen race track warriors. As soon as Farmer Fred had said the heads was in honor of Chet Siegel, I should have known. It practically *had* to be Fiesta. He'd hide the heads where Chet had breathed his last.

And I kept dropping the damn cans of dog food I was supposed to shelve, and messing up the rows, and trying to talk myself down. I'd pulled graveyard shift on Saturday, so I'd been awake to hear the clue. I'd been right under the speaker when the clue came. And Dirk had filled me in. If all that wasn't a sign that Zeus wanted to take a little R&R from Watergate and the India nuke test to be real sure that someone named Hank in Prado Diablo, California got his Vulcan of Speed heads, well, I didn't know what was.

•　•　•

I clocked out of Hardy's at 8:00 a.m. Usually I scarfed up some chow after a graveyard shift, but today I just hopped in my 'Cuda and went. Fiesta was way the hey out in the sloughs near

Union City. They opened the track at 8:00. I was going to be close to an hour late.

I got off the freeway and wheeled onto Cargo Road leading up to the track. The usual row of high school freeloaders was parked on the soft shoulder leading up to the main entrance, with teenagers standing on their hoods and rooftops, holding their hands over their eyes to squint in the sun glare so they could take in a free show over the fence without buying a ticket. As I drove closer I heard the BRRRRAAAAAAAUUUUUGGGHHHH of that good, good drag racing action, and glanced over the fence to see the front end of a righteous looking '55 blasting down the strip. They was probably a half hour into qualifications.

I got to the main entrance and pulled in behind the cars waiting to pay their way in, and took a gander at the vacant lot on the other side of Cargo Road. And got my first surprise of the morning.

They was hosting some kind of big hippy pow-wow there. Across the road from a drag race. I swear. Somebody had screwed up royal. There had to be five hundred longhairs milling around the lot, with a big banner proclaiming All is One or some other hippy crapola, and dudes with massive dreadlocks and giant Klondike beards that some lucky flea could raise a big family in, and dudettes who matched the dudes follicle for follicle except for the Klondikes. On their legs especially. Some of the long-hairs was clustered around tables piled high with Indian print bed spreads and dope pipes and other hippy junk, and others was standing around beaming at each other, like wasn't it just wonderful that Universal Love let them meet in a vacant lot that rodders chucked beer bottles at, and squish dried up cow patties through the toes in their sandals, and smell 110 octane racing gas, and try to talk over the BRRRAAAAAAAAUUUUUGGGH-HHH of blown V8s thundering down the drag strip across the road from them.

Typical hippies. I thought I was going to heave. The guy ahead of me in line pulled forward and I blipped the throttle to keep up, and looked across Cargo again. Now some of the hippy chicks was holding hands and dancing this Ring around the Ros-ie thing. Like kindergartners. A couple of them would've looked half-decent if somebody had turned a power wash on them, and maybe locked them inside a beauty salon for a month. Not that hippy men had the taste to appreciate mascara or eye shadow, or even basic femininity. Why did they have to? What I'd heard — and I wasn't ready to swear to it, but it had the ring of truth — was that there was a secret code among the hippies, and if you said it to a hippy chick her eyes would glaze over and she'd drop trou right there and give it up. It was a point of honor.

What I wanted to know was why Nixon didn't do something. His goose was cooked over Watergate. He had a free hand. He could send a Green Beret team out to plant some ICBMs under San Bruno Mountain State Park, and just nuke Frisco off the peninsula and turn it into a floating island. Then just shove the whole bunch of them across the Pacific to China so they could read the Little Red Book with the other commies. Minimal loss of life. Maybe I'd send the White House a letter.

•   •   •

I paid my admission and got in and found a spot for my 'Cuda and set all my various crook frustraters, and got out to look around. It was a pretty typical Saturday morning for Fiesta. There were some family member type spectators in the stands, but most of the hub-bub was in the pit area, because there was maybe eight dudes that had come to race for every one that had come just to spectate.

The tech inspections was still going on. I looked at Old Man Willis, with his track ID badge dangling off his belt, checking under the hood of a 427 Galaxy. Willis had campaigned a tricked out flathead at Santa Ana back in the early fifties. He'd known Chet. He'd known Chet good. So I started to walk over there, but then Willis got in an argument with the Galaxy driver about his fuel line, and all the racers lined up for tech behind the Galaxy started to look irritated, and I figured no. Willis wouldn't have the heads. Mr. C wasn't going to give Willis something else to do when he was running tech.

All around me was open trailers that had hauled in the strip-only racers, and then Chevelles and 'Stangs and 'Cudas like mine, and an old school Fairlane and a bitchin' 389 Ventura, and old old *old* school from-the-ground-up hot-rodded Willys and

❧ 7 ❧

Highboys. There were full on racers with roll cages and slicks, and then everyday street cars, with Edelbrock and Mr. C. and Weiand and Iskendarian decals and windshield stickers, with their race classes lettered in shoe polish on their windshields.

Some of the cars was just parked, and other cars had their hoods up, with guys dinking around with their carb jetting or timing. Race fans was kicked back in the stands, watching a rat motor Chevelle and a Charger doing their burn-outs on the track. I watched the burn-outs, too, and the burning rubber smoke cloud drift in front of the Christmas tree, and then watched the Chevelle and Charger get staged, and then listened to those engines roar as the yellow lights click click clicked down to the green. The Charger red-lighted, and the Chevelle pulled a five foot wheelstand, but he still got a good E.T.

It was shaping up to be another fine day at Fiesta, sunny and hot. I walked along between the cars, dressed in the Joe Cool attire I favored when I didn't have to get duded up like a fry cook in my Hardy's apron, with the heels of my Dingos clicking on the asphalt under my stovepipe jeans, and my leather gunslinger vest flapping on my Mopar belt buckle, and my gorgeous brown locks just a tasteful inch over my ears, unlike the Workers of the World types across Cargo. Where were those heads at? I had to be scientific about it.

•　　•　　•

And it was just as I was thinking that I had all day to look and could mellow out a bit, and maybe even spring for a chili cheese dog at the track cafe, that I happened to glance up at the stands, and saw a figure I wished to God I didn't recognize.

But which very unfortunately I did. Instantaneously, like you'd ID a big oozing bump on your cheek as a pimple, and the siren coming up behind you as a black-and-white about to give you a ticket.

Earl Howser.

Earl Howser, all five feet, eight repulsive inches of him, in his t-shirt and mirror shades and that damn windbreaker he had to wear everywhere, even to his sister's wedding. Stepping down the aisle and checking under the seats of every row he passed, real methodical.

Looking for something.

Earl Howser, who'd stepped on the backs of my shoes the whole time I was fourth grade line leader, and pantsed me in middle school, and told all the girls after high school that I was a blood relative of Charles Manson, which I'm not, so I could hardly get a date. Earl Howser, who I'd had to cashier with for one solid year at Hardy's, before he got the speed shop job he wouldn't stop bragging about, and who'd taken a break or shut down his cash register every single time a problem customer had come up, so Hank would have to deal with it. Like old man Bates. He carried all his change in his underwear, and held up the line for ten minutes while he licked his fingers and counted out all the wet, slimy nickels and pennies that had been jiggling all over town tucked under the family jewels. I didn't want to wait on Bates and handle those nickels anymore than you would. But Earl never had. He'd always made himself AWOL.

I froze. For ten seconds I gaped at him while my gut corded up and my neck went cold and my whole life flashed before my eyes, practically. Maybe there was some other explanation. Maybe he was just hunting for something he'd forgot up there.

But I knew better. Not from the way he was checking left and right as he went down the aisle, and eyeballing under every seat. And not from the set of ignition keys I knew he had jingling in his pocket, that fired up the 383 B series in his Charger.

Earl had heard that clue on KBXC, too. He was after my cylinder heads.

I almost panicked. I started walking twice as fast, twisting my head to check out every unlikely possible hiding place in sight. Not Earl Howser. My brain filled up with horrible fantasies, of Earl pulling into the lot at Hardy's when I was out on break, and everybody walking up and checking out those gold Vulcan rocker arm covers when he popped the hood, so I had to go over too, and Earl standing next to his Charger and playing dork of the month with one of his cigarettes.

That was his thing. His cigarettes. Oh, you're just so cool, Earl. He'd make a big deal of cupping his hand around his cig when he lit up even if there wasn't any more wind than the Sahara desert, and wave the match about ten times after the cig was lit, or use his dim bulb Playboy lighter that he said Hef had given away at the mansion, like anyone cared, and puff up a little cloud out of his fat mouth, and you'd get to look at your reflection in his aviators while he sucked the whole load back in through his nostrils. Like nobody else had ever done that with cigarette smoke before. Or he'd look away and tap his cheek with his fore-finger to make smoke rings come out. I swear, I'd actually seen him haul out a pocket mirror and *watch* himself make smoke rings, instead of looking at who he talked to. And he'd say "'Fraid not" a million times, and call everybody "Clyde," including me, and say "Arriverderci" when you finally got rid of him, and try to act like Steve McQueen in everything he did, even though Steve McQueen didn't say "'Fraid not" or "Arriverderci" or call people Clyde, and probably would've jumped out of a 707 with no chute if he'd known anyone like Earl even liked him. Earl had seen *Cincinnati Kid* about five hundred times and *Bullitt* about two million, and always talked about the car chase in *Bullitt*, like you couldn't see a movie for yourself, and the differences between his Charger and the Charger in the flick, and if he found those heads it would be worse than ever. He'd never shut up. He'd come by Hardy's for cigs for the next thirty years just so he could flash that monogrammed key chain at me while he dug out his wallet.

And now I felt like old Zeus had turned on me and set a trap, and was leaning out of his top fuel dragster in the wild blue yonder up above and thumbing his nose at me while I walked around like a headless chicken, and tried to spot the heads where they'd never be hid. Not Earl. I'd rather C had give the heads to the Sierra Club.

Two miserable minutes ticked by. I went into the track cafe and started peering behind the tables in there. Like Mr. C would ever stick thousand dollar cylinder heads where somebody could drip ketchup on them. I was trying to think clear, but it was like I was a coach of a football team down thirty-five to zip in the fourth quarter. My whole game was blown.

In the stands Earl had finished up two aisles, and was start-ing on the third. I couldn't tell if he'd seen me.

I made myself stop walking. For a second I just stood with my eyes closed. *Think.* I had as good a shot as Earl did. Where would C hide those heads? Think.

Then I remembered the hippies.

Of course. Of *course.* Hadn't C stashed a Dominator carb with a bag lady when he'd run the big Holley giveaway in Tampa? Wasn't it just like him to throw you a curve, and play a joke, and hide something where you'd least expect to find it? What self-respecting hot rodder wanted to go out there with the mud people and root around in their hippy wampum for a set of Mopar heads?

It was worth a try. *More* than worth a try. It was the best idea I'd had all morning.

I walked to the track entrance, and got my hand stamped, and crossed Cargo Drive.

If somebody had just told me then that I was taking practically the single most important steps of my entire life. That almost everything that happened in my life afterward unfolded from the decision to go where I went next.

•   •   •

It was some kind of hippy crafts fair. I saw that when I got closer. There was a table of longhairs selling peasant blouses and hemp purses and tie-died this and that, so you could walk around Frisco dressed like a damn Neanderthal, and another table selling incense, and another selling candles almost guaranteed to burn your house down. Somebody was playing some god-awful hippy sitar music that actually made old Merle on KBXC sound good, and I had to dodge around a couple of longhairs swaying along with it, and as I walked into the thick of things a tidal wave of patchouli and sandalwood and unshaven armpit body odor walloped me in the nostrils so bad I practically keeled over in the cow patties.

Near the main entrance a chick and a guy was selling hippy gee gaws from a long table. I figured I'd talk to them first.

The chick was about my age, twenty-four. She was decent enough looking. She had real thick, black hair that a baldie like Yul Brynner or Telly Savalas might have hated her for on sight, parted straight down the middle and falling around the ruffled shoulders of her white peasant blouse. Maybe Irish, or Italian, or Jewish. Maybe something else.

The guy next to her was the biggest hippy I'd ever seen. No. Sorry. Correction. The biggest *human* I'd ever seen. Practically the biggest mammal. I'd have to go to the zoo to check up. The two of them didn't look like an item. Maybe a chick would've laid down under him if she'd been big enough to play starting guard for the Packers, at least if you paid her first. Paid her a lot.

I don't mean to exaggerate his size. If you spend a couple of winters up in the Arctic, and canvas every inch of Alaska and the Yukon, you're bound to see at least four polar bears that big. He was pushing seven foot tall, and was damn near as wide as he was vertical, and had all his holy hippiness clad in a set of farmer blue denim overalls, probably because that was all that could fit him. With no shirt on under it. His shoulders were wide enough to bust through a couple of door jambs, and he had arms that looked ready to heave Al Oerter and the discus along with him clear out of the stadium, and his shoulders and arms was all coated with sweaty, curly hippy fur, so you could have just hung his whole carcass up on a rack at Carpeteria and used his body as an area rug. I could smell the sweat, too. Capital U Ugly. And he had a big Karl Marx beard that all the bugs probably loved to crawl around in, so they could dine on the left-over soup matted around his mouth, and a big mane of scraggly hippy hair.

On the table in front of the chick was a lot of hippy type jewelry: glass and topaz stuff, bracelets and necklaces and so on. In front of the gorilla, I swear, was a bunch of handmade soap. I thought that was rich. He sold it, but he didn't use it himself. Like a teetotaler who owns a liquor store.

In the background I could hear the track announcer blabbing about who was coming to the line at Fiesta, and the E.T.s of the cars that had just run. I walked up to the table.

"'Scuse me," I said. "I'm trying to find something in a contest. Did somebody happen to come by and drop off something here?"

The chick brushed back that thick hair of hers and looked up at me friendly enough. Maybe she had some Middle East in her. She had a strong, straight schnoz, like I thought somebody from back there might have, and high cheekbones, and brown eyes. Pale looking, though. Maybe part Spanish, or Mexican.

"A contest?" she asked.

Next to her Godzilla snorted and looked away.

"Yeah. There's a famous racer who's having a big giveaway today. Did somebody drop off, like, a big box here? Or a couple of cylinder heads?"

The chick looked thoughtful. "Cylinder halves," she said.

"No. Heads. They're called cylinder heads." I held my hands in front of my chest. "Couple of big metal blocks. With springs bolted onto the top of them. Cylinder heads. Or they might be in a box."

The chick sat back and sniffed at the air, like I'd just described something from Planet Klepton. Big Stuff snorted again, louder, and looked away, like he could hardly stand having me in front of his table, and was just hoping I'd go away before he had to look at me.

"We don't have anything like that here," the chick said. "I'm sorry."

"Well, did you see anybody wandering around here who didn't exactly fit in? Maybe an old guy with gray hair? Real sociable dude. Or anybody, carrying a big box, and like looking ..."

Big Stuff couldn't stand it anymore.

"Sir, I'm sorry," he broke in. "Sir. This is a crafts fair. Everything for sale here is of benefit to the environment and healthful. We do not have anything related to car racing. Nothing."

He'd turned his head toward me, but he was looking at my stomach while he talked, like I was so repulsive he couldn't stand to meet my eyes. His voice didn't go with the rest of him. It was high and reedy, like some Yale attorney waving his briar pipe around and saying "Be that as it may" and "As it were" on *Meet the Press*. Except Big Stuff would have popped somebody like that down his gullet like a soda cracker.

The chick sighed. Big Stuff was getting agitated.

"We do not have anything that could possibly interest someone like you. Please. Our fair never should have been booked for this location. A terrible mistake has been made. So if you would just run along now, and rejoin your fun little friends across the street, you can make lots of noise and not bother us."

I picked up one of the soap bars.

"Have you ever thought of using some of this stuff, instead of just selling it?"

"Attention, race fans!!" squawked the track announcer's voice over the loudspeaker. "Race fans! We have a special announcement!"

Big Stuff had a comeback for me, but I didn't pay attention. I put down the soap bar and took a step back and listened. A sick feeling was already spreading through me. Like I already knew.

"One of our lucky spectators at the track is a richer man this morning. He has just found two new, absolutely brand new Vulcan of Speed cylinder heads for the big block Chrysler wedge engine. These two high performance heads have been donated by Mr. C Enterprises in honor of the memory of Chet Siegel, who as many of you know ..."

And then the track announcer went on about Chet's death. I just waited. My gut was bonking around like a Maytag on spin cycle, and I felt green and bilious, but I still had hope. I'd listened to that cud-chewing country slop for one solid week for nothing. I already knew that. But as long as a certain disgusting someone hadn't won those heads instead of me. Please, I thought. Please. Not ...

"... and let's have a big round of applause for today's big winner: Earl Howser! That's Earl Howser, ladies and gentlemen!"

Some half-hearted applause came up.

I swung back toward the table slow and gazed off at the horizon. Earl. I thought I was going to die.

"Is that what you were looking for?" the chick asked.

I put my fingers on the table and leaned on my palms, and stared at a dippy hippy lanyard, and a dippy hippy bracelet, and a bunch of photos she had stacked up on her side of the table, with a shot of a St. Bernard wearing one of the dippy lanyards on top of it. Earl. He's got two new Vulcan of Speed heads, and I'm standing here looking at a shot of a dog wearing a hippy necklace. Up above I could practically see Zeus flip me off, and do his burn-outs, and launch his slingshot off toward Pluto. Earl. The whole universe had just used my face as an outhouse.

"Yes, that's what he was looking for," Godzilla said. "Somebody else won the cylinder heads. Oh, boo hoo hoo. You don't get to pollute the environment and make more noise. We're so terribly sorry. Now you can go back with your little racer friends and leave us alone."

"Jules, come on," the chick said.

"What are we *doing* here?!" Jules said. To her, not to me. "What was Mitchell thinking? That's a car race they're having over there, Evelyn. A car race. You know what those people are like."

He pointed at me, like I was something he wanted the handyman to be sure to scrape off.

"Just *look* at him. I'll bet all he reads are comic books!"

This last shot was fairly close to the mark, which didn't improve my mood any. I figured I might as well get into a hot-rodder-to-hippy insult fest, and let off a little steam.

I gave Evelyn a solemn look.

"Another thing Mitchell could do," I said, real slow, "is set up your longhair festival next to the Oakland Zoo. That way your friend wouldn't have to wander so far from his cage, and miss his morning feeding."

"I do not appreciate jokes about my size!"

I looked at Evelyn. "Or maybe you work at the zoo, and brought him out here for everybody's entertainment. What kind of tricks does he do?"

"Oh, har de har har," Jules shouted. "What a keen sense of humor! Oh, ho ho ho!"

Evelyn just looked mildly put out. Some of the soap-free set nearby was starting to sneak glances at us on account of the ruckus we was making, and at me especially, as I was about as out of place there as a Paxton supercharger on a VW Thing.

I picked up the stack of photos on the chick's side of the table and looked at the top shot of the idiot St. Bernard with the necklace, and then started to flip through the photos like I wanted to buy something.

"Where's the shot of him balancing the red rubber ball on his nose?" I asked.

"You'd really like to be in *Vietnam* right now, wouldn't you?" Jules shouted.

His cheeks was getting red. It looked like he'd been ticked off about their location all morning, and finally had someone from the car race he could holler at.

"Isn't that right? It's too bad the war's over, isn't it? You could be raping women and killing kids over there right now."

"Not until I see that shot of you with the rubber ball. I'm not going anywhere." I flipped through some more photos. "Or maybe there's one of you eating a banana."

Jules cussed me out some more. I looked at a shot of topaz earrings dangling off somebody's earlobes, and flipped to the next photo. I was just mad, that was all, from losing out to Earl and getting sniped at by Jules. So what if he clobbered me? He couldn't heave me any farther than the Bay Bridge. The water would break my fall.

The Evelyn chick looked nervous, for some reason. She was biting her lip and staring at the stack of photos while I flipped through them, and looked on the verge of saying something. Way, way in the back of my mind it dawned on me that maybe they was private photos, but I shook off that thought and kept looking. That was ridiculous. Why would she have had the stack out on the table with her jewelry crap?

I came to a personal photo, of Evelyn standing next to a guy in a kitchen somewhere. Then another personal shot, of a little kid with the clunky St. Bernard.

Jules was yakking about how some day I was going to be conscious and liberated despite myself, and realize what a big reeking pile of dog crap my mind was today. I tossed off a throwaway line about his size, and flipped through the shots. I was getting curious.

And then I came to the photo that changed my life.

It was a close-up shot of Evelyn sitting behind two things on a table. She looked a little blurred, because the camera was focused on the objects in front of her, and not her face. She looked sad.

One of the objects was a framed 8 x 10 of the guy who'd been in the shot with her in the kitchen. A semi-hippy looking dude, about her age.

The second object was a statue. Or a cup.

Maybe half the size of the 8 x 10. It was round, but with a flat bottom, so it could sit on the table without rolling around, and a flat top, too.

It looked like it was made of stone. A kind of mask was chiseled onto it, like an Indian mask. There was a ribbony looking shape on the forehead, and then symbols carved on the ribbon. Like religious symbols.

I almost flipped past that shot. I swear. My fingers practically closed on the edges and turned to the next one. My whole life afterward would have been different if I had.

But something buried deep inside my brain fussed at me not to. I stopped, and looked at the cup some more. The longer I looked at it, the louder the fussing got.

I'd seen it before. It wasn't just any cup. It was important.

"Excuse me," Evelyn said. "Could I have my photos back?"

And then things started to happen fast.

She stood up and reached for the stack. She looked more than nervous now. She looked downright frightened. I started to hand them to her — in a dazed way; where the hey had I seen that cup thing before? Where? — and then just as she gets her fingers on the stack the light bulb clicked on. I remembered the *Look* article and the TV interviews and the big shot TV news anchor yakking about it in his solemn national news voice, with a photo of the cup on the screen beside him.

The Cuauhtémoc cup. Oh my god. The Cuauhtémoc cup.

It was like she could read my mind. Like she could see the light bulbs going off, and that was why she was scared. She grabbed the photos and pulled and I should have let go, but I said wait, let me just look for one more, and then it seemed like we was having a tug of war, and then Jules got into it.

"Take your hands off her!" he roared, and now all the other longhairs are looking at us, and "I just want to see it!" I said, and Jules kind of grabbed me, and the chick has got her photos and is already pulling her hippy jewelry crap into a pile and getting ready to take off. Like me seeing that photo meant *vamonos*, but quick. And then Jules grabbed me, and all I did was try to put my hand on Evelyn's arm to get her to wait up a minute, I swear, that's all, and then "Assault, assault!" Jules yells, and slugged me, with a fist big enough to take first prize at the State Fair, at least if his hand had been a roast turkey.

The next thing I knew I was lying on my back trying to remember what galaxy I was in, and looking at the dusty bare feet and sandals of the hippies who'd gathered around me, and Jules is still bellowing about assault. He wasn't a guy who had to make an effort to hit you hard. It took me nearly a minute to decide I was still on the same planet, and struggle to my feet. Then all these hippies around me are glowering like I stole their gro-lamps and rolling papers, and this guy comes up who says he's Security, and informed me in no uncertain terms that I'd best skedaddle, but quick, if I knew what was good for me.

And I looked and looked all around, and Evelyn and all her stuff was gone.

Chapter Two

I drove back to Prado like I'd just picked up a full pre-frontal at Camarillo. Tailgaters drafted my bumper and cars cut me off, and the KBXC DJs kept annihilating my ear drums with a C&W barrage, and I was too dazed to touch the dial. I shifted and steered like I was in a video game I'd been playing for two days straight. The whole side of my face felt like a cheddar soufflé from where Jules had slugged me, but I didn't think he'd busted anything important in there, and might not have cared if he had.

The Cuauhtémoc cup. *THE* Cuauhtémoc cup. I remembered the talking heads giving some Harvard archeologist the third degree about that cup on TV, and the magazine covers, and how the local paper ran a story about Logos, 'cause he'd helped ID it. Maybe it hadn't been in the news for a couple of years, but neither had Roswell or Area 51. Every TV anchor from Bangor to Barstow would've hocked his teleprompter to get an exclusive on that cup.

And Hank Kruzenski had just seen it.

Or I thought I had. I told myself not to get a rupture. All I'd seen was a photo that looked like it. I knew I had to get Logos in on it, even if I was still P.O.'d at him 'cause of that cracked block. But I wasn't ready yet. He wouldn't help me if he thought I was just blowing smoke. I had to check it out first.

And maybe I was wrong. Maybe I was sure I'd just seen the Cuauhtémoc cup, and it was actually something else. But I still couldn't help imagining Hank's name up in lights, and what I'd say to Huntley and Brinkley, and swapping repartee with Johnny and Ed on the *Tonight Show*. I wondered if I'd have to drive to the studio, or if they'd spring for a plane ticket. I'd never been up in a plane before.

•   •   •   •

As soon as I stepped into the history department the librarian looked at me like there must be a busted toilet somewhere I'd come to fix. Then she saw I didn't have any tools, and started rummaging around in her desk like she had to have an old *Archie & Jughead* comic in there to feed me. Maybe that was what you learned in librarian school, if somebody who looked like me mistook the library for the DMV and came in by accident.

I told her what I wanted. She gave me a suspicious squint, like I ought to spell "cat" and "dog" first to prove I could read, but then she seemed to get all excited about Helping Primitive Man Find a Book, and walked me over to the card catalog, and talked at me like I still wore diapers while she helped me locate the title I wanted.

It was the old Centennial Heritage book about the Sioux wars, with the chapters on Chief Red Cloud and President Grant. I could have just gone home and fished out my old *Look* with the 1950s photo of Mr. C holding the cup at Bonneville, but you couldn't see the cup as good in that one, even if the shot was practically as famous as the flag shot at Iwo Jima. The studio photo taken after the Sioux Wars was way better.

I must have sat at that table and looked at that Centennial Heritage photo for ten minutes. I studied the eyes and the nose and mouth of the cup, and the marks on the ribbon on the forehead, every one, so I could tell them from memory. I rooted back in my head to what I'd seen of the cup in Evelyn's photo. My brain still felt fuzzed up, but I tried.

They looked the same. I felt the blood beating behind my temples, and my fingers shake as I held the book open. I tried to talk myself down. Maybe my eyes was playing tricks. But I was practically positive. The long, long lost cup, that Logos said was the single most precious artifact ever to come out of the ancient Americas. Hank Kruzenski had just gotten a lead on it.

•   •   •

I headed to the library pay phones. I hadn't slept for a solid day or eaten anything since the night before, but I felt like I'd just woke up. I wasn't on the roster to start my Hardy's shift until four p.m. I still had time left.

Unfortunately, the only number I had for Logos was for his notorious-all-over-Prado-Diablo lunatic family. That meant I'd have to talk to one of them and likely get dragged into the latest De Mello hullabaloo, but that was way better than actually going over there. So I called and crossed my fingers, but no soap. All I got was the recording for Frank De Mello All American House Painters, with the sound of the bombs going off and the actor with the big baritone reading the Declaration of Independence, and old man Frank yakking about house paint and patriotism. Which didn't mean nobody was home, 'cause they was usually too busy fighting each other to pick up the phone anyway. I had to go over there.

•   •   •

The De Mello household had to be the most infamous in Contra Costa county. Maybe they had some nut job in Pittsburg or Concord or Walnut Creek I hadn't heard of, but I doubted it. The neighbors usually put up with it 'cause Frank painted their houses for free, but I didn't think it was a good deal for them, 'cause people was always cruising by to snicker at the latest monstrosity Frank had erected on his lawn. Then there was the police. They wouldn't go out there anymore for anything milder than a serial killing, and with my own two eyes I'd actually seen the chief in plainclothes in his family station wagon — on his day off, with his family in there — cruise by the house just to treat his kids to a Har de Har on the latest De Mello shenanigans.

The problem started with old man Frank De Mello. He was one of those real ra ra immigrants who think the US of A is the greatest thing since sliced bread. He'd recite the Pledge of Allegiance if you looked at him sideways, and he still sent a pound of Omaha steaks every year to his old citizenship class teacher, even though he'd got naturalized over twenty years ago and the teacher kept telling him that he didn't eat meat. Which was pretty much Frank's mug shot in life right there, sending a hundred bucks of sirloin every year to a vegetarian.

But all that was fine. Or at least with me it was. If Frank had stopped there. But he didn't. He was way, way too gung ho about everything. Like Mom and me loved the U.S.A. too, but that didn't mean we had to paint the whole house red, white and blue, with *America the Beautiful* playing on low 24/7 from speakers next to the front door, like Frank had, or put up a flagpole on the lawn big enough to hook a low-flying Cessna. SFO pilots actually used that flagpole as a landmark. Or Frank's free speech thing. I was pro life. Kind of. Or I thought I was. But that didn't mean I was going to put a giant billboard on my lawn of a dead fetus, with klieg lights on it, and make the neighbors look at it for three months.

The De Mello wagon had really gone off the tracks when the next to oldest kid, Barry Goldwater De Mello, turned seventeen, and the boy's dean found about thirty womens' high heels stuffed in his locker. Then it turned out his bedroom closet was full of them, too, and there was slobber and bite marks on the toes and heels. So Frank insists that Barry needs a stint in juvie, and that got Barry P.O.'d, so he got an iron cross tattooed on his forehead for revenge. 'Cause he knew that would mess up the yearly photo for Frank De Mello's All American House Painters full page ad in the yellow pages. Getting that yellow pages photo taken was the highlight of Frank's existence, next to his Michelangelo lawn displays. He'd bring a pro photographer out and put up special lights on the front lawn, with the family in make-up and new clothes. Frank thought everybody in Prado Diablo was going to turn to that ad as soon as the new phone book came, and look at how his family had grown in the past year, and go "Awwww!"

Now Barry's got an Iron Cross. The photog said "That's okay," and posed Barry holding his hand up in front of his forehead, like he's blocking out the sun. But now the other kids are going south, too, and the next year the oldest kid, Spiro Agnew De Mello, has joined Voodoo Disciples and has a full-on biker beard. The photog tried to stall that out by having Spiro cup his hands in front of his chin. But that just made him look like he was about to barf, and then Frank threw in the towel. The yellow page photo the next year showed Frank kicking over a barrel of rotten apples, and the apples flying out of the barrel has got pictures of his kids on them, with a big dialogue balloon saying "Bad Apples!" coming out of Frank's mouth. Nixon's Veep had said that, about bad apples. Frank thought he was right.

Except Logos' picture, just Logos' picture, was on a cloud floating over Frank's head, with light beams coming out of it. That was one thing Frank had done that had paid off. Years ago he'd got all hot and bothered about the Children of Darkness, which was what Frank called kids in communist countries, and he'd adopted Logos out of Korea. Then it turned out the adoptee was strictly non-earthling in the IQ department, and was the only one of Frank's kids to turn out decent, too.

Logos thought that dealing with his fruitcake family was his cross to bear, which was part of why he hung around Prado. Not me. I had my own problems. I gave that house as wide a berth as possible.

• • •

But I had to go out there now. I parked my 'Cuda out of sight of the house and walked real careful to the corner and snuck a peek around. No soap. Frank was right in the front yard. Worse, he was working on this absolute monstrosity lawn display I'd heard customers snickering about at Hardy's. I'd thought they were joking. This was over the top even for Frank.

But there it was. Frank was still upset that Nixon was quitting. At the start of the Watergate trials he'd gone around hammering "Nixon's the One" signs onto his neighbors' lawns, and doing this martyr routine if anyone complained. But it looked like Nixon was quitting anyway, and for Frank it was like, 'Remember the Alamo.'

I don't know where he got this lawn display. He must've hunted it up out of a wholesale catalog, 'cause it would've looked huge even in front of a Sears. It was this big Christian Christmas thing, except it's still summer. Here are the apostles and here's the Virgin Mary and here's John the Baptist and here's a life size adult Jesus, too, with the robe and the halo and the whole nine yards, but guess who's standing right next to Jesus. I'd expected it, 'cause that's what the Hardy's customers had been hee-hawing about. You guessed it: it's Tricky Dick, life size and in a suit, and *he's* got a halo.

Frank was wearing one of his eight million sleeveless cardigan sweater vests. It was like his personal uniform. He was hunched over in front of Jesus and Nixon. It looked like he was trying to get them to stand closer together. Maybe Nixon didn't want to. I had to get past Frank. He'd know where Logos was, but no way I wanted to be caught dead talking to him in front of that thing. Somebody might have a camera.

❖ 23 ❖

Frank knelt on the grass to try to scrunch Nixon's pants leg closer to Jesus' sandal. I looked at the garage. Wide open. My chance. I slunk across the street and tip-toed down the sidewalk, and when I was close I made a dash for it. Frank yelled after me, but I was in the garage by then, and could pretend I hadn't heard him.

•　　•　　•

Poor old Mrs. De Mello was cooking up pasta in the kitchen, with her worthless son Barry standing at the counter, and her even more worthless son Ronald Reagan De Mello at the kitchen table. As soon as I barged in she went to wringing her hands and goggling up at me with these sob story eyes, like I'm the paramedic and she was expecting me twenty minutes ago.

"Oh, Hank. Hank, I'm so glad you're here. You have to help me with Spiro. Please, Hank."

She stood right in front of me, like I might try to duck around her and make a dive for the stove.

Barry sneered at me. All he had on was a set of hot pink posing trunks, with his poochy little pot belly hanging over the waistband, and oil dripping off his skinny white arms. A radio was going on the counter behind him. Barry was real into male physique contests now, in his own way. He didn't believe in special diet or exercise. He said he wanted to celebrate the natural look.

"Mrs. De Mello, I'm right in the middle of something important. I just need to get ahold of Logos. Can you ..."

"Hank, Spiro is going to lose his job!"

She dug her fingers into my arms and gave me the big moon-eyed look again. Damn fruitcake family. Spiro'd already been fired from more jobs than anyone in California.

So we get to wrangling back and forth, with me begging to just find out where Logos is at so I can clear out of there, and her digging skid marks on my arm and insisting I've got to burn rubber out to the Pilgrim's to check on Spiro. Some saint had appeared in a dream last night and told her that Spiro was about to get canned — which was about as risky a prophecy as saying a tourist would want to ride a cable car — and then Spiro had sounded discouraged that morning on the phone. She just knew his job was in jeopardy.

"Please, Hank. Spiro can tell you where to find Logos. You go see him."

"My mother is asking for your help," Barry says.

Real hoity-toity, like I'm a butler who won't put the madame's slippers under the bed.

"Why don't you help her, instead of standing around in your underwear?"

Barry sneered at me again and turned up the volume on a plastic radio on the counter. Then he started running through his muscle man poses. He'd been in about a dozen contests. He'd sign up for Mr. Fremont or Mr. Antioch or Mr. San Ramon or Mr. Wherever, and they had to let him on stage because he paid his entrance fee, but the whole auditorium would go deathly silent while he posed, and when he turned sideways it was real obvious that the posing affected him physically. If you know what I mean. None of the other contestants would stand anywhere close to him. Some famous Kraut bodybuilder had forfeited a sure win contest 'cause he wouldn't get on stage with Barry. At least it beat slobbering on womens' shoes.

From the kitchen table Ronald just gaped at me with his mouth open and pasta on his chin. He'd microwaved his brain on drugs, and about all he did now was eat and pick at his tattoos in the mirror. And be an audience for Barry, maybe. He was wearing a hairnet and a silver anniversary t-shirt for Alpo dog food.

Barry launched into a crab shot. He didn't have any more muscle than Don Knotts. I had to get out of there. The radio reminded me of the moaning and blubbering I'd been listening to on KBXC all week, and if Barry popped a woody I thought I'd heave. I told Mrs. De Mello I'd look up Spiro, and she promised me he'd know where Logos was, and I skedaddled, and cussed the family for being what it was, and sprinted past Frank on the lawn again, so nobody would see me near what he was building.

•   •   •

Spiro didn't like getting called Spiro. You could call Logos Richard Nixon De Mello if you wanted to, although nobody did, but saying 'Spiro' to Spiro was a good way of starting a fight. He'd named himself Greg.

Greg's latest gig was pest control. Not for Orkin or Terminix or any of the majors. They was too smart for that. Some old gin bag who'd gotten the boot for being drunk all the time had started his own pest control company, and hired other guys who'd gotten the boot for being drunk. I figured he'd be Chapter 11 in about two more weeks. Pilgrim's must have just hired them 'cause they was cheap.

I spotted Greg's pick-up as I wheeled my 'Cuda in, with his damn dog looking through the rear window, and there's Greg in overalls, tromping around in the shrubs near the entrance with a steel backpack spray rig slung over his shoulder. Spritzing around under the bushes like he had any idea what he was doing.

I figured I'd go in for the quick kill.

"Hey, Greg, where's Logos at? I gotta get ahold of him."

I stepped onto the red gravel ground cover crap next to the shrubs and gave him a hurried look, like I just wanted him to holler out the answer before I went in for a healthful Plymouth Burger. No soap. Greg grumbled something under his breath and crab-walked across the gravel to spray next to the sliding doors. I guessed he was mad at Logos for something.

"Hey, Greg. I said I'm trying to get ahold of ..."

"I don't know who you're talking about."

"Aw, come on, Greg."

The doors slid open and a Haystacks Calhoun lookalike waddled out swinging a carry-out sack in his pudgy fist. Pilgrim's didn't attract the Jack LaLanne set. Haystacks swung the bag into Greg's sprayer by accident.

"Hey, *fatso*! Why don't you watch where you're going?!"

Haystacks blinked at him.

"What're you eating here for anyway?!" Greg yelled. "Don't you see what I'm doing? There're *rats* around here. You want to eat that crap and get the plague?"

Haystacks' face turned white. A housewife coming up the walk with her kids froze and looked at Greg with her mouth open. Greg pointed his sprayer toward the garbage bins.

"They found two rats out there last week! Don't you even care about your children?"

• • •

Greg had probably been fired from more jobs than anybody in the Bay Area. I was surprised he was still a citizen, even. I thought Nixon had signed a special order to deport people who got canned that often.

He'd screwed up so many painting jobs that old Frank wouldn't let him on the truck unless Logos went out with him. Frank got him a job as a mortician's helper, but that only lasted a couple of weeks. Greg thought funerals were a big har de har. He'd crack one liners during the service and give noogies to distraught family members, and when everybody lined up to view the deceased he talked real loud about all the crap they'd stuffed the corpse with, and compared it with Thanksgiving turkey, and said how blue and shrunken the corpse had looked before.

So Frank got him another job handing out tract literature. How hard is that? Stand on a corner all day, give people Jesus pamphlets. But Greg only lasted four days. He didn't like taking back talk from non-believers. He told one atheist that maybe Christ would come into his life if he'd lop about eighty pounds of dead weight off his fanny, so he could fit through a door without turning sideways, and in the meantime he could at least wear a bag over his head when he prayed, so maybe the Savior would mistake him for someone who wasn't so obese. Like Rock Hudson and Raquel Welch. Greg said that Jesus always answered their prayers right away, 'cause they was attractive.

Greg's list of lost jobs just went on and on. Used car salesman, medical tester, paper boy, courier, bartender. He'd even got fired as part-time help playing Santa at a department store, 'cause he gave kids inside adult tips on how to cry and throw tantrums to get the stuff they wanted. Finally he was out picking up trash near the stadium for $2 a bag, and a stray dog took up with him, and Greg decided the dog was a divine sign that Jesus wanted him to go into business for himself. Greg called the dog Leg Humper. That was his big trick. That's all he did. Greg got a leash for him and took him into bars and told everybody he'd let Leg Humper do his thing on their shins for only ten dollars. Greg even made a no down payment deal on a 'Stang, 'cause he was so sure Leg Humper would be a big success. Well, they repo'd that

'Stang after two weeks. Nobody wanted to pay Leg Humper, no matter how drunk they was. The half price sale didn't help.

Most of the time now, Greg just went out and applied for jobs. He didn't think he'd actually get one. He'd put his feet up on the desk and eat lunch during the interview, and talk trash about the company and smoke and insult the interviewer, and say he'd just been curious to see if a job there could fit into his busy schedule.

• • • •

Greg had moved to spray behind the bushes close to the drive thru window, so we could smell the exhaust fumes of the cars pulling up, and hear Nancy do her sexpot routine while she handed over the orders. Nancy was the main reason guys came to Pilgrim's. She'd flash cleavage and lick her lips and wink, so she could get away with ripping off bills. She was a short change artist.

"Greg, I don't want to stand around with you in the bushes all day. Where's Logos?"

"Since when did I become Logos' personal secretary? It's not my job to keep his calendar."

"Aw, come on, Greg. You know he didn't do anything to you. What're you mad about?"

Greg swung around in the bushes to face the parking lot again. That damn Leg Humper saw him and started jumping around in Greg's pick-up and wagging his tail. He was a cross between a Welsh Corgi and a Great Dane. Can you even imagine anything that ugly?

Greg glowered at the lava rocks and spritzed behind the bushes some more. He was working up to unload on me. I could tell.

"How long do you think I've been painting houses?" he asks, finally.

"Oh, I don't know. It's your dad's business. Most of your life."

"Since I was six!" Greg said proudly. "Since first grade! Twenty years. I've done commercial, I've done industrial, I've done residential. Everything." He thumped the spray handle on his chest. "I'm past master, man. Past master. I should be supervising a paint crew right now."

I waited. Greg spritzed the bushes some more.

"So last week we're out on a job. Warehouse. They had this new type of dry wall composite. This lightweight, slick stuff." Greg paused. "Logos was there. Dad sent him out to help me."

Greg couldn't see me roll my eyes. To *help* Greg. Oh, sure. Oh, ho ho ho. Frank wouldn't even give Greg the keys to roll the truck down the driveway by himself.

Greg gave the evil eye to the bushes. Apparently this had been eating him up all week.

"The paint won't go on at all," Greg said. "The primer won't take, the paint's running. And I'm trying everything. Different primer. Paint extender. I mean, I'm a pro. Twenty years experience. I know what to do.

"And you know what that little gerbil did?"

Greg twisted his head back to look at me. Behind me I heard a car rumble away from the drive thru, and then through the speaker Nancy popping her gum and rustling the pages of the *People* she was probably reading while she waited for the next customer. She could probably eavesdrop on everything we was saying out there.

"I said, do you know what he did?"

"What'd he do?"

"One look at the label!" Greg snapped his fingers. "One look! Ten seconds." Greg imitated Logos. "'Gregory, I'm afraid we're going to have to take a different approach to sanding and priming.' You know how he talks. In tiny print at the bottom of the paint label, there's maybe half a sentence a chemist would write about changing the application procedure for this kind of drywall. I mean, come on! Who'd look at something like that? And he sees it in two seconds!

"A little know it all! That's what he is. He's got to be right about everything. How'd you like to have someone like that for a brother?"

Greg swung away from me and gave about five vicious spritzes to the restaurant wall, like he was trying to shoot it. I looked at the parking lot. Leg Humper was still watching us through the rear window. He wagged his tail when he saw me. I hoped the door was locked.

"It's not Logos' fault that he's smarter than you and knows how to read directions."

That hadn't been me.

Greg glared at the plastic speaker next to the drive-thru window. Nancy *was* eavesdropping on us.

"Hey, why don't you *shut up* and mind your own business? This is a private conversation."

From the speaker Nancy just snickered and didn't answer. There wasn't any drive-thru customers. Maybe Greg had scared them all away. After a second I heard her pop her gum again, and turn the page of her *People* or *Us* or whatever she was reading.

"Come on, Greg. Just tell me where I can get ahold of Logos. I can't stand out here all day with you."

"He's not here. He's coming back tomorrow." Greg shot me an impatient look over his shoulder. "Don't worry. You want to see him, I'll get the word to him. Don't worry. Sheesh."

"Greg, why don't you look on the bright side? You got a good gig here. Lots of people got pests. You've got steady employment. You work your way up, maybe you'll be glad you're not in painting anymore." I pointed at the sprayer. "You might want to wear a mask, if you're working with that stuff all day."

Greg got a faraway gleam in his eye. He looked at me over his shoulder and winked. Then he hoisted the sprayer and triggered a spritz right into his mouth.

"You *drink* that stuff?!"

"What'd he do?" Nancy said.

"Orange juice." Greg leered at me. "I'm not a life taker," he said. "I'm a life giver."

"What'd he just do?" Nancy said.

From the truck Leg Humper wagged his tail, like his special canine sense told him the end was in sight, and he'd have Greg back soon. Greg went back to spraying. From the speaker I heard Nancy gabbling with someone in the background. She sounded upset.

A second later the restaurant doors open, and the manager stomped out. Mr. Matthews. Or he tried to act like a "Mr. Matthews," anyway. He was only eighteen, and didn't shave yet, and his mom gave him a bowl haircut at home, and he wore a clip-on tie that Woolworth's wouldn't have sold for a buck 'cause he didn't know how to tie a real one. He overcompensated by trying to act tough, and calling everybody by their last names.

"What goes on here, De Mello?" He had a body like the Pillsbury dough boy, 'cause all he ate was Pilgrim burgers.

"I'm spraying," Greg said.

"I heard him say orange juice," Nancy said.

"Are you feeding the rats, De Mello?"

I got out of there. One thing about Greg: if he said he was going to do something, he almost always did it, at least if it didn't involve money. He'd get word to Logos. Mission accomplished. As for Spiro De Mello job number six hundred fifty-eight, or five thousand eighty-six, or whatever it had been: well, at least Greg could get caught up on his morning soap operas again, and poor Leg Humper wouldn't have to sit out by himself in the truck anymore.

•   •   •

My swing shift at Hardy's was as insanely thrill-a-minute as it usually is. Of course, Earl showed up. I'd expected that. He parked his R/T out back by the loading dock, so everybody he used to work with at Hardy's would practically have to go out there on their breaks to admire his wonderful new cylinder heads. Big wow, Earl. I'm so impressed. With the trunk lid open and the heads laid out on a blue tarp in there like they was a couple of Rembrandts, and Earl leaning against the fender in his aviators and that damn windbreaker and one of his Luckies going.

I snuck a look back there when I had to go out to the dock for a hand cart. Lefty and Mike was drooling over the heads, and Earl had his mouth open like a howler monkey so he could puff out one of his precious smoke rings, and was probably in the middle of this big LBJ speech about the Great Society plans he had for his 383 now that he had the Vulcan heads. Why didn't he just walk them through the meat department so everybody could give them a kiss? Made me sick.

I knew I had to put in an appearance. Earl knew about my 383 'Cuda. Lording those heads over me was probably eighty percent of why he'd come to Hardy's. I had it planned out. I'd sort of waltz over to his Charger like I was dashing between transatlantic jets on the Riviera, and take a quick peek, and sniff at the heads like they had tuberculosis, and say "Nice going, Earl" in as fake a voice as I possibly could, like I actually thought they was as interesting as a couple of tumbleweeds he'd hauled up from Bakerspatch. And then leave. Or walk over and look at the rust on the trash bins, like I thought that was more interesting.

I got my meal break at 7:30. Unfortunately, Dirk was already out there, leaning against the Charger and yakking with Earl about something. Probably the time he'd drawn down on a shoplifter with his full custom .45, with the competition sights and commando grip. Dirk had only told that story about eight million times. The guy had tried to walk off with some napkins. They both gave me the evil eye when they saw me coming. So much for my plan. Dirk had probably told Earl all about how I'd wanted to listen to KBXC all week. "So Dirk tells me you're a country western fan, Hank." That's what he'd say. I'd have to eat crow.

But even Hank catches a break every now and then. Earl went into his full-on Joe Cool act when I walked up, and took a massive drag on his Lucky, so he could blow smoke at me when I said hello. But he was so eager to see me humiliated that he inhaled too fast, and went into a massive coughing fit. Boy. Wasn't I broken-hearted. I said "nice heads, Earl" while he was still hacking and coughing away, and managed to get out of there before he recovered. Probably ruined his night.

·   ·   ·

I got home about 1:00 a.m. I shut down my 'Cuda in the driveway and went to the front door to let myself in. I figured I'd nuke up some leftovers and maybe flip through a *Batman* before I hit the hay. I wasn't that tired yet. I was still all psyched about that cup.

As soon as I opened the door I heard a car commercial blaring from the living room. Darling Dan's Quality Pre-Owned Dodge, seconds from the 4 on Antioch's auto row. Dan is the

Dealingest. I figured Mom had stayed up to watch a John Wayne flick. She said he was the last real man left in Hollywood.

But the living room was dark, and the sofa was empty. I went over and shut the set off. I was already starting to get that queasy feeling. I told myself just to let her lead her life, but her bedroom door was open and the light was on in there. I went over in spite of myself.

There she was sacked out right on the bed covers in the ratty old bathrobe that was practically all she ever wore around the house anymore. She was so tanked that she hadn't put herself to bed proper. A butt was still smoldering in the ashtray on the nightstand, with the latest fifth of whiskey beside it. She couldn't be bothered to even pour her damn medicine into a tumbler.

My gut started to wrench around. Just shut the door and leave her be. We was just roommates until one of our ships came in. But I thought of that smoking butt, and that it was going to get cold later. So I went in. I hauled a blanket out of the closet and spread it over her, and then went up next to her head to kill the cig. She was breathing through her mouth. Her make-up was all smeared. She still got herself duded up for her job at the gas station, but after work she never did anything anymore except beat up on her Old Arkansas bottles and watch the tube. Even five years ago it had been different. She hadn't exactly been a social butterfly since Dad had walked out, but she'd still had some money then from selling the ranch. Now the money was gone, and it was like it had took her self-respect with it.

As soon as I thought that I knew my brain was behind enemy lines, and I tried to haul it back, but it was too late. I shut off her light and walked out, but now I was all depressed.

Maybe I just needed a little late night medicine before I nuked up those eats. I still had some of that michoacan Tyler had sold me.

I went into my bedroom and hunted for the shoebox with my dope fiend paraphernalia. A picture of Mom breathing drunk through her mouth invaded my brain again, but I fought it back and found the shoebox and went out to the front step with it. I could sit and look at my 'Cuda if I smoked out there, and the moon and the stars and other natural scenery type diarrhea. The neighborhood was pretty much DOA at that time of the a.m.

Just treat myself to a toke and work up the munchies a little. That was the idea. I just wasn't taking care of myself.

I sat on the step and loaded the pipe and held the flame over the bowl, and leaned back against the door while I held it in. Michoacan. Har de har har. Sure it was. Like a loser like Tyler would ever get a line on anything except the gro-lite ragweed crap he always sold. But it was what I had, and I took a second toke, and then a few more.

But then I knew it wasn't going to work for me. Seeing Mom like that had left me too bummed.

If Dad had just give her some advice. I hadn't expected him to stick around. Even as a kid it had been real obvious that he'd thought of her and me both as a mistake he'd had to pay off, like we was a lemon car he'd bought. Okay. Fine. Be the big hotshot corporate jet salesman. I'm not going to hang on your coat sleeves. But couldn't he at least have told her, Helen, don't drop the whole nickel on some ding-dong timeshare deal. She'd landed eighty grand, eighty grand clear from selling the ranch, and now look where we was. The poorest block in Prado, just about. And I knew she was barely making the mortgage, even with the rent I paid. Other people who'd owned land anywhere near Prado Diablo when the boom had hit, man, landing on easy street had been about as tough as shooting apples in a barrel. But look at Mom with her gas station job, and me at Hardy's. And where we lived.

•　　•　　•

So I looked at the beat-up, saggy houses around us instead of the moon and the stars, and started to get seriously bummed, and my brain might have angled into even worse territory if I hadn't all of a sudden heard a rustling noise, and then something coming my way from down the sidewalk.

Right away I tamped out the pipe and shoved my doper kit behind the shrub next to the front door. I knew the hood of my 'Cuda was still warm. If it was Logos and he even half-way thought I'd been driving lit I could kiss any help from him on the cup goodbye. Logos was a total maniac about drunk driving. But then the sound got closer, and I saw what it was, and man, the relief just washed over me. If this wasn't a sign that Hank Kruzenski's ship in life wasn't finally pulling in, and that Zeus didn't want me having no bum trip, well, nothing was.

It was Ruby.

He trotted up and sniffed around our bushes for a couple of seconds, to keep tabs on the other dogs that had taken whizzes in there, and then came over to say hello. I koochy-kooed at him under my breath. Well. Wasn't *this* an honor. Ruby was the official good luck dog of Prado, at least for people my age. Nobody owned him. A couple of people had tried to, 'cause he was a nice dog and smart and sweet to kids, but eventually Ruby always got to feeling his wild oats and took off. He'd shacked up with at least ten people I knew of.

Ruby let me pet his head until he had me roped in, and then he rolled onto his back so I'd attend to his stomach. He was mostly Basset, but about the toughest Basset you ever saw, 'cause he also had some black lab and mastiff in him. People thought he was good luck. He'd slept in Phil Nester's shop the whole time Phil was building up his Chevelle for Super Stock, and Phil was just positive that was why his Chevelle had done so good. And Jamie Maris had took him out to Fiesta when he went under eleven seconds in his Willys. Jamie even wrapped a blanket around his head, so the noise wouldn't bother his ears.

Ruby had never stayed with me before. I'd have to rustle up some grub and a water dish in the kitchen, and put out some shop tarps for him to sleep on. Even if he wouldn't stick around for long. I'd still get bragging rights that Ruby had stayed with me.

Ruby rolled over and settled in to snooze next to my feet. I leaned over to rub his ears, and then I got all fixated on staring at the weedy gardening bed next to the step. Maybe I had got a little spaced on that dope. Even if it was rag weed.

Damn if I didn't remember when me and Mom had put that bed in. Second grade Explorers. I'd been hot to get some kind of pee-wee gardening badge. Mom had said there was too much clay in the soil, so she'd trucked me down to Galindo Hardware to buy peat moss and other junk to build a raised bed with. She'd learned about gardening growing up on the ranch.

Man, had those radishes come in huge. Man. I could still remember kneeling beside her and looking at those fat green leaves, and her quizzing me about when they'd be ready to harvest. 'Do you think they're ready, Hank? Should we wait another day?' Like it had been me deciding, and not her. She'd been a way different person then. She hadn't punished the bottle anywhere near as hard.

'Course, there wasn't anything in that bed now except weeds. Hadn't been for years.

Then my brain went behind enemy lines again, and I thought of how Mom had looked breathing through her mouth dead drunk, with the bottle next to her bed and her gas station cashier make-up all smeared.

I stood up. My hands shook a little. I walked to the side of the garage and switched on the two big 500 watt floods that aimed down at the driveway. Then I went back and sat on the step again and crooked my finger under Ruby's big floppy ear to massage his chin, and just drank in how bitchin' my 'Cuda looked under those floods, with those big Mickey Thompsons stuffed under the fenderwells, and the chrome vents in the hood and the gold hood clips, and the jet black paint gleaming like a wall of jagged flame.

What was I doing getting bummed about anything? I could go anywhere in that car. I could be out of the state in three hours flat. And didn't I have the official good luck dog of Prado resting at my feet? And who gave a rat's ass about the Vulcan heads if I'd just got a solid lead on the Cuauhtémoc cup, which was practically the most valuable missing artifact anywhere on planet earth?

So I thought about that, as Ruby snoozed at my feet and the planets and stars and galaxies winked at me from light years away, of all the legends and lore and mysterioso fables surrounding that cup, and how I'd first heard of it, which of course meant thinking of Logos, too.

Chapter Three

Logos gave me the low down on the Cuauhtémoc cup one night back in high school, while we was camped out up on Ripper's Hill. Or that was what everybody in high school called it. It was a top secret teenage hangout on the mountain, with a big oak tree for shade and a view you'd expect if somebody handed you the keys to Contra Costa County and named you emperor. You felt like you was sitting on top of the world up there, with the dark peaks of the foothills all around and the glittery lights of the 'burbs winking and twinkling beneath you like your own personal kingdom.

I'd got a hold of some Panama Red, and we went up there to toke up and sleep it off under the stars. This was before Logos went Steve Sobriety on us, and stopped using anything stronger than coffee. I loaded up a bowl and we goggled up at the Milky Way, and Logos got to yakking about what a big wow religious deal it had been to the ancient injuns. Like the Sioux had called it the Spirit Trail, and thought their ghosts traveled the Milky Way when they died.

Then that got him started on Red Cloud and the Cuauhtémoc cup. I felt privileged, really. Logos was the boy wonder who'd ID'd the cup in the magazine spread and got the Joe College archaeologists excited about it. Maybe he hadn't made the national news, but two local TV stations had interviewed him. He'd got so tired of answering cup questions that he'd mostly clammed up about it, and now here he was giving me the lowdown one-on-one.

• • • •

Red Cloud was a Oglala Sioux warrior who'd lived around the Black Hills in the middle 1800s. The Sioux was among the toughest Indian fighters on the continent, and Red Cloud was one of the toughest Sioux. He was just sixteen when he first 'counted coup,' which was the Sioux term for pulling off a major feat of derring-do in battle. He wound up counting coup seventy-nine more times. More than any other Sioux in history.

Think about that. Eighty separate times he'd got close enough to touch the enemy trying to do him in, or take a scalp, or kill a man hand-to-hand. Logos didn't know who to compare him to. Maybe some elite special forces type who'd run dozens of death defying top secret missions behind enemy lines, and had scars on half his body, and calluses and tattoos on the other half, and snacked on roofing nails instead of sunflower seeds, and who you'd cross the block to stay clear of. Maybe two blocks. Maybe a whole city. Red Cloud was a fearsome dude. No question.

•   •   •

Now, even drop outs like me knew how things went for Indians here in the 1800s: badly. The young U.S. of A. was spreading west. Wagon loads of prospectors and settlers and fortune seekers was tromping up dust on new trails. If some of those trails went smack dab through the middle of Sioux hunting grounds, well, the pale faces didn't much care.

The Sioux needed help, and they turned to Red Cloud to get it. He was the main war leader by then of the whole Sioux nation. He told them to fight, and they did, and they knew how, and they won. They harassed the whites on the Bozeman Trail so bad that a soldier couldn't squat to crap without fetching an arrow in the back. When Red Cloud finally signed a treaty at Fort Laramie, it was the treaty he wanted to sign. He was the only Indian in U.S. history ever to win a drawn-out war with the white man.

•   •   •

But you know what they say about fighting. Winning the battle don't mean you win the war. Sometimes, it takes winning a battle to show you that you *can't* win.

The U.S. President at the time was Ulysses Grant. He'd led the whole Union Army during the Civil War. He knew a little about fighting, too. Red Cloud wanted to come to D.C. to pow wow. Old Ulysses thought that was a fine idea. A *real* fine idea. They was both generals. He knew damn well what an Indian general would think when he rode behind a big smoking locomotive into East Coast cities bigger than anything he'd ever dreamed of, and checked out Uncle Sam's Gatling guns, and saw Yankee cannons big enough to take a nap in.

Red Cloud didn't let his feelings show. He called a big meeting two days after he hit D.C.; he bargained hard. But deep down, he had to be shook. Just what exactly was the Sioux nation going to do about people who built skyscrapers tall as mountains, and chugged down the Potomac in metal sea monsters? Maybe they could haggle for a few more acres. Maybe they could hope their enemy couldn't be bothered with them, 'cause the great white father didn't want to ship the heavy artillery to the Dakotas.

They was still sunk. It didn't matter that it wasn't fair, that the Sioux had been there first, that the Americans tried to wiggle out of every treaty they proposed. Red Cloud was a warrior. He'd cut his teeth sizing up battle odds. He was licked, and knew it.

• • •

Two nights after he got to D.C., when all this stuff had to be running through his mind, Red Cloud had a dream.

In the dream he was a young man again, chewing the fat at the trading post with old Tom Samson. Tom had been his favorite trader from the days when there'd only been a few whites out west, and the Sioux and the whites had been friends.

Tom looked regretful. The old Sioux way was coming to an end, he said. The whites was his friends now, but they wouldn't be soon. Tom was sorry. He wanted Red Cloud to drink from a special cup he had, so they'd both understand why life had to be as it was.

Red Cloud woke up as Tom put the cup on the table. It was the damndest thing he'd ever seen. Somebody had carved it in the shape of a human head, but it didn't look like the head of a Indian, or of any white man. Maybe it was a god. There was symbols carved into the forehead. Red Cloud recognized the thunderbird and four medicine arrows, but the rest of the symbols he'd never seen before. They wasn't Sioux, or Cheyenne, or Crow, or Ree, or Gros Ventres, or the letter symbols of the white man. They was like markings from another world.

• • •

The Sioux delegates went from D.C. to Manhattan. Red Cloud rode in a parade in Central Park, and gave a big speech at the Cooper's Institute. And then one evening a secretary from the Indian Peace Commission invited him to a special meeting.

It wasn't a government meeting. The secretary belonged to a spiritualist society. The meeting was a séance. Their leader was a big muckety-muck medium named Henry Towpfer, who drank some kind of weird tea and hypnotized himself so he could communicate with 'spirit contacts' in the afterlife. Henry's two main 'spirit contacts' just so happened to have both been big powerful native chieftains like Red Cloud, with a difference: they'd lived a lot farther south, and about three and a half centuries earlier.

Their names was Cuauhtémoc and Manco Inca. Cuauhtémoc had been the last emperor of the Aztecs. Manco Inca had damn near kicked Pizarro out of Peru, when he'd been boy king of the Incas. Cuauhtémoc and Manco Inca had been watching Red Cloud from the hereafter, the secretary said. They was sympathetic. They'd told Henry Towpfer to invite Red Cloud to the meeting. They'd *insisted* on it.

There was something they wanted to give him.

•　　•　　•

Now, Red Cloud was a skeptical dude. You could trust in God, but mostly you wanted to remember to hitch your pony, and if he'd had to choose between trust and the hitch, well, he'd take the hitch. But he was a guest and they was inviting him, so he went. The meeting was at the Maximillian Lodge near Central Park. Close to a hundred people was there. The regulars all sat at a long table, with a place of honor reserved for Red Cloud next to Henry Towpfer, and the looky-loos in the cheap seats at the wall.

Red Cloud spotted something on the table as he took his seat. It was some kind of cup. It looked familiar.

Henry Towpfer started the meeting. His spirit contacts Cuauhtémoc and Manco Inca had told him to invite Red Cloud, he said, and had told him how to get the sacred cup that now sat on the table before them. Together, they would drink from it. They would understand life better then, and why things had to be as they was.

Towpfer picked up the cup, took a sip and passed it to Red Cloud. It was the damndest thing Red Cloud had ever seen. It was carved in the shape of a human head, but the head wasn't of a Indian, or a white man, either. There was a ribbon shape etched onto the forehead, and then symbols carved onto the ribbon. Red Cloud recognized a few — the thunderbird, the four medicine arrows — but the rest he'd never seen before.

It was the cup he'd dreamed about.

.   .   .

From here, the account gets a lot fuzzier.

Red Cloud got his picture took with the cup. That was the picture I'd gone to the library to eyeball. He drank from it, and so did others at the table, and he took the cup back with him to the Dakotas. His wife Pretty Owl said so, when some college students interviewed her in 1920. The drink didn't change Red Cloud, but he still thought the cup was the most powerful medicine in the whole Sioux nation. It scared him a little.

But others who drank from that cup at the Maximillian Lodge did change. A lot.

Henry Towpfer never did another séance. He moved up to the Adirondacks and tried to live alongside the bears up there. Seriously. With the bears. The secretary of the society set sail onto Wallabout Bay in a sloop and never came back.

One after the other, bing bang boom, a full quarter of the believers who'd drunk from that cup at that séance gave away their property, quit their jobs, wandered off into the woods, walked naked in the Atlantic. Radical stuff like that. Some of them turned out fine afterward. A lot said they was happier, even. But they didn't give a hey about earth customs anymore. That drink had shown them something.

The *New York Times* printed more than a dozen articles on Red Cloud's visit to D.C. and New York. But they didn't run one word about that séance, or the cup, or about how some of Manhattan's finest was going bonkers after drinking out of it.

Henry Towpfer's wife wrote letters asking for help for her husband, and her friends kept those letters, and you can read them today. Ditto letters from the secretary's family. You've got a solid paper trail showing that at least twenty who drank from that cup went off on a rest-of-their-lives nineteenth century peyote trip afterward, *and* that the peyote trip traced from drinking from the cup at the meeting.

•   •   •

Red Cloud took the cup west, but it didn't stay with him. In 1874 it turned up with some Comanche who'd followed one of the last free buffalo ranges into Palo Duro Canyon. A couple of missionaries went in after them, and lo and behold, here's the cup again. The *Wichita Clarion* ran a shot of the missionaries and Injuns posing with the thing. The same types of stories followed. One of the missionaries married into the Comanche. Indians wandered off, left their tribes, went on lifelong vision quests. A journal at Fort Sill mentioned the cup, but the back East newspapers didn't touch the story, and how sure was anyone that you could even *see* a cup in a blurred photo someone had took with a box camera?

In 1877, Crazy Horse mentioned a dream vision of the 'Red Cloud cup' the night before he was killed. And then thirteen years later the cup turned up for sure with the messiah Wovoka, just as the whole Ghost Dance movement was kicking off. Two separate photos show the cup, one with Wovoka himself at Walker Lake. The *Sacramento Call* printed one. Maybe it wasn't the best photo, but everything else in the *Call* article spliced up with the cup's rep. If people drank out of that cup, they changed big time.

But the *Sacramento Call* wasn't the *New York Times*. The story died. Nobody had connected the cup at the séance to the cup with the missionaries to the cup at Walker Lake. They was all just separate, unrelated stories in the back pages of bohunk newspapers, next to the ads for livestock feed.

Which is how things probably would have ended. If it hadn't been for Logos.

•   •   •

Fast forward to the mid sixties. Mr. C had just took the checkered flag in two big races back to back, and *Rodder's Alma-*

nac figured that was excuse enough to run a retrospective on his career.

The first shot in the spread showed the young C at the Bonneville Salt Flats in the early fifties, with the blue streamliner that Perry McClendon had bankrolled. The C's standing at the front fender and McClendon's at the back, and then between them there's this beat-up Indian chick. She looked like a drinker. She was standing between the C and Perry with a weird drinker's smile and her hair all wild and her palms out in front of her, like she was holding out a birthday cake.

It wasn't a cake she had on her palms, though. It was some kind of statue. It looked like a cup.

The typical fruity rodder mag caption said:

> *Few savor victory's tangy thrill without first scarfing mouthfuls of defeat's bitter agony, and the big C is no exception. The dual-plug Baron heads, Magnuson supercharger and hand-crafted chassis gracing this ice blue streamliner — courtesy of bucks-up financier Perry McClendon, photo right — couldn't propel it to a worthy time at Bonneville. Nor could the peculiar Indian relic grasped by the damsel at photo center. Would'ja believe it: C and McClendon picked her up hitchhiking, and she insisted this trinket possessed supernatural power.*

Somehow, some way, a copy of that issue of *Rodder's Almanac* got to Logos. Maybe it was lying on the seat of a car he was riding in. Maybe somebody had left it at Pilgrim's. One way or the other, though, he saw that photo, and his built-in egghead geiger counter started ticking like crazy. He dug up the Centennial Heritage book and compared the shots, and put two and two together, and got on the horn with some archaeology types at Stanford and UCB.

A month later, that photo was national news. International news. The cup at Bonneville and the cup at the Maximillian Lodge was one and the same, all right, and finding that out prodded all the redskin buffs to root through their file cabinets, and pretty soon the *Sacramento Call* and *Wichita Clarion* clips and last vision of Crazy Horse was all tied up into it. Three separate confirmed accounts of people majorly flipping out after drinking out of the thing, and here was something else:

That cup's passport didn't check out. It was getting attention now. Experts was looking at it. First, no way it was Sioux. The Sioux was nomads. They didn't go in for making heavy stuff they'd have to lug along with the tipis. It wasn't Inca, either. The egg-heads thought it had to be Aztec, 'cause the Aztecs was sculpting fools and it had that ribbon thing on the forehead. That was the Milky Way for sure, right off the sun stone. The Milky Way was a big deal to the Aztecs, the Incas and the Sioux all three.

Okay, fine. It's Aztec. Mystery solved. But one little question: if it's Aztec, what are those other symbols doing on it? What's a nineteenth century Sioux four medicine arrows doing on a cup out of sixteenth century Tenochtitlan? And the Incans, man, they lived thousands of miles south of there. You don't think a hot shot injun expert with PhDs up the kazoo can ID a legit Inca cross when he sees it? How'd it get on the cup?

'Somebody must have copied it.' Okay, fine: how? The pale faces didn't even know Machu Picchu was there til forty years after the séance. Who knew enough to fake up a holey-moley Mesoamerican statue? And why'd Red Cloud have his big mysterioso dream that showed every detail of the cup before he ever went east? And most important: how come all these jokers are going out of their gourds when they drink out of it?

Oh, and there was one other detail:

Perry McClendon drank out of the cup at Bonneville. He did it just to tease the hitchhiker. She'd told him not to.

And after that, old Perry walked out to the highway, and thumbed a ride.

And disappeared. Nobody ever saw him again.

•   •   •

The reason people called Logos Logos was that he'd used the word a couple of times in high school, and it was such a weird word that he'd got teased about it until it set in as a nickname. Plus it sounded like 'Lego,' and that went with the cartoon-y and make-believe look Logos had about him, like he'd dropped out of a *Loony Tunes* re-run. He had big eyes and a round head and pudgy cheeks and no real jaw line to speak of. He wasn't a big guy. I think he went 5'2" and maybe 120 pounds. If that much.

The main weird thing you noticed right away was his race. Or races, plural. Logos thought his dad had been part Mex and part black and part Navajo, and that his mom had been part Korean and part European, although what part of Europe was anybody's guess. Maybe Ireland, because Logos could get an Irish sort of twinkle in his eyes when he smiled.

Or maybe English, or German, or Swedish, or French. You couldn't pigeon hole him. If you thought he looked mostly black, 'cause of his coppery skin and his hair, you'd notice how Oriental his eyes looked. Then if you decided he looked more Korean, you'd see how Latin his nose and his lips were, and decide, no, he looked mostly Mexican. Until he grinned, and you saw the European part again, or the Navajo part.

That was the whole *idea* of Logos. Nobody got to say he was one of theirs. He was one of everybody's. Or nobody's.

He wasn't good looking. I'll be honest: he was homelier than people who got made the butt of ugly jokes in high school. But with him it didn't matter. That 10,000 watt brain power just radiated out of him.

• • •

Logos and me was the same age, so he got dumped in my third grade class when Frank adopted him. His dad had knocked up a hooker on R&R leave, and little Logos had been left off at an orphanage near the North Korea border. Or that was what Frank heard. Don't get me wrong about Frank, by the way. Maybe he could be hokey when he carried on about his issues, but he had a good side to him, too. The Kiwanis gave him a big commendation for adopting a little kid from Korea, and he deserved it.

Mrs. Maples teamed me and Logos as seating partners. He only spoke a little English, so I nudged him along when we read *Velveteen Rabbit*. He caught on fast, though. In a couple of weeks it was him helping me on math, and not the other way around.

Eventually Mrs. Maples realized she had a major prodigy on her hands, and hustled Logos over to see the school psychologist.

We didn't see much of Logos for the next eight years. First they bussed him over to some special egghead class in Concord, and then Lafayette. He didn't get back til five in the afternoon, so we only ran into him on weekends, and by then he was a kid we hardly knew. I knew his messed-up brothers way better than I knew Logos. It was Greg told me that he was already taking UC Berkeley college classes when he was fifteen.

And then in our junior year of high school, Logos came back.

Nobody could figure it out. We thought he'd got in trouble, but he said he'd gotten tired of being treated special, and wanted to be in regular high school like everybody else. It was crazy. He was way, way ahead of the rest of us. But he'd made up his mind, so mostly he just hung out quiet in class, and helped other kids.

We made friends with him then. You got to remember, he was still a high schooler like the rest of us, despite the uranium enrichment plant he had going between the ears. He didn't have much of a love life, on account of his looks, but everybody liked him. He went cruising with us, and hung out at Pilgrim's.

I didn't find out for almost three years why he'd come back. I think I'm one of five people in Prado who know the story. He said he'd been at a Berkeley restaurant with a professor and some grad students, and the waiter had been some pruney old geezer who'd kept hitting them up with hokey Cal Bears questions while he took their orders. Like yakking about mascot Oski was going to coax a bigger tip out of a bunch of brains.

The grad students had thought the questions were dumb, and that he was pretty dumb, too. They'd made fun of him after he left. The prof had called him a prole.

The thing was, Logos had recognized him. Not well enough to say Howdy Do to, but still. Old Mr. Roney. One of his granddaughters had a big kidney problem. He'd had to come out of retirement and wait tables to help pay off the hospital bills.

So Logos had decided he'd just as soon live among the Roneys, seeing as how he'd been born among them. Plus his family was on tilt by then, and he almost felt like he'd been sent to Prado to keep an eye on them, and make sure they didn't slaughter each other.

•   •   •

A big difference between Logos and other high school kids was how he talked about history. To the rest of us it was just another subject in school. Caesar said 'Ett you, Brute,' and croaked, and Napoleon stuck his hand in his vest whenever he got painted, like his titties itched, and Washington always wanted to stand in front and hog the good view when he went anywhere in a boat. They weren't real people. You just memorized a lot of stupid dates so you didn't get study hall.

But for Logos it was way, way different. It was like he could see through time, like everything that had come before was this terrifying triple X rated horror flick that nobody his age should ever have been allowed to see. It wasn't just that the people was real to him. It was that they wouldn't stop screaming.

The only trouble he had in regular high school came one day when we had a sub in history, and she wanted us to make construction paper ships to celebrate Columbus Day. It was a pretty dorky assignment for high schoolers, but at least we'd get to have fun and flick glue at each other, and not read anything.

At first Logos didn't get it. In his usual polite way he asked the sub if she could explain the project again, like maybe he'd misheard her. So she did. She was just some poor old hen like my mom who probably cut coupons and watched soaps, and got her sub credential 'cause the professors got sick of flunking her.

Man, did he go off on her. 'You want me to honor the man who introduced slavery to the continent,' he said, like she'd asked us to make up Grand Wizard beanies for a Klu Klux parade. The sub said he ought to have more respect for American heritage. Logos stood up. I thought he was going to stand on his desk. He was trembling, he was so upset. The conquistadores branded the Indians' faces like cattle, he said, and then he started yelling — I mean *yelling*, with the spit flying out and his face all flushed, so the teacher next door finally bust in on us — about how one conquistador killed six hundred Indian children under the age of three, *six hundred infants*, and how horrible, *horrible* the whole thing had been, and the Aztec chiefs had been horrible, too.

They suspended him for three days. We thought it was a laugh riot. The ancient Indians was just cartoon characters who wore feathers and face paint in history books. How could you get worked up over that stuff?

•   •   •

Nobody understood why he stuck around after high school. It was like he thought some supernatural force had sent him to Prado Diablo, and given him all that brainpower so he could help out the people he'd grown up with. Like how he helped his nutcase dad run the painting business. Lots of people could say that they'd had the smartest human in the county up on a ladder in painter's overalls on the side of their houses, painting their trim. And he always seemed to be running into people who'd hit a rough patch in life, who he'd kind of tuck under his wing and pal around with until they got things straightened out. Other than that, he just drifted.

In high school I know for a fact he helped three kids soup up their cars, but after that he went Greenpeace on us, and wouldn't drive anything except the All American House Painters truck. He bought this big chart that showed all the eras and epochs of earth history, and yakked on and on about how us two leggers had just got here, basically, like in the last seconds of the fourth quarter, and how electricity and automation and the internal combustion engine and all the other tech stuff we took for granted might as well have shown up while you was reading the last paragraph, as far as the planet was concerned. We was like guardians of the earth, 'cause we was smarter than the other animals, and Prometheus had handed us the torch of knowledge, and instead of using it right we was fouling our own nest and flunking the big test.

After that he sold his car and went everywhere on the ridiculous transit system, or a damn bike, and stopped eating meat. Contra Costa Eco Boy. In some ways he could be a major ordeal to spend time with, but by then we'd all known him for years, so we took it in stride. Plus he'd clocked too many Prado years to think the rest of us was going to change much. He had a sense of humor about the whole thing. Maybe if he'd been stricter he wouldn't have filled in at Rosenfeld's Auto Salvage when old Abe's brain had gone south, and sold me that damn cracked block from a Road Runner. Never mind that I'd asked him to watch out for gear for my 'Cuda. That was what I got for buying car parts from Mr. Sierra Club.

Chapter Four

The phone got me out of bed at nine the next a.m. Greg. Logos was down in San Jose babysitting some poor Vietnam vet who still thought he was ducking artillery shells at Khe Sanh. He'd be back in Prado tomorrow.

I decided it was time for the great Hank Kruzenski to do some detective work. Maybe, *maybe* I could get Logos to use his 10,000 watt brain to help locate this Evelyn chick, but it would be a lot better if I could get a lead on her myself. I wasn't on shift at Hardy's til midnight. I had time.

I rustled up some chow for Ruby, and got on the horn, and damn if I didn't have enough Columbo in me to track down the hippy-dippy promotions outfit that had special evented the long-hair love fest on Cargo Way. They were over on Shattuck Avenue. People's Republic of Berkeley. So I piled Ruby into my 'Cuda and headed out there, and got to spend the next nine hours chasing down leads.

First the address for the promoter was wrong. Then I find the right address, but oh, no, sorry, we don't have the exhibitor's list. You'll have to see our events coordinator. He's on Solano. So I fire up the 383 again with Ruby hanging his slobbery snout out the window, undoubtedly so he can sniff at all the tie-died Berkeley fur balls gaping at my primo Formula S, and up to Solano I go, and after a half hour of cooling my heels in the waiting room, the list is in my fingers.

Except there wasn't no Evelyn on it. Only Jules. I'm real eager to see him again. Maybe this time he'd swat me clear out to Treasure Island. But I went to the address anyway, and as soon as I saw the house I knew Jules wasn't in it, because the bungalow wasn't tilting to one side 'cause of his weight. The chick who answered gave me another address clear across town. By now it's almost three, and the weather's taken a major turn for the worse, and Ruby looks like he's getting sick of getting chauffeured all over Woodstock West. I bought him some dog biscuits, but he still gave me a broody look, like a con who's thinking of making a bolt for the wall.

· · ·

To make a long story short, it was almost six-thirty before I tracked down Evelyn's house. It was full-on dark by then, and cold, and if the weather mid-afternoon had been ornery, it had grown vicious enough since to bite a nice chunk out of someone's ankle. I had my coat on, but that damn wind still ripped at my ears, and I kept rubbing my fingers together while waiting for the pinkos to answer the bell.

Finally, the door opened. The guy in front of me could have been Jimi Hendrix's long lost cousin. He had a 'fro on him like a boxwood hedge. I swear. You could've used him to scour an oven. But as soon as I went into my pitch he recognized Evelyn's name, and my heart starts going like a metronome on bennies, 'cause I think I'm *finally* on the right track.

But then he says:

"She just moved out, though. This morning."

Jimi blinked at me, like maybe I ought to flip him a hash brownie for all his hard brain work. I felt like wrapping his hair around my neck and hanging myself.

"Do you know where she moved to?"

Jimi shook his head. "She just split."

Great. Nine hours traipsing among the flag burners and communists, and I'd pulled a big fat zero. Just great.

But then Jimi said:

"I know where you can find her, though. If you hurry."

"Where?"

"The bridge."

Jimi gave me another searching look, like maybe I had his hash brownie treat tucked in my coat pocket. I thought he'd fit in perfect in the De Mello kitchen, right between Barry's posing trunks and Ronald's Alpo shirt. It wasn't skin color that made you a De Mello. It was your outlook on life.

"The *bridge*? Is that a cafe?"

Jimi smiled. "No, man. The Golden Gate Bridge. She goes out there once a week."

I stared at him. The bridge. Sure. It was freezing cold.

But Jimi looked serious.

"Why does she go out there?"

Jimi shrugged. "It's her trip. She just does. This is her night for it." He looked over his shoulder. "I think it closes at nine. If you want to catch her, you better get out there."

So I trotted back to my 'Cuda, mostly feeling sorry for myself, and thinking that a pointless walk across the Golden Gate Bridge on a freezing cold night would be a perfect capper to a waste-of-time day. But I knew I was going to go through with it, and I'd probably barely have time for a decent meal before my shift at Hardy's, and it was cold, and I was tired, and I was so busy boo hoo hooing my miserable plight that I threw the driver's door wide open, without remembering that I had some canine company.

Ruby did a flying Jim Thorpe past my hips, and was halfway down the sidewalk before I realized he'd pulled off the Great Escape. I called after him, but he just twitched his tail at me before he disappeared around the corner.

So much for the honor of hosting the great good luck dog of Prado Diablo. Ruby had decided to shed his good luck on somebody else.

•   •   •

I hadn't walked across the Golden Gate Bridge since Earl Howser had tried to shove me over the rail during a high school field trip. I wheeled my 'Cuda into the parking lot on the Frisco side, flicked the ignition kill switch under my dash and set off without bothering with the rest of my crook frustraters. Nobody was going to hot wire my 'Cuda. It was too cold. The wind was whipping the branches of the scuzzy little trees and bushes next to the lot, and blowing hamburger wrappers and coffee cups out of the trash and across the asphalt in front of me. A C Team Kydra would have been safe out there.

What the hey would she be doing out there? I buttoned my coat and shoved my hands into my pockets, and marched out on the walkway, with the cars whizzing by, and my nose and my ears going into deep freeze from the wind. The lanes were lit up, and the big thirties-style bridge lamps beamed pools of yellowy light on the pedestrian walkway, with shadowy gaps between them.

The farther I walked out there, the worse the wind got. Man. Any second I expected a patrol car to pull over, and for a cop to come after me with a straightjacket. But then on the walkway ahead of me this bundled up heaver came huffing out of the dark, with his breath making little steam puffs over his scarf before the wind whipped the puffs away. I wasn't the only one crazy enough to be out there. I passed another Icecapades exercise buff a minute later. Some people must like walking around in meat lockers.

I walked and walked and didn't see anyone who looked like Evelyn, and then I got up towards the south tower. The whole bridge is hung off of these two ginormous red towers stuck in the drink, with the steel ropes and truss work and chunks of roadway and other architectural diarrhea hanging off them, so the workers could slave away on top and not dog paddle around in the surf to get the bridge finished. The walkway goes around the towers, away from the traffic, which gives tourists a semi-secluded place to snuggle up on the rail and take their Alcatraz and Angel Island polaroids without being gawked at by all the motorists.

I followed the walkway to swing around the tower, and right away about ten decibels of the traffic roar cut out. I figured I might as well stop to enjoy the sights before I froze to death. I leaned on the railing and wondered what color my nose and ears were, and looked in at the bright lights of Frisco, where all the Frisco communists were hunkered down in their chi-chi North Beach cafes with their espressos and berets and Turkish cigarettes, and the hunky blob that Angel Island and Alcatraz made in the dark, and then the Berkeley and Oakland lights farther east.

Then I heard something behind me.

I turned. It seemed I had one of the deep freeze meat locker walkers right behind me. It was a chick. She was bundled up like an Eskimo in a beat-up pea coat, backed up against the red riveted tower wall so she'd have some protection against the wind. She must have been standing there when I'd walked up to do my sightseeing.

I was about to say something apologetic for blocking her view when I recognized who it was.

She must have recognized me at the same time.

Evelyn wasn't real happy to see me.

"What do you want?!"

Loud and super-hostile, like what someone would yell at a burglar just before racking a twelve gauge. She pushed off from the wall and whipped her hands out of her pockets, just in case she had to bean me with a set of brass knuckles.

I just gaped at her. Maybe I should have expected it. My mom had always said that women had to draft a emergency plan for how they'd deal with Sam the Serial Rapist, and that the emergency plan wasn't going to be anyone's idea of ladylike behavior. Here I was, chasing down Evelyn on the Golden Gate bridge in the middle of a freezing night, after she'd practically run off from me at the Fiesta. That ID'd me as a super villain.

"I said, *what do you want?!*"

I guess her emergency plan was better than most. She could've terrified a room full of Parris Island DIs.

I waved my hands in a lame way, and stammered like Ralph Kramden in the *Honeymooners* when Alice gets mad. I was pretty taken aback. The worst threat I'd been to women was when I'd wanted to go Dutch treat on dates.

"If you don't tell me I'm going to flag down a car and you can tell it to the police. Start talking *now*. What are you doing out here? Who told you I was here?"

A big wad of wind came in and sandblasted my cheeks, and my eyes watered up, and now I had trouble even seeing her.

"Your roommate told me," I sputtered. "I mean, sheesh, lady!"

I made a bleating sound, like some wimpy bookkeeper that Clint Eastwood would grab by the neck in *Rawhide*. I don't usually clutch that bad, but I hadn't expected to get the third degree.

"He told me you come out here. That's all." I wiped my eyes with my sleeve. "I mean, cripes, can't I even walk out on a public bridge without getting interrogated?"

I felt royally ashamed of myself for how wimpy I sounded, but that was probably the only reason she didn't try to flag down a car. She kept glowering, but she didn't move any farther away from me, either.

"Why didn't you just see me in Berkeley?"

"Because he told me you just moved out! I mean, cripes. He said you'd just hauled out of there, but that I could find you out here as long as I made it before the gates close. What else was I supposed to do? This was my last chance. You think I like freezing to death?"

Right on cue about twenty semis of wind blasted in, probably straight from Tokyo and picking up speed and icy cold all the way across the Pacific. Man. She had her back to the tower so she didn't get it much, but it hit me hard enough to nearly send me back into the rail. My hair whipped straight back and my eyes watered up, and I swear I felt that whole massive bridge wiggle and creak beneath me, like maybe the bozos who built it had still been catching up on their gin allowance after Prohibition and skipped some of the bolts.

"Sheee-sus." I held my hand up in front of my face. "I mean, what do you want to come out here for, anyway? Isn't your freezer cold enough for you?"

Apparently that question wasn't the key to her good side.

"What I'm doing here is absolutely *none of your business*," she shot back. "If I want to climb up on the tower and jump off, that's none of your business. My entire *life* is none of your business."

She was practically shouting. I wondered what raw nerve I'd hit.

"Okay, look ..."

"I don't even want to see you. I didn't ask you to come up to my table at the fair."

"Look ..."

"I don't even know who you are!" She waved her arm at the Frisco lights. "Why don't you go there and find someone on the sidewalk and bother her about her personal life? I'm not interested."

She shoved both hands into her pea coat and looked at me with her hair whipsawing around in the wind and her lips trembling a little over the big scarf around her neck. Her eyes were wet too, and I thought maybe the wind was getting to her more than I knew, but then wondered if they might be wet for another reason. Man. Talk about a weird chick.

Then I looked back the way I'd come, and saw that the bundled up heaver I'd passed earlier was puffing our way. Maybe he'd taken his evening deep freeze stroll to the toll gates, and now he was going to trot back to the north side and drive out to Fort Cronkite for a late night dip with the sea lions.

Evelyn glanced at him. I knew what she was thinking. If she said, 'Excuse me, this man is bothering me' to him when he came up, that would cancel my action right there, and maybe there'd be some sit down time that night with SFPD. She could pull damsel in distress rank on me, no question.

But the big heaver came up, and I got a look at the pimply shaving marks on his jowly puss as he huffed past between us, and Evelyn didn't say anything.

Then he was gone.

And that changed things. She'd had a wide-open chance to get rid of me, and she hadn't taken it. Maybe she talked tough, but she wasn't mean enough to buy me a ride in a cop car I didn't deserve. I could relax a little.

"Okay, here's what I'll do," I said. Charitable as all get out.

I backed up to the rail and slid down and sat on the walkway with my back to it, and crossed my legs in front of me. I felt like I was sitting on solid ice. Joe Martyr.

"I'm sitting down, and if you want I'll hang off the rail like a monkey, just so you won't feel I'm breathing down your neck. But I'm *cold*, lady. Okay? I came all the way out here to ask you a couple of questions, and I'd take it kindly if you'd hear me out just for the sake of human decency."

She rolled her eyes, and looked like she wished she'd asked the big heaver to call the cops after all.

"Okay?"

"Just tell me what you want."

"When I met you at the track, before your friend clobbered me ..." I figured I ought to work that in, so she'd feel slightly beholden. "...I was looking through some photos you had. Okay?"

I waited for her to answer. Well, I could go ahead and wait. She just glowered at me.

"Okay? And I think there were some shots in the stack that weren't supposed to be there. Personal photos. And maybe I wasn't supposed to see them, but I saw them anyway.

"One of the shots is of you sitting at a table. Okay? And there's two things on the table in front of you. One is a framed photo of a guy. And then there's a cup thing. It's like the bust of an Indian mask. And the cup's what I want to talk to you about."

"Why?" She shrugged. "Why not ask me about my coat, or my pants, or my shoes? It doesn't make any sense."

She looked like I'd just asked who won the Civil War. But old Hank had spent ten years swapping lies with hot rodders, and my B.S. detector was in fine working order, and I thought I sniffed something fake-a-loo around the edges of what she'd said.

"Do you know the photo I'm talking about?"

"Yes. Of course." Kinda defiant. "They're my photos. Of course I know which one."

"Who was the guy?"

"I'm not going to tell you!" She laughed. "It's none of your business! My entire life is none of your business. Look, I don't know how you got interested in this wild goose chase, but you're wasting your time. I'm sorry you came all the way out here for nothing."

"Okay. You're not going to tell me." I nodded and tried to look reasonable as all get out, like Walter Cronkite. "That's fine. He's the mystery man. Next question: can you tell me something about the cup?"

"Tell you what about it?"

"Well, was it yours? Did it belong to the guy you won't tell me about? How'd it get there?"

"I don't remember! It's none of your business!"

She laughed and brushed back her hair and looked past me at the bay and the Frisco lights, like she wanted to get back to her sightseeing in spite of me. Then she seemed to think of something.

"I think it was just a piece of tourist junk that someone had," she said. "That's all. This molded rubber thing. Like something you'd get at Fisherman's Wharf."

She nodded, like it was coming back to her.

"He liked it. He thought it looked corny. So I thought I'd take a photo of it next to his picture, and send it to him as a joke. That's all!"

She looked past me and nodded again, like she was searching her mind for the memory and nodding because she thought she had it right.

·   ·   ·

And for the first time all day, and maybe for the first time since I'd gotten clobbered by Jules, I stopped secretly suspecting that the whole hunt for the cup might be a typical Hank Kruzenski waste of time.

Because she'd just lied to me. She'd told it like someone who wasn't used to telling lies, but had thought she'd better cough one up in this particular case. She'd said it smooth enough, but hadn't been able to keep herself from looking a little nervous, and hadn't wanted to look at me when she said it, and my built-in B.S. detector was clicking away like a Geiger counter.

Why hadn't she just flipped me off, like when I'd asked her about the guy in the photo? Why had she looked so sad in that shot, if it was a joke photo? And if the joke was for him, why did she still have a copy of the photo in the first place? She wanted to get me off track so bad that she thought she had to lie to steer me in the wrong direction.

"That's all I remember," she said. "It was just ... one day. A photograph taken one day a long time ago. I don't understand why you care so much about it."

"And it was made of rubber?"

"Something like that. Or plastic."

She looked at me like I ought to know what a cheap tourist item would be made of, and went back to staring at the bay.

I figured it was time to explain why I was so hot and bothered about the cup. I told her about the old picture of Mr. C with the cup at the Salt Flats, and about how it had been my very own personal friend Logos who had ID'd it. I told what I remembered of all that Logos had told me, spliced in with what I'd picked up the day before at the library, of how the cup was maybe one of the most important undiscovered artifacts on planet earth, and how all the eggheads at Stanford and UCB and Harvard were slobbering over their pocket protectors to get their hands on it.

"So that's why I've been making such a big deal of it. I mean, I know you don't know where it is," I lied, "but that's why I went ape on you and tracked you down here. Logos would practically kill me if I had a lead on that thing and didn't follow it up."

That was my wad. I sat there with the icy bars of the railing doing the deep chill through my coat, and tried to give her the earnest Walt Cronkite smile. If she gave me a 'well-sorry-I-can't-help-you-and-I'd-like-to-be-alone-now,' I was sunk. I expected her to say it any second.

But she didn't. Damned if she didn't look a little shocked. I didn't see how anybody could have lived in the US of A without hearing about that cup, but maybe they hadn't had any TV reception up in the Hippy Heights Commie Commune.

She gave me a broody look for a few seconds, like she was trying to gauge if I was pulling her chain. Then she looked past me at all the nighttime postcard scenery, and then she seemed to damn near forget I was there. I could've been a pile of construction gear that the work crew left behind.

More than a minute went by.

She looked all bitter, for some reason. Had somebody tried to con her out of the cup once? Except she still had it now. Why would she look bitter and mad if she still had the damn thing, and it was the Cuauhtémoc cup, like I suspected, and she was just finding out that it was worth bales of money?

Maybe she was some kind of ding. I didn't know a thing about her, did I? Maybe she'd come out on the bridge 'cause she was thinking of heaving herself into the drink. A lot of these hippies were mental cases.

"Your friend Logos is the one who identified the cup?" she said at last. In a preoccupied voice, like she was still trying to figure out what she wanted to do.

"Yep. Logos."

"That's a pretty unusual name."

So I told her a little about Logos, and how people had started calling him that, and what a nut he was about history. She didn't look at me at all. It was like I was a recording she was listening to while she gazed out at Alcatraz.

"Are you still friends with him?"

"Well, yeah. I don't see him every day. But, yeah."

She tilted her shoulders back against the tower and shut her eyes. This time she didn't say anything for nearly two minutes. I wriggled around so I wouldn't freeze solid to the cement, and stared at the traffic droning behind her and the wind whipping her black hair around her cheeks. Don't mind me, lady. I love soaking in the polar chill like this.

Finally she opened her eyes and looked at the bay again.

"What's your number?" she asked me.

"What?"

"Your telephone number. What is it?"

I gave it to her. She said it back to me, slow, with her hands stuffed in her coat and her eyes casting out toward Angel Island and Alcatraz, and that angry, bitter look that didn't make sense.

"Okay," she said. "Thank you. I might call you."

So of course I said it might be better if she gave me *her* phone number, and a good time to call her, and her new address while she was at it, because this cup was a pretty big deal, and even though of course I believed her absolutely one hundred and one percent that it was just a rubber Fisherman's Wharf tourist thing, well, some other people might like to talk to her about it.

But I'd got as far with that chick as I was going to get. In a cold, even voice she said we were done talking. If I didn't get up now and let her see me walk back the way I'd come, she'd wave her arms until a car stopped, and I'd get to explain to the police why I wanted to bother her.

•   •   •

I left. The wind tore at me something ferocious all the way back to the toll gates. I thought of hiding out in my 'Cuda and trailing her on the sly when she finally came out, but figured I'd better not risk it. I wasn't no Kojak. She'd ID me for sure, and then I'd queer the whole deal.

No. Stand pat, Hankus. You've got at least an eighteen in the big blackjack game. Stand pat.

I got in my 'Cuda and rubbed my frozen stiff fingers to pump blood in there, and got the key in the ignition. The wind was pounding away so murderous my 'Cuda was creaking on its springs. An eighteen in the blackjack game. Maybe I could've played it better, but for sure I could've played it worse. She'd sounded straight asking for my phone number. Maybe she'd call me. If she didn't I could launch the big woman hunt all over again. And talk to Logos. The chips were going to fall where they was going to fall. There wasn't much percentage in trying to gauge what a woman like that would do about anything. She sure was a weird chick.

CHAPTER FIVE

When I got home Mom was all wrapped up in her favorite crime drama double header. Cannon and Barnaby Jones. She was curled up on the couch in the dark with the black-and-white tee-vee light flickering on this knowing leer pasted on her puss. Like any second old Barnaby was going to karate shop some joker who'd made fun of him for drinking milk.

I spotted the neck of the Old Arkansas bottle on the end table. She couldn't even be bothered anymore to mix it with soda. She just brought the damn fifth out to the living room.

Mom hollered that I had a letter. She sounded polluted. Just what I needed. I wanted to give her a low down on what to say if Evelyn called, and now she wouldn't remember anything. But I still went to the kitchen counter to fetch my mail, and damn if it didn't turn out to be the only thing that could have dragged my mind off the cup. The Wizard's Scribe had sent me a letter.

I took the letter into my bedroom and shut the door, so I wouldn't have to listen to Barnaby Jones solve crimes while I read, and looked at the Asphalt Monarchs monogram, with the top fuel slingshot dragster launching out of the wall of flame, and the New York City postmark. The Wizard's Scribe letters always came from Manhattan, even though a free range type like Mr. C wouldn't have spent more time there than it takes to transfer jets at JFK. The letters had to all get forwarded there.

The letter was typed real neat, with the same Asphalt Monarchs monogram and no XXXXXXXs for typos. I sat on my bed with the letter edges balanced on my fingertips, so I wouldn't get any smudges on the bond.

It said:

```
Brother Hank:
Here's the formula for
calculating carb size:
   engine cid x maximum rpm/3456 =
carburetor cfm
   You can turn 4,800 rpm with your
383. So you get:
   383 x 4800/3456 = 531.94 cfm
```

```
    I'd take another fifteen to
twenty percent off for a street
engine. So, 532 minus 15% = 450
cfm.
    If anything, that stock Carter
525 is too big.
    Brother Hank, your weak link is
your exhaust. Chrysler really had
to shoehorn that B-series big block
into the engine bay. You're going
to have to hunt hard to find a set
of fenderwells that don't heat up
your brake fluid or bump your front
tires, but I wouldn't touch that
Carter or the jets until you do.
Anything else is a bandage on your
elbow to fix a sore on your knee.
    A list of header manufacturers
is on the next page.
    Be good, brother.
    Sincerely,
    The Wizard's Scribe
```

I re-read the letter about five times, and then set it on the bed while I got my Asphalts Monarch binder out. I slipped the letter into a plastic page protector and the envelope into another one, and put the binder back up on the shelf. Then I stretched out on the bed and just looked at the big posters of Don Garlits and Bobby Unser I had taped to my ceiling, with the dippy Barnaby Jones theme song oozing at me through the bedroom wall, and my brain ricocheting around between the cup and my 'Cuda.

Well. Wasn't that mud on my face? Fenderwells. Even Earl had said I'd have to hunt up some fenderwells, but I'd still had to play the fool and cough up $25 for a big Mr. C Enterprises expert advice service to tell me the same thing. What had I expected? 'Oh, here's this magic ointment you can rub on your big block, it'll make it shrink like a 340 so you can bolt some regular headers in there.' There wasn't even room in there for a power steering pump.

From the living room I could hear old Barnaby holding some cop's hand at a crime scene. The poor dumb police couldn't do anything without his help. I chewed my lip and looked at my ceiling posters for awhile, and then I leaned off the mattress and poked around in the garbage collection on my floor and dug out a back issue of *Inside Rodder*. I opened it up to a big photographic investigation they'd done on a new lingerie car wash down in Bakerspatch. The Scribe letter had got me all aggravated. Maybe I'd distract myself with a little manly entertainment before I went to sleep.

The lead shot was of a Penthouse Pet type checking the brake fluid in her underwear. I looked at that shot, but I kept seeing header pipes instead of her legs, and exhaust manifold studs where her face was. Finally I just dumped the mag back on the floor. Fenderwells. How was I even going to get those in my damn 'Cuda? Five to one I'd wind up with a car I couldn't drive.

And my 'Cuda was street style. Frankly. Now if I'd won those Vulcans I would've held up Fort Knox to build a respectable engine, but this was different. Also I'd personally felt a difference just by screwing bigger secondaries into my Carter, even if that wasn't the by-the-book route for performance improvement. The Scribe didn't know altitude and humidity conditions in Prado. Every engine was different. Maybe mine just happened to need bigger secondaries than other 383s.

I got up and pulled the binder back out and sat on the bed reading that letter over and over, while a TV commercial pitchman tried to sell Mom on a new grout cleaner, so she wouldn't feel so ashamed. At least I'd have something to show off at Pilgrim's. That made the third Ask the Wizard letter I'd paid for from the C Team. Everybody always wanted to see it, even if they rodded a totally different make of car.

· · ·

You can skip this next part if you're a motorsports fan, 'cause you've probably already seen eight billion news articles and magazine spreads and TV shows about the C. But not everybody who reads this is a wrench. I ought to tell a little about the Mr. C living legend, and why he was such a big deal to little guy hot rodders like me all over the country, and maybe clear round the world, too.

First, there was how long he'd been around, and his track record. He'd already had a rep with Central California rodders when that Bonneville snapshot had got took, and since then his fame had just skyrocketed. The C was midway into his second decade driving NASCAR and Indy, and his third decade running Formula One, sprints and rally cars. He wasn't going to bow out any time soon, either. He was a top seed for the next Indy, and he was over forty.

But the wins was just part of it. There was the dramatic and death-defying way he did everything. Like those NASCAR and sprint wins he'd racked up after coming home from Europe. People had said a Formula One driver couldn't hold his own in a stock car. Well: he'd shown *them* who could hold his own. More than ten years after the fact, you could still hardly turn on a Sunday sports TV round-up without seeing a clip of his big come-from-behind win at the Rebel 300, or The Duel at Langhorne. That's all people called it now: The Duel. That had to be the most famous sprint car race in history, just 'cause of the C's performance in it.

All those driving titles and down-to-the-wire finishes would've made him a superstar no matter what, and got him those magazine cover spreads. But that still wasn't what made the C the C. It's 'cause he was down there in the trenches with us. No matter how famous he got. When was the last time you saw an Indy 500 winner at some bo-hunk nothing track in Truckee or Barstow or Cheyenne, drag racing head's up for a bar tab against a nobody hot rodder like me? I personally with my own two eyes had met a racer who had seen C at Truckee. Which is a stone *nothing* track. Mark Donohue wouldn't even have looked out the window of a plane flying over Truckee.

But C was there. Look at his giveaways. You think Roger Penske was going to give away customized heads at a hole in the concrete like Fiesta? Or Asphalt Monarchs and Ask the Wizard, so little guys like me could get advice from the big timers. Mr. C was at Le Mans and Daytona and Nürburgring. Sure. But he was standing right next to that Saturday hot rodder in Truckee or Cheyenne or Wichita, too. And for us, that's where it counted.

•　•　•

At work the next morning Dirk was all mad that I'd forgot my No Party at Hardy's button. That was supposed to be our new corporate slogan. "No Party at Hardy's." The Hardy's Madrigals yelled it out at you in all the TV jingles, including the Madgrigal with the Ice Capades gams who the director put in a different mini-skirt for every commercial, and it was plastered all over the weekly fliers, so if you was searching the ends of the earth for a good price on a premium ass wipe that didn't chafe and irritate and ruin your day, well, you'd see No Party at Hardy's, and know you could get that 24 pack of Charmin out the door and onto your toilet roll but quick. Any more than four customers in line was a party. And there was No Party at Hardy's. Get it?

"Where's the button?" Dirk says.

He walked up half-way through an order I'm ringing up. I mean, I'm busy, Dirk. I've got my mind on the undiscovered eighth wonder of the world. And I've got customers. You want to help, try bagging. As if you would.

"'Scuse me?"

"The *BUT*-ton."

He snapped his forefinger on my chest like he's flicking a gum wrapper into the trash. In front of the customer he does this.

The only thing that saved Dirk was that everybody at Hardy's knew he was psycho, and it was just a matter of time before Langley Porter sent the loonie bin truck with the net and the straightjacket. He was about 6'2", and looked like somebody who used to goosestep after old Adolf in the Munich beer gardens, with the storm trooper jaw line and the muscleman physique and the whole nine yards, except that his blue eyes had a weird twitch in them, 'cause he was so psycho he couldn't hold it in completely. Any day he was going to bring another one of his nine billion guns to work and hose down the store.

I said I was sorry. Dirk fished out one of the 'No Party' buttons and frisbee'd it at my apron like he's challenging me to a duel.

"You'll put it on now," Dirk says. His eye twitch was going, and he was starting to breathe hard.

The button was about as big around as a Oktoberfest beer stein. Real subtle and tasteful. No Party at Hardy's, white letters on red. I put the damn thing on. Dirk spun around and stalked off, with this big boing! boing! boing! in his steps, like he's got slinkies in his heels. He always walked everywhere on his toes. He was a big deal light heavyweight kick boxer, when he wasn't fondling himself with his gun collection. He said that was how boxers walked.

Later on I had a customer give me grief 'cause of that lame button. I'm on my knees stocking soup on Aisle 4, and maybe feeling sorry for myself 'cause my boss is a psycho and Hardy's keeps switching me from day to swing to graveyard shifts. Plus I've got the cup to worry about, and if Evelyn is going to call when just my damn Mom is home, and what I'm going to say to Logos.

Then this bozo harummphs over my shoulder, and I look up. It's Mr. Rotary Club at the Rifle Range. Maybe sixty, real meaty looking, like someone pasted a grey toupee on a giant ham and stuck it in tweed blazer with elbow patches, and I swear he was wearing a cravat too. A cravat. He had a couple of loaves of french bread. He snapped his fingers at me.

"Let's get a move on."

So I says gee, sorry, sir, but I'm stocking soup now, and I'm sure there's another Hardy's employee up front who will be only too happy to assist you. Like I'd be happy to lick his toes if it just wasn't against regulations. But he gives a backwards look to the registers, where there was maybe a little bit of a crowd forming, I'll admit it, and then he looks at me again.

"There's no party at Hardy's."

In this super solemn, serious voice, like he's Scout Master reminding me of the Boy Scout credo. I swear. Can you imagine anyone 14 carat dork enough to repeat a TV slogan to a supermarket worker?

So I fell all over myself apologizing, and got up and half sprinted to a register, like I was rushing out to meet an ambulance, and said 'Right this way, sir,' and rang him up.

It worked out for the best, though. In fact, it worked out perfect. 'Cause after he left and I was closing the register back up, I spotted a chick I halfway recognized coming through the sliding doors. She was maybe twenty-five, and wearing stretch slacks that are a majorly bad idea when you're as heavy as she was.

Her t-shirt stood out so much that you didn't look much at her slacks, though. The black print on it said:

I
PROMISE
TO DO
MY BEST
EVERY DAY

"I'm looking for Hank," she said.

I told her she'd found him, and then she said she had a message for me from Logos. He was at Rosenfeld's. If I wanted to see him, he'd be there all tomorrow morning.

•   •   •

That evening the phone rang while I was finger-scooping up the tapioca dessert from my TV dinner. I picked up before Mom could. If my buddy Todd could take my shift tomorrow, I could see Logos without using a sick day.

"Hank?"

I damn near cracked the receiver, from squeezing it so hard. No way I wasn't going to recognize that voice.

"Speaking."

She didn't answer right away. I heard her breathing through the ear piece, light and slow. Maybe she was trying to decide if she should continue.

At least ten seconds went by. From the bathroom I heard the clatter of Mom knocking something out of the medicine cabinet. Drunk. I wondered if Evelyn had heard it. I sat there with a death grip on the receiver and my pulse pounding in my ears, praying that she'd stay on and half-expecting to hear the click and dial tone of the line going dead.

Evelyn asked:

"Do you know where the Great Highway is in San Francisco?"

The Great Highway. What'd that have to do with anything? Why didn't she ask me where the cemetery was in Moscow, Russia, while she was at it? We wasn't rehearsing for some TV quiz show.

But I said:

"I can find it."

I heard her breathing again. From somewhere back of her a siren went off. Maybe she was calling from a pay phone. Maybe she thought I'd try to trace the call, if she rang me up from home.

Finally she said she wanted Logos and me to go to the Great Highway tomorrow night. 8:30 p.m. At the beach, at the corner of Great Highway and JFK Drive. 8:30 p.m. sharp.

Except I hadn't seen Logos yet. I tried to explain it to her. As weird as she was and as worried as I was about scaring her off. I was going to see him tomorrow, but I didn't have any idea if he could come with me.

But she broke in, cold and hard, and said she wasn't interested in arguing about it. Either we both showed up tomorrow, or the deal was off.

Then she hung up on me.

CHAPTER SIX

Rosenfeld's Classic Auto Salvage was way the hey out on Corgin Road, which was a two lane blacktop that just wandered off out near the refinery for about five thousand miles, before the road builder had come down off the LSD he'd dropped and realized nobody needed a road out there. You drove and drove and waved hi to all the bare hills, 'cause that's about all there was, and then finally Rosenfeld's comes up. Right afterward the road turned into a dirt path, like it was ashamed of itself and wanted to disappear without anybody noticing.

Up to five years before, it had done a pretty good business. Rosenfeld's specialized in the rare, unusual and hard to find.

Like let's say somebody wants, oh, the bumper for a '48 Chevy. I don't have any use for the bumper for a '48 Chevy. Do *you* want a bumper for a '48 Chevy? I didn't think so. But somebody does, if they're restoring one. They want that bumper bad. They'll pay through the nose for it. All Abe Rosenfeld had done was to keep an eagle eye on all the junked cars collecting rust on the West Coast, and figure out what parts somebody might want some day, so he could buy low and sell sky high somewhere down the road.

For awhile it had looked like he'd get rich. Abe knew his cars, and he could spot a trend. He bought up a half acre's worth of Porsche 356s before the artsy types went nuts about them, and he predicted the '50s Eldorados would make classic car status, even with the fins. For awhile Corgin Road got a nice work-out just from customers and tow trucks going to and from his yard.

But then his psychological problems caught up with him. At least that's what Logos said. Rosenfeld was a concentration camp survivor. You could still see the Auschwitz tattoo on his forearm. The Nazis had laid a real bad trip on him and he'd always been a moody guy, and when he got excited his accent was so thick you could hardly understand what he was agitated about. But he'd pushed all that stuff under the rug by burying himself in work.

What finally did him in, Logos said, was that a brother who'd been in the camps with him became a slum lord. He bought tenements in West Oakland and wouldn't fix the heat or the water, and then finally one little black kindergarten kid got pneumonia from shivering in the cold all day. And died.

And the brother didn't care. "Schvartzers aren't human." That's what he said to Rosenfeld about it.

After everything they'd seen in the camps. His own brother.

That really got to Rosenfeld. Or it was enough to push him over the edge, seeing as how he was already messed up. He'd always thought he had his people to believe in. Now he didn't even have that. He stopped calling around after those '35 Buick headlight assemblies, and customers bought up his inventory, and he didn't replace it with anything, and every year there was more open space at Rosenfeld's, and less cars. Logos guessed he had maybe a year before he went Chapter 11. Logos had been riding his bike up there for a few months now, greeting the once in a blue moon customer and handling basic stuff that Rosenfeld was too depressed to do.

·   ·   ·

When I motored my 'Cuda through the gates the next a.m. I spotted Rosenfeld in front of the rickety old shed he called an office. There didn't look to be any customers around. He was kicked back on an old sedan bench seat, soaking in the sunlight and petting the official Rosenfeld's wrecking yard dog, which looked about as ferocious as *Lassie*. He was a decent enough looking guy, for a camp survivor. Logos said he was just forty-five.

Rosenfeld stood up when I came in, and waited til he caught my eye through the windshield. Then he pointed at a clump of gnarly old sycamores on a little rise about a football field's length away. I guess Logos had told him I was coming.

I gave him a nod. Rosenfeld went into the shed with his dog, probably so he wouldn't have to talk to me.

The wrecking yard was maybe three acres total, basically just some semi-open space in the boonies that Rosenfeld had hung a chain-link fence around. I docked my 'Cuda and headed out toward the sycamores, and as I picked my way around the rusty axles and radiators and typical wrecking yard crap I went over for the millionth time how I was going to lay out my big pitch. I figured I had to be casual about it. Maybe I'd hardly slept the night before, 'cause I could practically see Dan Rather pitching questions at me on a split-screen on the national news, and the limos and the five star hotels and the whole nine yards, because no way she was going to give us a rendezvous if that thing wasn't legit, but even so: if I got to foaming at the mouth with Logos, he was going to blow me off.

I climbed the rise with the sycamores. The ground fell off steeper on the other side, and there was more wrecked cars scattered among the rocks and bushes on the down slope. The early a.m. sun cast a nice sheen on the crumpled up fenders and chrome bumpers.

A kid's tire swing hung from one of the branches. Miss "I Promise to Do my Best" was sitting in it, still wearing the same t-shirt and the bad idea capris. She gave me a shy smile.

Beached under the sycamore boughs was what was left of a mid-fifties Packard Caribbean. Most of the front clip was gone, and the whole roof had been ripped off. The interior must have been in good shape, though, 'cause I spotted a familiar-looking pair of feet crossed at the ankles and kicked up on the door sill.

I heaved myself up to sit on the front door facing him, and dangled my feet over the floor boards next to the steering wheel, and glanced at Logos, and gave the chick a pleading look.

"Why don't you make him wear a bag over his head, if he's going to read out here in the open? He's too ugly not to be covered up. All the crows and pigeons are going to get sick."

Logos stretched his runty little body on the back bench seat and peered up at me sleepily, like he'd been taking a nap. He had a big tarp spread out beneath him, and a big pillow bunched up behind his neck, and a nice stack of reading material on the floorboard. His own personal reading parlor. I spotted a bag of alfalfa sprouts next to the books, which was the kind of bird food crap Logos dined on.

He looked at the woman on the swing.

"Maria, please permit me the pleasure of introducing my dear childhood friend, Hank Kruzenski. Hank, Maria. Maria, Hank. Hank apparently thought it a matter of some urgency to travel here today to insult me."

Maria gave me another one of her shy smiles. She didn't look to be a big talker.

Logos fetched a bookmark from the stack on the floor-boards and fit it real careful into the book he'd been reading, so he wouldn't lose his place. Then he dropped the book on his runty belly, and folded his hands behind his weird little Afro — or semi-Afro, or whatever you wanted to call it, seeing how many human races had collaborated on his hair — and leered at me sociably. Today I thought he looked more Korean than anything else, but I knew that wouldn't last. Logos looked different every time you met him, like a kaleidoscope.

"I'm not insulting anybody. I'm just giving a health warning. You're the one who's so hot and bothered about protecting the earth." I made a show of looking around in the weeds next to the Packard. "I'll bet there must be at least three dead birds around this car right now, just from you going outside without your bag on."

Logos yawned. "Perhaps it's a genetic adaptation, Hank. It protects me from predators."

"What's that you're reading?" I squinted at the title. "*Theory of the Leisure Class.* Thorstein Veblen. Veblen! What's a Veblen?"

"A person who wrote a book."

"What kind of a parent would hang a name like that on a child?"

"You'll have to do a bit of time traveling to ask him, Hank. He died in ..." Logos flipped up the book to look at the back cover. "... 1929. Something of a lecher, from what I've read, and reportedly almost as rude as you are. I'm sure you would have liked him."

"I don't socialize with college types."

"As they no doubt regret not socializing with you." Logos showed me his pearly whites. "And now, Hank, as much as I enjoy swapping repartee with you, I'll admit to being curious. Greg said that you were quite eager to talk to me. It's time to reveal the mystery."

There was nothing to do but get on with it. I took a deep breath and made a quick mental thumb through of the different approaches I'd rehearsed, but I couldn't remember any of my own catchy phrases. So I just kind of lunged into it, perched on the door of the old Packard and trying to sound nonchalant, even though my pulse hadn't settled down since Evelyn's phone call.

I was asking him to hand over his afternoon and evening to me, basically. If he didn't go for the casual approach, I'd just have to beg.

It took me about twenty minutes. I gave the whole low down about going out to Fiesta, and explained about the Mr. C give-away, and why I'd checked out the hippy shindig across Cargo from the drags, and Evelyn's stack of photos.

When I got to the Cuauhtémoc cup Logos gave me a side-ways, cynical look that I didn't much like, but I hung in there. I told about my library expedition and looking up the Centennial Heritage book. By now I was trying to keep my eyes on the top of his head while I talked, 'cause he was looking at me like I was Tricky Dick giving the Peace through Strength spiel.

But I hung in there. I wrapped up with my big trek onto the Golden Gate bridge, and laid it on thick when I told how Evelyn had tried to BS me with the Fisherman's Wharf story, and how she'd done a big suspicious flip-flop after I'd talked about the cup. Then I told about the phone call the night before, and then I took another deep breath and got down to cases: Evelyn had made an appointment for us. 8:30 p.m., corner of JFK and the Great Highway. Tonight.

"I tried to tell her I hadn't even talked to you yet," I said. "But she just said, 'Be there with him or the deal's off.' You're the big cup expert. She wants you there, too.

"So, I was sort of hoping that maybe you could come out to Frisco with me this evening."

That was my wad.

• • •

Logos didn't answer right away. He yawned and did a slow, sleepy Siamese stretch on the back seat. Then he folded his hands behind his head and leered up at me some more. I made myself look at him eye-to-eye. I was in trouble.

"I sold you that engine block as is," he said, finally.

I rolled my eyes. "I know you sold it as is. What's that have to do with anything?" I tried to sound indignant. "This doesn't have anything to do with that engine block. Nothing. I happened to get a lead on what might be the most valuable historical thing-a-ma-jig on planet earth, that's all. I thought you might care a little. My mistake. So sue me."

Logos held up his hand. "I just want to be very clear, Hank, so there's no misunderstanding. I made no attempt to market that block to you."

"I know! Cripes …"

"You asked me to keep an eye out for parts for your Barracuda. I would have been a less than adequate volunteer had I not told you about that block, but I made it excruciatingly clear that I knew nothing of its pedigree. It was an 'as is' sale."

"I know! I know!"

"So if this story is part of an elaborate scheme to exact revenge for the sale of that block, you are striving to injure an innocent party."

"Would you get a load of this guy?!" I looked at Maria, like she might take up for me. "Who taught you to read back in third grade?"

"Not you."

"Okay, who helped you to sound out some new words?"

"Because I let you steal the Skittles out of my lunch every day."

"That was just part of the reason."

Logos wriggled on the tarp, like he was trying to buy his hips a good bite in a favorite easy chair, and re-crossed his feet on the door sill. "All right, *frère* Hankus, let's try a different approach. How would you gauge the odds that the single most sought after historical artifact of the ancient Americas — which has been missing since the Eisenhower administration, despite the best efforts of hundreds of amateur archaeologists — would suddenly turn up in the possession of a hippy jewelry vendor at a fly-by-night flea market?"

"Well, not so good." I shrugged. "But then why'd she act that way? Why'd she tell me an obvious, point blank lie about the cup, and then pull a big about face and say she'd meet us? If it wasn't real, why?"

Logos looked like he felt a little sorry for me.

"Perhaps because she really did want to be alone on the bridge, Hank, for reasons of her own, and her clumsy prevarications about a rubber Fisherman's Wharf toy had failed to get rid of you. So she pretended to take your story seriously, and asked for your phone number. That *did* get rid of you. Now all she needs to do to discourage your further interest is to be nowhere near JFK and Lincoln Way at 8:30 p.m. tonight. A long wild goose chase would discourage most any stalker. Practically a *fait accompli.*

"Don't you think that's a likelier explanation for her behavior?"

I started to jump in with a snappy come back, but my yap just flapped a couple of times, and no words came out. Damn. That was what I got for trying to do a sales job on a Brainiac. He had me.

I kicked my heels against the door insides some more, and looked at his books and his sprouts on the floorboards, and wondered how anyone could eat that stuff, and what I was going to barter with now that it was time to resort to out and out begging. But it turned out I'd give up too soon.

Logos twisted his head around to look at the tire swing.

"Maria, would you be up for a pilgrimage to San Francisco this evening? We would be honored to have you along."

Maria shook her head and smiled. She had braces. A real shy type.

"That's okay. I'll stay here."

"Are you sure?"

"That's okay."

"In that case, Hank, why don't we meet at..." Logos shut his eyes for a second, like he was trying to remember something. "... the transit kiosk at the junior college at 6:00 p.m.? That will give us plenty of time."

"Oh, hey, you don't have to do that." I said it fast. I knew what he was thinking. "Come on. This is a special occasion. I'll pick you up here."

But Logos just leered at me. I was sunk. You wanted to go anywhere with him, you paid a price. And we both knew what it was.

CHAPTER SEVEN

The big drawback to traveling anywhere with Logos was that he usually insisted on going there on public transit. I'm serious. Never mind that it's cold or pouring rain, or that you've got a car and even offer to *pay* Logos to get personally chauffeured around like he's the Duke of Edinburgh.

Oh, no. You go with Logos, mass transit was how you went. And usually not the easy way. I mean, we had BART now. The legislooters gave us our own billion dollar subway system. If we couldn't ride in my car like sane people, couldn't we at least take the new train to Oakland first before we had to transfer to the stinky bus and smell everybody's underwear?

But that was too easy for Logos. He had stacks of moldy schedules from AC Transit and Vallejo Transit and Middle of Nowhere Transit, and aside from reading his history books there was nothing the little muskrat loved doing more than picking through his mildewed timetables and figuring out some ridiculous new route from point A to B that you've could've done in five minutes in a Pinto, or speculating on how some earthquaking new development in the transit world was going to affect the other lines in the grid, like he was picking ponies at Santa Anita.

Like the Transbay Tube opening. Logos thought that was practically the Second Coming. The Marxist-Leninist BART directors was about to open this big tunnel under the bay to hook up the S.F. BART to the East Bay BART, so all the Frisco flag burners and drug addicts could hop the turnstiles and come straight to Prado to shed and molt and panhandle until their relief checks came in. I'd told Cindy and Mom not to talk to anybody within a block of that BART station. But Logos thought it was wonderful.

· · ·

"This route," Logos was saying, over the noise of the engine, "is likely to be cut after the Tube opens. Really, I'm glad you gave me an excuse to ride it. We're likely among the last passengers."

"I'm thrilled, Logos."

It was the MAVTA Freeway Flier. Flier. A bus. Get it? It *flies* on the freeway. Oh ho ho ho. Pittsburg to Lafayette and all the whistlestops inbetween, loop de loo around the transit centers and shopping malls like a drunk who can't read a map, until sometime before the next inauguration it's supposed to drop us off next to the Chairman Mao fan club on Market Street. Logos had been all hot and bothered to ride it. Never mind that we're on a mission.

At least he'd let me sit next to the window. We had a guy across the aisle from us who opposed soap and showers on religious grounds. I could smell his B.O. even with the vents open.

"I shall overlook the sarcasm in your tone, Hank. You're entirely too flip about these matters." Logos looked around the bus insides. "Transbay rail service is going to metamorphosize travel in the Bay Area. Half of our fellow riders may have to seek out a new route to work."

"You know damn well everybody in this crate is on welfare."

I held my hand over my eyes to block out the sun and squinted at the traffic in the lanes next to us. It looked like the Flier was going to chug onto the 680 after picking up more losers in Pleasant Hill. I figured we had close to another hour left in this stinker. Man.

"What's the score on the t-shirt chick?" I asked.

"Which 't-shirt chick' might that be?"

"Maria."

"I don't think it would be chivalrous of me to reveal the details of her life without her consent, Hank." Logos shot me a nice leer. "How would you feel if I were to tell strangers of your fabled gridiron exploits in Pop Warner?"

"Ha ha, Logos." He meant when I'd wet my pants and thrown an interception. "Very funny."

"She has panic attacks sometimes. I think I can tell you that much. We're keeping each other company for awhile." Logos lowered his voice. "I will confide, Hank, that I have hopes that an amorous spark or two may fly between Maria and Rosenfeld while I'm away. That would kill two birds with one stone."

"He's old enough to pay her allowance."

"She's thirty, Hank. Older than she looks." Logos hesitated. "He might be less aggressive than a younger man. I have hopes."

"What're you going to do if they get hitched? Treat 'em to a ride on this heap o' crap on their honeymoon? I mean, cripes, Logos. I got a car. I can drive. Why'd we have to go in this thing?"

I knew that was a mistake almost the second I said it. Logos shifted on the seat and launched into what I recognized from the git-go was Environmental Speech number 856 or 932 or 421, about how we didn't need to drive every place and had to use technology responsibly and couldn't just order up a fresh planetary habitat like a burger at Pilgrim's if we used this one up, and how humanity was pulling a big fat F in the late Holocene epoch report card, and blah blah blah. I'd only heard it about eight zillion times before, but once Logos got going, you were usually stuck.

Fortunately, today I got a reprieve. The shower boycotter across the aisle stood up and grabbed the back of the seat ahead of him. Big fat forty year old in a Goodwill reject overcoat, with his hair sticking out like an Einstein wig. Ten to one he slept in the ivy plants by the 680. I was surprised he hadn't brought his cardboard box along. Maybe he'd forgot it under the overpass.

He's got an itch. Standing up there with everybody glancing at him he goes to clawing away at his side, but dang, he can't get at it, so he pulls open his overcoat and yanks his shirt up, and out flops this giant, pasty white gut like you'd expect to see under a sheet at the coroner's, with pudgy red zits on it, and half the zits got hair sprouting out of them. Makes me want to heave. He goes in to scratching and clawing and raking away at his naked gut with the fat flopping like jelly under his fingers, while everybody sneaks disgusted looks at him, and he grunts and stamps his foot a little, and then a weird, sleepy smile spreads across his face. I swear. It looks like this is turning him on. Maybe I ought to introduce him to Barry. They could go on stage together.

That killed the Earth Boy lecture. Logos got a pained expression, and tried not to look at all the excited grunting and scratching next to him, and rolled his eyes up at the bus ceiling. I stared out the window some more. The turn onto Treat Boulevard was coming up and traffic had slowed to a crawl, and I looked out at the cars inching along in the nearby lanes.

Then an MG convertible zipped up in the lane right beside my window, and I had something to take my mind off the shower boycotter because there were a couple of stone, I mean *stone* foxes taking a ride in this thing. In bikinis. Free show. It was getting late in the day for sunbathing, but maybe they was on their way to a moonlight cocktail pool party in Lafayette or Orinda, with their California beach bunny locks streaming in the wind and their nekkid bare arms and thighs all slathered up with Coppertone. Man. Maybe this eco-friendly public transit had some perks I hadn't counted on, considering the view I've got, and just as I was slobbering over the one in the passenger seat she turned her head and looked up at the bus.

I knew her. Oh, cripes, it's Connie Dawson, Earl Howser's *cousin.* She looked right at the bus window. I swung my head back fast and scrunched down in the seat and held up my hand between my cheek and the window like I was trying to block out the sun, but I was just positive she recognized me, and that's all I needed. She was going to blab the whole thing to Earl and I was going to have him and his disgusting friends queuing up in my lane at Hardy's just so they could rag on me about what kind of ETs I could pull down in my smokin' public transit *bus,* and if I was going to let the bums ride in the public *bus* when I took it to the drag strip, and how Connie says she'd *love* to go riding with me in it, 'cause a public *bus* is such a turn-on. I could hear it already.

And I'd never been so humiliated in my entire life, and I tried to give a dirty look to Logos but now he was actually *talking* to the shower boycotter about something, like how quickly you could stink up a enclosed space if you skip bath time for a week. So I just sat there and glowered straight ahead, and reminded myself it didn't matter. We weren't on a wild goose chase. Evelyn was going to be there, and one thing would lead to another, and pretty soon all the drive-time traffic around us now would be listening to ol' Hank swap sound bites with Jim Dunbar on KGO, and watching me on a Huntley-Brinkley special segment, and staying up to see me on Carson, too. And they'd send a limousine to fetch me to the studio, and that and my 'Cuda would be all I'd ride from now on.

•　　•　　•

The Great Highway starts way up in the cliffs near the north-west end of S.F. and then takes a slow slalom turn downhill to ocean level. Then for about three miles it's a seaside thoroughfare, with the beach and the humongous big ass Pacific on one side, and on the other side all the masochists crazy enough to live that close to the ocean and get cremated 24/7 by wind and cold and fog and salt air.

The west side of Golden Gate Park butts up against that three mile stretch. That's where JFK Drive loops out of the park and meets the Great Highway. It felt like the middle of nowhere. At least that late at night.

Logos got us to the corner with twenty minutes to spare. We checked the street signs and crossed the highway to the ocean side, and sat on a short stone barrier thing that kept the wind from splattering sand all over the walkway. To the north the lights of the old Cliff House blinked at us out of the fog, and that got Logos to yakkety-yakking about some croaker with mutton chop 'burns who'd bought the Cliff House in 1883 and had owned a whole land grant worth of property up there, and had been one of the most generous and kind-hearted and wonderful and blah blah blah San Franciscans who'd ever lived. Sutro somebody. Like I cared. That's all it took to distract Logos. Something about history.

I nodded and unh-hunhed a lot, but my heart wasn't in it. It felt spooky out there. They get some serious fog on the west side of San Francisco. Tonight there was cargo planes full of the stuff, shellacked over the shoreline like Zeus had hooked up a giant dry ice machine out on the Farallones. It hung in a wispy white shroud over the highway, and filtered the light from the big streetlamps so it looked all pale and weird. Every once in awhile the drone of an engine would come up and two lights would swell in the fog, and then out of the pea soup some average Joe Citizen on a diaper run in his Rambler would roll by, like Logos and me was on a asphalt stage under a 360 degree curtain, and the car was crossing the stage in front of us and then disappearing in the fog curtain again.

Across the highway, and maybe a hundred yards to the south of us was a restaurant. I could make out the yellow lights of the windows through the fog. Once in awhile a car would troll out of the lot, and I'd watch the headlights spear off into the dark away from us. Maybe on another night the Richie Riches who forked over bread to eat in a swanky place like that would've taken an after dinner stroll by the ocean. Not tonight. It was too cold. Nobody was on that walkway but us.

I didn't like how I felt. I didn't know this Evelyn at all, did I? She'd handled me on the bridge like she'd had a ten gauge aimed at my gut. Maybe she wasn't so harmless. Maybe she and that guy in the photo was part of some big drug smuggling ring, for all I knew, and dumb old Hank had got to sniffing too close, and tonight they was going to get rid of me. And Logos too.

"A question about your friend, Hank. Did anything in her manner suggest that she might have ventured onto the bridge with suicidal thoughts in mind?"

I shoved my hands harder in my coat pockets and watched a couple of cars swoosh by. I felt Logos looking at me.

"Well, she seemed depressed. Now that you mention it. But I didn't think she looked suicidal. Not that I know what a suicidal person acts like."

"It's the number one bridge in the world for suicides. And you said she's in the habit of going out there by herself at night. That's unusual." Logos cast a mistrustful eye around us. "Why do you think she asked us to meet her out here? We're not exactly in the thick of things."

•   •   •

I didn't get a chance to answer. A big galoot in a dirty down jacket was shuffling up the walkway toward us.

He looked kind of like a hippy. He had a scraggly Fu Manchu hanging over his lip, and long black hair that he'd tied back in a ponytail. Maybe he was going to hit us up for tickets to a Dead concert.

But there was something off about him, too. I couldn't put my finger on what it was yet, but it was way off, whatever it was. Off in a bad way. I felt my stomach tighten up.

The dude walked up like he didn't have a care in the world, like he was out for a little mid-evening stroll by the ocean.

Then he got up to us, and sat on the stone barrier right next to me. Six inches away. Like he knew me.

"Did the 18 come yet?" he asked.

He had a gravelly voice, like the heavy in a *Godfather* knock off. From back east somewhere.

"'Scuse me?" I said.

"You don't read so good, huh?"

He cocked his head at the street lamp next to us. There was a wide yellow band around the pole, with a number stenciled on it. So that was how they marked bus stops in Frisco.

"No bus since we got here," I said.

"How long is that?"

"Maybe twenty minutes."

The guy grunted and didn't thank me, and didn't move any farther away, and stared across the highway at the once-in-awhile cars shushing through the fog. I looked at the leg of his jeans sitting next to me on the wall. There was a big jagged stain on the denim, like he'd spilled some Thunderbird on it a month ago and hadn't gotten around to a laundry run, and it had been collecting dust and crud ever since.

They were dirty jeans even for a hippy, and his down jacket was in bad shape, too, but that wasn't what looked off about him. Mostly it was his eyes. They were dead and glassy and stupid looking, like shark eyes. Like he'd got high or drunk or both for so long that he didn't remember what sober was, and just went through life like a zombie.

He had gloves on. Tight black gloves, so his fingers could move. They looked new.

I just sat there and acted freeze-dried. What were we supposed to do about this big gink? Evelyn hadn't said anything about meeting anybody. Maybe he was just an unlucky accident, and didn't have anything to do with her, and just happened to have walked up in time to maybe queer the whole deal, if Evelyn decided to bail 'cause she spotted three people on the corner instead of two.

But it was just about 8:30, wasn't it? And there wasn't anybody else around. Odds are he wasn't an unlucky accident. That he'd come there to see us.

Some kind of commotion had kicked up in the restaurant parking lot. I heard a car door slam, and laughter and giggly talk from some people across the highway. They sounded black. Like a bunch of black fraternity kids. Maybe they'd come out for a big Sigma Phi Delta Alpha something or other party, and were still carrying on while they came out to their cars.

I glanced at Logos. He was leaning forward and looking across me at the guy like he was the main attraction. Maybe he had ESP.

"Which one of you yo-yos is Hank?" the guy asked.

So that settled it.

"You got him," I said.

The guy nodded.

"Okay, here's how it's going down. Another few minutes, a bus is going to come. You two are getting on first. I'll sit down after you do."

He looked at me with his dead druggie eyes, like I was just something between him and his next fix. His cheeks was all pocked and cratered-up. Maybe he'd had bad acne as a kid. Either that or he lived on candy and fries and didn't care what it did to his skin. Up close he didn't look so much like a hippy. Maybe he'd grown his hair and beard out to make time with hippy chicks, and maybe the longhair community felt obligated to let him hang around, the way gung-ho Christians might try to act decent around a future death row inmate of the year who went to their church. But they wouldn't want to, and they wouldn't like the looks of this guy any better than I did.

"In the bus, I don't want you doing or saying anything that might look like a signal. You sit there and ride. You see me get up, you get up, too, right away, 'cause we're leaving. You got that?"

I said yes.

In the parking lot the frat kids were still carrying on. A horn tootled, and I heard the faint laughter again.

The guy looked across the highway toward the sound with his lip curled. He had bad teeth, to go with the rest of him.

"Nigger night at the beach," he said.

He made his black-gloved hand into a pistol shape, and pointed it at the restaurant, and jerked his finger up and down like he was firing off rounds.

"Maybe if somebody pumped a couple of slugs into them, they'd stay on their own side of the bridge."

. . .

The 18 came a few minutes later. I saw the headlights through the fog, and the white route letters in the head sign over the windshield.

"Let's go," Psycho said.

He stood up. Something heavy was weighing down one side of his jacket.

Now, maybe you've been thinking for the past few pages that old Hank had some reservations about this hiram. Well: that's an A+ on the report card for you. You just made the honor roll. I didn't know what crypt this guy had drug his chains out of, but I didn't like his black gloves or what he had in the jacket or anything else about him, and wasn't real keen on joining him on a late night oceanside cruise. Even if I was hot to see the cup.

But then that damn Logos had to hop up and look at Psycho like he was Cary Grant inviting us out on a yachting spree. Classic Logos. He made friends with the dings on the bus, right? Why not be buddies with this one, too?

I figured I didn't have much choice. My partner was in. I got up.

. . .

The 18 was almost empty. There was an old lady sitting close to the driver, probably so she'd feel safe, and then four or five others scattered around the inside. Logos led the way in and took a seat in the middle of the bus. I sat beside him. Psycho slid in behind us.

The bus pulled back onto the Great Highway. I couldn't see much through the windows with the lights on inside, and with the engine roar I couldn't hear much outside, either.

After awhile the bus turned left, and then south on a street a couple of blocks in from the Great Highway. In the dark I could make out the shape of the boxy little Frisco stucco row houses, with a few of the front windows lit up.

Psycho leaned in and put his hand on the grab rail next to our necks. I felt his breath on my ear.

"You see that house up there? The pink one with the green trim?"

I got a nice close-up of the stains on his jacket sleeve as he pointed between us. I saw the house. It looked like just another cookie-cutter box in the row.

"That's where old Granny got gangbanged," Psycho said. "You remember that?"

I did, kind of. All the TV news stations had covered it. It hadn't exactly been a story to give you a warm, snuggly feeling. Five sickos kidnapped and raped a sixty year old. Real swell.

"They grabbed her right out of that front yard." Psycho pointed again. "Five guys in a van. Man, that's cold. She was in the hospital for a month. Her privates was all lacerated."

I looked at him. He was talking to us, so I figured I could look. His skin looked like a slipper the dog had chewed on. He must've eat breakfast, lunch and dinner out of a candy bar wrapper to get skin like that.

"I think the FBI was in on it," he said. "It said on the news she was a red diaper baby."

His bad breath went off my neck, and his fingers slid off the hand rail. He settled back in the seat behind us.

Pretty soon I heard him giggling. Hee hee hee. Like he could hardly hold it in, like he was choking back the big laughs that would have come if he hadn't been on the bus with us. Nothing to tickle your funny bone like a quintuple rape of a senior.

He stopped talking. I tried to read the names of the cross streets as the bus motored past, just in case Logos and me had to make a dash for it.

Damn Logos for getting on the bus with this ding. Maybe he could go palling around with all the nutcases in the Bay Area. Not me. I mean, I was from Prado. There had to be some unwritten rule in life that psychos like this got crated up and shipped one way to Frisco or Oakland or L.A., where they could chew on fence posts without disturbing innocent suburbanites like me. This dude would have broke Freud's couch in half.

And the worst was yet to come, wasn't it? Psycho was going to want us to get off the bus with him. We could kiss our shot at the cup goodbye, if we didn't. And maybe kiss everything else goodbye if we did.

•   •   •

The bus hung a left and then a fast right turn, and then it hit a big street I actually recognized. Sloat. Where the zoo is. Oh, I get it. The bus driver's going to stop at the front gate, and Psycho's going to hop the fence and scamper back to his cage. He'd just gone AWOL 'cause they'd run out of bananas. But that didn't happen, either. The bus doubled back, and headed south past the backside of the zoo, where there wasn't many houses. Then the old lady got off, and so did another passenger. Now there was maybe only one other person on the bus besides Psycho and Logos and me.

Then the bus turned onto a highway. To either side was nothing but trees and bushes and telephone poles. No houses at all. I didn't even know there was a place like this in Frisco.

The bus motored on. I kept waiting to see lights and houses ahead, but there wasn't any. It was like we was on a road in the woods.

Psycho stirred behind us. From the corner of my eye I saw his arm move as he pulled the rope signal.

"This is where we get off," he said.

He stood up and poked me in the back of the neck.

"Let's go."

A couple of critical seconds passed. Where the old fickle finger of fate could have veered south to TJ or north to Squaw Valley, and taken a completely different break than it did, if I'd just thought faster, and if I'd been collected enough to say what I felt.

The bus pulled over. Psycho stepped past me. 'You don't seriously expect me to get out in the middle of nowhere with a knuckle dragger like you,' was what I *wanted* to say. But while I was wondering how to politen that up enough to say it aloud, Logos, the little bastard, Logos actually stands up and squeezes past me into the aisle.

And now they're both heading up toward the driver.

Psycho looked annoyed. "I said *let's go*."

So I did. I could have just sat there. I could have flipped him the bird, and told Logos not to go, and Logos probably wouldn't have if I'd said that.

But I didn't do those things. I got up and followed them out of the bus. With absolutely nobody to blame but myself, for whatever happened next.

•   •   •

We stepped off, and the bus pulled back onto the pavement, and once the taillights faded out of sight we could have been on a road twenty miles out of Fort Bragg, for all the signs of civilization I saw around me. No city lights, no houses close by, just the shadows of the hills and trees looming around us, and the smell of the ocean.

"What's next," Logos asked politely.

"What's next is we just wait here for a minute to see if the coast is clear." Psycho sounded irritated.

"I'm a little curious ..."

"You're not curious about anything. Just shut up."

He fished something out of his jacket. I spotted the pint label as he unscrewed the cap, and then I smelled it. Dick's Vodka. Great. That went with the rest of the package. Not even my mom drank that. He took a long swig.

Logos looked up at him politely, like he was waiting for Psycho to start a congressional address. The little gerbil didn't even have the decency to look scared. That was the thing about Logos. Nobody thought of him as brave, Logos included, but in some ways he was, more than practically anybody I'd met. He wasn't bothered by nut jobs. There was always a couple of people he was looking after, like Maria and Rosenfeld and the Vietnam vet he'd gone to visit — and his whole family, for that matter, though I didn't think Barry held a candle to Psycho. Logos just assumed that they all had a clogged fuel line upstairs, or a couple of fouled plugs, and what you wanted to do was look at life like you had a clogged fuel line, too, so you could see how the world looked through their eyes.

"Okay, here's how it's going to go down." Psycho nodded at the woods. "We're going up there. We've got a place picked out.

You're going to see what you came to see. But you're going to do it *my way*. Understand? If you don't, you're not seeing anything."

He took another draught of his medicine. Maybe I could fix him up with mom. He capped it and slid it back inside his windbreaker.

"I know what I'm doing," Psycho said. "I got experience."

"Yes, sir," Logos said.

Psycho nodded at the woods, on the ocean side. "That way. Get going."

Logos took the lead, and that left me in the middle, with Mr. Personality bringing up the rear. We walked away from the road and then stepped onto a narrow trail, that I could just make out under my feet in the darkness.

The trail turned sharp up a slope into the tree line. I felt sand mushing under my shoes. It was hard to climb on. Then we hit the tree line and it got a lot darker, with the trees rising up on either side of us. Big, gnarly old cypress trees. Logos was just a dark moving shadow ahead of me. At my back I heard Psycho's breath rasping out. Man, he was in bad shape. Just this little slope was making him pant.

"Stop at the top," he said.

Past Logos' head I saw sky and blinking stars where the trail came out of the woods. Then we hit the top of the rise, and were out in the open again.

We was in some kind of big ocean recreation or park place. At least from what I could make out in the dark. There was another sandy trail next to us now, and it was a lot wider. Even with the fog there was enough moonlight for me to see the trail curve up around a little hill toward the ocean. Miles and miles to the north the city lights blinked at us, maybe from the part of Frisco we'd come from. I could smell the ocean real good now. It was close.

I looked at Psycho just in time to see him haul the pistol out of his jacket.

• • •

It was a black snub nose. Maybe a .38. Not that it made any difference at that range.

He looked mad that I was looking at it.

"Just hold your water. Okay? This is for security."

"Sir, I can assure you that you won't need that with us," Logos said.

"Yeah. Maybe I won't, and maybe I will. But I got it." He nodded at the trail curving up the hill. "Get going. We ain't in the right place yet."

Logos set out, and I took the slot behind him. At least I didn't have to get in a big internal debate with myself anymore about following this nut job's lead. He had a gun on us. That settled things.

This wasn't turning out to be the most joyful night of my life. People didn't usually pull guns on me in Prado. Sometimes old Mrs. McDougall got torqued off that I wouldn't take her Golden Years at Hardy's Seniors card, which had only been expired for a half century, but she'd never been mad enough to haul out her Colt and take a bead on me.

I was stuck. I should have bailed when Psycho started talking to us. I should have bailed when he told us to get out of the bus. I should have bailed when he told us to walk away from the road. But I hadn't done any of that stuff, and now I was in a bad, bad way, and I'd got Logos in it, too. We couldn't yell for help. Nobody would hear us. We couldn't run. He could shoot us. All I could do was stare at my feet while I trudged up the trail, with my pulse pounding in my ears and my gut wrenching around like the lead car on the Matterhorn. Like we was walking to meet the firing squad.

We marched along for maybe five minutes, and finally we came out on top of a bare hill with some kind of low concrete fort built into the top of it. I couldn't figure out what the hell it was. It was about five yards around and circle-shaped, and stood maybe a foot off the ground. Chunks of concrete around the edges had crumbled off, and the steel rebar was sticking out.

"Sit on the ground there."

Logos and me sat on the ground on the ocean side of the thing. Psycho stood over us. With his free hand he rooted around in his jacket again. I thought he was hankering after another slug of his medicine, but then I saw metal glint on his fingers.

Handcuffs.

"Okay, here's what we're gonna do. I'm cuffing you guys together. We're not taking any chances on this. You do what I say, and then maybe you get to see your girlfriend. Okay?"

His voice had gone up an octave, and the nose of the gun was twitching at the ground. He had the shakes. Oh, boy.

"Sir, I can assure you that neither of us is going to try to escape. You don't need to handcuff us."

I looked at Logos. That made it worse. Now even Mr. Nerves of Steel looked worried.

"I *said* we're *putting the cuffs on*! Okay? That's part of the deal. I don't want an argument from you guys."

He was almost shouting. He took a step back and raised the gun a little, like he wanted to remind us he had it. Except he was still shaking, and I watched the muzzle twitch and jerk at the general direction of our midsections. Hoo, boy.

It took about five minutes. He tossed me the bracelets and told me to put one cuff on Logos' wrist, and then stepped up with that damn gun twitching over my legs while he looked to see if it was tight enough. Then he told Logos to loop the cuffed hand back behind one of the rebar pipes, and then he made Logos lean over to cuff the spare bracelet to my wrist.

Psycho clambered up on the concrete roof behind us, and bent down to cinch the cuffs on our wrists some more. Then he stood in front of us with the gun again. He looked like a village idiot who'd just won a spelling bee.

"You're fixed there good, huh? I told her! I know how to do this stuff."

He hauled out his pint and tilted a nice atta-boy wallop down his gullet. Then he shoved the snub nose back into his jacket.

"Wait here," he said.

He walked off. For a couple of seconds I heard pebbles scrunching under his feet while he moved away from us.

Then nothing. He'd left us.

"'Wait here,'" I said, after a minute. "I like that. Cuffs us to this thing, then 'Wait here.' What else are we going to do? Go swimming?"

Logos just looked off toward the Pacific. Even through the fog I could see it now from up high where we were, this monstrous black bastard stretching off to the Farallones and a thousand miles beyond, with about eight gazillion stars winking and blinking through the fog above. Probably all the extraterrestrials were spying on us and snickering. Dumb earthlings. Walked into a trap and breathing their last.

"Have you ever met a more psycho human being in your entire life? 'That's where old Granny got gangbanged.' What kind of diseased thing is that to say?"

"He did seem to be troubled."

"Troubled! I like that, Logos. That's rich." I rattled the cuffs. "And you called him 'sir.' I swear! 'Sir.' Would you like me to lift the rock you slithered out from under, *sir*? Would you like me to scrape the scales and puss off your boogery slimy skin, *sir*? I swear. What loony bin do you pry these people out of?"

Logos shrugged. He didn't seem to be nervous anymore, which just got me more agitated.

"Hey." I leaned against him. "Earth to Logos. Hey. Hello. We're locked up next to a concrete slab in the middle of nowhere. He had a gun. We're not waiting for the maître d at the Fairmont. It's time to *do something*. We got to get out of this."

"Hankus, I beg to differ." He almost sounded cheery. "We may yet come out of this unscathed, although we could be in for some unpleasant moments in the hours ahead. I don't think we need to do anything."

"Oh? I get it. The cuffs and the gun, those are the *good* signs. If we was in trouble, he would've had a machete."

"Think about it a bit, Hank. We are not worth kidnapping. The only goal in waylaying us would be robbery or murder. If he had intended to do either, he would have searched us by now for valuables, or would have killed us. That neither of these calamities has come to pass suggests that he is behaving in good faith, more or less."

"Oh? So you think it's a good idea to go following nut jobs off the bus in the middle of nowhere? Is that it?"

We went on like that for awhile. I was mostly P.O.'d that he wasn't as totally petrified as I felt. It was a miracle my undies was dry, frankly. I ragged on him for following Psycho on the bus and for getting off with him, and then asked where we was, like Logos was supposed to know, and then when the little Einstein actually did know got madder still. Fort Funston. The thing we were tied to was part of an old military installation.

So that set me off on another Frisco tirade. Fort *Fun*ston. This was how the commies got their jollies out here. Pull guns on each other, march their buddies out in the boonies and tie 'em to concrete slabs. What *fun* at Fort *Fun*ston. It was just a real good thing that J. Edgar had a file on basically everybody we'd seen since we'd crossed the Bay Bridge, and I was about to go into my ICBMs under the San Bruno Mountain idea, and why this was Nixon's last chance to pull it off, when I heard the pebbles scrunch behind us again.

I shut up.

Someone was coming up.

I started to crane my head around, but stopped myself. Psycho might not like that, if he was coming back. I sat next to Logos and stared straight ahead, and shook like a damn pinball machine while the *scrunch scrunch scrunch* of the footsteps closed in.

Evelyn stepped in front of us.

•   •   •

She was wearing her big pea coat again, and holding a flashlight. She looked like she'd looked on the bridge. Not nervous, or scared, or excited. Just a little depressed, like meeting us was just another thing she had to do.

She didn't turn on the flashlight. She stood in front of us, and looked at me, and here's what she said:

"Your dog won't go away."

Your dog. I stared at her.

"I went back to pick up some things, and he followed me. He just hangs out on the front steps. He's a nice dog, but he's not mine. He ate the cat food."

Oh. Ruby.

"Is that why you got us handcuffed out here?"

"I'm serious. How do we take him back? He belongs to somebody."

"He's not my dog."

Evelyn looked put out. "He jumped out of your car."

I wasn't in the mood to yak about an escapee from the animal shelter, what with our rendezvous with Psycho and the handcuffs. But she was a weird chick, and it was her show. So I gave her a quick rundown of how Ruby was the vagabond hound of Prado, and how some people thought he was good luck but that no one had ever been able to sell him on everlasting dog-to-human matrimony. Ruby had hung with me while he'd wanted to, I said, and when he'd jumped out of my 'Cuda in front of the hippy shack, well, that had meant we were quits.

Evelyn looked like she didn't believe me. Logos cleared his throat.

"If I may intrude," he said, formal as all get out. "Ruby is well known around Prado Diablo for just the reasons that Hank has described. He may once have had an owner. That is possible. Someone undoubtedly paid for his neutering. I know that some years ago he took sick, and was treated at length by a local veterinarian. That must have cost money, too, and the veterinarian likely retained a file on him. But Ruby did not reward any of these donors or chroniclers of his canine life with loyalty. He has always gone his own way."

Evelyn took a step closer to Logos. I thought she stared at him for a long time. I mean, he was new, so naturally he was going to get the once over, but I thought this was more like the twice or thrice over, from how long she checked him out.

Something dark and bitter slid over her eyes while she did it. For no reason that I could see. Maybe she was an unofficial Klu Kluxer, like Psycho, and didn't cotton to Logos 'cause he was 3/16th black, or whatever the mix was. Maybe her and Psycho were brewing up their own little racist longhair commune.

"So you're Logos," she said.

Logos nodded.

She flicked on the flashlight and put the beam right on his face.

Which surprised me. I mean, that was *rude*, flat out rude, to just train a light on somebody. She'd been plenty weird, but not rude.

Logos squinted and cocked his head to one side, the way you would if somebody aimed a big light square at your mug. I couldn't see her at all with that thing going. She held it on him for damn near a half minute. Then finally she shut it off, and Logos and me blinked while we tried to get used to the dark again.

"Why don't you tell me about the cup that Hank wants to find?" she said quietly.

Logos was still trying to blink his eyesight back, but he started talking. He gave her the whole history, with Red Cloud and Ulysses Grant and Cuauhtémoc and Manco Inca the spirit guides, and Mr. C at the Salt Flats. It took about ten minutes. He talked slow and picked his words, and after he got his eyeballs back watched her the whole time he talked. I knew him good enough to guess why: he thought she just might have something, and he didn't want to spook her before she laid out her cards.

I had the sense to keep my yap shut. Man, it felt weird to sit there looking up at her with our hands cuffed, like a couple of rustlers that Hoss had caught sneaking into the stables on *Bonanza*. I kept waiting for a director to step out and yell "*Cut!*" I looked past her at the tree shapes I could make out in the dark, and listened to the surf flogging away at the shore close by, like old Zeus beating dust out of a rug.

Evelyn listened. She didn't ask any questions, and when Logos wrapped up the story she didn't say anything about the photo she'd had of the cup, or her line of B.S. about it being molded rubber tourist crap, or especially about why she'd gotten help from the psych ward centerfold-of-the-month to truss us up.

She stepped in closer, and peered at where our wrists was hooked together behind the rebar, just to make sure her charming friend had put the cuffs on good. Then she stepped back again. I felt my pulse pick up. She set the flashlight at her feet and unbuttoned her coat, and reached for something inside of it. It was big, whatever it was, and she had trouble fishing it out, but eventually she did: this blocky lump maybe the size of a softball, all swaddled up in paper towels.

One by one, she picked the towels off. Then she had it uncovered. She held it on her open palm and stooped to pick up the flashlight with her other hand, and then knelt and held the thing in front of us like she was an altar boy holding the King James open to the Beatitudes, and flicked the flashlight on, and aimed it at what she was holding.

It was the cup, all right.

Son of a bitch if it wasn't. Or at least it looked like every picture I'd seen of it. I looked for the marks that Logos had spotted years before, that had started the whole fuss about the thing: the symbols that were Aztec and Incan and Sioux, that had no business being on the same piece of sculpture, but were there all the same. I spotted them all, or all that I remembered. Which didn't mean it was real. I knew it wasn't me that was going to ID the cup as the real McCoy, anyway.

It was just about the size of a softball, like I said, and a slate gray color. Or it looked slate gray in the light from the flash. I looked at the eyes and nose and mouth, and the spot on the top of the cup where it turned into a cup. The rim of the cup was darker than slate gray, almost black.

The longer I looked at it, the weirder I felt. I told myself it was just a sculpture. I didn't even know if it was real. If it was real and so all-fired powerful, how could she just lug it around in her pocket like a hunk of rusty bicycle chain without being affected by it? I looked at the steely gray stone eyes and mouth of the thing, and to me it looked real, and I thought of the super ultra-mysterioso power it was supposed to have, and of the people who had gone flat out crazy because of handling it, and I don't mind telling you that a part of me would have felt a lot more comfortable with that thing already in a museum, with little gallery lamps spotlighting it on a red velour pedestal, and a couple of inches of bulletproof glass between it and me, and definitely not on some hippy chick's palms right under my nose. Creeped me out.

After awhile I pulled my eyes off it, because I didn't think it would help the cause if Evelyn saw me getting the shakes. I snuck a glance at Logos, but that only gave me the willies worse.

I'd never seen him look like that. He was sitting far enough forward to strain the cuff on his wrist. His eyes were bright and locked on the cup like he was trying to memorize every part of it, with his lips parted and his nostrils dilating slowly in and out, in and out, 'cause he was breathing hard even though we were just sitting there.

"Could I see the back, please?" he asked.

She turned the cup around and trained the light on the back, and he stared at that for at least a minute. Then he asked to see the bottom, and even the top. His eyes was on fire, practically. Like that cup was the most important thing on earth.

"Miss, I have a small camera in my shirt pocket. Could I please ask you to unlock the handcuffs so I can take a few pictures? I give you my word that I will not assault you."

"I don't have the keys."

Logos licked his lips. He was looking right dead at her, like this was the biggest hand of the year in the Vegas poker tourney and he was going mano-a-mano with Amarillo Slim. Like he was cogitating on how she'd react to every single word he said.

"Miss, I'm very sorry if you have felt put off by any of the questions you have been asked about the cup." Logos shot me a quick glance. "I understand that it may be personally important to you. If we have seemed at all insensitive, I hope you'll accept my apology. It was not intended."

Evelyn just waited. She knew he was going to make a pitch.

"Could I please ask you to tell us just a little about how that artifact came to be in your possession?"

"No."

I held back a snicker. Ol' Brainiac was going to get about as far with her as I had.

"Is it possible, then, to tell us how long you've had it?"

She shook her head.

"Or where you acquired it?"

"No."

She turned off the flashlight. She bent to pick up the towels she'd dropped, and began to smother up the cup in them again. Logos looked like he was watching Amarillo scoop all the chips off the table. He started to say something, then stopped himself, then changed his mind again and said it anyway:

"Miss, I know I'm speaking out of turn, but an object of that significance deserves to be properly protected. If you were to fall or hit your pocket, it could shatter."

Evelyn thought that was pretty funny. She finished covering it with the towels and pushed it back in her coat pocket.

"You wanted to see it," she said. "You saw it. Dwayne will be back in a little while. He'll take the handcuffs off."

"Can you please tell us how we can get in touch with you?"

Evelyn smiled. It was the first real smile I'd seen out of her. Maybe she enjoyed tormenting eggheads.

"You can't," she said. "I go where I want to go. I might head up to Canada."

"Can you tell us your plans for the cup?"

"I don't have any." She laughed. "I'll take good care of it. Maybe I'll get in touch with you. Maybe I won't. You wanted to see it. You saw it. Dwayne will be back in a little while to take the cuffs off."

She left. I heard the pebbles scrunching as she stepped off, and then nothing. We were alone again.

"Real cooperative chick, ain't she?"

Logos didn't want to talk yet. He mumbled something about wanting to memorize what the cup looked like, and for maybe five minutes he just sat there with his eyes closed and his head up, like Sam the Celebrity Swami meditating on his chakras. Then he fished out a pen and one of his precious bus schedules with his free hand, and opened up the schedule on his thigh, and went to making about the most god-awful sketch of the cup imaginable. I didn't know why he bothered. How can you draw anything on your leg at night, with one hand cuffed behind you? But he wanted to try, if only to locate where the symbol dealies had been on the cup's forehead, and gave me a quiet "shhh" when I asked him about it.

After a long time our outpatient buddy from Bellevue Mental came back. Weaving on his feet a little. Maybe he'd had time to burn a couple of Klu Klux crosses on the trail, and had killed the rest of the pint to celebrate. He held the snub nose at his side and tossed me a little key ring.

"You take 'em off."

I did. He could've given me an easier assignment, what with it being dark and having to twist around to get the bit into the slot.

"Don't get up. Toss the cuffs over here. Slow."

I tossed the cuffs to him. The muzzle of his damn gun waved at us while he bent to pick them up. He was just drunk enough to plug us by accident.

He slid the cuffs in his jacket.

"Okay, I want you guys to just stay put for awhile. You get it?" He sounded drunk, too. "At least fifteen minutes. I want to get away from here. If I hear you walking behind me, maybe I get mad. Maybe I do something that none of us wants to happen."

That got him to giggling. Logos tried to chuckle along with him, and gave me a sharp elbow to make me chuckle too.

"Twenty minutes," Psycho said.

And then he trotted off. That was the last we saw of him. And I don't mind telling you: if there's life after death and I'm reincarnated about a dozen more times, and don't run into that big drunk doofus again until I'm chug-a-lugging a Strawberry Yoo-hoo in the Mars spaceport in the year 2822, well, that'll still be too soon.

• • •

Logos and me didn't get back to Prado until the next morning. We waited a full half hour, to be sure we didn't stumble into Psycho again, and then got fairly lost mucking around in the sand on the trails, and finally made it out to the highway just in time to see the taillights of a bus fading off into the distance. Logos checked his bus schedule collection, and gave me some terrific news. That had been the last bus til morning.

There was nothing to do but wait it out. We trudged back into good old fun Fort Funston, which I'd hoped to see again about the same time I ran into Psycho, and Logos found this giant-sized concrete meat locker thing that the GIs had built into a hill when they'd had an anti-aircraft cannon in there. Now it was empty.

We camped out there. Logos yakked most of the night like he'd just woke up. On and on about the history of the cup, like I'd never heard it before, and how unimaginably important it was, and how it was maybe the biggest sin on earth since the Inquisition that she was waltzing around with it in her pocket like a Zippo lighter, where anything could happen to it. He didn't want me to get him wrong. He wasn't sure. It could still be something else. But it sure in hey was worth investigating, and he knew at least four scholar types at UCB and Stanford who'd wet the bed about what he'd seen, and she had no right to play Mata Hari with something so important, and we had to track her down, and so forth.

.   .   .

The bus let us off back in Prado at about 10:00 a.m. Logos said he had a notebook in his bedroom with all his hallowed groves of academe contacts, including some big wow anthropologist at Stanford who was sure to start slobbering when he heard about the cup, and some other communist at Berkeley who was writing a thesis about the Aztecs. Did I want to come over and be on hand when he made the calls? Seeing as how I was the illustrious Hank Kruzenski who had ID'd the cup in the first place?

I said fine. Ordinarily I did everything I could to steer clear of the De Mello homestead, but I was plenty hot and bothered about the cup, too, and besides: what else was I going to do before my shift at Hardy's started? So I went, my fears of *Casa De Mello* notwithstanding.

.   .   .

Sure enough, I knew when we were a block away that another De Mello ruckus was going on. Apparently old Frank had ad-libbed a new addition to his Nixon-and-Jesus lawn display. This one had an anti-abortion theme. That was tried and true lawn display material for Frank. If no one complained about JFK in the coffin with the hammer and sickle or Earl Warren with the pitchfork and devils' ears, or any of his other conservative lawn display themes, well, all Frank had to do was haul out the plastic babies and fake blood. That was guaranteed to get the liberals screaming.

I spotted two of the plastic babies as we walked up. They was lying on the lawn grass between the sandals of the Jesus mannequin and Nixon's wing tips. I think this time Frank had put the babies out as an afterthought, like icing on the cake.

The main new addition was a mannequin duded up like a mad scientist. It had a wig of wild-looking, fluffed-out red hair, and a mad scientist type Halloween mask taped on its puss.

The mannequin was wearing a big 'Planned Parenthood' t-shirt. Frank had stood it up behind the Virgin Mary with its arms up and a giant surgical forceps thing strapped to its hands. Like Mr. Planned Parenthood was about to stab her.

As soon as I saw the mannequin I tried to duck behind Logos, and turn my head to block off anybody with a camera. Frank was standing next to Jesus in his latest cardigan vest. Fortunately, he was too busy arguing with his neighbor to notice. I thought I recognized her. Andrea Feldman. Logos said she was a social worker in Oakland. She was always getting into it with Frank. Somebody had given her the crazy idea she could buy a home in Prado Diablo without having to pull Nixon signs off her own front lawn. Logos said she volunteered with Planned Parenthood. Logos thought Frank was trying to get her goat 'cause he had a secret crush on her.

"...you need *help*," Ms. Feldman was yelling to Frank. Then something about gestalt therapy.

Frank just glared at her with his chin up and his hand on Jesus' shoulder and his chest stuck out. George Washington crossing the Delaware. Logos grit his teeth and walked right past them. Like he was going to make his phone calls to his egghead buddies no matter what, and wasn't going to let his nut job family pull him in on another caper.

Poor old Mrs. De Mello was wringing her hands when Logos and me walked in, and immediately asked if Logos could Do Something. But Logos grit his jaw harder, and said not right now, and went for the stairs.

I hadn't been in Logos' bedroom since high school. I guess he mostly lived at Rosenfeld's now, but at least once a week had to go back to put out a fire in his ridiculous family or help with a paint job, so he kept some stuff there. His mom kept the bedroom open out of gratitude. It still looked like a high school kid's room. I recognized posters he'd had in high school, and his desk and shelves and windowsill were still all piled up with books and notepads and magazines and newspaper clippings. So you could drop something in that mess and never find it again.

He fished the telephone out from under a pile of graph papers, and rummaged around in his desk drawer until he found a notebook. I figured it had to be the big rolodex of all his ivory tower friends, because he flipped through the pages and found a number and dialed it. Outside the yelling got louder. It sounded like Ms. Feldman was about to lose it. Logos looked real stubborn, like he had serious work to do and wasn't going to let his deranged family interfere with it.

Well, he tried. The number must have just rung and rung, so he pressed the cradle hook, flipped through the notebook again, found the next number he wanted and started to dial that, too.

That was as far as he got. His mom busted in.

"Richard, please!" Only the old man and his mom called him Richard. "Your father needs help! Please!"

Logos put down the receiver and tried to explain in this tight, forced voice that he had something very important to do. But then mom said that Ms. Feldman was trying to rip down Father's lawn display, and it was getting messy.

Logos looked about as exasperated as I'd ever seen him. He put his hands on the phone and shut his eyes for a second, like it took all his willpower not to heave the phone through the window. Then he mumbled something about 'being right back,' and stomped out after his mom. Which left me alone in there.

I took a perch on the edge of the bed and looked around for something to occupy myself. Maybe Logos thought he was going to 'be right back,' but past commotions at the De Mellos had gone on for days. I was likely to have the room to myself for awhile.

Logos had plenty of books, but they all had titles like *Mating Rites of the Estonians* or *Habitats of the Saskatchewan Beaver*. No, thanks. But I rooted around some more, and lo and behold: tucked under some books in the corner I found a big pile of *Hot Rods* from his early high school days, before he'd turned Eco Boy.

I grabbed the stack and plopped it on the floor and thumbed through the issues, hoping that maybe I'd find a cover story on a chop and channel job on a '49 Merc, or the gnarly flatheads they used to drag back in the fifties. But I got deep into the stack and nothing promising turned up, and then I found something else tucked in among the back issues. Almost like it was hidden there.

A folder. A manila folder with a bunch of pages stacked inside.

Well, curious me just had to open the folder for a look see. It took me about an eighth of a second to recognize the wand-waving wizard embossed on the letterhead, and the slingshot dragster with the big Roots huffer.

I must have grinned from ear to ear. The little bastard! So he'd been an Ask the Wizard subscriber too. He'd never told me.

There were a lot of the letters. Way, way more than I had. Some weren't even on letterhead. He must have been a subscriber for a long time.

I decided I might as well look at the letters near the end of the stack. I don't know why. I might just as easily have started at the beginning. Or I could have put the stack where it came from, and not read any more of the letters at all.

And if I'd just done that this whole story would have turned out differently, and my life would have, too. If I hadn't slipped my fingers into the stack and turned the top half over, and found myself looking at the particular letter I looked at next.

It was handwritten. A lot of the letters in there were handwritten. I'd never heard of anyone getting a Wizard letter that wasn't typed.

I started to read it.

By the time I was halfway through the whole bottom had dropped out from under my world, and I felt like there wasn't anything I could count on anymore, not anything safe, and I wondered if I'd ever be able to look at Logos again.

•　　•　　•

> Dear Logos,
> First: I hope things got better
> for you after you sent that letter.
> I just don't care that much.
> Maybe that means I'm questionable
> too and we should both see an
> analyst. So you think you're
> homosexual. (Or "gay." That's a new
> word for me!) It's like you just
> told me you're blood type A instead
> of O. That's how much I care.

Mostly I'm honored that you'd choose me to share the big secret with, if you've never told anyone else.

This man at college: what's he like? Tall, short, blond, brunette? What's so attractive about him? You can tell me if it's something superficial. (I get superficial attractions, too.) It doesn't sound superficial, though. I almost feel sorry for him: he's walking around with this halo of your adoration around him, and he doesn't know.

I have three Scribe letters left to write tonight, and one's about the AMC tall-deck block, which I'm not up to speed on. I'd better sign off. I just wanted to dash off a quick letter to let you know that I don't mind at all, and I hope you'll tell me more when you want to.

    S

CHAPTER EIGHT

Logos must have called my place a half dozen times in the next three days, and then nearly every day for two weeks after that. He went to Stanford for a pow wow with the anthropologist. He visited the guy in Berkeley, too, and some other scholar types. He drew up another sketch, and they compared it with the famous Centennial Heritage photo. But no matter how many fancy degrees they had between them, the only answer Logos could get was:

We're not sure. Maybe. It sure *looked* like the real McCoy, but that didn't mean it was. They couldn't say any more until they got their hands on it.

Logos was all wrought up. The Stanford anthropologist blew him off, but he got the Aztec thesis writer and a few of his history department buddies worked up, and they helped Logos hunt for Evelyn. They went back to Jimi's house, and gave everyone in his house the third degree about how important is was to find her.

But it didn't pan out. Evelyn was gone. She'd taken the dog with her. That was all anyone knew.

The police couldn't help. There wasn't a crime. No one had been accused of anything.

• • •

I found out all this from two telephone calls from Logos, and from a bunch of messages he left with my mom. A couple of the Berkeley history buffs called me, too. I learned how the great hunt was going between the questions they asked.

I didn't want to talk to Logos. That afternoon in his bedroom, I'd just put the letters back in the folder, and the *Hot Rods* back in a pile, and walked out. He'd been too busy trying to prevent World War III on the front lawn to pay attention. When he did get me on the horn a couple of days later, he was so excited about that cup that he talked and talked, and didn't seem to notice that I wasn't my usual self in what I said back to him.

That was fine with me. I just said 'yes' or 'no' or 'sounds like you're doing good,' and tried to keep the conversation short.

I was all wrought up inside. All the homo jokes I'd ever heard at parties and at work: he actually *was* one. I knew there was homos who lived in New York and Frisco, and a lot of hair stylists and decorators were supposed to be fags, but those were just the people the nightclub jokes were about. They were far away from me. Like maybe there'd be a feature about "Life among the Homosexuals" in some magazine, and there'd be a picture of some weirdsville guys on Fire Island holding hands, and maybe you'd cut out the photo and stick it in somebody's lunch box as a joke. That was how I thought about queers. Like they all lived in Borneo.

I didn't know what to do. I thought I should warn some friends, in case Logos tried to make a pass at them, but thinking that just made me all depressed. I couldn't do that to Logos. Not with all the Dudley DoRight stuff he did. I just couldn't.

I kept it to myself. I figured I hadn't had any business poking through his magazines. I didn't have any right to what I'd learned that way, so I'd pretend I didn't know it.

But I did. It changed everything for me. I'd been so hot and bothered about the cup before, about how it would change my life and make me rich and famous. Now I almost lost interest in it. It was mostly Logos' project now, for one thing, and now anything involving Logos gave me a sick feeling, like it was all contaminated by the secret I knew.

And for another, I didn't think they were going to get anywhere tracking down Evelyn. They had almost nothing to go on.

I was right about that. Logos' calls went from twice a day to once a day, and then to once every couple of days. He sounded plenty frustrated, but a dead end was a dead end. Evelyn was gone.

·   ·   ·

Then nearly four months went by.

Logos stopped calling after awhile. BART had finally opened the Transbay Tube. I figured that had distracted him a little, no matter how hot he was for that cup. Life more or less went back to normal. I put in my hours at Hardy's and hoped management would transfer Dirk down to Tierra del Fuego, but no soap. My ex Cindy called, but it turned out she just wanted me as a trampoline between boyfriends. She went AWOL after we'd hooked up twice. Maybe she found someone who'd stay up on his elbows more. I bought some Moon rims for my 'Cuda, and thought they looked dippy almost as soon as I had them bolted on.

The big change during this period had to do with my mom. Her drinking got worse. She'd gotten sloshed every night for almost as long as I could remember, but she'd always been able to stagger into her own room when Carson signed off. Nice and clean.

But sometimes now she was passing out in front of the test pattern. Not a lot, but it happened. One morning I'd come out for my a.m. Fruit Loops, and there was Mom sprawled on the kitchen tiles like a corpse. Man, I was scared. She'd come out of it when I shook her shoulder, but still. I didn't know what was wrong with her. Another time I'd had to bodily pick her up and cart her into her bedroom, with her babbling on my arm like a three year old.

"Nobody loves me." She'd actually said that, over and over. "Nobody loves me." What kind of trip was that to lay on me? I wasn't no psychiatrist. I was twenty-four years old. How was I going to help a middle-aged lady with her problems? It felt like one more thing in life that had dropped out from under me. Like what I'd learned about Logos.

•   •   •

One night at Hardy's I got my break at 8:00 p.m., and figured I'd go out to the loading dock to watch half the sky cave in. The biggest storm of the year had hit. Old Fritz McDonnell on Channel 12 had been panting and slobbering all week about low pressure system this and cold front that, and how one mother of a storm was blasting south from Canada to plow into the Bay Area, and cackling and making sick Noah's Ark jokes because of all the streets that would flood.

Well, he'd been right. The first sprinkles had hit by noon, and by the time I drove in for my Hardy's shift I'd had to run the wipers on high just to see twenty feet in front of me. And it had just been getting warmed up then. All during the 5 to 7 crunch time the wind had wailed like a banshee and shook the automatic doors, and the rain had pounded away on the roof of Hardy's like a tom tom, so customers made jokes about it as I rang them up, and shook the water off their umbrellas, and tromped around in the puddles the other customers had left in the checkout lanes. And it was still just getting warmed up. It was supposed to go on for two solid days.

I had a fifteen minute break. I walked out among the hand carts and produce racks and stacks of canned food, and hopped up on a pallet of soup boxes next to the dock. Then I just sat and watched the sheets of rain sweeping onto the cars parked behind Hardy's. The wind blew my hair back, and the rain was spattering all around the loading dock lip around my shoes. Dirk was going to give me grief if I walked back to my register with my shoes all wet. I knew I should take my break someplace else, but I wanted to be by myself. Nobody was going to come hang out at the loading dock if they didn't have to. It was too cold.

I didn't feel that great. Some bill collector had started calling us. For the life of me I couldn't figure out why Mom had had to go to Tire Citadel for her recaps, seeing as she only worked for a gas station. But that was what she'd done, and of course they'd been foaming at the mouth to sign her up for their wonderful store credit plan. Now she probably owed twice what the tires were worth.

"Put Helen on, please." That was how the collector talked. Nice and quiet and pushy, like our house was one of his branch offices. I didn't think she'd paid any of it. For the past week he'd called every night. So she's guaranteed to be polluted while she's on the horn with him, holding her ratty bathrobe shut and yelling about how her car isn't riding right with those retreads, *what does he think of that?!*, like a bill collector wants to go in a test drive in her rust bucket Caprice with her. It just showed how far she'd sunk. Eighty grand straight up solid USDA Uncle Sam cash money she'd got for those acres. She'd took me and two friends to Disneyland in junior high. Now she can't afford tires.

And it wasn't just her. After high school everything had felt la-te-da, life's all fun and games, but I wasn't nineteen anymore. Some kids I'd known in high school was way ahead of me. I mean, I *saw* them. I didn't like getting my nose rubbed in it.

What was I supposed to do, tell them not to come into the store where I worked?

Like the other day. Sean Davies. He hadn't had one thing in high school I hadn't had. Straight C student, strictly household current between the ears. Not like Logos. The other day he'd got in line at my register, and we'd got to talking. Damn if he hadn't already bought his own house. It was out in Bay Point. His own personal property house, with the title in his name and everything. He was shacked up out there with his fiancée. He was a HVAC tech. He even gave me a business card.

And here's what he'd said, as I'd handed over his receipt:

"Good old Hank, still holding down the fort at Hardy's. I can count on you."

Just trying to say something friendly while he fetches his grocery bags and heads out the door. I knew he hadn't meant anything by it. But, still. "I can count on you." Like I'd still be living with my mom and going nowhere ten years from now, like somebody with Down's who wipes tables at McDonalds. Maybe when I'm sixty he'll say "Good old Hank" when he pats me on the head and tosses me a Milk Dud.

It had bummed me out, that was all, just like the collection calls, and so I had all that on my mind as I sat out there on the pallet and watched the rain come down through the loading dock doors.

Then headlights showed through the rain, and a little Karmann Ghia rumbled up and pulled into a parking slot across from the truck bays. I watched while the driver door opened, and somebody dashed through the rain and came up on the dock with me.

I didn't recognize her at first. I'd only seen her three times, after all, and the last time had been four months ago. She was all bundled up, and I couldn't see her good in the dim lights on the dock. Honestly, all I thought was that some non-employee had come up on the dock for some nutty reason, and now I had to play security guard to get her out of there.

I hopped off the pallet. She stepped closer.

Then I finally got a good look at her, and the bells went off.

Ms. Mata Hari herself. Logos and his graduate student buddies had turned Berkeley upside down looking for her, and now she turns up out of the blue, and tracks me down instead.

"They told me you were back here," she said. "Look, your dog is real sick."

Just out of the blue, like we'd talked that morning. She wiped the wet hair back from her eyes and stood so close that I smelled the rain on her coat, the same grungy pea coat she'd worn on the bridge.

Her face was white and damp. I thought she looked pretty wrought up, but I couldn't get a good read on her face. The wind was making the big ceiling floods buck around on their chains, so that one second I could see all of her face in the yellow light, and the next half of it was in shadow.

Your dog is sick. I didn't have no dog.

Then I remembered how Ruby had took up with her in Berkeley. I started to say he wasn't mine, but then the swaying floods let me see all of her face again, and I decided I didn't need to. She wasn't thinking straight. She was all worked up.

"He just came back this morning. I don't know how he got out. I mean, the fence ..." She brushed her hair back again, like that would help her talk straight. "... but when he came back he was throwing up and bumping into things, and now I don't think he can walk anymore. He's in the car. Look, I just need to know who his vet is. Logos said he had a vet when he was sick before. I just need to know who and I'll drive him there."

Her words was all piled on top of each other, like she'd rehearsed a speech that she was too upset to say straight. I felt like I was dreaming. Maybe I would've expected a surprise visit at work from Logos, or my ex Cindy. Not from Amelia Earhart.

She took another step at me. Damn if she didn't look ready to cry. I made myself stop thinking about the cup.

"Lady ... Evelyn, I'm sorry." I tried to make my voice nice. "That thing with the vet, that was years ago. Nobody owns ..."

She shook her head. "He said he has a vet. Just tell me his name. You don't have to do anything. I can't just let him die."

She looked at me with her eyes wild and her jaw shaking. So I tried. I looked away so I could think without her eyes boring in at me, and rifled through all the stories I'd heard about that dog through the years.

"Well, there's that vet out on Rock Point. I think the name is Rock Point something, too. That might've been who Logos meant. If you look in the Yellow Pages ... "

She broke in to ask where the phone was.

I almost sent her out to the pay phones. I would've been plenty justified, and the whole rest of my life might have been different if I had. But she'd come all the way out in that driving rain to see me, and the hot rod dog of Prado Diablo was dying in her car.

So I pointed at the telephone next to the timecard racks. My stomach did a nice lurch when I did it, 'cause the phone and racks were strictly employees only. Dirk would fry my bacon but good if he caught us.

She rushed ahead of me and grabbed the phone book. A fresh freight load of wind had bored in, so the floods bucked over our heads like they was on ropes in a carnival swing ride, and the yellow light see-sawed over the book while she flopped it open and hunted for the name. I guess she had good eyes. She found the name and grabbed the phone and dialed.

And of course ten seconds after that, just as she bowed her head and started to talk, just like the S.O.B. had been waiting in the wings so he could barge in at exactly the right time, in comes Dirk.

"What is that woman doing here?!"

He stopped dead and looked at us like he'd caught Evelyn emptying out the store safe. In full on Mr. Indignant Supervisor mode.

"Dirk, we got kind of an emergency here ..."

"What kind of an emergency? This is an employees only area!"

I tried to explain about Ruby being sick. Evelyn had some-one on the line and was talking. Dirk stared from me to Evelyn and back again, with his eyes all bulged out and his No Party at Hardy's button twitching on the front of his apron.

"That's a *dog*," Dirk said.

"Yeah, but he's not just any dog, he's ..."

"It's a *dog*!" He looked at Evelyn. "You are in an employee's only area. Get off the phone. *Now!*"

But Evelyn had someone on the line, and didn't seem to know Dirk was yelling at her instead of me. She was bent over the phone and talking fast, and holding her hand over her other ear to block out the noise.

Dirk moved in. He tried to reach for the phone first, but Evelyn blocked him off, so he grabbed her shoulders and started to drag her off of it.

Well, what was I going to do? Chivalry 101 says you don't let guys attack chicks. You learn that in first grade, along with how to tie your shoes and eat paste. So I stepped in, and tried to push Dirk back, and of course you can guess what happened next, seeing as how Dirk was certifiably insane, and any shrink worth his prescription pad would have padlocked him into a straightjacket after hearing about his boxing career and his nine million guns and his stare downs, 'cause Dirk basically lived for a legal excuse to deck someone.

The next thing I knew, I was sprawled out on the concrete floor, with half of my face feeling numb from where he'd slugged me, and the whole storeroom doing a slow waltz overhead. At least he'd gotten Evelyn off the phone. Dirk waved the receiver at me.

"That was assault, Hank!" It sure was. "You are fired. Understand me? F-I-R-E-D fired! Both of you can get out of this market or I call the police!"

I tried to shake the fuzz out of my head and concentrate on standing up. Evelyn was shouting something at Dirk, but I was too woozy to hear what.

There wasn't much I could do. Dirk was the boss, and the Golden Era of Trial Attorneys and Lawsuits wasn't in full flower yet, and I wasn't some hot shot boxer. I got in some choice insults I'd had marinating in my cranium since I'd met him, but Dirk just looked imperial as all get out, and then told me in this Frosty Fred voice to Turn in My Apron. I thought that was pretty funny. Like I'm going to go out and have a wing ding at the Hyatt, and they'll put the Dom Perignon on charge 'cause I'm wearing an apron and they think I'm a Hardy's cashier.

. . .

A minute later, Evelyn and me walked out to her Ghia.

"Did you get ahold of the vet?"

She said yes, and got in. The rain was so bad that my shirt was almost soaked through by the time she opened the passenger door. I climbed in and looked at Ruby. He looked bad, all right. She had him stretched out on a blanket on the back. His eyes were shut and his stomach was swole up, and his furry chest was jerking up and down, up and down, like it hurt him to breathe.

I told her where my 'Cuda was parked. She said she could drive, but I told her I knew the roads in Prado, and maybe because I'd just gotten slugged she went along without giving me grief. It was starting to sink in that I'd just got canned and didn't have a job. I wasn't thinking too straight, but I still knew I didn't want to get stuck out in the driving rain in some duct tape and baling wire hippy wagon that was bound to break down on us. Even if this particular hippy wagon sounded good, I had to admit, as she drove us over to where I'd parked in the main lot. Maybe somebody's daddy had paid for a service job.

We got Ruby in the back of my 'Cuda and she locked her Ghia up, and maybe twenty minutes later we were at the vet's office.

Old Mr. Rock Point Pet Care didn't remember Ruby. He looked like he was still wearing his PJs under his khakis and lab coat. We'd gotten him out of bed, he wasn't making any secret of it. We hoisted Ruby onto the exam room table, and he checked Ruby's eyes and gums and even bent down to sniff his breath. Then he thumped Ruby a couple of times on his swole-up stomach.

Whatever he felt in his stomach must have told him what he needed to know. He stood straight and pushed up his glasses, and then he turned to us with that sad, practiced look that docs and vets use when they have to give bad news.

Liver failure, he said. Ruby might have eaten something when he escaped. That was why his eyes were yellow.

I asked if there was anything he could do. He shook his head. He was sorry.

Evelyn lost it a little. That damn old hound had worked his charm on her good. She tried to talk to the vet in the tough way she'd talked to me on the bridge, but the vulnerable part underneath was sputtering up through the cracks and sloshing all over the tough shell, so all she sounded like was a frightened chick who was going to lose her dog.

The vet was used to it. He told her that Ruby was in pain. He must have thought me and Evelyn was married.

"I guess we're going to have to put him to sleep," I said, finally.

Evelyn looked at me with her jaw set and her lips all quivery. Then she lowered her eyes and frowned at the floor.

The vet went to the cabinet and fished around for awhile, and came back with a giant needle. We knew what that was for. We held Ruby while he put it in, and a minute later the great good luck hot rod dog of Prado was no longer.

I asked how much all this was, and the vet said $50. Man, that hurt. That was almost everything in my wallet. I paid him. though. Then the vet started to clear Ruby off the table, and I realized that he was going to put him in an oven or something, and I said, no way, I'm taking him with me. I didn't even need to think about it. Ruby was going to get a proper burial.

That got me five of my fifty bucks back.

·   ·   ·

Evelyn and me carted Ruby back to my 'Cuda. By this time I was thinking in spite of myself what a royal mess all the rain and mud and pus oozing out of the dead dog was going to make in my precious car, but I tried not to let my brain go there, and after Ruby and Evelyn was in I went around to the driver's side and got in, too.

"How much did he say it was?" Evelyn asked.

I waved my hand. "Nothing. Free. My treat."

"No."

She flicked on my dome light and hauled up this giant canvas handbag she'd brought from the Ghia, which was hippy tie-died but otherwise just the thing only a woman would lug around, with enough crap stuffed in it to last through a Soviet nuke attack.

"Look, this was on me. I don't want your money."

"No, I want to pay!"

She practically yelled that at me. Just the typical crap I'd had to deal with from her from the beginning, and now she had the bag up on her knee and was rooting around inside it for her wallet.

And guess what I saw then.

Just guess.

Stuffed in among the tissues and maps and hair brush and sunglasses and lotion and other typical female crap, right smack dab in the middle of her handbag.

You just guess.

Give up yet? Try one more time. Just try.

· · ·

It took awhile to sink in. I went into 'shocked and stall for time' mode, and just told her how much the vet had cost without fighting the point anymore. She counted out the money and shoved it at me, and I watched her push her wallet back into the handbag right next to that cup. Then she reached up and turned off my dome light like it was her own car she was sitting in.

I told her I had shovels for burying Ruby in my garage. So we'd go there first. If she wanted to come. She said she did. It was like someone beside me was talking, and I was hearing myself say the words. She shoved her handbag on her lap and stared straight ahead, like she was riding with a chauffeur she didn't like.

I drove slow. My wipers was going a mile a minute, and I could still hardly see twenty feet in front of me. We didn't talk. I thought about what it meant that she'd actually bring something like that cup along in her handbag with her, stuffed in with her hair brush and her skin lotion.

It meant it was a fake, was what it meant.

All the big, big build-up, with her trying to grab the photos at Fiesta and playing hardball on the bridge, and her psycho friend and his handcuffs. All of it was because she was just a whack patrol hippy chick, who wrapped healing crystals around her fanny when she felt constipated and hid under the bed if her astrology chart was off, and took seaweed supplements and stuck willow bark in her underwear and all the crap they did, and it was my own damn fault that I'd taken her serious.

Sure, maybe *she* thought it was holy. Some quack in Sedona had given it to her after a roll in the hay, and told her it'd line up her chakras if she rubbed it a lot. Who knew what some nut job hippy chick thought? Because there was no way, absolutely no way at all, you were going to take something like the real McCoy Cuauhtémoc cup that Red Cloud had seen in a vision and that was key to some of the most mysterioso psychic events of the last century, that made the Mona Lisa and the Hope Diamond together look about as important as a 2 for 1 coupon for dental floss — there was no way you were just going to carry that around in your purse unprotected with your toenail clippers. Eff on that. That was *ridiculous*.

All that trouble, and it was all my own fault. She hadn't forced me to take her serious. I could have used common sense. I didn't have a job anymore, because Miss Space Case had driven all the way to Prado to hunt for a vet who didn't even recognize Ruby. The side of my face felt swole; so far two separate guys had busted me in the chops because of her. I had a dead dog oozing crap in the back of my 'Cuda, even if it was a dog I cared about, and mud and wet all over the insides of my car, and I was going to have to eat humble pie with Logos.

Logos, who was probably slobbering in the closet over Mr. America photos. A homo. Everything had dropped out from under me. Logos, and my mom, and my job, and Ruby, and all the ridiculous stuff I'd dreamed about the cup, all wadded up and shoved in my face. There wasn't anything I could count on anymore.

•   •   •

I parked in my driveway and left her in the car while I went in to hunt up the gear. Mom had too much of a load on to notice the mud I tracked in. I got on a decent jacket, and then I went over my plans while I hunted up the shovels.

Ripper's Hill was where we were going. No question. Even if it would be a bear to get to in that storm. I couldn't see burying Ruby any place else. With all the good times we'd had up there in high school, kicking back on that grassy hill under the giant oak at the top and checking out that great view. We'd played with Ruby lots of times up there. Now he'd get to be there forever.

I slid the shovels in the back and got in. She didn't even look at me. She sat with that dumb hippy bag on her knees and stared straight ahead, like I was a chauffeur who'd told a fart joke to the queen, and she was going to sit like an icicle until she could tell the boss and get me dismissed.

Well, that was her trip. She'd liked Ruby and she could help bury him, but after that she'd row her canoe and I'd row mine.

•   •   •

Soon enough we were out of the 'burbs and on our way to Ripper's Hill. The rain was worse than ever, sheets and sheets of it driving down on the road and the windshield. I felt like I was driving through a car wash. But I knew the blacktop to Ripper's by heart, and at least I didn't have to worry about other traffic. No one was out there with us.

"Where are you taking us?" she asked, all of a sudden.

In just the kind of loud, brassy voice I'd come to expect from her. Like there couldn't be any good explanation. Like I just had to be up to something bad.

I counted inside to three before I answered.

"A place called Ripper's Hill. We used to play with Ruby up there. It's a few miles from here."

She threw me a cold, hard look, like she'd accepted a ride with Charles Manson and he'd suggested a detour. She clutched her stupid bag and looked straight ahead. I kept driving.

But two minutes after that, out of the blue, like I hadn't even answered her question:

"I said *where are we going?!*"

"I already told you."

"There's nobody on this road. Where are you taking me?"

I pulled over onto the shoulder strip. I shut off the engine and the wipers and clicked on the dome light, and turned in the seat to look at her. We could have been parked in a spaceship on the damn moon, for all the company we had out there.

"Well, I guess it's time to fess up," I said. "What with this spicy weather we're having, and getting fired and beat up, and having a dead dog riding in the back with us, I've done gotten myself all excited. So I thought I'd drive us out in the boonies and have my way with you."

"There is nothing *out* here. Where are you taking us?"

"Ripper's Hill. I've already told you."

"I don't see a hill!"

"That's because we haven't gotten to it yet. You don't know Prado Diablo."

"Where's the hill? I don't see a hill!"

That should have told me how upset she was underneath her hard look and her tough act, because in that storm we wouldn't have been able to see the Queen Mary straight ahead, let alone a hill miles away. But my jaw hurt, and I was wet and cold, and sick of being sniffed at like I'd slunk out of death row.

"Okay, let's put it a different way," I said. Real quiet. "If you don't believe me, and you think I'm trying to pull something: What exactly are you going to do about it?"

She just stared at me, with her head back and her mouth set and quivery and her eyes wild and hard looking.

And then I thought of something.

"In fact ..." I said.

I reached over and grabbed the handbag.

Right quick she tried to grab it back, but I was too fast for her. I pulled it out of her lap and plopped it onto mine, and held it tight with my fist locked on the opening, and looked at her.

"In fact, if I take this big hippy purse of yours, with your fake cup statue thing in it, that you didn't make *any* attempt to hide, that I couldn't *help* seeing, if I take your precious cup *and* your purse and shove you out of the car right here and drive away, what exactly are you going to do about it? Tell me. I'd like to know."

She only glared at me some more, with her head up and her eyes still wild and the same quivery frown. Only now the frown looked more frightened.

"You couldn't do anything about it. Could you?" I shook the handbag. "Tell me. I want to know. What could you do?"

And I stared at her, and she stared back, and that lasted for maybe the count of seven. Which was a fair hunk of time, sitting alone on that road with the rain walloping the roof, just her and me and the yellow dome light and our dead friend in the back. At least he wouldn't have to take sides between us.

She kept her dignity, I'll say that for her. She sat straight in the seat and glared at me, with her eyes wide and her quivery frown looking more worried than frightened, worried and watchful and a little sad.

I hoisted the bag off my leg and plopped it back in her lap. Then I turned toward her.

"Okay, let's get a couple of things straight. I know you're upset about the dog. I'm upset about him, too. And I know I didn't have any business barging into your life the way I did, and that's why you've been treating me like I'm on the ten most wanted list.

"But this is different. You came hunting for me tonight. I didn't come looking for you. I'm done being treated by you like I'm not even human, and all I do is lie and cheat and steal because I don't have a big headband and hair down to my knees."

I fished out the bills she'd made me take earlier, and stuck them into her purse.

"Here. I'm not taking your money for the vet. He wasn't a hippy dog. He spent all of four months with you, lady. He was a Prado Diablo dog. We carted him around when we went cruising on Cherry Avenue, and he slept in Phil Nester's shop the whole time Phil was building up his Chevelle for Super Stock. And I've got no idea how much time we spent chucking branches for him up on Ripper's Hill. Okay? Am I making my point?

"I'll give you a choice. You can come up with me and we can bury him together, or I can turn around now and take you back to your car. It's your call. But if you come with me, I don't want you treating me anymore like my mug shot ought to be hanging up in the post office. I'm done with that."

I looked at her in the most determined way I could, and waited for her reaction. That had been about the longest speech I'd made since I'd had to read a paper on Magellan in junior high.

Evelyn looked a little shocked. She turned her head down a little, so she wouldn't have to look at me. She didn't look mad anymore, or even suspicious.

Okay, she said, finally. Without looking at me. She wanted to help bury Ruby.

I turned off the dome light, and fired up the car, and we went on.

•   •   •

The turn-out to Ripper's Hill was almost flooded. As soon as I pulled into it I hit a bog that almost splashed up to the headlights, but my back tires held and I got us out, and then I found a spot to park on a stretch of ground that looked solid and had missed the worst of the monsoon. We climbed out, and I pushed the seats back, and together we wrestled out the blanket with Ruby spread on it.

It was like handling a sack of wet flour. His tongue was hanging out, and if we didn't support his head it just dropped and hung, like a water balloon in a stocking.

I motioned for her to put down her end of the blanket, and then I got out the shovels and locked up my precious car, and we picked up the blanket again and started up the trail to the hill. All without saying more than a couple of words. It was like my big speech still hung in the air between us. I felt flustered 'cause I'd made it, and she seemed to have gone into a silent world of her own, and looked content just to follow my lead.

By the time we got halfway up the slope I almost wished she'd pulled a gun on me and made us go to a pet cemetery. It would have been hard to see the trail in a full moon, and now it was almost impossible. We kind of waddled up sideways, and I'd feel the ground ahead of me with my toe before putting weight on my foot, and even then we almost toppled into each other a couple of times.

Then there was the rain. Like any self-respecting storm, it had laid low and held its water until we were out in the open and couldn't protect ourselves. Then it shellacked us but good. We might as well have been showering at the Y. Or maybe Zeus had a yen to get in the car wash business, and figured he'd do a trial run with us. We were both soaked to the skin, and the blanket was water logged, too.

Evelyn didn't complain. It was like she'd made her deal in the car, and now she was going to soldier on no matter what. I was the one who had to stop twice to get a better grip on the blanket. Not her.

The peak of Ripper's Hill was like a rounded table top, with a massive oak tree at the center. The boughs were so thick and heavy with leaves that they blocked most of the rain. We set the blanket down next to the trunk, and I paced out a place maybe twenty feet from the tree canopy, so we could dig without hitting the roots. That looked like a nice spot for Ruby's ghost to gaze off at the foothills.

The rain had quieted down some, but as soon as it saw us dig in the open it went to slinging more torrents of water at us, so we were slopping around in muddy puddles before the hole was six inches deep. Oh, joy. But Evelyn dug steady beside me, and the main thing that kept me from slowing down was that she didn't.

It took nearly forty minutes to dig two feet. There were rocks in there, a lot of them, and the shovel wouldn't break through the big ones, so the only thing to do was pry with the blade around the edges until we could lever them out. The storm sent off to the Farallones for some take-out rain to dump on us, but then finally let up after we were soaked to the skin. Maybe it figured it ought to hold its load and go moseying off for some fresh victim to dump water on. Like maybe a corporate V.P. in a new Italian business suit, with no umbrella.

Then the wind beat on us for awhile instead, and then even that let up, and it was quiet. It wasn't going to last, but it was: quiet.

"Hey," Evelyn said.

She'd stopped digging. I couldn't hear her shovel chinking the rocks anymore.

"What is it?" I half-turned my head toward her.

"I'm sorry," she said.

I shrugged and turned away and swung my blade back into the mud. Sorry for what? Maybe she'd nicked the back of my boot with her shovel. Like I'd notice or even care.

I worked the blade in around a rock and started to lever up a scoop. But then she stopped me. Her fingers touched the back of my hand. Real delicate and shy, like she knew it would freak me out and she wanted to do it as light as she could.

I let the blade stick in the mud, and stood straight. She waited until I'd turned all the way around to face her, with both of us standing up past our shins in that soggy hole.

"I'm sorry," she said.

And this time I knew what she meant. The rest she said with her eyes. Locked right on mine, all naked and embarrassed looking, like she wasn't scared no matter how much she bared her soul, as long as I could see how bad she felt. Like maybe she'd been stewing on her apology for the past half hour, and had waited for the wind and rain to go on R&R before she'd spoke up.

"That's okay," I said. I barely mumbled it, but I guess it was convincing enough. This time she didn't stop me when I went back to digging. Pretty soon I heard her digging again, too.

I turned a little in the hole, so she couldn't see the side of my face.

Now I was all flustered. The way she'd touched my hand and looked at me. Nobody I knew acted like that. Like if she'd been two hours late, Cindy might have said how sorry she was that I couldn't appreciate her as a woman. That was my idea of a Prado apology. With some kind of dig in it.

Now I wondered if I ought to say I was sorry too, for grabbing her handbag. I'd known she was upset about the dog. I hadn't had to grab the bag. But I didn't know how to make an apology like that.

I started to put down my shovel so I could turn to her to say it, but stopped myself. It wouldn't come out right. I'd make a fool of myself. So I kept digging instead. We didn't talk anymore.

And it was just about then that I got the first inkling that maybe something was up there on that hill with us.

Something roaming around in the thick wet woods down slope from the bald spot where me and Evelyn was. Something stepping over the twigs and roots and leaves, and watching, and biding its time. I didn't hear anything out there. I couldn't have, with the wind blowing so hard.

I felt it.

I swung the shovel and looked out, but all I saw was the broody black shadow of the tree line and the night sky beyond. Well. Probably it was my imagination. 'Course, it could have just been the ghost spirit of Ruby out there, sniffing all the trees and bushes and paying his last respects before he jetted off to doggie heaven. Mom had always said a ghost stuck around long enough to see its own funeral. Maybe dog ghosts did, too.

But that wasn't what that thing in the woods had felt like. It had felt like something else. Like a *thought*, almost. Or closer to a thought than a ghost. A thought lurking out there in the woods, and watching, and waiting til it was time to come in and lay its trip on me, 'cause maybe I wasn't ready to hear it yet.

•　　•　　•

When we were four feet down I said I thought that was deep enough. We went back to the tree trunk and hoisted up Ruby, and real slow carried him back and got into the hole again so we could lower him between us. Then we shoveled the dirt back on top of him.

Evelyn wanted to put a cross on it. She pulled a couple of skinny branches off the tree, and broke off the ends until she had two twigs, and used one of her shoelaces to tie the twigs together into a cross shape. She carried the cross to the grave and pushed it into the dirt over Ruby's head.

The storm was still holding fire. Maybe it wanted to show some respect for the dead. More likely, it had found that V.P. with the Italian suit and no umbrella. Evelyn and me stood next to the shovels and looked at the grave.

"I guess we ought to say something," I said.

But that wasn't going to be easy. I still felt flustered. I cleared my throat.

"Ruby," I said, "you were a real special dog. A lot of people in town are going to miss you. There's nobody who didn't like you, except maybe the dog catcher. I hope you like the views up here when the good weather comes."

Evelyn's mouth shook a little.

"You were cute when you played fetch with little Nancy," she said. "She said she wanted to trade all her toys for you."

Evelyn's voice broke at the end, and she started to cry. I didn't know what to do. I still felt flustered, but you don't just let a woman cry without doing something. So I stepped close to her, and formal as all get out put my arm around her shoulder, with my fingertips barely touching her jacket, like I was a servant comforting the Duchess of Windsor.

And man, then I *really* felt that spirit thing or whatever it was, roaming around in the woods with its eye on us. I kept thinking it had to do with Ruby. Wasn't it Ruby we'd just buried?

But something told me it wasn't so. That I was in for a big surprise, when it finally came out and had its say. 'Cause right now I wouldn't believe it.

•   •   •

Back at the bottom of the trail we dumped the shovels in the back and heaved our muddy and sopping-wet bodies into my 'Cuda, and then I couldn't get the starter motor gear to mesh up with the flywheel teeth. Perfect. Just what we needed. I turned the key and the thing shrieked at me, 'cause the gear couldn't get a bite on the teeth, and just as I was starting to get hot and bothered Evelyn said she knew a trick her dad had taught her, and told me to put it in gear and get out and rock the 'Cuda a couple of times. And what do you know, that did it. Son of a gun. Learn something new every day.

So that made me grateful, and so without thinking it through I offered to let her shower up at my place before driving her back to her Ghia. Which was only decent of me. We both looked like a couple of dirt clogs.

Evelyn said yes, thank you. Thank you very much.

And then I remembered my mom.

What if she wasn't asleep yet? Or passed out on the sofa in front of the TV, so Evelyn would see her as soon as we walked in?

I sat forward to squint through the rain as I drove, and racked my brain for a way to back out of it. Oh, I'm sorry, I forgot, the Prez and his wife are sleeping over, and there's Secret Service everywhere. But all the different lies I came up with were as obvious as something a kid would say.

Finally I came up with a plan. We could go in the back door of the garage. That would lead right through the kitchen into the hall. Evelyn wouldn't see Mom unless she stuck her head all the way around the kitchen cupboards. And I could ease in and block off her view.

We pulled into the driveway. Evelyn looked at me funny when I led her into the little service alley next to the house, but I told her we'd tramp in too much mud if we went in the front. She shrugged and followed me, and we stepped around some old paint tins, and then she was dripping water on the back patio next to me while I tried to get the key in the back door in the dark.

•   •   •

It was like the whole thing had been choreographed, like you'd set up a scene on stage. Just so it would be the most shameful and embarrassing thing that could happen to me.

If Mom had been anywhere else in the kitchen, I would have seen her when I walked in. I could have blocked off Evelyn and made an excuse and gotten her out of there. But Mom just had to be at the counter, next to the sink. Just had to be. The one part of the kitchen I couldn't see until we'd stepped in far enough to see around the fridge, and the back door was closed behind us. When it was too late.

"What'd'ya want?" Mom said.

She was standing at the sink in her rat-colored old bathrobe with her hands braced on the counter so she wouldn't fall over. The latest fifth was next to the sink, and an empty tumbler and an ice tray. I could hear the TV going in the living room. Maybe old Ed McMahon had trotted onto the airwaves on a Clydesdale to try to hustle some Budweiser, and Mom had figured she'd pour a refill during the commercial. But she was too stinko to pour. She was swaying on her heels and holding onto the counter, and maybe waiting until a sober moment clicked in, so she could trust herself to pick up the bottle.

I heard Evelyn breathe in sharp.

"Comp'ny?" Mom said. "We got comp'ny?"

She pushed herself away from the sink and turned toward us. Totally polluted. As soon as she took her hands off the counter she had to lean onto it hard, so she wouldn't keel onto the floor. Her ratty old bathrobe was half undone, and I saw we was in for a free nudie show underneath it. She glared at us, with her head quivering on her neck like a bobblehead doll, and her pruney lips smacking together, and her eyes so bloodshot and fogged over she could have been staring at us through a couple of coke bottle bottoms.

"Comp'ny?" she said again.

Then she squinted at Evelyn, and started to get mad.

"Who is this *slut*?!," she hollered. "You can't whore with no *slut* in my house!"

She tried to push herself off the counter and come at us. She made it one step, and then she started to fall. Evelyn got her arm, and I stepped in under her chest before she could keel onto the tiles. The robe fell open and out flopped an old boob, and I got a snootful of her stinky hair spray and her damn liquor as she slobbered and spit on my chest, and I fought to keep her upright.

We got her into her bedroom. The mud got all over her robe and her hair, and the bathrobe came open all the way. Mom thought that was funny. "I'm naked!" she screamed, like some nutcase in a psych ward, and "I'm embarrasin' Hank!" Like she could read my mind.

Then she went into her nobody loves me bit. We had her on her bed by then. "Nobody loves me," and snuffling and blubbering while we did our best to wipe off the mud.

I caught Evelyn looking at me while we were pulling the blanket on Mom's shoulders. Real serious and watchful, like she was a doctor who'd learned some important new thing about a patient, and was cogitating on the notes she'd put in my file.

She lowered her eyes when I caught her, but that moment had been enough. All the shame and fear and embarrassment I felt was writ on my face like letters on a neon sign. I'd never wanted anybody to see me like that.

• • •

I told Evelyn she could shower in the bathroom next to my room. I just went in the backyard and stripped in the dark and turned the hose on myself like I was washing a dog. That wasn't the most dignified way I'd ever cleaned up, but I finished ahead of her, and by the time she was done showering I'd put on fresh duds and carted our muddy clothes into the laundry room and got the washer going.

Evelyn wore a bathrobe I'd handed in to her. I went to the kitchen to sop up more of the mud. By the time I came back she was sitting on my bed with her shoulders braced against the wall and her calves curled under her thighs, looking up at the hot rod posters on my walls.

I almost sat next to her, but that was too intimate. I felt weird even having her in my bedroom, but that was the only place we could talk without maybe waking up Mom. I said 'scuse me and went to fetch a chair out of the kitchen, and then sat on that across my room from her.

"You really like cars," Evelyn said, matter-of-factly.

"Yeah. Yeah, I guess that's true about me, all right."

"That one looks like yours."

She pointed at my poster of Cam Knight's righteous 383 launching off the line at the Winternationals. So I said, well, yes and no, and started prattling about the difference between Super Stock and a street car like mine, about slicks and a full race cam, and how Cam Knight's car went everywhere on a trailer. I knew she didn't care, but it gave me something to do with my mouth. I had the heebee-jeebees bad, from the scene with my mom. I mean, real bad, serious bad, and I could tell Evelyn knew it, and that just made it worse.

So I squirmed on the chair and rubbed my legs through my pants, and looked at the floor instead of her, and yakked like a total dip about how Cam's 'Cuda was a '68 and mine was a '67, and the incredibly important differences between the models, and so forth. Evelyn looked at me like a librarian listening to a guy trying to explain the book he wanted. Then I thought I could show her my Ask the Wizard letters, so she'd stare at those instead of me, and rooted around in my closet until I found the binder, and handed it to her.

There, I said. If you want to know what *started* all this, it's 'cause I'm a Scribe Subscriber, and that's why I was at Fiesta and met you in the first place.

She looked at the letters like you'd look at two carousels of slides your uncle just had to show you of his golden anniversary trip to Niagara Falls. But she still played along and leafed through them. I sat across from her and fidgeted some more, and wondered how else I could kill time during the wash cycle.

I snuck looks at her. She'd found the hair dryer, and her long hair was fluffed out on the bathrobe. She had real thick, black hair, like an Indian or a Mexican, except with auburn streaks in it.

Was she part Mexican, I wondered? Or even Indian. She had a strong, proud sort of nose, like I thought an Indian might have. Or maybe she was Jewish, or Italian. She always looked so serious, with her big, broody dark eyes, and her full lips set the way they were. She wasn't a half bad looking woman, I had to admit, at least for a hippy chick.

Then I looked at her calves, curled up beneath her. Man. No razors or Nair for this chick. Her calves were damn near as furry as mine. The Prado fashion police would have made her gossip topic numero uno if she'd gone anywhere with her follicles hanging out like that.

I guess I stared too hard.

"It's hair," Evelyn said quietly. "It grows there."

So I said 'scuse me, and went back to my fidgeting. I squeezed my knees and scratched at an itch on my thighs I didn't have, and took a big studious survey of all the crap I had stacked on the floor, like there was something I actually had to see down there.

But she was still looking at me when I snuck another glance at her. Not like she was mad about me ogling her calf hair. Just looking at me in a gentlefied way, with her brown eyes all sad and soft, like it made her wince to see a hurt she couldn't fix.

"You're embarrassed because I saw your mother drunk," she said.

I puckered my lips in a kind of whistle and shrugged, and fidgeted in the chair, and scratched my neck, and looked at anything in the room except her, and hoped my face wasn't as red as it felt. How could she come out and say something like that? You didn't talk like that about someone's personal affairs. Like if

Cindy had been there, she would have said, Hank, you're acting like a total spazz. That was how you talked to a person.

She put my Wizard's Scribe letters on the bed and clasped her fingers on her knees. She started to say something, then stopped herself. Like she wasn't sure what words to use.

"Hank, we got off on the wrong foot," she said, finally. "I'm ... sorry we started out as we did. The things I thought about you were wrong. Could we just start over? Please? I'm not your enemy."

Oh, sure, sure, I mumbled, and did more of my lame fidgeting.

We were quiet for a few seconds. Evelyn started to say something else, and stopped herself again. Then I guess she decided to go ahead and tell me.

"My husband was an alcoholic."

She gave me a sad little smile. Like she was telling a story where the joke had been on her, about something that had happened a long time ago.

"He was the one in the photo you saw at the drag race. With the cup. See? We're starting over. I'll tell you who he is now."

She slid around on the bed and lay on her side, with her elbow dug into the mattress and her cheek resting on her palm, and her feet dangling over the edge. Not even the least bit self-conscious about being on a man's bed. She looked all caught up in her memories for a second, and then she smiled, like she'd hit on the perfect thing she could share with me.

"One time ... I was seeing a therapist then, and Jennifer ... that was her name; my therapist ... just insisted that all I was doing with Ricky was acting out. That's the term they use. Acting out. Like a gambler going to a casino. Because I complained so much about Ricky's drinking.

"But I said, 'Oh, no, no no.' Maybe Ricky had gone on the wagon for a week. Of course, I thought it was going to last forever. 'Oh, no, no, no, Jennifer. It's not like that. You're wrong about him.'

"Finally I *insisted* that Jennifer meet him. Insisted. It was all my idea."

She laughed and crooked her cheek on her palm to look up at my ceiling, which probably would have been a lot more inviting to gaze at without the poster of Big Daddy losing the wing at Gatornationals. Then she lowered her eyes again, and traced a thoughtful little figure 8 on my sheet with her forefinger.

"So the big day came. I wore my best dress. I was all jittery. You know: 'What's Jennifer going to think of him? How's it going to go?'

"Ricky was already there. I knocked on the office door, and Jennifer let me in. She looked like someone had died in there.

"He was drunk, of course. He stunk of it." She sounded a little amazed, like she could hardly believe what she remembered. "He'd actually thought it wouldn't show.

"It was horrible. Ricky kept talking about how he cherished me. 'I really need to cut back on my drinking. I know Evelyn deserves better.' And he's *drunk* while he's saying all this. Jennifer kept staring at me. Like I was the most pathetic, hopeless patient in her case load.

"Finally she threw us both out. She said he was obviously intoxicated, and that she was enabling him by listening. So I had the honor of being kicked out of my own therapist's office with the husband I'd insisted on showing off.

"I never saw her again. I knew what she would have had to say after meeting my drunk husband. So I didn't go back."

She rolled onto her back and lay looking up the Swamp Rat poster. I thought of getting up to check on the wash cycle, but I put a cork in it and stayed put. Not while she was telling me all this personal stuff.

So she'd had to deal with a drinker, too.

She wasn't in a hurry to start talking again. I looked at her proud, Injun-sort of nose, and those soft brown eyes of hers gazing up at Swamp Rat, and her long black hair spread out on the bed cover. Pretty soon I could swear I got another visit from that spirit thing. This time at least I knew it wasn't physical. It was there, but it wasn't there. It still wouldn't tell me what it was. It was just biding its time, and tip-toeing in the weeds behind the fence posts at the border of my thoughts, and waiting, 'cause I still wasn't ready to hear what it had to say.

"If I tell you a little more about the cup," she said, "can I tell you just the part I'm ready to tell, and not all of it?"

I shrugged.

"I know it's not fair. Can you promise not to ask any questions about what I tell you? I don't even want to say why I don't want to answer the questions. Could we do it that way?"

I said okay. She turned sideways on the bed again, facing me, with her elbow crooked into the mattress and her cheek resting on her palm.

"Ricky wrote a bad check," she said. "I was working in a health food co-op. He waited until I was off shift before he went in. He knew they'd have to cash it. He was my husband. They all knew him. And of course I was the one they turned to when it bounced.

"That was the last straw. You come to where I work, you shame me in front of my co-workers because you want to buy alcohol. That was it.

"It was ugly. I yelled at him. I pulled my wedding ring off and threw it at him and said he could go sleep in the park, for all I cared. We were through.

"He just looked at me in that misty-eyed way he had. He didn't argue. When I finished he said he was sorry, and left. I think he took one day's change of clothes. He left everything else.

"And I never saw him again."

Her lower lip trembled, and she wiped her eyes. I thought she was going to cry, but she fought it back. She stared at the floor and went on.

"I didn't hear from him for a month. And then one day a box came for me special delivery. It was the cup. Ricky had sent it, with a letter. He wrote that he'd remembered how I'd talked of it and had decided to see if he could find it, and had, and that he hoped it would help make up for what a terrible husband he'd been. I checked it out. He'd camped out at the flats and spent days hunting for the cup near where the photo was taken. Just for me. Just to show he could do one thing right.

"Then a week after that, the San Francisco police called. Ricky had killed himself. He'd jumped off the Golden Gate Bridge at night, right at the south tower where you met me. That's why I go out there."

She curled up on her side, with her knees bent under the robe and her hand clasped under her cheek to support her head. She stared off at nothing. Her eyes were moist, but I didn't think

she was going to cry anymore. She just looked sad, the way you'd
be sad about an old piece of bad news that you'd already got ac-
commodated to, that had weighed you down for a long time.

After awhile I said I'd better fetch the wet clothes and plunk
them in the dryer. When I came back she was sitting up on the
bed again. Like she felt awkward about having let her hair down
so much, and wanted to look more formal.

We talked about this and that. She asked a couple of quiet
questions about my mom's drinking, but that obviously sent me
off into heebee-jeebee land again, so she backed off. Then she
asked a bunch of questions about Logos. I thought she was pretty
curious about someone she'd talked to for five minutes and hadn't
seemed to like much, but then I realized she was probably just
trying to steer my brain away from Mom.

After awhile she said she was sorry again that we'd started
out on bad terms, and then I finally managed to cough out an
apology of my own. I'd intruded on her personal life in all sorts
of ways I hadn't had the right to intrude, I said. And I shouldn't
have scared her by hijacking her bag.

Then she asked if I wanted to look at the cup with her.

I didn't know what to say to that. I'd still written the thing
off as a fake. But here she'd gone and opened herself up to me.

In my closet I still had the big boxes that the dippy Moon
rims had come in. We stood those up on the floor between us,
and then she asked if I had a candle, and I remembered this orange thing on a glass saucer that Mom had won at a bingo parlor.
I brought it in from the kitchen and set it on top of the boxes, and
lit it, and then Evelyn asked me to turn off the lights.

She sat up on the edge of the bed facing me, with the stacked
boxes and candle between us, and hauled over her big hippy bag,
and pulled out the cup. She put it on the boxes next to the candle.

"Just look at it and let your mind go free," she said. "And see
what you feel."

She'd set it up so that the face of the thing was staring right
dead at me. I looked at the mouth and the nose and eyes, and the
ribbon shape on the forehead and the mysterioso marks carved
onto the ribbon, and everything tallied up with what I'd seen in
the photos.

I started to feel creeped out again. What if it actually was real? It was like working near a high voltage line at a construction site. It doesn't smell or hum or hiss or do anything to show you it's live, but if you touch it, Jack, you're instant past tense. One way express to Arlington Memorial. What if water had somehow got in the cup, and it fell over, and the water got on my lip? That would count as drinking out of it, wouldn't it? That was when all the supernatural stuff was supposed to kick in. I knew I was being ridiculous. But I still wanted to sit farther back, and keep my lips pressed together. Just in case.

Then I thought of how Logos was going to annihilate me for letting the cup out of my sight, and then I looked past it at Evelyn. I watched how the soft yellowy light moved on her cheeks and nose as the candle flickered, like sunlight glinting on stream water, and how it shone on the auburn streaks in her hair, and made her eyes look even bigger and softer than they already was.

And that was when I could just swear I felt that damn cup laughing at me. It was like the Cup Spirit had hooked up with the Other Spirit that had followed me and Evelyn down from Ripper's Hill. The Other Spirit and the Cup Spirit had had a nice pow wow out in spirit land, and the Cup Spirit had said, 'Ah, so,' and was leering at me. Because it knew just what that Other Spirit was, and what I was in for.

•　　•　　•

I fetched the clothes out of the dryer, and we dressed, and I drove her back to the mall parking lot. The rain had let up. It must have thought we'd be in the house all night, or it would have hung around to dump more water on us.

Evelyn looked a little nervous. I thought I knew why. Maybe I'd copy down her license plate number and give it to Logos. Or even tail her car.

So I stopped at the far corner of the lot, and told her I'd stay as far back from her car as she liked, to respect her privacy. She smiled and said, no, no, that wasn't necessary, but the way she said it told me I'd guessed right.

I promised not to copy her license number. She said thank you, and I drove her the rest of the way to her car. She smiled at me, this great, beaming smile with all the sun and warmth of her heart in it, because she trusted me now.

She said she was glad we'd gotten to be friends for awhile. Then she leaned across the seat to give me a hug. I smelled the young woman smell of her fresh-washed hair on her neck, and felt her soft fingertips on my shoulders.

And then I was watching the Ghia accelerate away, and then she was gone.

•   •   •

That night — or maybe partly that night and mostly the next morning; it was pretty late — I had one of those strong dreams that come along only once in a long while. That you remember after you wake up, and can still remember years later.

It started off ordinary enough. Logos was in it. He was standing in front of a class chalkboard in a lame-o white mortarboard cap, and giving one of his big speeches. Except it wasn't about history, or anything he'd ever talked about in real life. He was talking about how people hook up and have babies, and jabbing at the board with a teacher's pointer. On the board there were pictures of cells dividing and plant seeds and a cow nursing its calf, and then five words in big block letters: The Birds and the Bees.

Then I saw Evelyn again. Sort of coming out of the dream darkness at me, because I wasn't in the classroom anymore. Logos was gone. I wasn't anywhere. Just floating. I saw those beautiful brown eyes, and felt the gentlefied way she'd touched me, like no woman ever had, absolutely no woman ever had in my entire life, and smelled the woman smell of her hair on her neck, and saw her smile again. And then she sort of stepped aside, and I finally, *finally!* saw that Other Spirit thing that had been stalking me so slow and quiet and patient ever since we'd first jabbed our blades in the ground on Ripper's Hill.

And knew who it was:

Cupid. Not no nice, cuddly, little boy Cupid, either. A big, burly, leering bastard with a five o'clock shadow and a lot of bald real estate up top, with his hairy old gut hanging over the pins of his crap-stained diaper. Like he'd just sort of hung out in the ethery spirit world since Roman days, smoking bad cigars and knocking off shots of gin and getting old and gnarly and pot-bellied, but also real good at tracking down bozos like me, and hitting what he aimed at. And the bow he had wasn't no cute little kid's Christmas toy, either. He'd chucked that one when the Visigoths had moved in. It was maybe seventy pounds draw weight and as tall as a Great Dane, and had an arrow ready to go in the string that would have lopped the head clean off a charging rhino.

But she don't even shave her legs, I said, in the dream. She don't even use eye shadow.

Cupid just sneered and shoved the cigar to one corner of his mouth, and hauled off with that massive bow, and let me have it.

•　•　•

And I woke up, lying in my real life bedroom, staring up at Big Daddy in Swamp Rat 16. With a big, sticky mess under the sheets. I'd never actually had that happen in a dream. I saw those sad, gentlefied eyes, and the curve of her soft lips when she'd smiled at me, and I smelled her hair again, and I swear I saw the stalk and the feathers of that rhino-annihilating arrow sticking straight up out of my heart as clear as if it had actually been there.

Because I was done for, Jack. She'd got me good. Flat on my back and knocked out cold. I was in love.

CHAPTER NINE

My story didn't go over real good with Logos.

"You promised not to copy her *what?!*," he said, when I told how we'd said goodbye at Hardy's. Like I'd just said I'd fobbed off the Hope Diamond 'cause I'd wanted to see what a hock shop would give for it, and then lost the pawn ticket.

I tried to explain how it had been. That we'd sorta become friends, even if she was a hippy, and that I'd promised not to run a big Sherlock Holmes trip on her. And the cup was a fake anyway. Come on, Logos. The real Cuauhtémoc cup wasn't going to be bouncing around in a hippy tote bag.

"So now you're an artifact authenticator," Logos said, and then the conversation really went south. Do you have any idea how important that cup could be? And you won't copy her license plate number?!

He was sputtering. I practically had to hang up on him. How could I explain how I felt about her now? I wasn't going to tell Logos about Cupid, or the dream, or the fact that I still felt like I had that arrow in my chest. You show me one man who'd give a tinker's damn for a precious mumbo-jumbo anything after he falls for a woman.

The next week some of Logos' Joe College egghead friends called. One wanted to pay for me to see a hypnotist, so I could remember the Ghia's license number. I even got a call on a crackly phone line from some jasper in London, England in Europe, who said he was a big muckety-muck authority on Indian artifacts. He wanted to rake me over the coals, too. I'd never talked to anybody on the phone farther away than L.A.

But I just got rid of him. And then after that it was mostly Mom's bill collector who called, so I let her get the phone.

· · ·

The next six months didn't go that good for me. I slid pretty far downhill, if you want to know the truth.

I know six months doesn't seem like a long time. You say Happy New Year to some joker in January, you don't expect him to be that different when you run into him watching the fireworks show on July 4. Maybe a different haircut. Maybe a few extra pounds around the belt. That's about all.

But it can be a long time, if the cards aren't going your way in life's big poker game. You can make that last bad bet and go bust in six months. Or maybe just a couple of bad poker hands can add up, and take their toll that way, and change you from the inside out. So you're not the same person you was before, and don't see life the same way. Even if you wish you could.

That's what happened to me.

. . .

Dirk didn't exactly give me a rave job review. I'd let a non-employee into an unauthorized area. I'd assaulted him when he'd tried to interfere.

That was his version. He stuck to it. Maybe he was in CYA mode, on account of slugging me.

I had to go out on interviews with that in my job record. The unemployment worker practically laughed in my face. You think our cowboy governor Ron Reagan's going to send you a check every week if you "assault" your boss? Oh, ho ho ho. And I had maybe enough in my wallet to gas up my 'Cuda and put food in my face for a month.

. . .

The only job I could get in a hurry was at the big HM&F plant, way out off Route 4 near Antioch. They manufactured big structural parts for commercial jobs. Like maybe you're planning to put up a barn, you don't want to chisel up the girders on the spot from a fir tree. That's what HM&F made. Stuff like that.

Now, maybe you're not from Prado. HM&F doesn't mean anything to you. Okay: you talk to any guy who lived in the county back then, and you ask him how he would've felt about a HM&F job. It was strictly last resort. If you had two legs and two arms and could spit, they'd take you. Maybe you wouldn't have those two arms after you'd been working there a month.

For the first couple of days, I tried to pretend it was a joke. Like, here I am pulling into the parking lot for my shift at HM&F,

and any second Allen Funt's going to step out and tell me I'm on *Candid Camera*. But Day One went by, and then Day Two, and the TV crew didn't show up, and nobody else trudging up to the time clock thought there was anything to chuckle about.

By then it had sunk in how bad the job was. I wasn't no William the Woodworker. I hardly knew how to run a table saw. They couldn't put me in a skill position. Mostly they assigned me to sanding or the glue room, and man, was that bad. Man.

The first day after I clocked out I just drove home and slept for twelve hours. I thought I'd get used to it. I never did, though. Not really. And I looked at the faces of the guys I was working with, and they all looked as bushed as I felt.

I wore it around with me 24/7. I didn't want to work on my 'Cuda anymore, or do anything fun, or even change clothes or shave, if I could help it. I just wanted to watch TV and sleep.

•   •   •

Two weeks into the job, somebody made a serious theft attempt on my 'Cuda in the HM&F parking lot. He ripped up the driver's door and stole my Hurst shifter, and would've taken the whole car if it hadn't been for all the crook frustraters I'd rigged up. HM&F had a lot of workers with rap sheets.

That scared me bad. My 'Cuda was practically all I had left. But then Tyler told me I could carpool with him and his bong buddies if I chipped in for gas.

I'd known Tyler since high school. He was a big, dippy guy with his ears and nose about three sizes too big for his chin, who told the same jokes five times before he realized you'd already heard them, and was usually the only one who thought they was funny. He sold weed to a lot of plant workers. That part of long-hair culture had made it to Prado, at least. I don't think he made any money at it. He just did it to pay for his own stash, and so people would hang out with him.

At first I tried to pay my buck a day car fare and not get involved with them. But then it was, 'What's with Hank, he's got a bug up his butt, he won't get high with us.' I didn't want to come off like that. Pretty soon I was toking up too. And I was lonely, if you want to know the truth. I didn't feel good enough to hang with regular people anymore. At least with them I didn't have to put on airs. They worked HM&F just like I did.

We'd watch Monday Night Football at Tyler's dump. He had buckets all over the living room, the roof leaked so bad. Tyler would haul out his personal stash shoe box and pick through the stems and seeds for a decent bud, and tell us, oh, this is Panama Red or Guadalajara Super, when it was just the same rag weed crap he always got. Then we'd pass the bong around. On the tube Frank and Howard and Alex would be yakking about how the Pats got to play ball control offense and dominate the line of scrimmage, and how the road to the Super Bowl leads through Pittsburgh this year, and every once in awhile I'd spot a cockroach scrambling over the dust bunnies tangled in the extension cords behind the set. Man. And Jamie's trying to hold down the hit he took, and Tyler and Dean is laughing 'cause his eyes is all bugged out, and maybe Tyler jokes about how somebody had doper's cough coming back from break today, and how the supe looked at him. Ha ha ha. You know. We're not HM&F losers. We get stoned. We're cool.

And I laughed, too, but underneath it I kept remembering something Logos had said about why it was so easy to get drugs in prison. It was because nobody cared what convicts did to themselves.

• • •

One afternoon on the way back from HM&F Tyler hit a dog. Jamie was passing him the doobie, and I guess Tyler took his eyes off the road. He was in no shape to drive anyway.

I was in the back seat. I felt a big WHOOMP, and then I spotted a sheep dog staggering off the road into the gulley next to the soft shoulder.

Tyler floored it. He ditched the roach and checked the rear view and kept the accelerator pegged, with a real hard charger look on his face, like he's a big time border running drug dealer staying clear of the cops.

C'mon, you gotta check on the dog, I said. But he acted like he didn't hear me. He didn't slow down for a half mile.

Then they tried to make a big joke out of it. Tyler had the shakes bad. "Hey, Tyler," Jamie calls out: "Bang, zoom!" Like Ralph says to Alice on the *Honeymooners*. Bang for the punch, zoom you go flying. That got Tyler to smile a little, so Dean yelled it out too. "Bang, zoom! Bang, zoom!"

They started laughing about it. Can't you at least see if you killed the dog?, I said, but it was like I wasn't even in the car. Tyler even had the roach going again. He was sweating so bad I could smell it, but they still wanted to sweep it under the rug and make it a big har de har. You know. We're the Fabulous Furry Freak Brothers. We're Cheech and Chong. It's just another doper lifestyle adventure. It was just a dog, right? Dogs are five bucks at the pound. Mellow out.

•   •   •

When we hit a stop light I told them to let me out. They didn't ask me why. They knew.

It took me a half hour to walk back there. By then it was getting dark.

It was dead, all right. It lay in the ditch like an Orphan Annie doll, with a big red stain on its ribs. Some kind of sheep dog. Its fur was real clean and white and fluffed up, like it had belonged to somebody who brushed it a lot. It had a collar, too.

I copied the number on the dog tag and went to a pay phone. A girl answered. Oh, great. He killed a little kid's dog. She sounded like she was still singing the damn ABC song in grade school.

I asked to talk to a grown-up. She got her mom. I told her mom real fast what had happened and where the dog was, and hung up before she could ask me anything. I didn't have the guts to stick around. I was afraid she'd bring the kid out there.

I hitchhiked home. I bought a canvas car cover with a lock, and rigged that up on my 'Cuda on the HM&F lot before I clocked in. Tyler and me didn't look at each other when I saw him at the time clocks. So much for Hank in the car pool.

•   •   •

But man, that accident ate away at me. If only the little kid hadn't answered the phone. I kept thinking of how it must have been her dog, and how she must have looked when she saw it in the ditch. I shouldn't even have been in the car with them. I'd known he was in no shape to drive.

And it was one more thing that ate away at me, one more hand in the big card game that had cost me a lot of chips, so the old Hank I'd been before seemed farther and farther away from me.

．　　．　　．

A lot of nights now I just conked out in front of the little TV in my bedroom. One evening I was in there watching *Mannix* when the phone rang. I figured it was the collector, but Mom was asleep. I went out to get it.

It was my dad.

I must've stood there with the receiver stuck on my face for fifteen seconds before it seeped in who I was talking to. He hadn't checked in for at least five years.

"Hank, it's Roj." Nonchalant as all hell. Like we'd just talked yesterday. "I understand you've got the big Two Five coming up, Hank. That's a pretty big birthday."

The rest of it was a blur. He'd be tied up in Chicago for a few more days, but next week he'd be on the West Coast to finalize placement of three Gulfstreams with a corporate client in Santa Clara. "Right in your neck of the woods, Hank." Would I give him the privilege of taking me out to dinner to celebrate my first quarter century?

I felt dazed. I had maybe two memories of him eating dinner with us or tying my shoelaces before he'd divorced Mom. After that he'd mostly just been a name on the child support papers. It had felt like Mom and me was a mistake he was paying off, like if he'd backed his car into a fence post. Maybe every fifth Christmas or every third birthday he'd remembered he had a kid out west, and had his secretary pick out a gift. Then the next few years he hadn't called or sent anything.

．　　．　　．

We met at the Tarryton out in Lafayette, which was one of the fanciest restaurants in the county. I drove Mom over in my 'Cuda. No way we was pulling up in Mom's rust wagon Caprice. Tarryton's would have towed it.

I smelled trouble. I knew I shouldn't have asked Mom to come. It had seemed like the decent thing to do, but I hadn't known how she'd deck herself out for it.

Don't get me wrong. I was duded up, too. I had the blazer on with the crest on the lapel pocket, which hadn't been out of the closet since high school. But Mom had stuffed herself into this sex pot outfit. I could read her mind. Maybe the old embers would fire up again. She'd never said one good word about him in twenty years, but he was still Mr. six figures jet-setting corporate account representative. The guys she'd hooked up with since had been way lower than him. Way lower. Not that there'd been anyone for a long time.

Dad had rented a brand new Vette. An LS6. Cherry red. Man.

"Hank, how's the boy." With a big hearty handshake, like I'm too mature now for a hug. He looked like a *Wide World of Sports* announcer.

Then he turned to Mom. "Helen." And kind of waved his lips at her cheek. By now the smell of trouble was so bad I could practically taste it. I knew her. Maybe her outfit had reeled him in when she had the beach bunny body to put into it, but now she looked ridiculous, with all the veins and pudge showing under her mini-skirt. And she's still so mad at him, too. It's like maybe he'll be so enchanted with her fifty year old cleavage that he'll fall to his knees and slobber on her toes and beg for her forgiveness, and maybe after he sobs and pleads for an hour she'll say okay and be Mrs. six figures jet-setting corporate account representative, but in the meantime she's going to act like it's a tax audit.

Dad had a table reserved overlooking the reservoir. It was the whole nine yards in there. You could smell the fresh cut flowers on the table. I could hardly believe they'd leave out silverware like that. Everybody was wearing fancy clothes.

Dad chit-chatted about the corporate world for awhile. I'm afraid it's back to Tokyo after this, Hank. He rolled his eyes. Fifteen hours flight time. You know how those airlines are. Just miserable. "I can just imagine, sir," I said, and then he goes in to grilling me. Well, Hank. The big two five. Only three days away. I'd give anything to be twenty-five again. You're in the golden years. Tell me everything.

Real slick and debonair, like he's explaining the Gulfstream cabin features to the VP at Paramount. But at the same time he's checking me out, and his smile keeps flickering dim as he sees how high my blazer sleeves ride up on my forearms, and the yellowy stain that wouldn't wash out of the collar, and especially my fingers. HM&F had put me in the glue room all week. You don't just rinse that gunk out from under your nails.

Mom's sitting there with her freeze-dried face. She's already on her second highball. He'd gave her a look when she ordered it, too.

"What kind of work are you doing, Hank?"

Glancing at my fingernails again. I felt like I couldn't move them off the table, he was looking at them so much. Exhibit A: my kid's a loser.

"I work at HM&F."

"Oh? I'm afraid I'm not familiar with that company."

"It's a construction manufacturer, sir," and then I went on about the stuff they turned out, like I was on the board of directors and had just suggested to the prez how we could promote our product line on the East Coast. I felt so stiff I could hardly breathe.

"What are you doing with HM&F?"

I tried to shrug. "Well, this and that, sir. I have different assignments. Different projects they put me on."

Mom killed highball number two and motioned for the waitress.

That was the end of it. Maybe deep down she did it for me, without knowing it. One minute more, and I would have had to tell about the glue room.

"We haven't started our meal yet, Helen," Dad said.

In a weak, strained voice, like he's embarrassed and doesn't want to say it but just has to. Like, would you please not stand up and hold your cheeks apart and pass gas as loud as you can in the restaurant, Helen? The odor is unseemly. People are staring.

"Are you going to lecture me, Roger?"

From there it was straight downhill. She went off on him. I know we haven't started our meal. You don't think I know if we've eat or not? If I have food in my stomach? What's that supposed to mean? If you're too cheap to pick up the tab why don't you say so?

"Helen, please."

And he's already shooting nervous glances at the people around us, like everybody in the Tarryton was thinking of buying a corporate jet off him and now he can see his commissions going adios. Mom just got louder. Don't tell me how to drink. I'm not one of your little sluts. If I want a drink I'll get a drink.

Dad got up. By then everybody in the Tarryton was staring. His cheeks was pink. He fished his wallet out with his hands shaking and peeled out a stack of greenbacks and flipped the stack real disgusted on the table, like he was paying off a crooked bell hop in one of the exotic cities he traveled to. He didn't even look at me when he left.

•   •   •

All the way home Mom yelled about what a SOB he was. She happened to want a drink with dinner. Was that a federal crime? Yelling with her face all red under her special occasion hair-do, and her voice so loud she was pulling in stares from drivers in the next lane. He thought he could walk out, and leave her high and dry, and then come back for a big reunion, and pull exactly the same stuck-up hoity toity routine he'd pulled twenty years ago. Humiliating her in front of people in her own home county.

As soon as we walked in she went for the liquor cabinet. She grabbed a glass out of the sink and poured in a stiff shot and chug-a-lugged it, and bought herself a refill, and stamped around the kitchen with the special occasion high heels marking up the tiles, and the liquor spilling out. That bastard. After everything she'd done to prepare. Nobody told her how to act.

Then she decided she was going to go out and paint the town red. Totally polluted. Her lipstick was smeared bad and her eyes was all bloodshot, and she'd already fell once. But oh no. That wouldn't stop her. She staggered into the living room and hunted for her purse. Try to tell me what to do. You watch me.

All I could think of was that dog Tyler had killed. I never got into mom's business. That was how we survived. But I kept thinking of how that little girl had sounded, and how it would feel to get your dog killed when you were little like that.

Mom got her purse and rooted around for her keys. I'm gonna go out and get laid, she said. I swear. You're too drunk, I said, and I snatched the keys out of her fingers. Then she went ballistic on me. Swearing and trying to slug me, and now we're wrestling on the floor like a couple of five year olds. She's yelling the whole time. I mean really yelling, loud enough to make the neighbors call the cops if she kept it up, and I kind of grabbed her arm and pushed it on her mouth. "Would you quiet down?," and I'm so locked up in what I'm doing I don't know I'm hitting the back of her head on the tiles. "Would you quiet down?"

And I'm banging her head, and I don't know how hard I'm doing it.

Finally she started to cry. Nobody loves me. Nobody cares. And went limp. At least I got her off to bed.

When I came back from her room I saw the little smear of blood on the floor. I'd actually hit her head that hard. My own mom.

I got a wash rag to wipe it up. I felt like I was about two feet tall. I'd just hurt my own mother. I didn't see how much lower I could go. Everything in my life felt so out of control. I was turning twenty-five, and everything seemed to be whizzing past me like 200 mph fastballs I couldn't see, let alone hit, and I didn't know how to make the pitcher stop or slow down the balls or change anything. I was just a bum who worked at HM&F. No wonder Dad had ditched us.

· · ·

I mostly tried not to think about Evelyn. Sometimes I did anyway, though. At odd times. Like maybe I'd be wiping the steam off the mirror in the morning before I scraped a razor across my face. I'd get to thinking about married couples I knew, and how they shared everything, and had to step around each other in the john in the morning while they both got ready for work.

Then all of a sudden I'd imagine myself married to Evelyn. I'd think of how she'd looked that night in the bathrobe, with her brown hair fluffed out. I'd imagine us married, and her maybe touching my shoulders as she stepped around me at the sink, and catching the smell of her wet hair and skin after her shower.

I tried to chase thoughts like that away. They hurt. I got all depressed, if I thought those things. But sometimes my mind went there anyway.

I'd basically decided she was out of my league. At least in the birds and bees department. Even if she was a hippy. I'd gotten a glimpse through a door that just wasn't supposed to open in my life, that was all, and the sooner I closed that door the better. Cindy was more my speed. Maybe I'd have to ask her to take the gum out of her mouth before we kissed, but she'd go to car shows with me, and tailgating parties. I figured I'd get hitched to someone like Cindy eventually. I ought to get used to the idea.

•   •   •

But one Sunday I didn't have anything to do, and figured I'd go to Berkeley. I told myself it was to help hunt for the cup. Sure it was. All the way over there on the freeway, though, that's what I told myself.

I spent about two hours walking on Telegraph. That was East Bay hippy kingdom ground zero back then. They was all lined up selling their beads and jewelry and dope pipes and incense on the sidewalks, and there was other hippies panhandling or giving out leaflets for the different causes they wanted you to support. A year ago my brain would've been cooking up eight million put-downs for them, but I didn't feel that way anymore. All I knew was that they was closer to her than I was, and that she might be among them, and that I might be able to steal another look at her thick brown hair and that proud nose, and look into those gen-tlefied brown eyes again. That I'd never really stopped thinking about, that were in the back of my mind night and day, no matter what I told myself.

She wasn't on Telegraph. I took the long way home, on side roads near Briones. Every time I took a turn or crested a hill, I half expected to see a blue Karmann Ghia pulled over on the soft shoulder. Maybe she would've just happened to have taken a drive out there that day. Maybe the Ghia would be broke down, and she'd be standing next to it, and I could help her.

• • •

One day after work I was at the McDonald's near HM&F when I spotted Sean Davies and the wife he'd told me about. Or I figured by now they was married. Sean had said they'd be getting hitched when he'd talked to me that day back at Hardy's, when he'd told me about his HVAC job, and the house he had up in Bay Point.

I was camped out at one of the plasticky tables with a Big Mac. So that's Sean's old lady, I thought, and kept waiting for them to look my way so I could wave. They was in the order line.

McDonald's was kind of a splurge for me. HM&F paid minimum wage. But I was so tired after my shift. And I figured I could always go to McDonald's, no matter how bad I looked. I'd gotten real lax in the grooming department. I usually wore the same clothes to work all week now, even though I could smell myself by Friday. And hardly shaved. It didn't matter there. I could have gone in covered with fur, like Bigfoot. Or as out of it as Tyler. As long as I could work a glue gun.

Sean's wife was a blonde. I thought maybe she ought to lay off the Big Macs, and then I realized different. She was pregnant. Maybe five months along. They was both duded up a little, like they was going out to hit the town. Maybe his HVAC job was going good, and this was Friday night, so they'd do a quick takeout and then go out to a movie.

I kept watching them move up in line, with my smile and a wave all ready to go, but Sean never looked at me. It was weird, that he'd stand in line and never glance at the dining section. But he didn't.

It wasn't until they'd gone out that I figured it out. He'd seen me first. He'd spent the whole time trying not to look at me.

CHAPTER TEN

One late afternoon I was out in the HM&F parking lot when I spotted Logos. Usually I was never out there longer than it took to get the cover off my 'Cuda and split, but today there was a big "optional" meeting that management had wanted us to go to. They'd let everyone in my department off an hour early.

I'd skipped out on it. I was out there next to my 'Cuda at the far side of the lot, staring through the chain link fence at all the scenic litter and gravel and weeds alongside Greely Road. Then I spotted a figure hoofing up toward me on the other side of the fence, and recognized who it was. Logos.

I turned away, and looked for something I could duck behind so he wouldn't see me.

I wasn't in the world's greatest mood. I figured I was about to get fired, or maybe assigned to shifts even worse than I already had. The "optional" meeting was about some horrible dastardly union that wanted to organize HM&F workers. A guy who'd gone to the same meeting for his department had told me about it. HM&F brass gave you a big speech about how union leaders raped crippled blind dogs in back alleys, and then they wanted you to sign this petition for continued independent corporate leadership.

Well, not me. No thanks. Even if the union was sleazy. Just two months ago some poor bastard had got two fingers sawed off 'cause they put him on a table saw with no shield. Typical HM&F. You showed them a corner, and they'd cut it. I wasn't going to nod my head like a bobblehead doll at everything the VIPs had to say, and sign a petition so a union couldn't even twist their arm on safety regs, and somebody else could lose fingers next year.

And I knew about where that put me. Maybe there was some legal reason they had to call the meeting "optional," but anybody who thought HM&F was going to give you an hour to twiddle your thumbs on their dime had another think coming. I'd counted all of four other guys out there playing hooky with me in the parking lot, and half of them was about to quit anyway. No way they wasn't logging attendance on this. I figured next week I'd be assigned to licking the underside of the president's Mercedes. If I still had a job then.

• • •

Logos looked like he was out on a hike. I was about to try hiding behind a big Econoline, but it was too late. He'd already seen me.

"Hankus."

There was nothing to do but walk up to the fence and nod 'hi' at him.

Logos stepped up to the Greely side and hooked his fingers through the chain links. I hadn't seen him since we'd got back from Fort Whatever It Was. He looked his usual cheery self.

"So it's come to this."

He tilted his head at the HM&F plant.

"Well, Hardy's canned me. Like I told you. I had to get a job. This is what I got."

"Please accept my condolences, Hank. I'm afraid I've yet to hear a positive word about your new employer. I doubt you much relish your time here."

He leaned his little shoulder on the chain link fence and gave me a sympathetic look. It ticked me off. Even if he was just trying to be nice. He'd never have to work at a place like HM&F. Not with his brain. He could just waltz through life doing whatever he pleased, and earn spare change tutoring other eggheads at Stanford, and then maybe pick up a gig as chief brain surgeon for the Mayo Clinic if he wanted a regular paycheck.

Or maybe he'd get a job from some secret homo friend. Every time I thought of that letter I'd seen, it was like an electric jolt reminding me I couldn't feel safe around him anymore. It felt like he'd done something behind Prado Diablo's back, like stealing from the treasury. Something he didn't have any right to do.

• • •

"You're out pretty far for a nature stroll," I said. Just to have something to do with my mouth.

❦ 147 ❧

"It's not much of a stroll." He nodded at the road. "I have a half mile to the bus stop. Greg dropped me off."

"Where you headed?"

Logos looked a little sheepish. "I thought I'd take another stab at locating the elusive Evelyn, Hank. I've done quite a bit of sleuthing these past many months. Perhaps I should open a detective agency."

He twisted his fingers on the link fence. "I've got a new lead in Berkeley. Maybe it won't pan out. None of the other leads have. But it's worth a try. You're welcome to come, of course. If you don't think that would violate the spirit of the compact you struck with her."

"Well, thanks anyway," I said. "I'll pass. I can't leave here 'til 5:00 anyway. I'm going to go back later and clock out."

"They just want you to guard the parking lot until 5:00?"

So I had to tell him about the management meeting. I didn't want to. Even his taking my side was going to grate on me. Oh, you poor doggies, they treat you so bad at the pound. Thank heavens I'm not a dumb doggie like you.

But I went ahead. As I talked I could see him finally register how old Hank had changed. I was pushing five days on the same set of work clothes. And I looked tired and worn out, like everybody else in there. I knew I did. I saw it in the mirror every day.

Him eyeballing me like that ticked me off even more. He was checking me out like my dad had at Tarryton's.

I didn't need it. And I sure didn't need it from some secret fairy who'd never have to go through what I was going through.

Sure enough, when I was finished he said:

"You have my sympathy, Hank. I'm afraid that sounds par for the course for your present employer."

"I guess."

"I know an attorney who dabbles in labor law. I could put you in touch with him, if you like. He might be able to offer advice."

"Well, tell you what, Logos. You want to help out, maybe you could start some kind of business and give us HM&F peasants a job. Maybe that'd interfere with your scholarly book reading time a little. But you could do it. Then I wouldn't need no lawyer."

· · ·

I hadn't intended it to come out mean, but it did. I could hear the edge coming into my voice, and I couldn't fight it down.

He blinked and stepped back from the fence. He looked a little shocked.

"I'm not much of an entrepreneur, Hank. I'm sorry."

"You could learn. You could try to."

"I don't think I'd make much of a go of it."

"Well, okay." I shrugged. "You know yourself best. It was just a suggestion."

I stared past him at Greely, like I hadn't just sounded as ticked off as I knew I had, and like I was just fascinated with all the rusty cans and hamburger wrappers on the soft shoulder. So I wouldn't have to look at him.

But I could feel Logos watching me.

"I hope you're not angry with me," he said.

"Angry? I'm not angry about anything. You can see what a great job I've got. My employers are deeply concerned about my personal welfare. Why should I be angry?"

But I was still looking past him at all the breathtaking roadside garbage, and I could feel him tallying up the fact that I wouldn't look at him while I talked. I made myself look at his face.

He looked hurt. He knew for sure now that something was wrong. It hurt me and made me madder at the same time seeing his face like that. He was such a dinky little dude. He looked about fifteen years old.

"Hank, it's almost five o'clock. Why don't I wait here until you punch out? Then we could go over together."

"No, man. I already told you." I looked past him at Greely some more. "I made a deal with her that I wasn't going to go tracking her down. And that thing's fake anyhow."

"Then perhaps you could just accompany me while I look for it. That wouldn't violate your agreement with her." He was quiet for a second, and when he went on his voice was more careful. "I think it would be good for you to hash things out with someone. I'd like to offer a sympathetic ear. We don't have to take the bus. We could travel in your car, at least if you'll permit me to compensate you for mileage."

And for some reason that made me madder than anything else he'd said. You practically had to put a gun to his head to get him to set foot in a muscle car. But now poor dumb old Hank is so bent out of shape that he's just going to have to humor me. Aww. Poor Hank. I could just see him prodding me to talk and maybe putting his dinky hand on my shoulder, and hey, who knew, maybe he'd try to turn me into a fruiter too. Maybe that was how they operated.

Because I believed he had done something wrong. The more I thought about it. He didn't have to be some kind of pervert, not with how everybody he'd gone to high school with looked up to him. He'd betrayed us. It made me sick. I felt dirty just being around him.

"Look, I don't want to be letting my hair down with you. Okay?" And I looked right at him, and now I was so mad that I didn't care how bewildered he looked. "Why don't you work on your own problems? Maybe if you spent a little more time fixing yourself instead of worrying about other people, you'd be a little more *normal*. Okay? You ought to try it. Seeing as how you want to psychoanalyze everybody else."

"Hank, I'm sorry. I don't know what this is about."

And I knew I'd already gone way too far, from how he was looking at me. But I went on anyway. It was funny. Once as a little kid a neighbor had asked me to watch over her poodle, and she'd given me an electric prod in case some big German Shepherd tried to mess with it. And I'd just had to try that prod out on that damn dog. Being seven years old. I'd known it was wrong. I'd known I shouldn't do it. But I could still remember holding that thing and putting the prongs on the poodle's fur, and knowing I shouldn't touch the button, but touching it anyway. Like there was a part of me that just wanted to do harm, with no sense behind it. Harm to myself, too. Because I'd felt way worse than that poodle did afterward.

"Well, maybe you ought to try re-reading some of your own personal mail, Logos," I said. "You got a nice stack of letters in your bedroom that tells a whole lot about you."

Logos stepped back. If I'd wanted a rise out of him, I was getting it. His eyes opened wide.

I went on. Still pushing the button on the electric prod, just for the sake of making hurt.

"I didn't have anything else to read while you was out there trying to keep your dad out of the evening news," I said. "I thought I was just going to see some Scribe advice. Well, excuse me.

"Why didn't you tell us, instead of writing off with your secrets to somebody half way across the United States? Okay? If you think you're a queer. Maybe somebody here could do something for you. Why ..."

But that was as far as I got.

He took another step back. He looked different now than in all the years I'd known him, clear back to being tablemates in third grade. Naked, and hurt, and frightened, and not even fifteen years old anymore. More like ten. Staring up at me like I was a big brother he'd trusted, who'd just played a dirty joke on him in front of a bunch of friends. Something he'd counted on me not to do.

"Hey, Logos, wait ..."

Now all the ugliness and meanness was out of me, and I wanted to take it back. But it was too late. He was stepping back, moving away from me. With that look on his face. I couldn't follow him. The fence was in the way.

"Come on, Logos. I didn't tell nobody ..."

He didn't answer. He didn't say anything. He gave me one last hurt, confused look, and turned, and then with the setting sun slanting on Greely Road I watched him walk fast away from me.

CHAPTER ELEVEN

The next ten days wasn't exactly the happiest of my life. HM&F canned me for skipping the meeting, just like I'd figured they would, but I was so miserable about Logos that I hardly cared.

As soon as five o'clock had come, I'd gone chasing down Greely Road after him in my 'Cuda. But no soap. The bus must have picked him up. And I knew I couldn't track him down in Berkeley if I didn't even know what part of town he'd gone to.

So I went in person to the De Mello household — which said a whole lot about how bad I felt, considering the wide berth I gave that place — and met up with Logos' mom, and asked her to tell Logos that I wanted to talk to him. Please. Because it was important. Without mentioning to her the scene on Greely Road.

She said fine.

But Logos didn't ring me up that night.

•   •   •

Well, I figured, maybe he wasn't even staying at his folks' house. Maybe he was out at Rosenfeld's. I'd have to be patient. Every time I thought of what I'd said and how he'd looked I felt sick, like I could hardly feel normal until I apologized. But it was only one day. I could wait.

But Logos didn't call me the next day, either.

•   •   •

I rang up Mrs. De Mello again. She said Logos had left a phone message with Barry. He'd be "away for awhile." That was all. "Away for awhile."

Well, that wasn't so bad. Logos traveled. Maybe his Vietnam vet friend in San Jose had gone off the deep end.

I waited. But it was like a part of me already knew he *wasn't* visiting any Vietnam vet friend this time, or anything like he usually did. That I'd caused just the hurt I was most afraid I'd caused, and maybe made him do something I'd never forgive myself for.

I waited. Then it was five days since Greely Road, then six. Then seven. HM&F gave me the pink slip. I went out to Rosenfeld's, but it was all locked up. Maybe old Abe had sold out.

•   •   •

By day ten I was straight up miserable with worry. I went out to the De Mello's again, and as soon as I saw Mrs. De Mello my heart really sank. Now *she* looked worried, too.

No, Logos hadn't called. No, this wasn't like him. He'd never done anything like this before.

I asked if I could go up to Logos' room to look around. Maybe he'd left something behind that would tell me where he'd gone. It was the best idea I could think of.

Mrs. De Mello said that was fine.

•   •   •

Logos' bedroom looked about the same. He'd been there in the past month, though. I recognized the headline on a newspaper.

I shut the door and started fishing around in the keys and spare change and other stuff-from-your-pockets crap on his desk. Then I turned to a stack of books on his bed and rooted in there for awhile. *Life among the Inuit*. Maybe that was a clue. Maybe he'd moved in with the Eskimos.

It felt hopeless. What was I supposed to do if I found a piece of paper that had a name and a phone number on it? He might have written that down two years ago. I didn't have any idea what I was looking for, but it was either try my best or go out and be miserable some more.

Finally I decided I might as well read through the stack of Scribe letters. I thought that showed how desperate I was, seeing as how old anything in there was bound to be. But reading that one letter had told me more about Logos than anything else I'd seen. It was worth a try.

I went to the stack of *Hot Rods* and pulled the manila folder out of the pile. I sat on the edge of the bed with the folder on my lap, and opened it up, and started reading through the letters one by one.

It took me about a half hour of reading to figure out what was going on.

I wish there could have been a hidden camera in the bedroom, to tape the look on my face when I finally figured out what the score was. I'd like to look at it now. Just to see me sitting on the bed with those letters on my lap and my jaw hanging open, as I finally caught on to what a royal, and Jack, I do mean *royal* hunk of wool that chick had pulled over my eyes from the start.

I'd never suspected it. Not from her selling her hippy wampum right next to Fiesta, where the giveaway was. Not from her pulling an about-face on showing the cup right after I'd mentioned Logos' name, or all the questions she'd asked about him in my room. And not even from that damn Ghia of hers, which had sounded like the lead engineer in Stuttgart had set the valve timing. No way a hippy wagon VW was going to sound like that.

It had still never occurred to me. It was like you meet a chick and she acts like anybody else, and you invite her over and talk and argue a bit, and think whatever you think of her, and go your separate ways.

And then you find out she's practically the Queen of England.

CHAPTER TWELVE

Brother Logos:
A happy hot rod b-day to your buddy
Charles! I think this is the first time
anyone has paid for an Ask the Wizard
letter as a birthday gift.

Some racers do cut bores oversize and
install thinwall nodular iron sleeves.
This *can* produce a strong bore that will
resist detonation, but it's a lot easier
to install the sleeves incorrectly than do
it right, and you're guaranteed to have
head gasket problems if you do it on the
wrong block.

I'm sorry if this is bad news for your
buddy, but I don't think this is the
best way to fight detonation. He'd be
better off paying attention to ignition,
carburetion and compression ratio. He also
should plan to check the plugs regularly
for signs of detonation after the engine
is built. (Look for tiny purple-black
spots on the ceramic or electrodes.)

Believe it or not, sometimes I think hot
rodding is a little silly, too. Even if no
one around here agrees with me.

Sincerely,
THE WIZARD'S SCRIBE

•   •   •

Hello again, Logos:
Yes, I remember you. We save all the
letters to Ask the Wizard. You have your
own file here now.

I would never build a high performance
engine without budgeting for an align hone
with a Sunnen Hone Master, or something

similar. On a racing engine, not getting the align hone done is like throwing away twenty or twenty-five horsepower.

The align hone must be done with a head (or torque) plate in place, to match the stress that will be put on the block by the cylinder heads in the finished engine. (Well, maybe I shouldn't say 'must,' but you'd be wasting your money if you didn't.) You'll also want to use the same fasteners and head gasket that will be used in final assembly.

Are you still helping your friend Charles, or are you helping someone else? If you're being paid, I'm supposed to charge you a different rate. It doesn't sound like you are from the other things you wrote, but I still had to ask.

You didn't offend me by comparing hot rodding to courtship behavior by male bowerbirds. You made me laugh pretty hard, though! I don't think anyone has ever sent a letter like that to us before. I'm tempted to show it to Claude, but he might not take it the right way. I'm not like most of the other people who work here.

You're right, it's just a hobby. It can be a fun hobby, though. You enjoyed it in high school yourself, as you said.

Sometimes I wish I could say that in some of the letters I write. "This is just a hobby! There's more to life than your car! Look at the clouds for once!"

Actually, this is the first time I've ever said it in a letter. So, thank you for the opportunity.

If you have any other questions, I hope you write back.

I'm supposed to say 'brother' at least
once in every letter I write, so:
   Until next time, brother,
   THE WIZARD'S SCRIBE

·   ·   ·

   *First, estimado Hankus, as understandably
anxious as your readers must be for the sor-
did details of my long-postponed showdown with
Evelyn — and in some respects it really was a
showdown, an excruciating and shameful thing
to endure, as richly deserved as my suffering was (and worry not, Hank, every oozing
and purplish detail of this suffering shall
be related forthwith) — I must not neglect my
manners:*
   *Thank you, old friend, for inviting me to
contribute a guest chapter or three in this
life story you have underway. I am honored,
and touched. I hope I ruffle no feathers by
admitting that you were the last of all Prado Diablans I expected to become an author.
Please remember me after Oprah puts your name
in lights, and please do remain a gentleman if
she is overwhelmed by your manly allure, and
chases you about the table during the commercials. You will have our hometown's honor to
uphold.*
   On with the matter at hand:

·   ·   ·

   *You have written that you agonized over
my psychological state when we parted company that unfortunate gray afternoon at HM&F. I
know you are the sensitive sort, Hank, and do
not want you to wince as you read this account, but must admit that my consternation*

likely was greater than you expected. For two
reasons.

First, I was a much more thoroughly closeted fag than I think is the norm today. I
had revealed my suspected homosexuality once
and once only in an impulsive letter to my
faithful pen pal Sarah, and then had responded to her irreproachably sympathetic reply by
abruptly severing all ties with her.

Grok that, Hank. Put that in your pipe and
take an experimental puff or two. I am not a
rude fellow. You know that. I think my uncon-
ditional cauterizing of this link to Sarah was
the cruelest thing I did in a decade, and it
was nearly as cruel to me as it was to her; I
agonized over every subsequent letter she sent
beseeching me to renew our friendship. But I
could not bear to communicate with the one
person I had invited to peep inside the closet
and look around. I was not closeted only from
Prado Diablo. I was closeted from Logos. I
steadfastly regarded my homosexual feelings as
a phase.

Second, my westbound mission that evening
was not only in pursuit of the cup, although
you have correctly presumed that I held far
more faith in its likely authenticity than
you did. I intended to kill two birds with
one stone: to pursue a lead that would likely be another dead end (as all the other Evelyn leads had been), and then to hasten to
San Francisco, where I could hover skittishly
near the entrance of a gay newcomer's meeting
then convening weekly at a storefront off Polk
Street. I had no intention of entering; rather, I would audit it (in my own repressed way)
by haunting the sidewalk across the street,
and observing the pedestrians slipping inside

*as a pet beagle might balefully regard a for-
bidden beef briscuit on the kitchen counter.*

*This was what I had _really_ been on my way
to do that night, so confident was I that the
Berkeley lead would fizzle.*

*And now you had confronted me. Not on pa-
per, as Sarah had. Man to man. Face to face.*

I was reeling.

•   •   •

Logos:
I remember you. I admit that I don't
always remember the people who write, but
I'm just as much a flesh-and-blood person
as you are, believe it or not. I actually
cry sometimes and have feelings. Isn't
that amazing? I remember letters that
stand out. I don't just think about cars.
Nobody told me I had to spend the rest of
my life thinking about cars when I was
born.
Also, I don't answer all the Ask the
Wizard letters. Each of us here has a case
load. You're in mine.
Your letter sounded a little confused.
You say that you've given up hot rodding
for environmental reasons, but still
wanted to write to thank me for the advice
I gave you, and to let me know why you
wouldn't be writing again. Why? If you're
not going to write anymore, isn't it
unusual to write to say that you're not
going to write? Isn't that like knocking
on a door and telling the person inside
that you don't need to come in?
I'm afraid it made me a little angry
that you're so sure I don't care about
the environment. You don't know me, do

you? There might be a lot of things
about me that would surprise you. If you
sent me an article about how cars harm
the environment, I wouldn't "throw it
away in disgust," to use your phrase.
It's not fair to make all these personal
assumptions about me just because I work
here.

This is my job. Okay? The reasons I'm
working here would take a long time to
explain.

I am returning your check, as your
letter didn't have a mechanical question
in it.

I don't mean to give you the impression
that I didn't like hearing from you. You
seem like a very interesting person, even
if you made me pretty mad! Please write me
again soon, if you'd like.

Sincerely,
SCRIBE

P.S. — Please don't show this letter to
anyone else.

•   •   •

Dear Logos,

I don't know where to begin. I've been
staring at the page for the past half-
hour, and just keep tapping my pencil
point on the paper. ~~Maybe I secretly think~~
~~the words are hidden~~

Are you trying to test me? I wrote to
you that I don't just think about cars.
So now you send me this ~~horr~~ intensely
personal letter about Ingrid. ~~Are you~~
~~trying to taunt~~ Are you trying to taunt
me by implying that I really do just think

about cars, and that I'll run away from a
story about someone like her?

It's good that she trusts you, but if
she was abused ~~she should~~ I think she
should talk to a professional. It's good
of you to try to help, but it sounds like
she needs to see a therapist who has
studied ~~the issues the problem~~ that sort
of abuse.

I'll think more about this and write
again tomorrow.

Have you thought of calling a help line?

The reason I'm not returning your check
this time is that I tore it into little
pieces and flushed it down the toilet.
It is absolutely, disgustingly <u>insulting</u>
to write a story like that and then send
a check with it. Just thinking about it
makes me shake a little. If you wanted to
make me mad, you succeeded. Don't do that
again.

Please do not ask me any more questions
about auto mechanics. Ask someone else.

I didn't put your letter in your file
and am not using a typewriter anymore
because this has nothing to do with the
scribe service. I don't like typewriters.
I like to feel the words come out of my
fingertips when I write with a pencil.

At the bottom of this letter is a
different address you can write to. (I
know: it's a long way from New York City.)
Please don't give this address to anyone
else. Please.

Sincerely,
Sarah

P.S.: Please don't show this letter to
anyone else.

P.P.S.: I'm Claude's daughter.

•   •   •

I had a bus to catch. I hot-footed my way
along Greely Road, sometimes glancing soft
shoulder-ward as I stepped around beer bottles
and other roadside bric-a-brac in the deep-
ening twilight. Occasional cars roared past,
illumining my brisk-striding form in the headlights. I squinted when the bicephalous lights
bore down, like a guilty-as-sin cat burglar
in the precinct show-up. Which seemed appropriate. For I was guilty, wasn't I? You had
caught me.

"If you think you're a queer."

A queer. My memory of your words fairly
throbbed in my mind's eye as I hailed the bus,
boarded, fed bills and change into the fare
box and took a window seat at the bus center,
behind a weary-looking young Mexican in a security guard's uniform. <u>If you think you're a
queer</u>. The bus joined traffic, bore westward.
BART was at least fifteen minutes distant. I
slouched in the seat and observed the passing
sights as if through a gun turret, not wanting
to be seen over the window sill. Perhaps you
had already gone on the intercom at HM&F and
solemnly informed the proletariat there of my
faggotry. Perhaps there would be a warrant out
for me.

Would you tell? You had been in poor humor.
I guessed that this had been much more about
your tenure at the notorious HM&F than about
me, but what if I had been wrong? A single moment of rumor-telling at the HM&F water cooler
could have incited a conflagration of gossip
that would have made my life in Prado unbear-
able. I can't make light of my psychological
state, Hank; I was terrified.

Gradually, however — as the bus lumbered through town, consuming BART-bound riders like a blue whale engorging krill — I persuaded myself that I was probably safe. I enumerated four reasons supporting this view.

One: you hadn't told already, even after many months.

Two: you had told me you hadn't told, even as I was bolting away from you at the HM&F fence.

Three: your manner and countenance had indicated no malicious desire to tell.

And four: it just wouldn't have been like you, Hank. You have never been a gossip.

I needed to settle down.

I let my head droop against the window glass, felt the synesthetic vibration of the bellowing engine against my temple. Gradually, I persuaded my enfevered mind to contemplate a more pleasant matter: the newcomer's meeting, and the object of my latest giddy crush.

• • •

Dear Logos,
Okay. You win. We don't have to talk. You're so infallibly brilliant about everything else, maybe you're right about this, too. It would change the dynamic between us. We wouldn't tell our secrets so easily.

"Why do you think there's a screen in the confessional booth?" Nice line, Logos. Touché.

Never mind that we have been writing each other for *two years* now, that you have a *stack* of letters from me, that I've told you what I fantasize when Ricky is about to come and why I was afraid of

light switches when I was five, and a few
dozen other things I've never told anyone
else. Never mind. We'll just keep being
pen pals. The 7-11 cashier will get to see
you and hear your voice, but I won't.
     You win.
     I'm too irritated with you to write
anything more today.
     Love,
     Sarah

· · ·

     Dear Logos,
     I'm sorry if this is hard to read. I'm
writing this on a rickety gray card table
next to the janitor's supply closet, which
is the only place I can write anything at
the co-op without a lot of people milling
around and looking over my shoulder. The
table keeps dipping and making the letters
squiggle.
     I smell. Literally. My clothes smell. My
charming precious husband raided my hand
bag to make a liquor store run, leaving
me with exactly twenty-seven cents until
pay day. The twenty-seven cents were in my
jeans, or he would have taken that too.
     Undoubtedly with one of his beautiful,
doomed, quirky little smiles. "Isn't it
just terrible the way I am?" He actually
says things like that.
     I don't have laundromat money. I
washed my panties and socks in the sink
and ironed my jeans, but I could smell
my blouse when I put it on. It's *gross*.
I feel like everyone at the co-op is
sniffing at me.

I need to see a therapist. A good one.
Even if it costs a lot. I can do Scribe
work again.
If I just kick Ricky out he's going to
go lie in a gutter somewhere and die. He
won't make any effort to help himself. He
won't talk about the war at all. It's like
whatever he did or saw or didn't stop in
Vietnam was so horrible that it's beyond
anything he can forgive himself for, and
so he exists and gets drunk and waits for
his heart to stop beating. If I ask, he
just makes these dark, cryptic, doomed
remarks. Am I really so pathological
because I want the man I married to stay
alive?
This is a terrible letter. I'm sorry. I
shouldn't dump all this on you.
Love,
Sarah

•   •   •

*The newcomer's meeting would be my third. I
had stumbled across the first only a month earlier, while wandering about Polk as part of my
ongoing, self-prescribed therapy for my homosexual thoughts. I mean this seriously, Hank.
I thought of my gay desires as a sneering
military psychoanalyst might: an acting out,
a self-abasement, a neurotic purging of unfinished business with the more significant actors
in my delirious family. I believed I could
treat myself without revealing my sickness to
a confidante, as a therapist might self-pre-
scribe for a personal phobia. I would lance
the boil by giving it some rein.*

*Thus were born my solitary expeditions to
gay San Francisco. (Always to Polk. The Cas-*

tro was too hardcore for me.) I would start at Polk and O'Farrell and then meander north, stealing discreet glances at the uncloseted gay men promenading about me, and nervous- ly rehearsing the excuses I might recite if an AWOL Prado neighbor happened to spot me in front of the Kokpit. ("Is this where the cable car stops?") I could not seem to rid myself of my shameful homoeroticism; so, I would indulge it, would wade knee deep through the heartland of gay culture, until I became bored with mustachioed fags in Tom of Finland get- ups, and developed a wholesome letch for Ra- quel Welch. The long-anticipated Transbay Tube was open, after all; my San Francisco forays had become almost effortless.

That was the plan. I never entered a gay bar; that would have been unimaginable, far too much. I just walked, endlessly, from af- ternoon into the night, swiftly averting my gaze if one of those Tom of Finlanders regard- ed me with intent, even as my pulse raced at the prospect his eyes offered.

• • •

Dear Logos,
No, I don't mind writing about Claude. Ask away. I'll tell you anything. Maybe one of these days I'll persuade you to actually talk to me, so I can bore you with all my problems on the phone instead of in letters. (Hint hint hint)
Anyway.
I *worshipped* my father when I was little. Every time I asked where Daddy was, Cora would pull out her little clip collection of her wonderful son racing in Europe. "*That's* where your daddy is,"

she'd say. I thought he was like Superman,
off battling Brainiac and Lex Luthor.
I made Willard teach me how to take off
the air cleaner in his truck, so I'd have
something about cars to show Daddy when he
came home.

But he didn't come home. At least
once a month there'd be a beautiful toy
in a box covered with international mail
stickers from some exotic city in Europe
that he was racing in, but he didn't come
home until Willard's cancer was stage IV.
Then I think fate intervened. I think
Claude would have kissed the coffin and
gone straight back to Europe if he hadn't
attended his high school reunion while
he was here, and had his famous identity
crisis. (Incidentally: none of the
articles about that reunion or identity
crisis mention that Claude had a daughter
in the U.S. I guess motorsports writers
aren't any more interested in parenting
than Claude was.)

You know what I think? Deep down inside,
I still think that an angel who watches
over small children set up everything
that happened at that reunion so one
race driver's daughter in Fresno would
occasionally get to see her father. I know
that sounds silly.

My pathetic doomed husband just walked
in with two new pals from the bar, and I
have to get out my rolling pin. I *hate*
playing that role. My life is a disaster
and I don't know what to fix.

More tomorrow.
Love,
S.

• • •

I discovered the newcomer's meeting one night while traipsing about Nob Hill. Ahead of me on the sidewalk appeared a propped-open doorway, exuding bright light within. Beside it stood a self-appointed concierge of sorts, a broad-shouldered twenty something with the golden-haired mane of a young Thor, bearing a stack of mimeographed fliers. I watched an apprehensive CPA-type turn toward the door, accept a flier, disappear within.

I thought it was a political meeting. I continued my unconcerned way along, observing another passerby exeunt the sidewalk throng and disappear inside, and also observing how the passer-out-of-fliers' rich saffron locks contrasted with the rusty wool tendrils of his gorilla hair sweater.

As I drew abreast of the door, the golden-maned concierge turned toward me. Our eyes met. I thought I was about to get an Impeach Ford handout.

He, however, seemed to regard me with all the wisdom in the world, although he was no older than twenty-three. I saw now that he was more than ordinarily good-looking; he was stunning, and my primal electric response to his looks seemed to merrily uproot all my patient efforts to reason myself out of my faggotry, as a mischievous child with hand outstretched would knock down a row of soda bottles.

He seemed to see through me, Hank, in that one instant. It was as if the whole sad folly of my self-prescribed Polk Street safaris were as shimmeringly clear to him as the color of my shirt. His understanding was kind, unmalicious. He could help.

He smiled. He offered a flier.

I dared to look at it when I was a block away.

The flier described a weekly gay newcomer's meeting, a new outreach project of a student gay rights group at S.F. State. Some dewy-eyed undergraduate had decided that his fellow collegians should rent an off-campus storefront to offer succor to angst-ridden fence sitters like me.

The project perished within a year, but it was bristling with health then. They met weekly. Same time, same place. If you thought you were gay or wanted to learn more about the gay experience, this was the place to come.

• • •

Dear Logos,
After I got rid of his friends last
night Ricky vomited all over the kitchen
floor and would've passed out in his
own puke if I hadn't dragged him to bed.
I am freaking out. He's getting worse.
He's *trying* to get worse. Whatever
happened over there, he's given himself
an uncommutable death sentence. The only
person trying to keep him alive is me.
It's sick. I know it's not just him.
There's something wrong with me for being
in a relationship like this. I'm afraid
you're going to realize what a loser I am
and stop writing. Please don't, Logos.
Okay. Enough. Stop, Sarah.
Back to Claude.
After he came back to the states I
decided in my crazy little grade school
way that I was going to steal my superhero
daddy from the world and make him mine.

As soon as he opened the shop in South Fresno, I nagged Cora to take me there. Boss got a big crate for me to stand on, so I could watch him rebuild the Offenhauser in their sprint car. I must have learned more about mechanics before I was ten than I ever learned afterward. I was going to make Daddy proud of me.

The first bubble burster was in fifth grade. We'd just moved up about eight income brackets to our house in the old Fig Garden neighborhood, and I was terribly self-conscious about being the girl from the wrong side of the tracks in a new school with all the rich kids. But everybody was impressed by my starting-to-get-famous father, and Claude was in town for once, and I got him to promise to come to my school one day to answer questions.

Well, he just blew it off. I don't remember why. Any development with one of the team cars would've been enough to make him forget a visit to his daughter's elementary school. Trust me.

I was devastated. One p.m. rolls around, and no Claude. All the upper grade classes had come to the auditorium to see him. One fifteen, one thirty, and no Claude. Kids are starting to snicker and sneak glances at me, because I was the one who'd set the whole thing up. I got teary eyed. I felt like a pathetic poor kid who'd just tried to con everybody into thinking she had an 'in' with a race driver.

What made it a turning point was how my teacher reacted. I blamed myself for the whole thing, because Daddy was a superhero and superheroes can't ever do anything wrong, can they? But it was very, very

obvious that Mrs. Elson thought it was
totally Claude's fault. She even drove
me to his shop after class, so she could
basically tell him off about not breaking
promises to children. I still remember how
I felt standing next to her, and watching
him try to blow *her* off too, and finally
beginning to question the superhero
fantasy.

   My hand is getting tired. I'll do one
more installment tomorrow and mail three
letters together. Then you'll have to send
three letters to me, too. Ha ha ha!

   S.

· · ·

*Thereafter I thought of my golden-maned
doorman obsessively. I saw his image in my
mind's eye almost constantly as I did my Mary
Worthing with my feckless family members, as
a votary would imagine a likeness of a deity
sculpted into the bumps and furrows of a cloud
head. He had arrived. He was in the know. He
had transcended all the sturm und drang of my
sorry grappling with my sexual identity, and
with serene sympathy gazed upon me from the
Other Side, omniscient, transcendently kind.
Beautiful.*

*The next week I just happened to find my-
self on another subway to San Francisco, and
just happened to navigate precisely the boule-
vards that would deposit me across the street
from that bright-lit open door as the meeting
began. He was there again, dispensing fliers.
It was warmer. He wore a work-shirt, cornflow-
er blue, the blond locks cascading about the
collar. I did not dare venture to that side
of the street, Hank. He might have recognized*

*me, might have spoken to me. What would I have
done? Instead I moseyed about in front of a
shuttered antique store across the street,
innocently, as if I were waiting for someone,
and stared at him fiercely whenever I felt sure
he wouldn't catch me.*

*He didn't look at me. After a half-hour of
dispensing-of-fliers, with the meeting well underway, he turned into the bright doorway. He
didn't reappear.*

*But my thirty minutes of discreet ogling
had been more than enough to nourish my fixa-
tion. I was enmeshed in fantasies of him as
I hiked along Greely Road, Hank, and spotted you at HM&F. And now to him once again my
mind returned, as I convinced myself that Hank
Wouldn't Tell, and looked forward to continuing to Polk once I dutifully investigated the
latest Evelyn lead, and found it to be another
red herring.*

•　　•　　•

Hi:
They gave away bags of these luscious
carob snacks at the co-op today, and
little me is determined to put on
ten pounds before I mail this letter
documentary. That's what the chocolate-y
stains on the margins are. Carob. Not
chocolate. Organic-y health food store
junk food, not corporate America candy
rack junk food.
Excuse me for using Asphalt Monarchs
stationary. Again. I'm too cheap to buy my
own paper.
It's weird. The more famous Claude got,
the lower my own opinion of him became.
Frankly. Not because he was famous, but

because of all these behind the scenes
things I saw that the public didn't know.
It was like Goddess was giving me a drawn-
out lesson in how meaningless fame is.

After my grandmother Cora died, Claude
shipped out a parade of floozies to look
after me. I think he'd take his pick of
the track pit poppies and have his roll
in the hay, and if they showed even a
smidgen of maternal instinct they got
a one way ticket to Fresno. These were
supposed to be my *parents*. Even when I
was eleven I knew that my new "mom," quote
unquote, wasn't supposed to ask what kind
of lingerie would make Claude hot. Or hock
some of our stereo gear for liquor store
money.

It was chaos. I could have eaten
nothing but ice cream, if I'd wanted to.
And at the same time, this larger-than-
life superdad I was having all these
mixed feelings about was starting to get
seriously famous. His name really went
into lights after some of the NASCAR wins.
I'd be sitting up with one of the pathetic
floozies watching TV, and dear old Dad
would come on.

The moment of truth came for me after
a sprint car accident I saw back east.
Claude had started yanking me out of
school to go on road trips to watch him
race. I was his good luck charm. Sprint
car racing was like organized Russian
Roulette then. No roll cages. The cars
would do horrible somersaults down the
track, with the drivers flopping around
and getting smashed. Claude had *no*
business in sprints. He was famous. He
didn't need it. But: anything for his

fans. He'd put himself in a wheelchair for the rest of his life just to make them happy.

Claude sent me into the grandstands with another racer's grandmother and two of the racer's children. I think they were four and five years old. Practically babies. They didn't know what the race was all about, but their Daddy was in it, and Daddy was wonderful and they wanted Daddy to win.

The little boy was all dressed up in Sunday School clothes. I have no idea why. Maybe his grandmother hadn't known how hot and dirty it would get out there. He was *so cute*. He had his blond hair all combed and parted, and a cute little blazer jacket and clip-on tie. Like a little man. And he sat right next to his little sister in the stands with his hand on her shoulder the whole time, like her protector or squire or something.

Well, Daddy got in a horrible wreck. Not my daddy; *their* daddy. Another car clipped it on a turn, and it went cart wheeling down the track, with their father's head and arms slamming onto the dirt. *Slamming* onto the dirt. Right in front of us. There was no way he wasn't dead or crippled for life. No way.

As long as I live, I'll never forget the expression on that little boy's face sitting next to me. Five years old, with his arm around his little sister's shoulder, sitting up in his little blazer and looking at the track and trying to be brave while we stared at the mangled car turned upside down on the dirt, and his father's body sticking out lifelessly from

underneath it like a crumpled rag doll.
It had all happened for *nothing*. Racers
aren't policemen or firemen, risking their
lives to save people. They just want to
make their cars go fast.

Within *three hours* of that race, Claude
had blown the whole thing off. Don't get
me wrong. He was contrite about it. He
said the right things. He donated his
whole race purse to the family. Which
was very, very typical of my extremely
generous father to do. Don't get me wrong.

But within *three hours*, he was back
to yakking with Boss about the rear end
slipping out while he was broadsliding,
and grooving the tires differently. Stuff
like that. Because that was racing.
Accidents happened. Always to somebody
else. You didn't dwell on it.

Logos, something changed in me after
that. I decided that part of the world
was insane, and my father was a leader in
the insane part, and that I should feel
ashamed for not being happy and insane
like everybody else.

And now I'm an adult, and my life is a
disaster that I wrecked all by myself, and
I'm still like a planet orbiting around
Claude, because I need Scribe money and
he's much more successful as a lunatic
than I am as a sane person. If I am sane.
And he keeps calling me, because he feels
guilty for all his parenting lapses, and
thinks I'm the only woman he can trust,
and that I'm good luck besides.

So that's me.

Carob all gone. I can practically feel
my hips expanding.

S

P.S.: I forgot to answer one of your questions.

Only Ricky knows who my father is. Nobody at the co-op does. I have my old tools and fix cars I have to drive and *sometimes* fix friends' cars, but mostly lie low. I am *very* good at pretending I don't know anything about mechanics. I once seriously told a gas station mechanic that I thought that pressing on the accelerator made gas spray on the tires and turn the wheels around.

.   .   .

I left BART at the MacArthur station, hot-footed it to the bus pad, caught a rumpled AC Transit local motoring north on San Pablo. At Ashby I stepped off, a few blocks from San Pablo Park. It was full night by then. I fished out my little black book, and paused under a street lamp to check the address I had scribbled. Only a few blocks away.

A lead. That was all. A friend of a friend of the next-to-last person I had interrogated on the phone about Evelyn. Just worth pursuing. Unlikely to pan out. I checked my wrist watch and continued, past squat bungalows and boxy apartments, the night air cool on my neck, through the shimmering phosphorescent pools cast by street lamps. I had just enough time to dispense with the red herring and hustle on to S.F.. Maybe tonight <u>he</u> would glance my way. Maybe something would happen.

I turned left on a side street, and passed a cottage almost dwarfed by a motorhome shoe-horned into the driveway. Sarah had lived near a motorhome like that. She had mentioned it in one of her letters.

Quickly, almost by reflex now, I arrested the thought, ruthlessly thwarting memory of my long-lost pen pal before the pain could begin.

It was done. I had cut all ties, couldn't think of her now; there was no going back. I had done what I thought necessary. Perhaps she was still in Denver. Perhaps she was attending to her maniacal dad, in a relationship almost comically similar to my caretaking of the diverse members of the De Mello clan, although the père of Sarah was an international celebrity. Perhaps she had found a new beau. I hoped she had. I wished only happiness for her.

But she was somewhere far off. Of that I was sure. Certainly she was nowhere close by.

•   •   •

Logos:
So it's been a week and you still haven't answered the letter I wrote after you told me about ~~your gay~~ who you're attracted to, and I'm worried.

I'm sorry if I'm being clingy. You probably just got bogged down with one thing or another, and it doesn't have anything to do with me. But I've become pretty dependent on on these letters. Maybe that shows what a pathetic person your little Sarah is behind the scenes.

Did you blurt out something you weren't ready to tell me? Or maybe you're worried about someone else seeing the letters. (Or maybe it's nothing, and I'm being clingy.) We can use generalities. Your "romantic tastes." How's that?

I just don't *care* very much. Look: my father races sprint cars, where people get

killed and dismembered for no reason, and
in the world's eyes he's perfectly sane.
To me he's nuts. But he's rich and famous,
and has zillions of fans, and maybe they
think *I'm* maladjusted because I don't
want to get third degree burns or maimed
for life in a sprint car accident, too.
Everything is turned upside down for me.
To me, frankly, you seem like one of the
sanest people I know, except that you have
unusual romantic tastes. Big deal.
    Could you please write back as soon as
you get this, just so I won't worry?
    Sarah

•   •   •

*   The domicile corresponding to the scrib-
ble in my address book turned out to be a
close cousin of the other Berkeley homes I
had visited while hunting the cup, and, indeed, of many, many other homes in the circa
mid-70s San Francisco Bay Area: an unrepen-
tant hippy house, a Craftsman gone willfully
to seed, with great clumps of crabgrass shooting up through the drunkenly leaning pickets
of a fence famished for paint, a roof nearly
bald of shingles, and, inevitably, some sort
of paisley bedspread crappery hanging behind
the windows in lieu of store-bought drapes.
I'm skeptical that Reagan or Goldwater ever
thought of unleashing a nuclear cannonade at
the sight of such a house, as you once whim-
sically suggested, Hank, but do think that
the FDR-era workingman who once raised a family there might have winced to see his former
homestead so neglected.
    Behind the paisley crappery a light shone.
The hep cats were in. I unlatched the gate*

and picked my way up the walkway, already
anticipating the conversation I expected to
transpire seconds hence ("Evelyn? No, sorry,
no Evelyn here. Somebody must have told you
wrong. Peace.") and my subsequent liberation
to continue to San Francisco to do more moon-
ing after gorilla sweater.

Interior footsteps responded to my lofted
knuckles and brisk rappety-rap-rap; the door
swung open to frame a fairly generic Summer-
of-Love type, bare-chested and bare-footed and
sporting an impressive Mediterranean Afro. He
wielded a ladle, regarded me with the polite
impatience of one interrupted while preparing
dinner. The earthy smell of a stew-in-progress
wafted out from behind him. In the gloomy interior I spotted a couple ensconced on a rumpled thrift store couch, their faces illumined
by light messages flickering from a portable
TV.

I launched into my Evelyn inquiry.

The chef waved the ladle brusquely at the
stairs.

"Upstairs, last door on the left," said he,
and turned back to the kitchen.

I blinked, and stared numbly after him as
he trotted back to the kitchen. A full five
seconds passed before I roused myself to shut
the door behind me like a decent guest, and go
as directed to the stairs.

Here the couple on the davenport could no
longer see me. I took the stairs slowly, giving my startled synapses time to rearrange ex-
pectations for the evening, and to conjure up
a strategy for the crucial minutes before me.

So I was <u>not</u> on a bum lead. (Which also
meant I was not going to see gorilla sweater,
but this I would just have to live with, fixated though I was.) I was about to be cara a

cara with the likely possessor of one of the globe's most important historical artifacts, for which the curator of the Museo Nacional in Chapultepec Park would have happily swapped a dozen Aztec sun stones, <u>and</u> that histori-cal artifact might very well be with Evelyn at that very moment in her about-to-be-en-tered room. If I played my cards correctly, if I persuaded her as I had failed to persuade her in the starlit wilds of Fort Funston, the moment of space-time in which I now resided might become the subject of reverent documen-taries in decades hence.

As he ascended the stairs, De Mello struggled to collect his thoughts, and rehearsed the arguments he might offer Evelyn for sharing the cup with the public.

I'd have to put together a press kit.
The upstairs hall was quiet. I paused at the indicated door, rapped shyly.
"Come in."
I took a deep breath, made a last mental run through of what I'd say, and turned the knob.

•   •   •

Logos:
That's *ridiculous*. You're going to stop writing and throw me to the dogs because you wrote something you weren't ready to share? I'm sitting here shaking, I'm so angry and scared. You're going to cut me off and wound me and take away the one thing I look forward to because you let someone in on your big secret, which I've already said *I don't care about.*

"I initiated an intimacy I'm not ready to sustain." Well, that's wonderful. So I get to rot in the gutter and deal with Ricky and my crazy life on my own, and as long as you can use elegant therapist language you get a total bye to leave me cold.

Your romantic tastes *don't matter to me.* I don't care.

Will you even read this letter now? You said you won't write again. It's so senseless. Did I offend you, in something else I wrote? If I did, PLEASE accept my apology, Logos. Please, please, please.

Please write back. Please. *You* started us off, when you wrote to me as Scribe years ago. You don't know what I'm going through with Ricky. I don't have anyone else to talk to. *Please.*

●　●　●

It could have been a college dorm room, or the room of a traveler who had unboxed and unbagged her things, and arranged them well enough to find clothes and toiletries for a few months before moving on. Homely cinder block shelves teetered precariously against the walls, heaped high with stacks of jeans, books, bric-a-brac and shoeboxes brimming with smaller items of stuff, all of it looking as if the shelves could have just gone up that morning.

Against the opposite wall was a twin bed — or, more accurately, box spring and mattress, sans headboard or bed frame — shoved into the corner beneath a bare window. A ceiling lamp was on, as was a large, rusty-looking floor lamp next to the bed.

Sprawled on the bed, with back braced against a wadded-up army blanket and a threadbare lounge pillow, was Evelyn. She had been reading.

I paused in the doorway in my best tremulous Boo Radley manner; I was prepared for a hostile reception, perhaps a violently hostile one. But Evelyn regarded me with so little expression that I wondered (for a ridiculous moment) if she even recognized me. She closed her book and dropped it on the blanket beside her, and looked at me with neither friendliness nor hostility. It was as if she had expected me.

"Can I come in?"

This will show that I can say stupid things, Hank. I already was in.

She nodded at a chair supporting a spaghetti-like tangle of unwashed clothes. I shut the door behind me and — after interrogating my memory for the appropriate etiquette and deciding that there wasn't any — bent to hoist the clothes gingerly toward a shelf.

"Just shove it on the floor."

To the floor the tangle went. I took my seat.

She clasped her hands behind her neck and continued to look at me with neither friendliness nor hostility, as if I were a new piece of furniture that someone had dropped off, or a scene in the television program being watched by her housemates downstairs. I guessed that I hadn't caught her on a good day. Her eyes looked heavy and insomniac; I wondered if she had been crying. An almost palpable aura of depression hung about the room. I reminded myself of how little I knew of this woman, and that your second encounter with her had been on the Golden Gate Bridge on

a night better suited for suicidal leaps than
for sightseeing.

You have already shared with your readers the painful torch you carried for Evelyn,
so I will tell a bit more of my impressions
as I surveyed her for the first time in a decent light. She did look, as you have written, a bit Irish, or Italian, or Jewish, and I
agree that her high cheekbones, dark eyes and
strong nose hinted at a Native American branch
in her family tree. She wore jeans, a blue
sweatshirt, no shoes, not a speck of make-up,
and was too deliberately sturdy a girl to be
thought conventionally attractive. The coif-
fured, poodle-like beauty of a Liz or Marilyn
was not for her, but she might have helped
carry Liz or Marilyn's furniture, if asked
nicely.

"I hope I haven't interrupted anything."

"No. I thought you might turn up eventually."

I flexed my mouth corners into an unctuous
salesman's smile, largely to conceal my per-
plexity. 'Thought you might turn up eventually.' The safeguards preceding our meet at Fort
Funston had been worthy of an assignation with
Klaus Barbie. Now she acted as if she had as
much as left the door unlatched and the porch
light on.

Which meant she had surely stashed the cup
somewhere I couldn't find it.

But no sooner had I concluded this, Hank,
than I spotted it, as I let my eyes troll
over the bric-a-brac piled high on the cinder
block shelves, and wondered idly why Contra
Costa Republicans never seemed to go in for
such hoarding. There it was, one of the most
valuable historical artifacts extant on terra firma, all of three precarious inches from

the edge of a rickety shelf, between a can of baked beans and a box of sanitary napkins. Any self-respecting museum curator would have put it in a gallery of its own behind layers of security glass, with an armed guard at the door. But, there it was on the plank shelf, unguarded and unshielded and right next to the Kotex. I couldn't be mistaken about the hiero-glyphics on the cup's brow. An almost orgas-mic thrill of recognition shivered through my neural pathways. In its presence was I, once again.

"There it is," said I, sociably, with a nod at the shelf.

She didn't answer. I cleared my throat.

"It might not be my place to say this, but that shelf might not be the safest place for our illustrious friend there." I nodded at the cup. "If you don't mind my saying."

She ignored this as pointedly as if I hadn't spoken. She turned onto her side to-ward me, buttressing her elbow onto the lounge pillow and resting her cheek on her palm. Her hair fell about her face. She lifted the black tresses with her fingers and pushed them behind her ears. But she didn't look at me, although she had deliberately turned in my direction. Moodily she gazed at the floor at the foot of my chair, making no effort to mask the depres-sion that I felt sure I had intruded upon, her countenance at once grim and bitter and (yes, this too, and this utterly bewildered me, Hank) faintly ashamed, as if she found it in-explicably humiliating to host me in her room.

<u>A weird chick</u>. I did not usually sum up my fellow homo sapiens with that kind of lan-guage, but your words still echoed.

"Why don't you get on with what you want to talk to me about?" she said quietly.

*So, I did. Perhaps I hadn't really expect-
ed to see Evelyn that night, but I believed
with all my heart that she should make the cup
public, and had no trouble assembling my arguments into an off-the-cuff speech. I began,
my voice quiet, ingratiating, familiar, like
a rural alderman squeezed among constituents
in a coffee shop booth. I recapped legend and
lore about the cup, explained why it was only
decent to share it with the world.*

*She didn't look at me. Resolutely she
stared at the foot of my chair, her lips grim
and determined and inexplicably, confoundingly
ashamed, or embarrassed, or humiliated, sur-
mised I with increasing certainty as I took
her furtive measure while I spoke. It made
no sense. What reason would she have to feel
ashamed with me? All the bargaining chips were
on her side of the table. A weird chick was
right.*

*Once again I let my eyes meander among the
clutter heaped upon the shelves.*

*Not far from the cup, I spotted a scissors
jack.*

*Now, <u>that</u> was an odd thing for a woman to
have. Perhaps she dated a mechanic. I doubted
she would even know what such an apparatus was
for.*

•   •   •

Logos,
 This probably isn't going to do any
good, because it's been almost a month
and you haven't answered any of the other
letters I've written. Maybe I'm just
writing to myself.
 It's getting really heavy here. Ricky
is getting totally wasted every night. I

can't take it anymore. I'm going to have to throw him out, but he'll never survive on his own. I might as well shoot him.

Maybe you think I'll just muddle by. I can't believe you don't care. I wish you knew how much you've hurt me. I think you'd stop, if you did.

I guess I should stop banging on a door that won't open anymore.

S.

●　　●　　●

"A friend of mine at UCB lives only a few miles from here," I was saying. "Very straightforward fellow. Not pushy. I could call him right now. Or we could take a cab over. My treat. Or walk, if you wish." I cleared my throat. "One look from him, and we'd both know far more about that cup than we know now. He'd never overstate. He's a trustworthy friend."

"A trustworthy friend," said Evelyn, softly.

As if there were something in this homely phrase that warranted repeating. She watched her finger trace an idle pattern on the bed spread. Her eyes looked heavier, moist.

Why, she looked as if she were about to cry.

"Well, yes." I swallowed, quite nonplussed. "I think he is."

"Are you a trustworthy friend?"

She regarded me directly for the first time since I'd come in. And it was here, Hank, that I felt the first icy, icy premonition that all was not well in Denmark, that there was some key element in our duologue that she saw and that I remained blind to. She was obviously close to tears, and yet also looked bitterly, furiously amused with me.

"Well, yes." I may have flushed. "I mean, I can't be objective about myself, can I? I try to be."

She lowered her eyes to the floor again. She looked disgusted. I forged ahead, my discomfort notwithstanding, eulogizing the knowledge and amiability of my Berkeley friend, and the significance of his studies of Native American history. As I spoke I continued to discreetly take her measure, and resumed my careless survey of the clutter on her shelves.

On a shelf near the ceiling, almost at the corner, I spotted a ½ inch drive socket set.

Well. Her mechanic boyfriend had to be on close terms with her, to leave something like that in her room. Such tools were expensive.

"Evelyn, I don't think I can make a better argument than I've made thus far. I know that I'm intruding." I hesitated. "I also sense — and I hope you don't mind my saying this — that I've caught you on a difficult night."

I took a deep breath. Time for the big pitch.

"If I call Andy, will you consider visiting him with me this evening? Or letting him come here?"

She didn't answer. The social niceties clearly weren't for her, at least not that evening. Questions could go unanswered, silences could drag on indefinitely. She stared resolutely at the foot of my chair, and now — in growing dismay and confusion, although I had met my share of troubled folk over the years — I watched an obvious tear slide from her eye corner down her cheek.

Followed by another. She was going to weep in front of me.

"I'm sorry if I've upset you."

She didn't speak. Once again I let my eyes rake across the mounds of hippy stuff on the rickety shelves, as I furiously interrogated myself for a reason for her mood.

And then, Hank, it happened.

You _know_ it happened. You have waited patiently for me to get to it, and now To It I am. I ain't no dumb bunny, Hank. Sooner or later I was going to figure things out, and get what I had coming to me.

Secreted among the clutter on a shelf near the closet door, its chromium snout protruding from a velour carrying sack, lay a torque wrench.

Not an el-cheapo beam type torque wrench. No: an expensive, precision, click-type torque wrench, and every mechanic from Bodega Bay to Bangor knows the marque: Snap-on. A professional tool.

For perhaps two seconds after spotting that wrench, Hank, I remained unmolested in my innocence. I could have been strolling across a frozen lake moments before the ice splintered.

Well!, thought I: her mysterious suitor had to be a _very good boyfriend indeed,_ to leave such a high quality tool behind!

But that didn't add up, did it? Nothing else in the room indicated habitation by a man. Nothing. Only the tools.

And there hadn't been just one stray tool. I had already spotted three.

Hey, Logos! Golly gee whiz! Maybe they _aren't_ a boyfriend's tools.

Maybe they belong to her.

And that was when it hit me, the whole enchilada. The missing puzzle piece snapped all too crisply into place, and perhaps a vengeful god observing my comeuppance took me by

the nape of the neck and held me firm, so I'd
have to look at the picture thus completed.
The tears, her inexplicable humiliation, her
change of heart on the bridge after you mentioned a friend named Logos, and the fact that
she — _of course_ it would be her, of course —
would possess a cup last publicly linked to a
certain world-renowned race car driver.

Hank, it was as if I'd been doing ninety in a fifty-five, and had just caught my first
glimpse of the whirling rooftop light in the
rear view mirror. Everything that follows is
anti-climactic. Isn't it? Almost unnecessary.
The siren, the looming black-and-white at your
rear bumper, the pulling over on the soft
shoulder. The cop's approaching footsteps, the
rolling down of your window. The first sight of
the rooftop light is what counts. From that
moment on, you know what you're in for.

I must have been silent too long.

Evelyn — or should I say Sarah, or Sarah
Evelyn — looked at me.

I can only guess at how I appeared: eyes
idiotically protuberant, mouth slack in primal fear and shock, a perfect platitudinous
deer frozen in the harsh glare of headlights
that had in a heartbeat revealed to whom I'd
been yakking so foolishly for the past umpteen
minutes. I looked between her and the torque
wrench, as if it were the bloody dagger hauled
freshly from Caesar's shoulder.

Evelyn followed my gaze. Her expression
did not perceptibly change, but (as you shall
see presently) it was in this instant that she
must have seen that whirling rooftop light,
too, and realized that the jig was finally up
for her fickle pen pal Logos.

She did not glower at me, or crack a bitter smile. She wriggled toward the foot of the

bed, extended a bare foot toward the shelf and neatly scissor clamped the shank of the torque wrench between her big and index toes. She bent her knee, hoisting the wrench as a crane might hoist a girder, and transferred it to her fingers. Then she flopped back on the lounge pillow and pantomimed an earnest study of the wrench as she held it over her face. As if she had just happened to decide to amuse herself with it while I spoke, as a child might doodle while listening to a bedtime story.

"You've stopped talking," observed Evelyn, after a moment.

She didn't look at me. She lay on her back on the lounge pillow, as she had lain when I had entered. She fished the wrench out of the velour sack and turned the gleaming shaft about in her fingers, as if rediscovering a neglected trinket.

"Go ahead. I was listening. You were telling me why we should go see your friend Andy."

Nothing was what I said, nothing. I felt as if I could hardly breathe.

Nearly a half minute passed. That is a long time, Hank, to sit in such silence. I had begun to feel physically ill.

She turned her head toward me on the lounge pillow.

"What do you suppose I have this for?"

She looked at me matter-of-factly, as if we had gone spelunking in a junk yard together, and she hoped I could identify a rusty hood ornament. Her eyes were still moist. Her lips trembled. Ever, ever so slightly, Hank, just enough to show the seething, lava-like acres of long-suppressed emotion that churned behind the dam. Oh, I was going to get it. Oh, was I.

I didn't answer. She didn't expect me to, knew I wouldn't. The rooftop light still twirled. I as much as heard the squad car door open, as much as saw the striped khaki cop leg step out, commence its way toward me.

She looked at the wrench again. She fingered the knurled handle, pinched the nipple-like socket holder.

"It looks like some kind of tool. For mechanics." She glanced at me. "But why would I have something like this? I'm a girl."

She frowned at the wrench, squinted at the torque markings.

"Look at all the funny little numbers on it. It must be for measuring something. Maybe someone left it here."

She placed the wrench beside her and tilted to the edge of the mattress to gaze at the bric-a-brac scattered on the floor. She plucked a plastic case from a heap of underwear, popped open the latches and withdrew a business-like looking something else. Then she lay on her back again and regarded this new object as she held it over her eyes, like a child comparing selections from a toy box.

This one was a Starrett micrometer. Maybe three hundred bucks. As likely a hippy chick trinket as a vial of uranium-235.

"But, look. I have this too. I guess there must be some reason."

She put the micrometer back in the case and returned it to the floor. She turned on her side again, facing me, almost in a fetal position, with her cheek pressed onto the lounge pillow, as if she might nap in front of me. She didn't look at me. Her lips had begun to tremble again. She stared at the foot of my chair.

She cried. The tears slid down her cheek, dripped on the bed. Her expression fractured, as an expression will when tears come. She covered her mouth with her hand.

"Stop," I said. "Please."

I fidgeted on the chair, my cheeks hot, bending forward as if to offer comfort and then lurching back, horrified that I had thought of touching her. I was in agony. I have striven to lead an exemplary life, Hank. You know that. I had helped my fellow sufferers far more than I had hurt them, and the hurts had been minor, save for what I had come to think privately of my One Great Sin: the breaking off with my confidante Sarah, simply because I could not bear to continue writing to someone who might know me as a secret fag. The knowledge of my sin had never really let me alone, in all the intervening months and years, and now here was my victim bawling piteously in front of me, and I am at least enough of a gentleman to be scandalized by a woman's tears, particularly when I was the cause of them.

"Please!" I said.

But she didn't. She couldn't. Her chest heaved beneath her sweatshirt; her mouth corners twisted wretchedly behind her fingers as she sobbed on her palm. I felt I might vomit. I had never, ever, ever spoken to a single living soul about the gay business, and she <u>knew,</u> and she was right in front of me, crying because of me, the woman I had sinned against. I was beside myself.

"I did nothing unethical," I cried, finally.

Yes, I cried out this inane remark, like a rally slogan.

"I wrote to you. I explained myself." I jerked about on my chair like a marionette. I was almost yelling. "I told you why I could not continue. I had every right to discontinue

our correspondence. There was nothing unethical!"

This self-justifying tack was so preposter-
ous that it managed to startle her out of the
worst of her tears. She withdrew her hand from
her mouth and flopped back on her back on the
lounge pillow, glowering at the foot of the
bed.

"I did nothing unethical," she pantomimed,
disgustedly.

"I did not!" I came close to thumping my
fist on the chair. "I had the right to stop
writing to you. It was too painful. What would
you have done? What if you wrote to a person
for a perfectly innocent reason, and all these
secrets came up, and you hardly knew the person you were writing to? It was too painful."

I checked myself; I was practically shouting.

Evelyn said nothing. She glowered resolutely at the foot of the bed, as if I were no
longer worthy of being looked at. But her eyes
were still wet, and even as I regarded her
fresh tears appeared.

I folded.

"All right, I'm sorry," I said hoarsely.
(And would have been amused by the rapidity of
my own 180 degree about face, had I not felt
so overwrought.) "I apologize. Please. Please
don't cry. It was my fault. I'm here now. You
can throw me out, if you want to, but I'm
here. Please don't cry. I can't stand it."

My voice had risen again, but I decided
that the stew-eaters downstairs likely at-
tributed this to peyote, if they attended to
it at all.

Evelyn still did not look at me, but no new
tears emerged.

* * *

I haven't slept for two days. Ricky left. We had it out one last time, and he said he didn't want to give me any more grief, and the next morning I woke up in an empty bed.

He's as good as dead. There's something he's always said he wants to do for me before he dies and maybe he will, and if he does maybe that will give him hope to stay alive, but I don't think so. He's going to kill himself. I've never had an intuition this strong turn out to be off.

Why do I keep writing to you? You won't write back. Maybe you care. I can't believe you don't. But you'll never answer. You've said you won't.

Okay, Logos. You win. Goodbye. I'm so sorry I shared my messy little life with you, and so terribly sorry you showed me a messy place in your life, too. You'll just have to clean it right up, so you'll be perfect.

* * *

We were silent.
After awhile Evelyn rolled onto her back and wriggled toward the foot of the mattress. I watched in mute disbelief as she delivered a swift toe kick to the belly of the plank supporting the cup, which, of course, sent one of world's most valuable artifacts somersaulting toward the mattress. Why I didn't swoon, I still don't know. It was like watching a five year old pebble skip the Star of Africa across a swimming pool.

But she caught the cup before it hit the bed. She sat back on the lounge cushion, sneered at me — to be sure I understood that she had fetched the cup in this fashion to horrify me — and then held it on her sternum, as a mother might hold an infant. She pressed her fingers on the sides, gazed at the symbols on the forehead. I watched her look at it.

I've forgotten which one of us broke the ice. I think I asked which name she preferred. (Rather formally, as if we had just been introduced at a cocktail party.) She said that both were hers — 'Sarah Evelyn' had been on her report cards in grade school — but that Sarah had been Ricky's name for her, and she had gone by 'Evelyn' since his death, and also to separate the private Berkeley Evelyn from the Sarah who sometimes still gigged with Dad. I started to express the usual diplomatic condolences about Ricky, but this was a blunder; Evelyn glared at me so ferociously I thought I might yet be expelled, and we were silent for five minutes more.

Eventually, I asked if she had played a role in the hiding of the ported cylinder heads at the race track. Evelyn nodded with unconcealed disinterest; I decided to save my remaining questions about this incident for another day. She then surprised me by offering an apology of her own. Dwayne — a.k.a. 'Psycho,' who so memorably shepherded us that night by the coast — had been a last minute substitute for a much more reasonable friend who had chickened out at the last minute. Dwayne/Psycho had been a last minute stand-in. She was sorry if his manner had frightened us. It had frightened her a little.

And then we went on that way, Hank, with one shy step after the other, I suppressing

*the urge to apologize more abjectly than I al-
ready had, and she (I now think) trying con-
sciously not to forgive her long lost pen pal
too quickly. She asked what had brought me to
Berkeley. I started to say I'd journeyed there
only to track her down. But then I remembered my romantic hopes for San Francisco, and
stopped myself — I had done enough dissembling
with this woman — and, hesitantly and with
cheeks aflame, confessed my pursuit of gorilla
sweater. Hank, I must have paused with every
third word, and stammered a-plenty. I had never spoken of my homosexual feelings to anyone.*

*But this turned out to be the right thing
to do. Evelyn was quite solicitous. She turned
toward me on the mattress, with the cup upend-
ed on the sheets in front of her, and braced
her elbow on the lounge pillow. She smiled
encouragingly as I spoke — I had been entirely forgiven by then, I suppose, for daring to
reveal so vulnerable a spot in conversation —
and ignored my stammering, and asked playful-
ly coquettish, fellow conspirator, one desir-
er-of-men-to-another questions about gorilla
sweater. Did I feel ready to talk to him? What
might I say? She was still angry with me, I
shouldn't make any mistake, but, just the
same: she would be willing to travel to San
Francisco with me to provide moral support. It
was too late now, though. The newcomer's meeting was surely about to wrap up.*

*She had a sleeping bag. No one at the house
would mind if I ate with them tomorrow. Why
didn't I just hang out with her for awhile,
and we could go to San Francisco tomorrow to
find out what we could? Or another night, if I
still didn't feel ready. There wasn't a rush.*

CHAPTER THIRTEEN

After a half hour I figured I'd better put the manila folder back where I'd got it. Maybe I'd known Logos since third grade, but that didn't give me call to set up shop in his bedroom. One of the De Mellos would be rapping on the door if I stayed much longer.

I found Mrs. De Mello in the kitchen. I wasn't sure, I told her, but I'd got an idea from snooping around Logos' room, and I wanted to play gumshoe a little more to see if I was right. I didn't think there was anything to worry about.

Then I took off. I felt better than I'd felt in months. Maybe I was wrong. Maybe Logos had left the 'being away for awhile' message for another reason. But I didn't think so. Everything clicked too good, the way I had it figured. I just knew.

Man, had I ever made a fool of myself with that chick, yakking about cars. Man.

*   *   *

The next morning I mailed off special delivery the first 'Ask the Wizard' letter I'd written in a long time. On the envelope I wrote:

IMPORTANT! GIVE THIS LETTER TO SAR-AH EVELYN, MR. C'S DAUGHTER! IMPORT-ANT!

... and then I scrawled the same thing on the front of the letter inside, too:

> *Evelyn,*
> *Well, did you have me fooled. Very funny. You could've at least dropped a hint, so I wouldn't make a fool of myself talking about cars.*
> *Well, the jig is up. I know who you are. There's no use denying it. Never mind how I found out.*
> *Please contact me ASAP. I know your dad is going for a Indy win this year, and maybe you are with*

> *him, lucky you. Someday maybe I'll go to Indy too. But*
> *please contact me ASAP no matter what. Logos' mom*
> *is worried and so am I. I think he's with you. Please*
> *contact me even if he's not. This is serious.*
>
> *Remember, I kept my word and didn't tell Logos all*
> *the things you told me.*
>
> *Hank*

Four days went by. That's all. Just four days.

On the morning of the fifth day I was camped out at the kitchen table in my BVDs, thinking that maybe the waffle I was chawing on wouldn't have tasted like a cylinder head gasket if I'd maybe glanced at the mix instructions first, when some communist rang the doorbell. 8:30 a.m. Man. I cinched on a bathrobe and went to see who it was.

Standing on the doorstep was this Dapper Dan type who looked like he gave handsome seminars to GQ models. Maybe 6'2", God's gift to women looks, and a sharkskin suit that looked like it would have been plenty comfortable if it had just stayed on the mannequin, and you didn't try to sit or walk or reach for anything in it.

Big Secret Service shades. He was taking a nervous look at his cuff links when I opened up, like he was worried that the air molecules of our cow patty house might corrode them. He was holding an envelope.

A brand new Eldo was parked behind him. Brand new. Not a speck on the white walls.

"Hank Kruzz ..." He took a squint at the envelope. "Hank Kruzzennsker."

"You've got him."

He thought that was pretty rich. He curled his lip and looked me up and down, my hotty bathrobe especially, and snickered, like he couldn't wait to tell the other male models about me. Then he handed me the envelope.

My pulse ticked up a notch. I couldn't mistake that Asphalt Monarchs logo in the corner for anything else. The Wizard had answered my letter.

My address wasn't on the front this time. Instead somebody had just scrawled "To: Hank Kruzenski" in jerky block letters, like a first grader who'd had too much rum candy.

Dapper Dan shot me an impatient look. I opened it up. Inside was three crumpled pages in the same loopy print, with oil stains on the edges. They looked like somebody had written them with a grease pencil on a tool chest.

> **TO HANK KRUZENSKI:**
> **AGREE MANY SENTIMENTS**
> **EXPRESSED PREVUIOS**
> **CORRESPONDENCE. MEEGHAM**
> **SPEED PRODUCTS 100% JUNK. I KNEW**
> **THAT OLD CROOK WHEN YOU WORE**
> **DIAPERS. DITTO FREZETTI CAMS,**
> **ACORN HEADERS, MANY OTHERS. BUY**
> **THE BEST AND CRY ONCE. <u>NEVER USE</u>**
> **FOREIGN KNOCK-OFF PARTS IN PROUD**
> **USA CARS. WE HAVE FOUGHT TWO**
> **WORLD WARS FOR THAT RIGHT.**
> **YES, I AM ENTERING MAY CRUISE**
> **IN INDY AGAIN THIS YEAR. VICTORY**
> **GUARANTEED. UNSER AND FOYT**
> **JUST THINK THEY'RE GOOD. YOU**
> **ARE COMING. ACCOMPANY BEARER**
> **THIS LETTER FOR TRANSPORTATION**
> **AND TRAVEL EXPENSES. RIGHT NOW.**
> **IMMEDIATE DEPARTURE MANDATORY.**
> **IF YOU ARE STILL STARING AT THIS**
> **YOU ARE ALREADY LATE. LETS SHAG IT**
> **KRUISER.**

I'd gotten a half dozen Scribe letters, and they'd all been signed the same way. Not this one, though.

The signature at the bottom was a giant black C.

The man. The man had written it.

Underneath the signature was a P.S., in different handwriting:

We're sorry you were worried! Please come, Hank.

The P.S. was signed Evelyn and Logos.

·   ·   ·

"Is there a phone in this place?" Dapper asked me.

He shot a disgusted look past my hotty bathrobe, like maybe there'd be a telephone in there with the rats and cockroaches and black mold and whatever else a peasant like me had in his house. I hooked my thumb at the Princess on the kitchen wall. Dapper slid past me careful, so he wouldn't have to touch anything.

I hardly noticed him go in. I felt dazed. A personal, handwritten letter from Mr. C. I could frame it. If I died that instant, my life would've been worthwhile.

On the kitchen phone Dapper was already yakking away with someone. He'd borrowed a napkin to lift the handset off the hook, so he wouldn't have to soil his manicure on it. He probably made chicks show a cert from the clinic before they kissed his bunions. I overheard him say "He's here" and "Pretty pathetic, frankly," and then he hung up and eyed me up and down.

"Are you going in your bathrobe?" he said.

"Going where?"

He rolled his eyes at me. "What he said in the *letter*. Are you *going*?!"

I stared at him for a long count of three. Then I looked at the C letter in my mitt, and remembered the new Eldo out front. I shrugged, and went to crawl into some duds.

·   ·   ·

Fifty minutes later, Dapper wheeled onto the lot of this ultra high end sports car dealership over by the 24 in Lafayette. Exotics Exclusively. I'd walked past Exotics real slow at least a dozen times, like any other self-respecting car nut in the county, but I'd never been any closer than the sidewalk. At least once a year they'd get some wisenheimer who'd try to act like a Getty heir so he could score a test drive in one of their Lambos, but it never worked. Exotics could smell your net worth from the off ramp.

I kept thinking that somebody had slipped something into that waffle mix. Nobody had ever sent me a letter before telling me to get out of town, basically. Of course, I'd never got a personal letter from the C before, either. I kept on racking over what I'd done so far and wondering if I was getting set up, but it just seemed most sensible to play along until I could draw a bead on what this was all about. Dapper was exactly zero help. All during the drive he'd glanced at me like maybe he'd have to get the seat sanitized now that I'd sat on it.

We got out of the Eldo. There was some kind of big commotion at the back of the Exotics parking lot. I spotted a TV truck back there, and a couple of TV reporter looking guys clambering out with a camera you could have anchored the Queen Mary with, and then maybe a dozen people milling around something near the service entrance. Then I caught a glimpse of a front fender and grille between their legs, and knew what it was.

Well, no wonder. Damn if they didn't have a C Team Kydra back there. There was supposed to be only five in the whole country. Nobody was going to waste any time ogling a Ferrari or Lambo with one of those around.

Dapper walked me toward the dealership and caught the eye of somebody on the other side of the picture window, and pointed at me like I was a garbage can he was delivering. He jerked his head at me to go in.

Inside they had a bunch of Rodeo Drive type sports cars arranged on the floor tiles, the way they do in auto showrooms, and another GQ type by the door. He curled his lip at me and held out his hand for me to stay put, like I might roll off with my lid up and start collecting trash on my own, and bustled off to knock on a mahogany door at the back with a big gold name plaque. Somebody inside answered and GQ2 said something and then out comes this middle-aged Mr. Big who obviously runs the joint. He looked like somebody cut him out of the Princeton yearbook. Lots of tousled silver hair, like he just couldn't be bothered to comb it after a day on the catamaran. Family crest on his blazer. And there I am in my hanging-out-in-Prado duds.

Well. Princeton stops dead in his tracks and gapes at me up and down, and for a second I'm positive he's about to upchuck his chicken flambé. Then he throws up his hands and rolls his eyes, like it just can't be helped, and motions me to follow him into his sanctum.

"You're Hank Kruzenski," he said, when he was behind his desk. Like that was part of the joke.

"Speaking."

That got another eye roll. He yanked open his drawer and hauled out a clipboard with a stack of triplicate forms on it, and dumped the whole enchilada on the desk.

"Driver's license." He flopped his palm out at me.

"What?"

Princeton blinked at me a couple of times and showed me the teeth. Not in a nice way. Too bad I'd forgot to wear my leash and flea collar. Maybe he wouldn't have minded me being indoors so much.

"Your California Drivers' License," he said sweetly. "The little card the state sent you that permits you to drive. I'd like to see it, please. If you don't mind terribly."

"I'm not buying a car here."

Princeton threw up his hands in a big fake shock act. "Oh, my goodness! You're not buying a car here. I'm stunned. Mr. Hank Kruzenski, visiting us in an unwashed Pendleton and a t-shirt with a mustard stain on the front, isn't buying a $60,000 Lamborghini from Exotics Exclusively. I'm *terribly* disappointed. Nonetheless, may I still please see your driver's license, so we can continue with this charade? Please?"

He had a voice like J. Paul Getty would have sounded if J. Paul'd had some real money. Now, who the hey was this Jasper to tell me what to do? I gave Princeton my best squinty-eyed Clint Eastwood stare, but that just made his salesman's grin get even tighter and sicker looking. So I shrugged and took out my wallet. In for a penny, in for a pound. And they'd had that C letter.

Princeton held my license like maybe I'd blown my nose on it, and copied the number onto the triplicate forms. Then he shoved the stack at me.

"Sign," he said.

I picked up the pen he flicked at me and eyeballed the forms. Man. Enough legalese in there to sign off on a shopping center.

"Please sign the forms!!"

I signed.

Princeton grabbed the clipboard and chucked it in the desk. Then he pulled out a white envelope and started to hand it across the desk. I reached for it. He pulled it up away from my fingers.

"You're an Ask the Wizard subscriber," he said, "and you've always wanted to see the Indianapolis 500. Isn't that right?"

In a real sweet, slick voice, like I'd better read between the lines, or else. With more of the charm boy smile.

"Well … yeah." That was true enough. Sure I'd always wanted to see the Indy 500.

He shook his head at me.

"No 'well.' Let's lose the 'well.' You're an Ask the Wizard subscriber, and you've always wanted to see the Indianapolis 500. It's a lifelong dream. Yes or no?"

I nodded. He lowered the envelope. I put my hand on it. He wouldn't let go. Looking right dead at me.

"Nothing about your friend," he said. "And nothing about Claude Winters' daughter. That's not public information. One more time: you're an Ask the Wizard subscriber, and you've always wanted to see the Indianapolis 500. Are we clear?"

That almost got to me. Damn. Who'd told this blueblood about Evelyn?

But Princeton had his eye on me, so I nodded. Sure. Fine. Maybe now you'll tell me what's going on.

Princeton handed me the envelope and trotted around to my side of the desk. I glanced inside. Money. And something metal, too.

"Don't count it now," he sniped at me. "There's three thousand in there. Let's go. We're late."

I followed him outside.

• • •

The Kydra was gold. I thought that was a good color for it. Maybe if they discovered a brand new lode up at Sutter's Mill and you were first in line with the pan and cradle, you might scoop up enough gold to buy one. Supposedly the C had masterminded the whole Kydra project because he was all hot and bothered about the Shelby Cobra. The Cobra was modified from an AC Bristol frame, see. A foreign car. The C was a gung-ho super patriot.

I'd seen magazine spreads on the Kydra, but no way I'd ever expected to get close to one in 3D. It wasn't a regular production car. Supposedly Boss Maryland and the C Team had designed the whole thing, and the C test drove every one personally. It looked like a cross between ten percent assembly line sports car, and ninety percent something you'd launch out of Cape Canaveral.

As soon as we walked outside Princeton slapped on a big fake-a-loo smile and threw his arm around my shoulder. He walked me over to the crowd around the Kydra. All around there's Porsches and Ferraris and Lambos and Maseratis, and I swear nobody's paying a bit of attention to them. They're all like Golden Gloves boxers after Muhammad Ali shows up. If a car could look ashamed of itself, those cars did.

"Here's the lucky man," Princeton said.

The crowd slid out of the way to let us in.

By this time it had pretty well soaked in through the old Kruzenski gray matter that I was going to Indianapolis. Maybe I had a lot of clay in the soil up there, and it took awhile for stuff to percolate in, but it did eventually. The C letter, the chauffeured Eldo ride, this wisenheimer Princeton dude. It added up.

And don't get me wrong: I was plenty excited. Even if they were just going to buy me a Greyhound ticket and a seat in the grandstands once I got there. I'd never been out of state before, and it sure beat hanging out in Prado and watching Mom beat up on her whiskey bottles.

I liked getting so up close and personal with a Kydra, too. Don't get me wrong about that, either. I just didn't understand what it had to do with my Indy trip. Maybe they wanted to back the thing over me a couple of times to break in the tread.

The guy with the Queen Mary camera swung it around in my direction. I tried to duck, to get out of the way of whatever they wanted to film, but Princeton put a Andre the Giant crush hold on my shoulder to hold me up. Then this blow-dried dude leaned in and stuck a mike at me. I recognized him from the TV news. Shane Viscount. He'd done the big undercover investigative probe on topless waitresses.

"Why don't you get in, Hank?" Shane says. "See how it feels."

Princeton chuckled for the camera, like there was nothing they wouldn't do for dear Hank, and did some more deep finger work on my shoulder. I reached for the door handle. I kept expecting alarms to go off if I so much as touched the car, but I got the door open and eased myself onto the bucket seat. Shane and the camera man scooted around so they could film me through the driver's window. I sure hoped I could get a copy of the tape, so I could prove I'd sat in a Kydra.

"How does it feel, Hank?"

Shane was leaning in beside the camera lens with the mike under my chin. His hair looked like it had come out of a giant toothpaste tube. I slid my tootsies around on the steering wheel and touched the gear shift. Maybe they'd ask me to wipe off the prints later. The dashboard didn't have any more gauges than you'd need for deep space exploration or time travel. I kept looking for the switch that would take me back to see the dinosaurs.

"Sure is a nice car."

"Why don't you start it up?"

Through the windshield I could see Princeton and everybody else in the crowd beaming at me, like I was a third grader about to blow out the candles.

That's when it finally hit me. Finally. Took me long enough.

The paperwork and my driver's license, and the metal thing in the envelope. I felt it again with my fingers. It was a key, all right. Damn straight it was.

I was going to drive the Kydra. For real. Me. That's what all this fuss was about. This was the C's idea of transportation to Indy.

Real slow I held up the envelope and fished the key out and aimed the tip at the ignition switch. Like in slow motion. I was feeling seriously strange. All I'd basically done was send a letter asking about my buddy. Then this male model shows up and chauffeurs me to meet Princeton, and after they both finish sneering at me they put me in this unbelievable car. Why didn't they just chuck Ford out of the White House and put me in the Oval Office, while they was at it? It was just too much weirdness. I was going to have a brain seizure.

The engine fired up. BRRRMMMM brmm brmm. Real lopey idle. Radical cam. The shifter and steering wheel vibrated. I blipped the go pedal. BRRAAAUUUGGGHH. It sounded like it wanted to go out and murder a Mustang. I tried to remember what kind of NASA engine the C had put in this thing. As soon as I got my foot into it at all, I mean at all, the cam was going to get in range, the secondaries would kick in, the supercharger would come on, and that Kydra would slam me into the seat and rip all the stuffing out of my vertebrae like blowing feathers off a piñata. How was I going to get this monster on the 24, let alone to Indianapolis? This wasn't real. I'd never been in a car like this. Any second I was going to wake up and be in the kitchen with my waffle mix again, and Mom watching a *Let's Make a Deal* re-run in the living room.

"How's it feel, Hank?" Shane asked me. The mike and the lens was practically right in my face.

"It sure feels special." I put my hand on the shifter and watched the needle vibrating on the tach.

"Think you can drive this all the way to Indianapolis?"

"I can sure try."

Princeton was all smiles. Heh heh heh. I'd signed the paperwork, right? His insurance was covered. So what if I cremated myself? Maybe he'd give Shane a nice speech after I left, about how Exotics Exclusively was always eager to help out lower life forms. Just the other day they'd sent off an orangutan in a GTO. Shane told me to wait a sec, so the camera could get in position for a shot of me taking off. He and the camera guy hustled over and set up the Queen Mary rig to my left.

"How about a nice wave, Hank?"

I waved. I put off the handbrake and let in the clutch and put it in gear.

·   ·   ·

The next twenty minutes was near about the hairiest of my life. I'm going to tell you something: you've got a half hour to spare and want to do something useful, write your Congress critter *now* that nobody ought to be let near a car like that without a diploma from Bondurant racing school. I mean it. That thing was a full on race car with a license plate hung on the bumper. I didn't have any more business in that Kydra than I did hauling in a 747 at SFO.

Somehow I got out to Mount Diablo Boulevard, and in the rear view there's Princeton and Shane and the TV crew waving goodbye. Good luck, Hank. Maybe if you pull a fatal a half mile away from here, we'll be able to get the footage without sending out another truck. I hit the turn signal. The exhaust is bellowing in my ears. BRAAAAUUUUGGGH. I'd been in rat motor Chevelles and big block 'Stangs and Hemi chargers, and I'd never rid in a car that felt or sounded anything like this. Like everything from the main bearings to the rod caps to the hose clamp on the radiator has been weighed and specced out and torqued in, the way the chief engineer at Cape Canaveral locks the Rocketdynes into Saturn V. I pulled out and got in the lane for the freeway approach. The steering wheel's humming under my fingers and the needle's twitching on the tach gauge, and across Diablo there's two guys in front of a liquor store and a woman with her kids, and they're all stopped dead staring at me. One of the kids is pointing. Look. It's a Kydra. Look.

I got on the onramp and tried to just tickle the gas to get around the curve, but now I'm coming up on the damn 24 and I've got to lean on the go pedal. That's when it got majorly aggro. The cam and the secondaries and the supercharger all kicked in, just like I figured they would but way, way stronger. Like driving an ICBM. Zeus reached in with a Zeus-sized paw and slammed me onto the seat back, and I was holding on for dear life with both mitts locked on the wheel, and the whole car's trying to go supersonic on me. It was all I could do to stay in my lane. All around me traffic was scattering. Maybe it was all the 'Stangs and Chargers, jumping over the guardrail and hiding in the ivy plants.

Somehow I got to my exit and headed home. By now I think the Kydra had figured out that it didn't have A.J. Foyt at the wheel. I mean, I know cars can't think. Or they're not supposed to. But I sensed it. Like it was disgusted. I thought I felt the seat twitch under me. Maybe there was a James Bond ejector seat dealie in there. Maybe it would just chuck me out through the roof and go cruising off by itself down to the Unser spread in Albuquerque, and wait for Bobby or Al to show up.

I was back in Prado now. Every street I turned onto people was stopped and gaping at me, like the Prez had lost his marbles and gone on a one man motorcade in the 'burbs. And finally, I'm starting to feel pretty good. Maybe I'm not going to total the Kydra, or at least not in the next five minutes. Maybe they're not going to realize their horrible mistake back at Exotics until I'm out of state. I'm in a Kydra. Paul Newman can get in his Ferrari and cruise out to Prado to make time with our woman life, and next to me he looks like Howard Cosell.

I flashed a swift little Joe Cool salute to a couple of chicka-dees giving me the once over, and turned onto my street. There's fat, bald old Mr. Snavely filling up his porta pool in his Play-boy mansion swim trunks. He thinks he's a hot retiree. Checking out my Kydra. I clicked off another Hollywood A-list salute and pulled into the driveway. Mom's already at the door. She's gawk-ing between me and the car like the DTs have finally struck.

"What're you doing with that car, Hank?"

Mom, it's a long story. I've got to pack. I'm going on a trip.

"You tell me who you stole that car from. Did you rob a bank?"

I shook her off and got a couple of paper bags out from be-hind the fridge and started tramping around the house stuffing in traveling stuff. Mom keeps following me around. Did you kill somebody, Hank? Do the cops know? Then she gets all hot and bothered about my house rent. You're not going off on some big crime spree and leaving me short of the mortgage. So I pull out the envelope the key came in and whip out the roll. Come on, Mom. I've got three Gs in here. Just hold your water til I get to Indy. My rent's not due for two weeks.

And then I see that there's a little 3 x 5 file card in there with the greenbacks. With something written on it:

Check in with Phil ASAP. Call collect.

and then a phone number.

•   •   •

I tried to give Mom a hug goodbye, but she took a kick at the family jewels and said she'd fry my bacon if I didn't get the rent in. Okay. Fine. I love you too. I headed out to the Kydra. Now old Mrs. Snavely's out there. Another hot senior. She's wearing pink shorts with lace fringe. Mom says she's a swinger. No, thanks. I did my little salute again. Jet setting Hank Kruzenski. Drops in to see the little folks, then back to life in the fast lane with the beautiful people.

BRRAAUUUUUGGGGHHH I got that vicious bastard onto Vincent Parkway. I'm feeling no pain. Sidewalk left and sidewalk right, Prado Diablo, California is checking out Hank. About time I got some respect around here. You can shove this Rodney Dangerfield treatment. I'm done with it. Just give me time to pick up an Interstate map, and off to the Benicia Bridge and a straight shot to the 80. And I gotta call this Phil dude. Wonder what he's like. BRRMMM BRAAAAUUUUGGG- HH and I pushed in that powerhouse clutch and ratcheted that diamond cutter precision machine work shifter into second and tried to picture this all pro C team racer named Phil, with a friendly twinkle in his eyes and a kindly man of the world 'been there, brother' smile, who was just waiting to give me some cheery advice on how to ride to Indianapolis.

Prado Diablo Boulevard. Gotta get that map. The nearest place for sure I could pick one up was Dale's Auto Accessories over on Highland and Fourth. Now, major tragedy, that just *accidentally so happened* to be where Earl Howser worked. 'Course I'd never in a million years dream of going in there to lord it over Earl that I'm in a Kydra. No, sir. Not Hank. That would be crass. Now, if circumstances just so happened to *require* me to drop in on Earl and show him the Kydra, and the key to it, and the three Gs in the envelope, and the C letter, with the invite to Indy in it, and make him understand that I was on my way to auto racing nirvana while he was stuck selling tire valve caps to boogery high school kids, well, I'd just have to swallow hard and do what I had to do.

•   •   •

The lot at Dale's was empty. I pull the Kydra in. Through the sun glare and posters on the picture windows I can see the racks of leather steering wheel covers and auto air fresheners and license plate frames and other auto parts diarrhea they got in there, and Linda Vaughn draping those Godzilla mams over a Hurst shifter, like she'll drop trou and get majorly carnal with you if you just bolt a new shifter in your Volkswagen. Sure. I shut that monster engine down BRRAAAMMMMMM and get out and walk in like John Wayne.

It was just Earl in there. He'd already jumped off his stool and rushed around the counter to gawk at the Kydra. Then old Hank sauntered through the doors, and the poor bastard saw who was driving it. He froze. His ugly little mug puckered up in a pruney little O. I could read his mind. He's practically in cardiac. Where's the defibrillator? It's Hank. Hank's driving a Kydra. His arch rival just scored a major grand slam car status victory. His life's passing before his eyes.

"What's up, Earl?"

Just as slick as can be. Like I drive a Kydra 24/7. If my Gulf-stream wasn't in the shop, I would've parachuted in from the upper troposphere. I walked past Earl to the counter and started scoping out the maps. Behind me Earl's still in deep medical shock. He wants to go out and slobber on that car so bad. But it was Hank driving it.

Finally he came back to the register. He had to. He worked there.

"What'dya want?"

I picked a map out of the rack and flipped it on the counter. "Just a map, Earl. I'm going on a little trip."

"Where'd you rent the *kit car*?"

Practically grunted it at me. Worst thing he could think of to say.

I slid him a buck and he rang up the map and practically frisbee'd the change back at me. Boy, was he hacked off.

"Oh, the Kydra?" Like I'd just remembered I was driving it. "That's not a kit car."

"Sure it's not."

"Really. You can watch Shane Viscount tonight. It's a real Kydra."

"Kit car."

.   .   .

I left. Outside was a rack of phones by the side of the store. I figured I'd make my big check in call to this Phil character now. Not that I wanted to torment my old friend Earl by keeping the Kydra there. It just couldn't be helped. I got out the envelope and pulled out the card and fed a dime in and dialed, and when the operator came on read off the number I wanted her to ring for me. I had this guy Phil totally visualized in my mind. Veteran racer. Elite C Team member. A hot rodder's hot rodder. Well, Hank, old boy, how does it feel? Did we tell you that we're putting you up in the Conrad Hilton tonight, Hank? With Beluga caviar for breakfast? Don't worry about a thing, Hank. Leave it to us.

The number rang. A dude answered.

Not Phil. He couldn't be. It was this cynical old Southern-sounding guy.

"Collect call from Hank Kruzenski."

"Put him on."

I heard the operator click off.

"Hi, uhh, this is Hank. I've got the car here, and ..."

"I know who it is. The operator just told me. Are you deaf? *Where've you been?!*"

Through the receiver I heard him sucking on a cigarette. Well, this was some kind of mistake. He had to put Phil on.

"Is Phil there?"

"Who do you think you're talking to? I asked you a question. Where've you been?"

"Well, I just got the car here ..."

"What do you mean, you just got the car? You picked up that car over an hour ago. That note said to check in ASAP. You know what ASAP means?"

It went downhill from there. He hadn't seen me on the tape, but he'd heard from Exotics that I'd looked like a complete hayseed. What business did I have going on TV dressed like a coal miner? I'd better burn my behind getting to a department store to buy some decent duds, and I'd better not pay too much and save the receipt, too, and every other receipt for everything else I spent, because he was going to check every receipt personally once I got to Indy, and I could count on a police visit and some time in the slammer if the numbers didn't add up. Sentry Security Service in Las Vegas was waiting to check in that Kydra from me no later than eight p.m. tonight and he had a motel picked out only a mile away, and I had a appointment with KRZB news in Las Vegas at 9:30 sharp the next a.m., and I'd better believe I was going to call him again first and go over everything I was going to say to the reporter so I didn't make an idiot of myself like I'd apparently just done in Prado. This wasn't his idea but if I thought some rinky dink like Hank Kruzenski was going to flush C Enterprises team money gallivanting across the country, I had another think coming. And God help me if I put a wrinkle in the paint on one corner of that Kydra. Did I hear him?

Click.

That was Phil.

Through the picture window Earl was still hunkered down glowering at me from behind the register. Kit car. I got in the Kydra and opened up my new map and tried to scout a route to Las Vegas. This beat working at HM&F. That was for sure. But maybe not by as big a margin as I'd hoped.

CHAPTER FOURTEEN

First, dear Hank, at the risk of marring the flow of your story, I must thank you again for permitting me to stitch the chevron of junior author upon my sleeve, and heave my two cents into your saga. Certainly, this is a vastly more ambitious undertaking than any of your childhood fellows would have expected from you, given your fondness well into maturity for what today's literary lights call "graphic novels," which we knew no better than to call "comic books." You impress, Hank. Faulkner and Selby certainly never anticipated competition from such an unlikely quarter.

Still, I must note: by chance or design, you assigned me the one chapter requiring real research. I paid no fewer than five visits to SFPL Central to gather material for what I am about to write, and suffered all manner of eye rolling from the card-carrying tree huggers employed therein, who may have expected me to confine so déclassé a research project to Prado.

But, enough of my complaining:

• • •

By the time we made his acquaintance in Indianapolis, the C had been well known to motorsports cognoscenti since the middle fifties, and nothing less than a household word for the past decade. Racing business people calculated that his appearance at any Indy, NASCAR or sprint car race guaranteed a bonanza at the box office. Strip malls and gas stations hawked C Cola, C chewing gum, even C chips (which tasted to me as if the potatoes sacrificed in their making had been cultivated under a canopy of moldy undershirts, but perhaps I have simply failed to develop a gourmand's palate for such delicacies). I could not travel three blocks in Indianapolis in our month of May visit there without a reminder of his existence: the C logo on the cap, belt buckle, chest or underwire-buttressed bosom of a passing race buff; the trademarked C flames on a license plate holder; a hydrocephalic and likely unlicensed head shot of the man himself on a billboard towering high above Georgetown Road, solemnly professing faith in the probity of a West 16th Street used car dealer.

Inside the Speedway grounds, I could not travel ten paces without such a reminder. Not ten paces. He was as ubiquitous and omnipresent as sweat, sunshine, oxygen.

Where in the story does one begin? I have only a single chapter to limn the highlights of a life that warranted nearly 200,000 words in Granger's seminal _They Call Him the C_. Should I follow Granger's lead, and start with the sad history of how he learned to drive? Claude was only eight; his dipsomaniacal father taught him to operate clutch, brake and gas so he would have a personal chauffeur to squire him home from his nightly revels in Fresno's dive bars, while he snored off his ingurgitation in the back seat. Or perhaps I should take a cue from Walt Bessler's hagiographic _Nothing Less than the Best_, and join the story in junior high school, when the popular and athletic twelve year old Claude threw a protective wing around a shy new student with a speech impediment and harelip. Many automotive journalists also dwell on this first encounter between the C and young Boss Maryland, as the Boss would become as storied a crew chief as was the C as a driver.

But I will be bold, and draw my own conclusions. My hours spent among the tomes in the car nut wing convince me that the seed of today's living legend was not germinated for a good fourteen years more: seven years after the Bonneville jaunt that produced the historic cup photo with Perry McClendon; six years after the birth of Evelyn, the C's only child; four years after Claude and Boss wrapped up a couple of happy post-high school seasons on the midget and sprint car circuits; and four years after the gadabout young racer bought a one way ticket across the Atlantic, to gratify his inner gypsy, chase continental lasses and perhaps talk himself into a race car while overseas. Claude Winters would have been remembered as a gifted driver without the event I am about to relate, and perhaps even a great one, but never so hallowed a figure in American folklore.

The event was his high school's ninth year reunion. Claude was in town for the occasion only because his father had taken ill, requiring a hasty flight back to the states to hold the old man's hand on his death bed, and to visit the daughter he had entrusted to his parents' care practically from birth (and to what dubious care could be provided by the girl's mother, of whom you will undoubtedly tell more as your story progresses). The gold-filigreed reunion invitation had been delivered to the family farm only a day after the globe-trotting young racer had stepped off the transatlantic plane. Willard probably would have chucked it in the circular file, if it had come earlier. It was as if the fates had stage-managed the events preceding the reunion, to insure that the future C would be on hand to attend.

By then Claude Winters was a cheerfully successful twenty-six. Shortly after arriving in Europe, he had sweet talked his way into a pilot's seat at the Targa Florio, where his derring-do had so impressed observers that a Palermo team owner bankrolled his first Grand Prix start at Imola. Claude had spent the next four years piloting Formula One cars at the most storied tracks of the Old World, from Rouen-Les-Essarts to Barcelona to Nürburgring to Le Mans. Motorsports journalists knew him as an up and comer. He could brandish clips (in languages he found incomprehensible) from Gazzetta dello Sport, Dagbladet, Le Monde. But his fame was all east of the Azores. Like the two years older Dan Gurney, he was a celebrity abroad and a stranger at home.

By all accounts, the reunion was an ordinary enough affair. Claude said his hellos, twisted and hully-gullied with old girlfriends across the half court line, small-talked by a punch bowl on a crepe-hung table under the basketball hoop. No voices were raised, or insults exchanged, or blows thrown. Everyone was too mature for that.

It simply became apparent as the evening progressed that Claude was not especially welcome. His cohorts responded with polite diffidence to his anecdotes about hailing a cab in Paris, puzzling out directions from the beach of Tamariz to the Autódromo. They would permit him to intrude upon the nostalgic little coteries they formed under balloons and bunting, but did not invite him in of their own accord. A couple of chance comments revealed why: the C had "gone European" on them. What was a Formula One driver to a Fresnan? He might as well have taken up fencing.

One former classmate with thick eye shadow finally dropped the bombshell, a line reprinted in both of the biographies named above and in several others, although I may be alone in attaching such import to it.

"Claude," she said, "it's like you're not even an American anymore."

Not even an American anymore.

This would not do.

Claude Winters left his old high school gym that night a changed man. It was as if a group of Louisville teens had told the young Cassius Clay that he seemed like a "white boxer" after his stint at the Olympics. Claude reacted as strongly. Not an *American* anymore!?!? What did the trophies and glories of all Europe matter to him, if he was not first a hero in his own home town?

Two days later, a telegram informed a Formula One team owner in Madrid that his star American driver would not be returning for the 1960 season.

The day after that, the telephone rang in the Glendale apartment of a brilliant young mechanical engineer already bored by his well-paid work in the aerospace industry. Rex Maryland was delighted to wax nostalgic about midget racing with the visiting expatriate on the line. He *did* miss it; Claude was right; they'd had plenty of fun in those few years after high school. And you only lived once; Claude was right about that, too.

Perhaps it wasn't too late to pick up where they'd left off. In fact, Rex had an idea: this time around, maybe they could bring in a third classmate from their Fresno high school years. Phil Shay was toiling for an ad agency in nearby Pasadena. Sure, Rex agreed, Phil was a grumpy little tightwad, but a genius at raising money. You needed plenty of cash to campaign a race car. If they could put up with Phil, he could help them get it.

They might make a good team.

• • •

In the racing season that followed, the stars of the sprint car circuit learned that they would have to beat off a rabid and spit-frothing pit bull from Fresno to collect their customary share of winners' trophies. Claude drove like a man possessed, manhandling the bellowing Offenhausers that Rex built around the perilous curves of the most notorious tracks in the country: Dayton, Winchester, Salem, Langhorne. Phil persuaded a Marina del Rey advertising tycoon that a manly-man race car sponsorship was better therapy for mid-life angst than another chin lift or tummy tuck. The money came in, and Rex knew what to spend it on.

Trophies followed, many of them. But what made Claude Winters into the legendary C were not the sprint car victories, or the first foray at the May classic — even though Claude nearly won the damn thing in his first year out, in a second-hand roadster that Rex had worked his magic on — but a come-from-behind finish in the Rebel 300 so stunning that it quickly became a "must include" in any television anthology of stock car racing. Thirty-two thousand Carolinans stood as one to watch the C's searing red 409 savage the curves of Darlington: drafting, trading paint, threading through traffic, gaining the fourth spot, then third, then second, and at last — as Darlington thundered its approval, its awe — first for the checkered flag, in a down-to-the-wire sprint for the finish line, with only feet to spare. A wire services cameraman who thought to point some long glass at the stands left the track that day with a single Tri-X frame that would be reprinted in every sports journal on the continent. It showed not the car, or the driver, or the competition, but a trio of high school aged spectators who were veritable caricatures of Southern womanhood in the JFK era: sequined cat eye glasses, beehive bouffants, one clutching a Sugar Daddy candy bar, staring in slack-jawed, glazed-eyed disbelief at the track.

The caption said it all: "Watching the C at Darlington." Soon no caption was needed. Photo editors didn't bother with it. Everyone knew the shot. Everyone.

And who was this novitiate who could so stand on the gas, and steal a sky full of thunder from the Pettys, the Roberts, the young Foyt? A disdainful, tea-sipping furriner? No. Hardly. The strapping young Californian with crew cut, cobalt blue stare and stars and stripes stitched on his uniform breast was a perfect good old boy: simultaneously courteous and unpretentious, charismatic and gregarious, and ready to sign autographs and pose with the fans until the track closed. They didn't have to know how eager he was for their acceptance, how earnestly he sought to pulverize the misunderstanding that had weighed on him since the reunion. Not <u>American</u> enough. Not American!

"Don't you bother with Claude," he told his fans (as he slouched against the hood of the meteor-red Impala, scrawling his signature on receipts, programs, anything that would hold ink). "I don't care what you call me, so long as you buy a ticket. Just call me the C."

. . .

Only a little more in this chapter, Hank, before I return the reins to you. I do hope you'll allow me a few more paragraphs later in your story to wrap up.

The Legend — and no other word will do; if anything, 'legend' is a word barely large enough — that emerged in the decade following that Rebel 300 was primarily the work of Claude Winters' sincerely beneficent nature, and Phil Shay's eagerness to exploit that generosity for profit. The more famous Claude became, the larger swelled his hunger to metabolize that fame into dispensations to his faithful. He could not rid a teenage fan of his abusive parent, or cleanse his skin of acne, or send him to the prom with the girl of his dreams. But he could give him a set of mag wheels, or chrome rocker arm covers. And wanted to. And did.

Phil Shay had merely convinced him that it had to be made to pay. Santa Claus required funding. Thus were begotten the Asphalt Monarchs, and Ask the Wizard, and the Speed Warriors, and the other endless promotions and campaigns that flogged the C brand name and imprimatur into the collective American psyche. The C did not even return to the tracks of Europe until a quietly-commissioned Phil Shay survey revealed that his fans would forgive him for such intercontinental philandering.

. . .

I was quite helplessly impressed to see the real McCoy in person, Hank, despite his shoddy treatment of me, of which I'm sure you'll inform your readers in chapters hence.

CHAPTER FIFTEEN

Five days later and three time zones east, your fearless hero was tromping south on Georgetown Road in flat-as-a-pancake Speedway, Indiana, with the world's biggest stadium sticking out of the plain ahead of me like a giant metal erector set that Zeus wrenched together after too many martinis. On the big grass parking lots to either side of the street, race-crazed Hoosiers was docking their pick-ups and station wagons and sedans and tromping south along Georgetown with me. We was still at least a quarter mile away, but man, you could hear that REEEE-AAAUUUUUGGGGHHH of those big turbocharged Offenhausers jetting around the track as loud as an air raid siren. The first practice week had begun.

Physically, I'd had better days. I was hot, for one thing. In Indiana in May they've got this clammy wet stuff called "humidity" that Governor Brown mostly outlawed in California. The Disco Dave sports shirt that Phil had made me buy was sticking to my pecs and my pits, and the sweat was dripping off my forearm onto the wadded-up Hardy's shopping bag that still held all my earthly possessions outside of Prado.

For old el numero dos, I was tired. Phil had booked me into some of the mangiest hotels this side of Bangladesh. The night before, I'd got to sit up late watching the roaches wage a Rommel vs. Patton campaign on the bathroom floor. I hadn't slept decent since I'd left home.

Plus I was nervous, because I didn't know where to go in that humongous metal stadium, or how I was going to get to the C team once I was inside. Phil had lost all interest in communicating with me after I'd done my last TV spot and checked in the Kydra that a.m. The Hoosiers could have barbecued me up with the ribs at a tailgate party, for all he cared.

But don't get me wrong. Hank K. was feeling no pain. They say that every dog has its day. Isn't that right? Maybe Nanuq the Eskimo huskie has to pull the drunk fisherman's sled 24/7, but there's got to come a day when the fisherman's too hung-over to roll out of the igloo, and Nanuq gets to frolic with the girl huskies and bark at the sea lions all day.

Except for getting yelled at by Phil every night, those five days on the road had mostly been mine.

•   •   •

The Kydra had been a repo. Phil had told me that much, so I'd understand why an untouchable like me had been let behind the wheel. Some Hillsborough zillionaire had crapped out in the commodities market, and Exotics Exclusively had needed to get their Kydra back, and then my letter had come along, and the C or somebody else had cooked up the idea of a loyal Ask the Wizard subscriber driving the wonder car back east for his first Indy 500. With lots of Phil-arranged publicity along the way. I'd met TV crews in Vegas, Denver, Kansas City, St. Louis, and Terre Haute, and my beautiful Grecian profile was about to be beamed all over Indy, too, at least if WABCDEFG whatever it was aired what they'd shot of me that morning at Meridian Kessler Autosports.

Phil had made all the phone calls to set up the spots. His opinion of me hadn't elevated much in that past five days. I'd sure never read about anyone like him with the C Team. He hadn't actually seen one interview I'd been in, but he was convinced that I was about as photogenic as a sewer rat, and talked like one, too, and that it was a crime and a sin that a born washroom attendant like Hank Kruzenski had been relieved of wiping the bowls long enough to even touch a Kydra, let alone drive one. None of this had been his idea. Frankly, he didn't think I deserved to get dragged to Indy from the back bumper of a Greyhound. But somebody else had made the decision, and by God he was determinated that they at least make some money off the deal, and that meant publicity. Anybody who'd seen me on the tube had one more reason to buy a Kydra t-shirt or key fob or wallet, or something else from C Enterprises.

I'd had to call him every night, and he'd spent most of the time promising me a one way ticket to San Quentin if I so much as wrinkled the Kydra's finish or didn't turn in every receipt, and yelling at me about how I was supposed to sound grateful and appreciative on TV, and not mention him at all, or anything else he didn't tell me to say, because I was too stupid to ad-lib. Oh, and I was supposed to sound spontaneous and unrehearsed, too. Did I get that? Then every night I'd had to check in the Kydra with some fancy five star Barnaby Jones type security service that probably charged a arm and a leg just to stare at the front bumper all night, while old Hank got to shack up in the Motel Calcutta. The only exception was St. Louis, because the Heritage Point Inn paid fifty bucks and comped me a room so they could be a trip sponsor. If it hadn't been for the fifty, I could have slept on the sidewalk.

So I'd taken a few lumps, and I sure wasn't looking forward to meeting Phil in 3D. But don't get me wrong. That had been one happy trip for me.

•   •   •

You've got to understand: after I'd bought some decent duds and sat for a hair cut, nobody could tell anymore that I didn't belong in that Kydra. True, McDonalds burger slingers had turned up their noses at me a week earlier. I'd been a HM&F glue worker. The lowest of the low that didn't chug-a-lug lunch out of a Thunderbird bottle.

Okay. *You* know that, and I knew it, but with my new duds and 'do, nobody *else* knew it.

Damn if I didn't get treated like the visiting Sheik of Araby. Here's Hank stepping off the 80 for a fresh tank of Sunoco 260 in Whistlestop, Utah, and every man, woman, child, dog and flea is gawking at me like I'm Max Magnum movie producer. I couldn't pull in for a microwave burger at the 7-11 without collecting a crowd. Or starting a mini-riot, in some cases. Near Topeka one pot-bellied old tycoon offered me seventy grand and the pinks on his Ferrari if I'd swap for that Kydra. I swear. Seventy grand plus the car. Nobody bothered to look at his Ferrari with that Kydra around. Him included.

I'd had people ask for my autograph, and ask if they could get their pictures took with the car, and with me. Plus I'd seen the Rocky Mountains for the first time in my life, and the Great Plains, and basically the whole USA out of Prado.

It had done something to me. I felt like the big guy upstairs was giving old Hank a second chance. I'd messed up everything in my life pretty royal, and painted myself in a corner, and even got myself fired from HM&F. And now this.

I was going to parlay this into something. Maybe I wasn't going to be driving a Kydra for the rest of my life, but I wasn't going to be sucking dust through a face mask at HM&F, either. This was a new start for me. I wasn't going to be a loser anymore.

·   ·   ·

Man, had she ever pulled the wool over my eyes. Man.

What had she said the first time I'd talked to her at Fiesta? "Cylinder halves." Ten to one she'd been the one who'd planted those Vulcans in the first place. And the way I'd gone on in my room about my wonderful 'Cuda and what a big hot rodding expert I was. What had she been thinking, with me shooting my mouth off like that?

And then there was that damn mysterioso cup of hers. My whole take on that had changed, now that I knew who she was. Nobody on earth was likelier to have that thing than Mr. C's daughter. It probably *was* real. I'd had this mundo precioso historic dohitsit sitting on the nightstand in my bedroom, right under the Big Daddy poster.

And I was going to meet the guy who owned the car I'd been driving. Evelyn was his daughter. He'd writ me a personal letter, for Pete's sake. I was going to be one on one with him, and all these other big pro race team guys. What was I supposed to talk to them about? How I put moon rims on my 'Cuda?

·   ·   ·

Every once in awhile a banished thought about Evelyn would sneak in. About how she'd touched my arm that night when she'd apologized, and how her hair had smelled after the shower, and the way she'd looked at me.

Well, she was totally out of my league now. Any idiot could see that. Mr. C's daughter. Come on. I'd just do my best not to let my brain go there, that was all. And maybe not hang out with her too much, so I wouldn't do something crazy, and make a fool of myself.

It was weird how she'd got in this big letter-writing relationship with Logos. She knew a side of him I'd never seen. I still felt plenty uncomfortable with the homosexual stuff. I knew I'd have to deal with it now, too. It was out in the open.

I figured Evelyn and me could team up to get him some help, so he could have a girlfriend like a regular person.

• • •

Maybe I didn't know where I was going, but the race fans around me did. I asked a Ma and Pa Indiana type the best way to get to the garages, and they pointed out an entrance way the hey down the road, where lines of cars and people was queuing up to go in through a tunnel.

I walked down there. More time to freshen up my Joe Cool disco shirt with a fresh load of sweat. On my left was the chain link fence and the huge metal bleachers looming up, and then inside the fence in the shade under the bleachers Hoosiers was milling around buying soda and popcorn and fries and burgers and other healthful nutrients from concession stands. Then they wonder why they've got so many lard buckets per capita in Indiana.

I made it to the entrance after five minutes of walking in the heat and more horrible suffering, and got in the line like an ordinary citizen and bought my ticket and followed everybody else in through the tunnel and inside.

I don't know if you've ever been to Indianapolis, so I'd better tell you about the Speedway.

Think size. Biggest stadium in the world. No lie. Either real estate was seriously cheap in 1909 or the builders was seriously rich, because this thing just goes on and on and on. You get in a car on Georgetown and drive by the track, and the bleachers go on and on, and you pass in a car on West 16th and they do some on and on there, too, even though that's the short-end-of-the-oval side.

It's not like Candlestick or Dodger Stadium or another regular stadium place where you only park on the outside, and then inside there's just the seats and the field. At the Speedway they've got some of the parking lots *inside* the racetrack oval. They've even got a damn golf course in there. Plus the Pagoda, and the garages, and Gasoline Alley, and a big new museum they was building, and this giant grassy area inside of turn 1 that the C personally told me stay clear of, called the Snake Pit, which I'll get to later.

It's all *inside* the track and the stadium. Like a little town in there. Go look it up, if you think old Hank's lying to you.

•　　•　　•

Anyway, there I was on the inside. Finally. I'm in the middle of a big State Fair atmosphere, except for the occasional REEEEAAAUUUUUGGGGHHH of a race car zooming by on the track. Which I couldn't see yet. Looming up above was this blocky silver and glass thing I ID'd as the pagoda, and then branching out to either side of the pagoda was the backs of the clunky metal bleachers that blocked my view of the track, and then tucked under the bleachers was more concession stands.

And above all, people. Loads and loads of people. It was only the first week of practice. They was just testing out their cars. But there's Ma and Pa Hoosiers and their kids lugging in styrofoam picnic coolers from the inside parking lots, and bodacious young sexpots lining up for sodas and popcorn in their halters and short shorts, like they was just grabbing a bite to eat before they tried to knock Linda Vaughn out of the Hurst car, and race fanatic dudes in shades and muscle car shirts sneaking peeks at the sexpots, the same as race fanatic dudes did in California, and tourist types clucking over souvenir T-shirts in the gift stalls, and even long-hair biker and Joe College types, too, way more than I'd expected to see in Indiana. They'd mill around and go in under the bleachers to get to the seats and then come out and mill around some more. Just thousands and thousands of people, so I couldn't walk more than ten feet without sidestepping to get out of someone's way.

I walked up to a Snuffy Smith looking grumpus in a yellow track worker shirt and asked how to get to the C Team. He gave me a slow, head-to-toe once over before he answered. Like he was working security on Pennsylvania Avenue, and I was a wino asking directions to the Oval Office.

That took some of the wind out of my sails. Really, I'd felt the wind going out for the past two hours, ever since I'd dropped off the Kydra and the MK Autosports sales manager had showed he really didn't care if I crawled to the Speedway now that the TV spot was done and they had the car checked in.

Grumpus nodded his head at a chain link fence about twenty yards ahead of me. I spotted the marquee letters hanging over it. Gasoline Alley.

I walked over. Through the links of the fence I spotted a bank of payphones, and then the two long, low, cinder block buildings I'd seen pictures of in car magazines, where the eighty-eight garages was, where Boss Maryland and George Bignotti and A.J. Watson and some of the best mechanics on planet earth worked on the cars. Some of the garage doors was open. They looked like horse stalls. Race cars was sticking out of them, with mechanics' tool chests next to the cars, and stacks of tires next to the garage doors, and guys in race team shirts bent over the engines. In the long alley between the buildings crew members were bustling around, and now I spotted my first race driver. I even recognized him. Bob Harkey. He was a big sprint car champion back east. Always a bridesmaid, never a bride at Indy. I remembered the article I'd read about him.

Harkey was wearing a full race outfit, with the Nomex face shield thing pulled down around his neck. Maybe he'd just taken a test run on the track. Big All-American looking guy. I half expected to see his car next to him, like a horse hitched next to a cowboy. He was standing next to a stack of tires and yakking to some executive type in a business suit. Seeing them got to me, for some reason. It was like I was that wino again, and I'd somehow got close enough to the Oval Office to spot the Chief of Staff in a hallway. What was I going to do back there? This was where the C and A.J. Foyt and Bobby Unser belonged.

Another yellow shirt was standing by the Gasoline Alley entrance. I sauntered up to him and flashed my ticket quick, like I could hardly be bothered, and started to breeze past like he was some peon holding the velvet rope for Prince Charles. That works sometimes.

Not today.

"That's not good for garage access," he said.

He was a hobbity-looking middle-aged dude with one of the most massive combovers I'd ever seen. Seriously. It looked like he'd let all the hair grow over one ear since the Cuban missile crisis and then dumped about five bottles of contractor-strength spray on it, and then tack welded the whole magoo over on the starboard side of his scalp. It looked like a giant furry spinnaker. It probably made him ornery to have to truss up that big coiffure every morning, unless he just slept in a helmet and didn't take showers. It looked like he wanted to take it out on me.

"I didn't know."

"You do now."

From behind me a Steve Suave type stepped up and pointed to something metal clipped to his shirt. Combover waved him through. Then he made me and some other fans step back while a crew brought one of the race cars out. That's why it was called Gasoline Alley, see. It went straight to the track. First came four guys in crew shirts riding a golf cart, and then a rope hitched to the back of the cart, and then the giant tires and air scoops and engine of the race car hitched to the rope, with another crew dude sitting inside to steer.

Combover waited until the rear wing was clear of the gate before he'd pay attention to me again. I figured it was time to haul out the heavy duty BS. I gave him the gazing-out-from-the-pulpit look I'd used on Hardy's customers when the 'on sale' stuff was sold out, and went into a Dwight Eisenhower rap about how I personally could care less if I saw where the C and A.J. Foyt and Bobby Unser had their cars — really, I found auto racing rather tiresome — but I just so happened to be on a deathly urgent errand for the C team, and he certainly had the right to say no, in which case I'd go off quietly and slit my wrists, because life as we knew it would be over.

Combover leered at me. He'd heard it all. And I was thinking I was going to have to go out and call Phil again, when among all the crew members bustling around in that long alley in front of me, guess who I spotted.

She was halfway down between those two cinder block buildings. It took me so long to recognize her that she almost got too far away to hear me yell. I knew Evelyn was the C's daughter. I'd come to Indianapolis expecting to see her right where I was seeing her now. But I couldn't make it register in my brain that the hippy chick I'd buried Ruby with and this race crew member was one and the same.

She was pushing a tool cart. Wearing the unmistakable emerald green C team shirt, which the C picked because half his competition was superstitious about green. All that thick black hair that I'd spent hours thinking about was balled up under a C team cap. She almost looked like a man. I knew she had to be the only woman on a race team here. They'd only let chicks in the pits a couple of years earlier.

"Evelyn!" And then I remembered her other name, and thought I'd better holler that, too. "Sarah!"

I yelled it as loud as I could. Combover shot me a dirty look, and a couple of fans turned to stare at me. It worked, though. I saw her turn, and then she smiled and left the tool cart where it was and walked over.

I don't mind telling you, I felt my heart pick up. Even if she was duded up like a guy, and didn't look much like the star of my secret fantasies. That arrow Cupid had drilled into my chest was still stuck there hard and fast, even if you couldn't see it.

Up she walked with that beautiful smile of hers. She flashed a quick gesture to Combover that I was okay, and Combover frowned and stepped back to let me through the gate. It would've been a lot more fun if she'd asked him to call the cops, and he'd got to see me arrested.

She hugged me. The way all chicks think they can just hug any man any time without it having an effect on them. Then she stepped back, and brushed a lock of hair off her forehead, and beamed at me in a shy, curious way.

And here's what she said:

"What size are the secondaries in your Barracuda?"

.   .   .

Peaceful and matter-of-fact as all get out, like that was the most perfectly natural thing in the world to ask me after I'd unmasked her top secret true identity, and drove two thousand miles cross country to see her.

I stared at her. For a second I tried to tell myself that I hadn't heard her right. Then I wondered if maybe Combover had a 'Cuda too, and if she she'd been giving him mechanical advice before I walked up.

But Combover was just standing to one side and trying to act like he wasn't eavesdropping.

"The what?" I said.

She shook her head quick, like I was trying to get out of talking about something.

"The secondaries. The secondaries in your Carter. What size are the jets?"

A little leer was flickering way back in Combover's eyes now. Maybe he'd get to eavesdrop on something juicy. I kept staring at the woman. The secondaries in my Carter carb. Under the hood of my car in Prado Diablo, two thousand miles away.

My mouth must have been hanging open. She gave me the impatient head shake again.

"You were in my case file," she said. "Every single Scribe letter that you showed me came out of my typewriter. It drove me crazy riding around with you, because I couldn't say anything. What size are they?"

Just the most natural thing in the world to ask me about after I'd drove cross country. It was real obvious my secret romantic feelings for her was mutual. I could tell by her choice of conversation material.

"Ninety-fives," I said finally. In a voice you'd use to answer somebody if you were both running away from a burning building together, and he kept asking you about the color of your socks.

She rolled her eyes.

"That's much too rich. You should have told me. How did your plugs look?"

My plugs. I felt my cheeks getting pink. From the corner of my eye I spotted Combover leering at me.

"My what?"

Evelyn looked impatient. "Your *spark* plugs. Just tell me how your plugs looked, and I'll leave you alone."

I tried to look dignified. "Maybe I don't happen to go around checking my spark plugs every day of the year."

Combover snorted, the rude bastard. Evelyn looked at me like I'd just said I stuck Crisco in my fuel line.

"You didn't check your plugs."

I held out my hand and waved my palm slow in front of Evelyn's face.

"Hey. Hi. Hello. It's me, Hank Kruzenski. I just drove out from California. That's where my car is. We're in Indiana now. I'm sorry I didn't bring my spark plugs with me. If you want, I can go back home and get 'em. I thought we'd have other stuff to talk about."

Evelyn held up her hands. "Okay. You win. I'll stop. I've just never met anyone I wrote Scribe letters to before." She stepped back toward the tool cart. "Let me drop this off, and then we'll get you set up at the credentialing office. Just give me a minute."

She went back to the cart, and I watched her pushing it down the alley past the stacked up race tires and horse stall garages and people bustling every which way. I felt a little hacked off. I mean, maybe I'd had a pretty righteous street machine — not like the Kydra or anything, but still — and wrenched on my 'Cuda a lot, but you couldn't expect me to do *everything*, could you? I didn't belong to some major league Brainiac auto racing family. I didn't run a compression check every time I stopped for gas. She didn't have to rub my nose in it. I had a life. Maybe I wasn't so all fired serious about it as some people. I mean, gee whiz. Frankly.

"What kind of engine you got in your 'Cuda?" Combover said.

He was leering at me some more. Watching a girl make Hank look dumb had made his day. He'd have to empty out another can of spray on his combover to celebrate.

"383."

"I wouldn't use one of those to weigh down a bathtub. And you don't even read the plugs in it?"

•   •   •

Evelyn came back and separated me from my dear friend with the clipper rig hair-do, who'd already thought of two more insults for my car which he'd never seen, and was working on a third, and led the way. She knew her way around in there. She walked us past the garages outside the chain link fence, and then down another road toward a little building with a first aid sign on it.

We were clear of the infield bleachers then, and I could finally see part of the track, where it banked up under the outfield bleachers toward one of the turns. I was staring at it and I heard the RRRRREEEEEEEEEE coming up of one of those turbocharged Offenhausers, and it got louder and louder until the Indy car flashed into sight, with the sun glinting on the paint and the engine so loud for a second I wanted to clap my hands over my ears, and moving fast as all get out, like a dragster at the end of a quarter mile. Then the sound tapered off, and it was gone.

Evelyn marched us along. We got past the first aid building, and then I saw off to my right this big grassy strip on the inside of one turn of the track that had what looked like a rock concert crowd camped out on it. There was jalopies and vans and Harleys, and people stretched out on blankets on top of the vans like they was sun bathing, and people sacked out on towels on the grass between the parked cars. They were half watching the cars practice and half just hanging out.

Evelyn kept walking us toward the new Speedway museum. I lagged a little behind, watching her. She didn't wear the C crew shirt too good. Or the cap covering her hair. I couldn't put my finger on why. It was like seeing her in a burger flipper uniform. It was something she had to wear.

"Can I ask you a question?"

"Go ahead."

"Was it you who planted those cylinder heads at the Fiesta?"

I figured we could have a nice ho ho ho about it. But Evelyn threw me a sad look I couldn't figure out and stared straight ahead again. Like I'd brought up something embarrassing.

"Of course it was," she said.

She kept walking us along. I heard the RRRR-REEEEEEEEEE coming up again and then another Indy car flashed by, hugging the same part of the track in the corner as the car before.

We were up to the museum they was building and the big empty parking lot there, and the little plaza with the fountain in it. One whole turn of the track was off to our right now, and the bleachers beyond it. I spotted a couple of yellow shirts nearby, but almost nobody else was around us.

"I must've sounded ridiculous, yakking about all my hot rod magazines."

"I didn't think you sounded ridiculous."

And she gave me that sad look again that I couldn't read. A little voice warned me there was something simmering under the surface I didn't understand, and that I ought to keep my yap shut. But dumb old Hank was just too excited to be talking to the great Mr. C's daughter with her secret identity exposed.

"Man, I should've suspected something from the way your Ghia ran. That was the first thing I thought of when I realized you was the C's daughter. That little Volksie you drove up to Hardy's in. You take a typical hippy Volkswagen, it's gonna run like a two stroke lawn mower."

She stopped walking, so sudden that I almost shot past her. She didn't look mad, or irritated. Just embarrassed again, and a little resigned, like she'd realized she'd have to say something that she would have rather had me figure out on my own.

"Hank, I'd like to ask you a question."

I waited. Off on the grassy infield stretch I saw some dude stand on the roof of his van and stretch, and then rub suntan oil on his arms. It looked like a earthier crowd in there. Then the RRRRREEEEEEEEEE came again, and the guy stopped basting his arms while he watched the track.

"Do you think you met the real me when we talked in your room after burying Ruby, or is this the real me now, wearing this team shirt?"

She gestured at the big C Team logo on her shirt. In an almost humiliated way, like she was a teenager wearing a dorky dress her parents had made her get. Car nuts all over the world would've paid half a week's salary to wear that shirt.

I didn't answer. I don't think she expected me to. She stood in front of me with her heart on her sleeve, in the naked, embarrassed way she'd looked at me when she'd apologized while we was burying Ruby.

"Hank, I'm here because I'm a failure. My husband killed himself, and I've made a mess of my life, and my crazy father thinks I'm good luck. I don't know how to say no to him, and I need the money, so I come along, even though I hate racing and wish he'd never do it again. What do you think that says about me?"

She winced, like it hurt her to think about it. "I shouldn't have asked you that question about your jets. I like you, and that was something I could offer that might help. And I know that Claude is very famous and that all of this is new and impressive, but please try to understand how different it looks to me. Please try."

On the track behind her another Indy car swooped around the turn, and we stood looking at each other while the RRRR-REEEEEEEEEE sound swelled up and then faded again. In the infield a fat guy with no shirt snapped a picture of the car, then looked at his camera like he wanted to make sure he'd had it set up right, and flopped back on his lawn chair.

"Well, okay." I felt awkward. "I mean, sure. Whatever you want. But we're kind of in the car racing capital of the whole world right now. If you don't like racing, there are friendlier places you could hang out."

At least that got her to smile. She nodded, and looked a little shy, and started leading us again to wherever it was we were going to get my badge. RRRRREEEEEEEEEEE went a car, and a he-man voice on a loudspeaker announced the lap time, and some in the menagerie in the infield broke into applause.

And to me she was like the queen of it all, the whole thing, and she didn't want to be.

•   •   •

The silver badge is the big deal at Indy. This year it was shaped like a cock-eyed triangle, with a big shock absorber on it and the Monroe logo next to the shock. You could buy a brass badge that would let you get in the Speedway and the garages every day til the race started, but the silver badge is what got you in the pits and Pagoda and press room and everywhere else. The veteran racers and crew members got them. They figured that if Jackie Stewart had almost won in '66, they probably could trust him to walk around the pits without breaking anything.

We went into the office and Evelyn picked up my badge, and then we walked back toward the garages.

"Just show it whenever you want to go anywhere," she said, while I was pinning it to my shirt. "Please don't lose it. They're numbered."

I checked the badge on my shirt front. She thought I was going to lose it. A silver badge at the Indy 500. I'd probably put it on my mantle for the rest of my life.

"I know I'm supposed to treat you like I did in Berkeley," I said, "but I can I ask you what your job is? Are you like the crew chief?"

That got her to laugh.

"The crew chief at the Indy 500!" She gave me a disapproving look, like I'd told a bad dirty joke. "That's Boss Maryland, Hank. You don't get to be crew chief if you don't walk, talk, eat, drink auto mechanics. I'm one of the lowest of the low here."

"How's Logos doing?"

"Badly."

We were coming up to the chain link fence surrounding the garage area on the parking lot side. A whole slew of humans was crowded up there, hanging or leaning on the chain links and watching the crews bustling about in the garages, and yelling if they saw a racer they recognized. I spotted at least three chicks who'd dressed to get noticed, if you know what I mean. They looked like groupies at a rock concert.

"He's just here for me, Hank. You know how he feels about cars and the environment." Evelyn looked embarrassed. "My father dragged me out here for good luck, and so I drag Logos out to keep me company while I'm here ..."

She let her voice trail off. She looked a little defensive, like there was something else she thought I should know that she hadn't decided to tell me. We walked along by the fence. I watched the race fans checking us out, looking at her crew shirt uniform and then at me, like I just might be worth a second look if I was with a team member.

Then I guess she decided to spring it. She went on in a lower voice.

"I think our crew knows about ... what he's going through sexually." She sounded ashamed of herself. "It slipped out in an argument with my father. It was my fault. I told Dad, 'You'd better keep that to yourself,' but I think he must have told Boss or Phil. They've all known each since before I was born. Then maybe it spread from there. The crew will hardly talk to Logos. It's terrible. They stare right through him, like he's not even there."

We were almost up to Combover. Evelyn stopped and gave me a pleading look.

"Hank, why don't you keep him company for awhile? He's out in the stands somewhere. It will do him good to talk to you." She checked her watch. "Come back at six. Dad said we're all going to go out to dinner then. He might change his mind, but ... please come back then. I can introduce you to everybody." She touched my arm. "Please be gentle with him. This is a very difficult time for Logos."

She gave me another hug goodbye. I felt the girl muscles of her back under her shirt, and smelled her hair, and then I watched her walk past Combover into the garage area. With the purse thing jiggling a little around her waist while she did. Probably because she just happened to have the ninth wonder of the world tucked inside it, maybe alongside some Kleenex and a Chapstick tube.

•　　•　　•

The metal bleachers wrap most of the way around the outside of the Speedway. On the inside of the track circle, though, in the infield, the only bleachers are on the west side, to either side of the Pagoda. Maybe they'll put up more infield bleachers eventually. I think they've only got 400,000 permanent seats now. Hardly enough for a decent cook out. The track staff is probably worried half to death about what they'll do when they sell ticket 400,001. The poor guy might have to stand.

I walked in through Gasoline Alley with my magic silver badge pinned on my shirt, and squinted up in the sun at the bleachers ladder-stepping up toward the pagoda. Then I realized that finding Logos might not be so hard. A humongous crowd of Hoosiers had come out to watch practice, no question, but the yellow shirts had only opened some of the bleachers to spectators. I wouldn't have to hunt all over the Speedway.

I was right next to the pits, with a passel of guys in team shirts behind me sweating over a car before sending it out for a practice run, and at least a thousand fans stacked up on those ladder-stepped bleachers. They was sucking sodas and beers and leafing through race programs, and some were clicking off times with a stopwatch and writing the lap speeds on scorecards, even though the he-man announcer was reciting the stats for them. Maybe they didn't trust him to get the times right.

I held my hand over my eyes and squinted up there for Logos, and then I spotted him. Away off by himself in the top row under the awning, so he'd be out of the sun. At least three rows away from anybody else. Like he'd picked a spot by himself on purpose.

I clanked my way up the metal steps. He was sitting with his elbows on his knees and his feet hitched up on the metal bleacher seat in front of him. I grinned up at him when I got close, but he stared stonily straight ahead as I climbed up, even though there wasn't anybody else in the way, and he couldn't have missed seeing me. I started to feel weird. We hadn't exactly parted on the best of terms at HM&F.

Fortunately, I'd worked out this absolutely wonderful ice breaker joke on the drive east.

I stood in front of him with a big leer and my hand cupped in front of my crotch, like I was poster boy in a queer bar in Frisco.

That was my big ice breaker.

Well, I should've left that one back on the interstate. A hurt look flashed across Logos' face, and then he looked real serious and determinated, like a priest ignoring someone who tries to tell a joke during catechism, and kept trying to stare past me like I wasn't there.

Hank, old boy, I told myself, you watch yourself; you watch yourself good. Things is different now. Evelyn was right.

I sat next to him on the bleacher seat and gave him a friendly poke on the shoulder.

"You could at least say hello. It wouldn't kill you."

"Hello," Logos said.

Frosty as all get out, like J. Edgar saying howdy-do to the Zodiac Killer. I kept my trap shut. I sat like he was sitting, with my feet up on the metal seat ahead of us. For awhile we stared out at the track. There wasn't any cars out there now. That's how it went on Practice Days. If a team needed to see how that latest camber change shaped up, they took the car out for a spin. If not, you got to stare at the empty asphalt for awhile until somebody needed to test something.

"How did you figure out where I was?" Logos asked.

I shrugged. "I went back to your place and asked your mom if I could snoop around in your room. Then I read through the rest of your big letter collection. I'm sorry for getting in your business, Logos. I was worried."

Logos nodded and looked grim. He still hadn't looked at me.

I chuckled. "Man, if she just hadn't swore me to secrecy about the stuff she told me that night we buried Ruby. If I'd told you that story about her drunk husband going off to hunt up the cup, we would've both put two and two together way earlier."

"I'm sure we would have."

Still in the Frosty Freeze voice. Nixon showing the kitchen to Khrushchev. I couldn't stand it anymore.

"Look, would you lighten up? You only known me for more than half your life. I'm not going to treat you different. Growing up in your family, it's a miracle you don't fondle yourself looking at livestock catalogs. Frankly. At least you don't oil yourself up and go onstage like Barry."

Logos shot me a quick glance, and looked a little resigned, like somebody who had to loan out a door key he'd just as soon keep to himself. He watched himself clasp and unclasp his fingers.

"She wants me to tell my parents."

I didn't say anything. He pushed his fingertips together in a steeple, and frowned at them, and let the fingers fall loose again.

"She feels that I'm living a lie, and that I won't be capable of real happiness until I unburden myself. She thinks I should call them from Indianapolis."

"Well, I guess you could. That's an idea."

Logos gave me a skeptical look.

"How do you think my father will react to the news of my suspected homosexuality?"

"Oh, nothing too serious. Just take you out back and shoot you. That's all. Or hire a firing squad, so he can get the whole thing photographed for his yearly phone book ad."

Logos nodded. "I don't know what to do with myself, Hank. I'm in limbo. You know what Prado is like. I can't conceive of myself sharing this with anyone there. So I trail after Evelyn like a spoor, because she already knows and wants me here, even though I'm as welcome on the team as an IRS inspector. You'll see when we meet the others. I'm not doing any tutoring work, so I'm practically broke. I'm just drifting."

"What's she said about the great missing wonder of the western world?"

"A great deal." Logos looked at his fingernails. "And I'm afraid I'm not yet at liberty to divulge a word of what's she's told me. She's sworn me to secrecy, just as she swore you to secrecy the night you buried Ruby." He looked at me. "I believe she plans to tell you all eventually, but it will have to be in her own time."

We did some more gazing off together at the speedway.

Well, that was funny how things had worked out. With all the chasing we'd done after that thing, and practically getting killed by her maniac errand boy, and now neither of us was going to do anything about it, even though it was likely the real McCoy. She had us both under her thumb for different reasons, without her even trying to put us there.

A car came out for a practice run. I'd have to get a program later so I could recognize them. It did a couple of slow laps on the inside to get warmed up, and then RRREEEEEE picked up speed, and the announcer started getting all hot and bothered about the lap times. I'd already decided he had the hardest job at the track. He had to make practice laps sound interesting.

Logos winced a little every time the racer ripped by. Maybe the noise bothered him. I snuck a look at him out of the corner of my eye. It was finally starting to sink in for old stupid Hank what a tough time he was having.

But it wasn't going to do him any good to have a royal cow about it, so I said:

"Look, Logos, I know you're going through a lot. But why don't you try to lighten up a little? I mean, half the people in Prado is brain damaged anyway, from what they watch on TV and from what they buy at Hardy's. I know. I used to work there. And I'll still be your friend. Hell, I know you ain't going to make a pass at me. You can't afford me."

That finally got him to crack a smile. Maybe it wasn't the biggest one I'd ever seen, but it was something.

We talked more regular after that, sitting up there under the awning and watching the racers. After awhile I even went down to get us some eats, and swore at him when he wouldn't eat the greasy fries, just like I would've done back home. There's nothing like being somebody's homie since third grade. It's hard to go too wrong, even when you practically try to.

CHAPTER SIXTEEN

A competitive Indy team requires a money man, a builder and a driver. I can't imagine a serious go at the checkered flag without a superlative functionary to consummate each of these roles, Hank, but the who and the how of consummation are up to the team.

Mario Andretti worked for Clint Brawner until team owner Al Dean died. Then Andretti bought the team and became Brawner's employer. The two got along. A.J. Foyt and George Bignotti, in contrast, quarreled so bitterly that one may wonder if both have staggered into senescence on the hope of seeing the other expire first, so the survivor can heap insults on his adversary's grave at the funeral. But both Brawner-Andretti and Bignotti-Foyt won the 500, differing styles or no.

There have been cool, calm and collected Roger Penske team owners, and emotional Andy Granatellis, and owners somewhere between the two. Eddie Sachs may have known little more about cars than the typical Cosmopolitan *subscriber, but still nearly won; Mark Donohue, who did win, knew more than many crew chiefs. The contest didn't care.*

Like Patrick Racing, Vel's Parnelli Jones, All American Racing and every other top seed at Indianapolis, the C Team provided for the tripartite essentials in its own unique way.

• • •

The litmus test for separating C insiders from outsiders was probably acquaintance with the team's money man: Phil Shay. Although some group or individual fulfilling this function is absolutely indispensable — racing costs money, buckets of it – Phil recognized himself as an especially unattractive financier, and avoided scrutiny. A USAC newsletter once published a cartoon of Phil chasing a nickel into the gutter; I believe this was his only media mention. Repeat interview requests by trade magazines were refused.

Phil insisted on taking his yearly 'vacation' at the 500, although he relished only the buck grabbing he could do as team marketer, and enjoyed neither racing nor its fans. He was a fixture on his stool by the phone at the back of the team garage, where he could fish a succession of Pall Malls out of his inevitable cardigan sweater, pick at his bulbous nose and hairy LBJ ears, and complain constantly: about his joints, if it was cold; the fetid air, if it was warm; the food, no matter what had been brought for him to dine on; his hotel; the smell and sound of race cars; and especially, his unflagging suspicion that someone somewhere was about to request an unnecessary centavo from C Enterprises. When he was not complaining, he stared humorlessly into space, likely brooding over promotional angles yet to be exploited, reporters yet to be manipulated, and sponsorship pockets available for the picking that he had not yet wriggled his fingers into.

But Phil Shay was a marketing Einstein. This is important to understand: each core member of the tripartite C Enterprises isotope was an unquestioned genius in his field. No matter how foul his humor, Phil roused himself regularly from his roost for beady-eyed strolls among the commonalty in the "Snake Pit," the Rabelaisian throng on the Turn 1 infield that you passed with Evelyn in your first day stroll here. Phil loathed these folk as

passionately as the C adored them; he wished
only to survey their fickle vagaries of fashion
first hand, to better chisel a dime out of an
unsuspecting wallet in the next C Enterprises product catalog. His eye was keen: Ask the
Wizard, the Asphalt Monarchs, the fruity Ro-
manesque names for C Enterprises speed equipment (Vulcan of Speed, Empyrean of Speed), the
logo and team color scheme, the sponsorships
that obviated dependence on a single bucks up
sugar daddy, and the endless free P.R. from
the press were all the doings of the grumpy
old fellow on the stool by the wall. And he
had gone to high school with the C and Boss in
Fresno. They trusted him.

Phil also insisted on sheltering the second core C Team member from public view: the
builder, the mechanic's past master, Boss
Maryland. Speed equipment ads (generally conjured up and certainly all approved by Phil)
showed the same heavily retouched, Mount Rush-
more-like shot of a granite-jawed Boss staring resolutely at the horizon, proud moustache
bristling beneath an imperious Viking probos-
cis, as if contemplating crankshafts and connecting rods with Thor and Odin in Valhalla.
Even the moniker 'Boss' was a Phil Shay inven-
tion. Phil probably guessed that Boss' frail-
ties might be best camouflaged with an especially inappropriate nickname.

In truth, Boss was shy, retiring, taciturn
— owing to the speech impediment and cleft
palate, which the moustache had been grown
to conceal — and so immersed in mechanical
thoughts that he had to be reminded to eat.
Only with the C could he have survived as such
a naïf. Behind the scenes, the Bignottis and
Brawners are usually required to be team leaders: contending with financial matters, hiring

and firing drivers. But Boss was one of the original Fresno trio, and turned a wrench for just one team. He could live with his head in the chassis, and did.

. . .

Lastly, there was the man himself.

The living legend behind the scenes was simultaneously authentic to the nth degree, and a conscious fraud. Authentic, because he cared passionately for his fans — adored them, brooded about them, contemplated their shifting moods as obsessively as a love-struck teen might agonize over every wayward glance of a straying paramour. He could spend hours haggling with Phil over some Santa Claus-like giveaway that might cost C Enterprises an unrecoverable $50,000 to sponsor, only because it might bring a smile to the lips of someone like, well, a Hank Kruzenski, toiling away at his Prado Diablo cash register. But he was also a fraud, because he regarded his fans a bit like children. Emblematic of this duality may have been his private views of the racing he had left behind in Europe. His fans wanted him in stockers and sprints, and in those cars he would sit forever, if they wished, but to Boss and Evelyn he might confide (almost in a whisper, a sad one) that he thought nothing the equal of Nürburgring, and no racer a match for Fangio.

I can't say he had no parallels as a driver, but certainly no superiors. His vision still tested at 20/10 at age forty-two. His decades-long relationship with Boss was an immense advantage in setting up the car, and like most of the best drivers, the C paid close attention to mechanical matters. (And

here too his simultaneously adoring and yet
sympathetically condescending attitude toward his fans was apparent: neither he nor
Phil wanted to disturb the theatre staging
of his public image by permitting a too candid glimpse of his constant back-and-forth
with Boss about camber, caster, stagger, toe,
the other learned rites of race car setup;
both the C and Phil understood that his fans
didn't want him to be as smart as anyone that
good had to be.) He had superb race craft:
the awareness of the vulnerabilities of the
vehicle beneath him, the ability to nurse an
ailing ride to the finish line, to push tires,
chassis, engine to their screaming limits, and
no further. And when occasion called for it,
he could stand on the gas as hard as anyone in
racing.

The C had never married, fathered only one
child and participated in only one long-term
relationship, a one-sided and pathetic affair
of which you shall surely tell more in future
chapters. 'Pit poppies' are plentiful in the
racing world; the C had his pick of them, and
among thousands of other women: he was handsome, accomplished, wealthy, charming. But
there was only one woman who mattered to him,
and only one whose heart he couldn't win, and
only one who cared for him as more than a race
car driver, and it was in his conduct towards
this one that the C may have been at his most
unfathomable. At once, he pushed her away — by
continuing to race, which she would not accept — and sought her forgiveness, even as the
behavior she regarded as sin continued.

This single, aloof, unavailable woman was,
of course, his <u>best girl</u>: his daughter Evelyn,
our mutual friend, and perhaps the C's only
Achilles Heel.

CHAPTER SEVENTEEN

The C turned out to be a leaner-looking dude in person than I'd expected. He had some gray in his crew cut and some gray stubble on his chin, too. And you could see the long scar next to his ear from the crash at Talladega. I'd known it was there, 'cause I'd read about it, but it didn't show up in photos.

I spotted him when Logos and me went down to the garages. It was six o'clock and the track had closed for practice, and as we walked down there fans was shuffling out of the bleachers and clogging up around Gasoline Alley and the Pagoda, lugging their styrofoam coolers and picnic crap out to wherever they'd stuck their cars. But things was still plenty busy in the garages. Most of the teams worked until nine o'clock at night, at least. They'd work all night if they had to, if they'd hit the wall in practice or if a new engine had come in.

All the horse stall garages looked the same to me, but Logos knew where to go. Down we walked between those long cylinder block buildings, with me trying to sneak looks inside while crew members in team shirts rushed around us. The big elite racers had garages right alongside the little guys. You'd pass the garage of William Wannabee, who'd scraped together all his spare change from twenty years of running tow trucks so he could field one Indy car that had as much chance of qualifying as Nixon had of making the Berkeley city council, and then in the garage right next to him there's Johnny Rutherford, or Foyt Gilmore, or the Gurney team. Freaked me out.

The C team garage was near the end. And damn if the man wasn't right there next to it, pow-wowing with a bunch of fans. I didn't know how they'd got in there. Maybe they was with some special tour group, or buddy-buddy with the Hulman family. Gasoline Alley was strictly off limits to John Q. Public.

The C was wearing his race suit, with the Nomex head sock thing pulled around his neck. He was standing next to a go kart parked between his garage and the next one over, holding a burger that nobody was giving him a chance to eat and yakking it up with his admirers. There was close to a dozen in front of him. I tried to catch his eye, so I could at least wave and say thanks for the Kydra, but he was too busy.

A beefy Iowa tractor salesman type was blocking off everybody to get his race program signed, and then there was some dudes and dudettes crowded behind him who might've all come from the same fraternity. One of the dudettes looked like somebody had airlifted her from Hef's round bed at the Playboy mansion. Put together. Seriously. Annette Funicello 'do, big fake black eyelashes. She was looking up at the C like she thought he was Moses.

"You think you'll get pole this year?" one of the dudes was asking, as me and Logos came up.

I figured we'd walk around them. Maybe I'd get an intro later.

But old Zeus had plotted out a bigger day for me than I'd thought. As I was stepping past, a hand comes out and hooks me by the shirt sleeve.

The next thing I know, I'm eyeball to eyeball with the man himself. The tractor salesman and Ms. Playboy Grotto and the fraternity types are all staring at me.

"How'd you like that Kydra, Kruiser?"

That same big voice I'd heard so many times on radio and the tube.

Fine, sir, I said. Or something like that. I might've just babbled.

The C handed the pen and race program back to the tractor salesman. He stepped closer and pulled something out of a pocket of his race suit and held it under my nose. I blinked at the threads and the insulator. A spark plug.

"We check our sparking candles around here, Kruiser. My best girl told me somebody's not with the program."

I gave him another fine sir. The tractor salesman looked impatient. He wanted his autograph. The C turned back to his fans.

"Welcome to Indianapolis."

•　　•　　•

The inside of the garage was jammed with tool chests and parts trays and mechanic's stools and an air compressor and everything else you'd expect at a corner garage, except what was on the set up pad front and center wasn't a Buick in for a oil change:

❧ 247 ❧

it was the bright green, 1,000+ horsepower Valkyrie, with the sponsor names in yellow and white on the sides.

Evelyn was cleaning parts at the solvent tank. She wiped her hands off when we came in, and introduced me around. I actually shook hands with Boss Maryland. She just called him 'Boss,' like you'd say 'Jim' or 'John' or anybody else's name you worked with, living legend or no, and he got up from his stool next to the Valkyrie long enough to say hello. I'd seen his giant moustache in magazines and ads for as long as I could remember, but now I could see what it was covering up. He had some kind of big gash in his upper lip. He said 'hello' like he was talking underwater.

Next up was Eldrich, this dapper looking Kraut dude, which maybe doesn't count from me 'cause I thought anybody with a Europe accent was dapper, and then blond, already-going-bald Luke, who looked and talked like somebody I could have pulled a wrench with in Prado. He had a little gold cross dangling around his shirt collar, and shook hands like he was welcoming me into his church. Evelyn said there was two more I'd meet later: Nash, another mechanic, and Caspar, the son of a family that Logos and Eldrich was staying with.

Sitting next to the phone by a bench in the back was a cantankerous looking old string bean with a pack of Pall Malls hanging out of his shirt pocket. I sure didn't need anybody to tell me who he was, not after getting yelled at for four nights straight, but Evelyn still took me back there.

"Phil, this is Hank."

Phil stared at me up and down like I was a horrible fungus that had growed on one of the tires, and didn't pay any attention to my hand. He looked at Evelyn.

"Why do we have to put him up at Caspar's? He can sleep on the garage floor."

So that started an argument about where I was going to sleep. Man, that guy. Before my face he told Evelyn I didn't deserve the bed she wanted to book me into, and that I could sleep next to the air compressor, or better yet on the ground outside the doors, 'cause then I couldn't get in to steal anything.

Then he started bitching about the receipts, and Evelyn said never mind and got me away from him, and said that we could go out now and get me set up at Caspar's. The team wasn't going to go out for dinner after all. They were having problems with the car. They'd wanted to clock laps in the 190s, and hadn't hit any better than 185. They had to be ready for practice tomorrow, and couldn't skip a night of work.

That was my introduction to the C Team.

When we went out I saw that the C had moved off next to a trash bin about five feet away. His back was to us. It was after closing now and everybody in the tour group had left except for Ms. Playboy Love Grotto. The C was leaning in close to her, and staring down at something farther south than her face, and looked like he was talking at her the soft, smooth way a pastor does when he wants you to slide your hand on the Bible next to his. Except maybe the Bible wasn't what he was selling.

She was looking up at him with her lips parted. She looked nervous. She might've been twenty. I guess the C thought that was old enough.

Evelyn glanced at her dad, and when she figured out what he was doing she frowned and walked fast toward the gate, so Logos and me had to hustle to catch up. She looked like I looked when I saw Mom polluted.

It was funny. As totally wide-eyed and awed and star struck as I was, I could still catch the first tiny whiff that being the C's daughter might not been the fantastic deal I'd thought it was.

There was something else that felt off about that first trip to the garage, too. I didn't realize what it was until I thought about it that night.

Nobody had said hello to Logos, or even looked at him. They'd acted like he was invisible.

•　　•　　•

"Caspar's" turned out to be the house of Caspar's widowed mother, Mrs. Rosabel Henderson, on a little street about four blocks from the track entrance on Georgetown. She'd been following the C for about eight million years, and all her kids except Caspar was growed and gone, so she rented their old rooms to the C's crew for next to nothing.

Eldrich was staying there, and Logos, and now I'd get the last free room. It turned out that a lot of crew members shacked up with families in Speedway, which was basically the suburb of Indianapolis right around the track. The Indy 500 wasn't any bigger in Speedway than the second coming. It wasn't hard finding families to rent rooms.

It was a brick ranch house with an American flag on the lawn, on a street with a dozen other houses that looked like it. Eldrich had the mother-in-law cottage in the backyard. Logos was in the bedroom next to mine. At 6:00 every a.m. Mrs. Henderson called us out to breakfast. All she talked about was racing. She was heavy enough to smash a bathroom scale and had enough hair on her upper lip to fake her way into a mens' room, but she obviously didn't give a damn, her kids was big and her sexpot years was over and now she was free to follow motorsports. She knew NASCAR, she knew sprint cars, but first, second and foremost, that woman knew the 500: what Foyt Gilmore was running in the Coyote, how Bobby Unser had took the pole in '72 eighteen miles an hour faster than Revson in '71, the custom chassis that George Bignotti had ordered up for the Sinmast cars. She'd quiz Eldrich about the Valkyrie while he was forking up pancakes, with a cigarette going in the ashtray next to her coffee.

Mine was the last room she rented out 'cause it had been her son Walter's. He'd died in Vietnam. There was photographs of him all around the room, and his framed high school diploma and medals he'd won, and before breakfast every morning we sat still while Mrs. Henderson led a prayer for him.

She wouldn't look at Logos. She'd ask Eldrich or me to pass the milk, but if it was in front of Logos she'd get up and bustle around to his side of the table, so she didn't have to talk to him. Once right in front of him she led a prayer asking for vengeance against the Vietnamese "gooks" who killed her son. Even though Logos was part Korean, on top of all the other human races shoveled into him.

But Mrs. Henderson sure liked Hank Kruzenski. She ruffled my hair and told me dirty jokes and made sure I had plenty of grits. I was a rodder and an Indianapolis good old boy, as far as she was concerned, even if I'd spent my childhood a few thousand miles outside the city limits.

•　　•　　•

Evelyn got me hired as "pit support." That was a fancy sounding two words for the lots less fancy "gofer," which is what it meant in my case. There must've been fifty million race fans in Indy who would've done the C's errand running and clean-up work for free. But I didn't have a job, and the Kruzenski investment portfolio wasn't looking too diversified.

Phil hated it. He called me the official team grocery bagger while he shoved some forms at me to fill out, and said I was the first Indy crew member in history who didn't believe in reading spark plugs. But Evelyn was the boss' daughter.

I had my picture took for a team ID hard card, and got three green C team shirts, and practically every night before I hit the hay I'd stare at myself in the bathroom mirror in that shirt with the ID card clipped to it, and lie on the bed tracing my fingers over the wings in the Monroe logo. No matter what happened to me for the rest of my life, I'd have that badge and card to show people. Nobody could take that away from me.

I called Mom collect so she'd know she was going to get my rent money. She still thought I'd robbed the Federal Reserve. I had to make her call me back, so she'd see the Indianapolis area code.

·　　·　　·

Evelyn knew five times as much about auto mechanics as I did. Maybe she didn't like racing and maybe she was with Logos on the eco stuff, but if Luke or Boss asked her to pitch in she could hump it like any other pro mechanic. It was a little humiliating. I'd never seen a girl work on a car like that.

But next to Eldrich and Luke she was a stone rank beginner. It just kind of snuck out, how good they was.

Eldrich was from Berlin. He'd got his start in some fancy race mechanic apprentice program in Austria, and then after graduating he'd crewed for Formula One teams. Luke was a high school dropout. But he'd won two science fairs in Des Moines before he'd run away from home to crew for a sprint car team, and was damn near as natural a mechanical genius as Boss. There wasn't any rule book for how you got hired. You either had it or you didn't, and if you did you was part of the circuit. The other teams knew about you; they'd fight to steal you, if they could.

Like they'd be working on the suspension set-up, and they'd go to the work bench with Boss and sweat over these drawings and charts with math stuff that I couldn't make head or tails of. They might as well have been designing the next H bomb. I could follow along a little when they talked about the turbo and boost and wastegate and other parts of the engine, but as soon as they got into the chassis I didn't get four-fifths of what they was saying. They could have been talking Portuguese.

Once when I came back from a chow run and they was scarfing down the burgers I'd brought, they got to comparing the food at other tracks they'd worked at. It turned out they'd both been all over the world. Eldrich said he'd gained five pounds eating the parmigiana at Emil's in Monaco. Then Luke said what about the so-and-so in Buenos Aires, if you wanted to talk fattening food, and Eldrich nodded, and while he was chewing Luke said that the worst place had been Gabby's in Melbourne, 'cause they wouldn't make anything without pouring a ton of their sauce on it.

That was three continents in five minutes. Then Eldrich talked about some restaurant that 'Emmo' had liked, and Luke nodded. It turned out they meant Emerson Fittipaldi. They was just casually yakking about the two time Formula One world champion like he was the neighborhood bartender. It showed me. Maybe Luke acted like somebody who could have taken over my register at Hardy's. But he wasn't. He lived in a different world.

•   •   •

Mostly, though, they talked about the car. The crew finally went out to dinner together a couple of nights later, but for all the conversation changed they might as well have brought the Valkyrie along and plunked it on the table with them. If they wasn't talking about the chassis they was talking about the turbocharger, or about the wing, or about the stagger, or about the Cosworth that the Parnelli team had brought, or the Gurney Eagle, or how Bignotti had gone back to a long stroke in the Sinmast. It was like Evelyn said: anybody at that level just walked, talked, ate, drank and slept, racing, racing and more racing. Luke said he'd even thought about caster set ups in bed with his wife.

If Boss said anything, they hunkered in and listened to that strangled voice of his like they were trying to hear Ford give a presidential decree on a bad loudspeaker. Nobody but C ever interrupted Boss or talked over him. Ever. He was the guru of the guru's guru. Of all the mechanical geniuses from all over the world who'd come to Gasoline Alley, only a couple had that kind of rep. George Bignotti. A.J. Watson. Smokey Yunick. Boss Maryland. Maybe I was too stupid to know how good he was, but Luke and Eldrich wasn't.

· · ·

Once I tried chiming in with a mechanical suggestion. Boss and Luke was going over a drawing of the turbocharger set-up, and I thought of a tip I'd heard about setting up turbos at Fiesta. They was all being so friendly and treating me like one of the guys. What if I happened to know something that could help, and didn't throw it out there, and hurt the team?

Well, bad idea, Hank Kruzenski. Boss got a pained look and shut his eyes, and Luke looked real nervous, like I'd just told the mother of all tasteless Polack jokes. After a second he blurted out something else about the turbo, like I hadn't said anything, just to change the subject. I figured he was trying to do me a favor.

· · ·

I was errand boy. I usually got to the track first, so I could plug in the oil warmer and get the coffee going and see what they was running low on in the fridge. Then I spent the day toodling around Indy in the C team van, cussing out traffic and picking up eats at Charlie Brown's or just plain McDonalds, if that was what they wanted, and making runs for hardware. You'd be amazed how much an Indy team needs from a plain old hardware store.

Maybe I was low gnat on the totem pole in the C Team garage, but I was a VIP around Indianapolis in that C Team van and my green team shirt. Everybody asked me how the C car was running, or who I thought was gonna get first on pole day, which is when they decide what car starts first in the race, or how much looking over our shoulder we was doing at the Gurney Eagle or the Sinmast car or the Foyt Coyote, or Johnny Rutherford.

They'd yak for hours about it, even though the race was weeks away. The closer you got to the Speedway, the more practically guaranteed it was that every two legger you met was nuts about the 500. There were Speedway specials at restaurants and department stores, and "Welcome, Indy racers!" signs strung up in storefronts, and checkered flags flapping under street lamps, and posters and souvenirs for sale in gas stations and auto parts stores. The "month of May" was what they called it. Like a spell that eased in on May 1 and got more and more hot and bothered through Memorial Day weekend. If you stopped five people on the street, at least one could tell you the fastest lap that Gordon Johncock had run.

•   •   •

On one side of the garages there was a separate building with a welding shop and a rack for front end alignment. One morning Boss sent me over to pick up some parts, but then he must've decided I'd find some way to screw it up if I went alone. So he asked Evelyn to go, too.

She was in a good mood. The guy at the welding shop must have picked up on it. Maybe if she'd looked sour, he wouldn't have made the joke he did.

"You bring your boyfriend along to do the heavy lifting?"

He winked at her. Evelyn laughed. She hooked her arm through mine, and patted my hand.

"I sure did!" she said. "Hank Kruzenski, my husband to be!"

The welding shop guy said that was what you wanted to do with men, train 'em early so they'd know who was in charge. Evelyn joked around with him some more. I tried to go along with it. I held my mouth like I was laughing too, and hoped she didn't notice my flushed cheeks.

All the rest of the day, man, if I wasn't messing up Luke's lunch order, I was picking up the wrong stuff at the hardware store. Phil yelled at me something ferocious.

❦ 254 ❧

If she just hadn't said 'husband.' If she just hadn't put her arm through mine, and touched my hand that way. I knew I wasn't on her level. She'd been joking and it was stupid of me to take it serious and think about it for more than five seconds after it happened. But I'd never met anybody who could talk in that gentlefied way, and look at me the way she did. Like she saw all the way through me. Like I didn't need to hide anything. And it just seemed with my whole life turned upside down and inside out and things happening to me I'd never dreamed possible, maybe somehow even *she* could happen too.

All that night I thought crazy things. Maybe I'd win a sweepstakes and become a big millionaire, and sponsor my own Indy team, and be in her league. Maybe some murderous convicts would break out of the Indianapolis pen and try to take over the track, and I'd be alone in the garage with Evelyn, and could save her life.

•   •   •

Logos mostly kept to himself. He'd sit way up in the stands, or go wandering the streets near the track. Sometimes he came down to see Evelyn, and the two would go off on some personal pow-wow. He looked like the unhappiest person at the Speedway. There were the bikers and stoners in the Snake Pit and racing-for-Jesus types and fanatics who'd come to the track every year since the Korean war, and the 500 was such a carnival atmosphere that they all managed to fit in and find a niche. But not Logos. I didn't understand why he stuck around.

Once Phil muttered the word "fag" under his breath after Logos left, and I knew for sure that the team knew. Eldrich and Luke and Nash didn't say anything about it, at least not to me. I mean, they were big time elite crew members. They were getting paid to help nab that checkered flag. Period. They mostly pretended he wasn't there.

But then Caspar showed up, and I stopped thinking that Logos was going to get off easy.

He was Mrs. Henderson's youngest son. He'd been in Kentucky for an off-season football camp. I couldn't help being glad

❦ 255 ❧

that the team finally had somebody who knew even less about mechanics than I did. Caspar was strictly heavy lifting.

He was a varsity defensive tackle at ISU. Phil griped about paying extra for Caspar's C-team shirts, 'cause of his size. I didn't understand how he could drive the team van without putting a couple of hundred pounds of ballast in the passenger seat. It should've tipped over. He was friendly enough, though, at least to me, and didn't seem to mind that I was doing most of the work that he usually did, even if Phil minded plenty.

But Caspar didn't like Logos. Maybe his mom had told him about the gay stuff, or that he didn't like car racing. Or both. Every time Logos came to the breakfast table, Caspar glared at him like a bailiff watching an axe murderer come into a court room. He wouldn't talk or smile while Logos was there. He just watched him. Like he was waiting for Logos to give him an excuse.

•　　•　　•

Once Logos came down to the garage looking for Evelyn right after she'd left. Logos stood at the door looking awkward, until Phil called across the garage that she wasn't there.

Logos turned to go. And then I heard:

"Bye bye, Brucie."

In the girly-girl lisp voice that comedians all over the country used when they told their fag jokes.

Caspar was standing with his broom next to the fridge, glowering at Logos' back as he left. He'd said it plenty loud. He hadn't cared if Logos heard. He'd wanted him to.

CHAPTER EIGHTEEN

The first week at the Speedway was all practice. Teams hauled their cars off the trailers and hit the track to see what kind of lap speeds they could run and get their chassis dialed in. It was free form. You could run just one lap, or two, or take a damn Speedway summer cruise. You could cut practice runs late in the afternoon when the track was cool, and crank up the boost on the turbocharger, and nail speeds you'd never hit during the race, and get all the fans clucking and chattering while they wrote your stats on their scorecards.

Or you could not go out at all, if your car wasn't ready. Sometimes the fans sat up there for a half hour with their coolers and stop watches and race programs and shades and sunblocks without seeing a car come out.

What everybody was gearing up for was Pole Day, at the end of the first week. Saturday, May 10. Pole Day was the first day of qualifications. The drivers drew lots on Pole Day to see which cars went out first, and hoped they drew low or high, because the track would be cooler and faster early and late in the day, and then when they got called they went out alone to clock off four laps with every speck of speed and horsepower and go fast they could muster, with damn near a fifth of a million fans up in the stands watching and the announcer jabbering the lap speeds on the loudspeaker.

The average speed for those four laps was their qualification score. The driver with the best speed hauled in the Pole Day prize money. Two weeks later, he got to start the race in the pole position: first row, closest to the track, with the second and third fastest qualifiers filling out the front row next to him.

Not making pole wasn't the end of the world. Johnny Rutherford had qualified with the twenty-fifth fastest time the year before, and started the race in the ninth row. That hadn't stopped him from winning. But everybody wanted pole anyway. The most dangerous part of the race was the start, when the pace car rolled into the pits and thirty-three bunched-together race cars all got that big green flag at the same time. The front row was the safest place to be. The TV crews and out-of-town reporters filing Indy

500 stories to L.A. or New York or Paris or Peking all wanted to meet the pole sitter. He was the man in the limelight.

•   •   •

There'd been five favorites to make pole when I showed up early in that first practice week: the C for sure, in the C Team Valkyrie, A.J. Foyt in the Foyt Gilmore Coyote, Bobby Unser in the Gurney Eagle, and either Gordon Johncock or Wally Dallenbach in the Sinmast Wildcats. But that had been when I'd got there. By Thursday, nobody was predicting the C would take pole. The Valkyrie was having problems.

They couldn't get the chassis dialed in. It was a new design from Donohue Engineering, with the hub centerline front suspension that Bob Riley had worked up for the Foyt Coyote and the Bignotti Wildcats, and then a brand new rear suspension that Donohue had put together with Boss in '74. In Trenton it had handled fine. That had been the race before Indy on the USAC circuit. The C would have whupped A.J. at Trenton if the distributor rotor hadn't broke. But Indy was a different story.

Sometimes it pushed in corners, and you could hear the tires shrieking even in the stands, and when the C came back to the pits he said the Valkyrie felt like it wanted to run into the wall. So they'd take it in and put it on the set-up pad, and let air out of one tire and pump air in another, and tweak the suspension. Then the C would take it out again, and this time it was so loose it wanted to spin out. They couldn't get it right. Luke said it was like trying to write a prescription for a patient who was already taking a basketful of meds. Every change made something else go bad.

They'd still been easy going about it early in the week when I'd showed up. Phil had griped and moaned about everything, which I learned was a good sign; he knew enough to clam up when the team had problems. The C had done a lot of his famous horsing around with fans. He led a big C Team cheer from the pits, and went into the stands next to the Pagoda to sit right alongside the regular race fans with their score cards and stopwatches, and applaud when a little guy racer hit the track, and get everybody laughing while he booed when another A-list driver came out. Sure, they was running into first week glitches, but every race was different. They figured they'd get it sorted out.

But then May 8 rolled around, and then May 9, and the Valkyrie still wouldn't corner.

•   •   •

A.J. Foyt wound up taking the pole. His team waved him off on his first attempt, but he went back out late and qualified at 193.976. Gordy Johncock took the number two spot, at 191.652. Bobby Unser filled out the front row at 191.073.

The Valkyrie wasn't in there at all. Later the C said that when the wind hit the Valkyrie in turn 3 it was all he could do to keep it in the groove. He told *us* that. He didn't tell any of the TV people or news reporters, who crowded around him as he clambered out in the pits and wanted to know how the great legendary top seeded C felt about qualifying just shy of 186. "How do you expect me to drive if my underwear itches?" he'd complained, and said he'd have to shop for some decent BVDs to wear under that scratchy Nomex suit. Come Race Day, he'd still whup everyone.

But that was the C being the C for the public. Inside our garage, the mood changed. Those big horse stall doors stayed closed more often. The team didn't want to deal with lookie-loos if the Valkyrie wasn't running right. Phil sat on his stool and smoked his Pall Malls, and watched, and was quiet. Eldrich and Luke nodded when I brought in their lunches, and didn't joke with me, and went back to work. Boss stood at the work bench going over the drawings I didn't understand, and the C himself camped out in there with us and got Donohue Engineering on the horn, and got into deep pow-wows with Boss just like when they was teenage hot rodders in Fresno.

It showed me something. Maybe for John Q. Public the C put on his big I-can-hardly-be-bothered act. But he wasn't like that behind the scenes, and the team wasn't, either. They hadn't come just to get in the field. They wanted that checkered flag, and nothing else but. Second place was first place loser.

•   •   •

Sunday, May 11 was another qualification day. Wally Dallenbach punched in the second Sinmast with a 190.648, and then a bunch of racers made the field with 182s and 183s. Then the next practice week started. The teams had five more days of tuning and testing and tweaking before the last two qualification days on the 17th and 18th.

If you'd clocked in faster than 183, you was safe. Nobody was likely to run hotter than 183 the next weekend and knock you out of the line-up. But if your four lap average had been in the 181s, well, you spent a lot of that next practice week looking over your shoulder. Only thirty-three cars got to roll behind the pace car come May 25 race day. If enough drivers ran faster than your 181 the next weekend, you got bumped out of the line-up. They called the last qualification day "Bump Day" for a reason. If you got bumped, you got to clean out the garage and pack your thoroughbred into the trailer and git. You'd paid your entrance fee for nothing.

After they'd qualified, some of the top seeds practically closed up shop and twiddled their thumbs until race day. The C Team couldn't. Not with those handling problems, and not with a qualifying time eight miles an hour south of the pole sitter. The horse stall doors stayed closed. Boss told me to tape some newspaper over the window panes so nobody could look in. The team chucked a kitchen sink worth of changes at the Valkyrie, and the C hit the track for one practice run after another. Nothing worked.

•　　•　　•

One afternoon a big commotion started up outside our garage as the team was getting ready to take the Valkyrie back out to the track. I'd just got back from my latest official Indy 500 gofer run, and was hunting for a place to stash a giant jar of pretzels.

Phil told me to see what it was.

"And keep the door closed!" he crabbed at me. Like I didn't already know that.

It turned out to be a TV news crew. There was a dude with a film camera that must have cost more than our whole house in Prado, and damn near weighed as much, and a reporter I already knew from the local news. Hard Charging Harry Hicks. That's what they called him on the WXOX promos. This meaty looking middle-aged dude.

I slipped out and held the doors shut behind me and asked what the deal was. Harry looked impatient. His suit looked like Dupont had cultured it out of a petri dish. With some glittery sequin stuff in his tie. When I'd seen him on TV with the I-team, he'd almost choked out some old kindergarten teacher who'd been selling Avon on the side in the faculty lounge.

Harry said the C had personally promised him a interview. He didn't look happy about waiting.

I closed the door behind me and told the team what Harry wanted.

The C swore. They had the Valkyrie on the set-up pad and Cole Donohue on the phone and was up to their earlobes in the latest chassis experiment.

"That ugly bag of pus," the C said. "I told him *maybe.* I didn't promise him anything."

"Just go out and get rid of him," Phil said.

But C said he wasn't going out for a slobber session with Harry, and Boss and Luke and Eldrich waited to see what the C would decide, with Luke holding his hand over the phone mouthpiece.

Then C looked at me.

"Hank Kruzenski, official C-team spokesman," he said. He snapped his fingers at me. "Get out there, Kruiser."

"You can't send him out!" Phil looked shocked. "Hank's an idiot!"

Luke cracked me a shady leer. The C's mind was made up. "Official team spokesman," he said. "Let's shag it, Kruiser."

So I went out there. I felt weirded out. I knew I was team gofer, and if they wanted me to jump through the flaming hoop I'd try to do it without getting my clothes singed, but this didn't make a lot of sense. Team spokesman. They might as well have stuck me in the Valkyrie and sent me out to beat A.J.'s best lap time.

Harry didn't look thrilled to see me again. He was holding a microphone in front of his tie now, and his partner had the giant camera ready to roll. I guess they'd been positive the C would come out. In Gasoline Alley behind them people was already shooting looks over Harry's shoulder to see what was going on.

I shut the double doors behind me, and told Harry I was official team spokesman.

The next five minutes wasn't the most dignified of my life. First, I'd forgot to leave the pretzels in the garage, so I wound up clutching the big econo-size jar on my chest during the interview like a kid holding a teddy bear. Second, there was Harry. He wasn't like the creampuff TV reporters Phil had booked me with during the Kydra trip. I think WXOX usually gave him stories where he basically got to bite people, like the kindergarten teacher, or another I-Team investigation where he'd ambushed a cabbie who'd been relieving himself in a Mason jar while he waited for fares at the airport. Harry probably didn't like having to do regular news Indy 500 stories. Maybe he figured he'd take out his bad mood on me.

Harry asked me why we'd qualified at just 185. Is this going to be for everybody to hear?, I asked, and in a snarky voice Harry said that was probably why he was holding the microphone, and why the other guy was pointing a camera at me. Oh, I get it. Very funny, Harry. So I hemmed and hawed and gave my jar of pretzels a nice squeeze, and said you never could tell. Maybe the Valkyrie was having mechanical problems, like some people said, but maybe the C had held back for strategic reasons.

"A secret strategy not to take pole?" Harry asked. Then he wanted to know how long I'd been official team spokesman. With a lot of snippety top spin on the word 'official,' and practically rolling his eyes when he said it. Snide as all get out. He was the type who would've got annihilated in a bar in two seconds flat if he hadn't had that big camera and plasticware suit. I said I'd been appointed spokesman only very recently. I was starting to get mad. "Recently, as in the last two minutes?" Harry came back at me. Then he simpered at his own joke, like he could hardly believe what a droll guy he was, and it was just a catastrophe that some big station in Manhattan hadn't stuck his dippy Julius Caesar hair-do and baggy jowls in front of the greater New York audience, so he could do his exposes on second graders who copied each other's homework or men who impersonated Santa in fake wigs for all the back east slickers instead of a bunch of Hoosiers toting manure buckets in overalls.

Finally I got hacked off. He'd just asked me for the third time why I was holding the pretzels, and I told him maybe so I'll have something to take a whiz in like that airport cabbie, and he could come follow me to the crapper with his damn camera if he wanted to do an investigation on that, too, and at least I didn't dress like a Macy's mannequin and style up my hair with silicone caulk, or whatever he'd used to gum it up like that.

•   •   •

Well, damn if they didn't run my big interview on the 5:00 o'clock news. I'd thought for sure they'd trash it after I gave Harry all that lip.

We had a clapped-out Sylvania in the garage. All of a sudden Caspar said "Get a load of this," and pointed to the screen.

There I was. Caspar cranked up the volume. And what do you know: I guess the TV editors hadn't liked Harry, 'cause they'd made the whole thing into a joke that made me look good. All of Harry's snotty questions was in there, so he sounded as snippy on the tube as he did in real life, and when I came back with my line about the pretzels I looked like the put-upon hero.

Luke and Eldrich actually applauded. Even Phil smiled. Then the C told Caspar to shut the set off, and the living legend came up right next to me and told everybody to listen up. Kruiser here just beat out Harry Hicks fair and square, he said, and with style, too. And if Kruiser can do it, maybe the rest of us can roll up our sleeves and make this race car run like a lady, and send our friends Foyt and Unser and Rutherford home empty-handed come Memorial Day weekend.

•   •   •

A half hour later when they broke for dinner it turned out that dumb old Hank had missed Luke's order. Usually that would have got me a groan, at least. But Luke clamped his hand on my back, and told everybody he wanted to take the official team spokesman out to the concession stands to buy us both a burger.

We went out. It wasn't six o'clock yet. Fans and pit poppies was pressed up against that big fence around the garages, with the sun glinting on the cameras and pens and race programs they held, and the pit poppies' halter tops and make-up, while they stood with their fingers curled on the chain links and tried to get a glimpse of the big time racers and mechanics in where we was.

Luke waved at them. "Official team spokesman!" he said, and threw his arm around my neck, and gave me noogies, and a couple of fans yelled 'woo-hoo,' and one of the pit poppies half smiled, which was a lot, 'cause usually they only looked at the drivers. Luke marched me up Gasoline Alley. There were a couple of race cars next to the garages, and crew members milling around, and they grinned at us as we walked up, 'cause Luke still had his arm around my neck. And then there was Bob Harkey, the racer I'd seen on my first day there. Wearing his race suit again. He was driving the big black Dayton Walther 33 this year.

I swear, I thought he smiled at me. Maybe it was my imagination. But still. Maybe he'd seen me get Harry's goat on TV. It meant something. This was his fifth start at Indy. Three weeks earlier I'd been swinging a glue gun at HM&F. Now maybe an all-pro Indy racer like Bob Harkey knew who I was.

Luke marched me out of the gate. "Official team spokesman!" he shouted to the fans, and threw another headlock on me, and the fans laughed and made way and flashed the "C Team" sign when they saw the emblems on our shirts. Then we straightened up and rounded the corner to the concession stands.

And that's when we spotted Logos.

He was walking up through the crowd, nearly a foot shorter than some of those big Hoosier race fans around him, in one of his Earth Day t-shirts. Maybe he was on his way to hunt up Evelyn. Maybe he'd run out of places to roam around to.

Luke tightened up. He slid his hand off my shoulder and frowned straight ahead, like he didn't see Logos.

Logos studied Luke for a second, and then he turned to his old buddy Hank from his hometown.

I stared at the ground, and pretended like I didn't see him, either.

• • •

It wasn't fair. There was my big moment, and he'd ruined it. Now I felt all torn up. Why didn't the little gerbil go celebrate his eco holidays with the homos on Fire Island? If that's what he thought he was. Or go see a psychiatrist and get straightened out. Why'd he stick around at all? He had to know I was never going to get another chance like this. Did he want me to rush up and give him a big hug, so everybody would think I was a fairy too?

I hardly slept that night. I tossed under the covers, and kept looking at those photos of Mrs. Henderson's dead son in the moonlight. He looked like he wanted to shoot me for bringing a homo into the house.

I mean, Logos had a disease. Didn't he know that? Why didn't he take care of it? What right did he have to stick around so I'd feel I was doing wrong, for not standing by my friend, and feel all ashamed of myself?

•   •   •

But then the next morning something happened that made it easier for me to see where I stood.

It happened while I was pushing a stack of tires over to the Goodyear shed. They was stacked up high on my cart, so I had to crane my head while I was pushing to make sure I didn't plow into any of the fans or crew members. I must've been hid pretty good behind that stack. Maybe Evelyn would've acted different if she'd seen me coming.

She was standing by the bank of payphones near the fence, leaning on one of the glass cubicles with her back to me and talking to a guy who looked like somebody had cut him out of an *Esquire* fashion spread. Don Preel. One of the drivers with no car. Him and the other ride shoppers would hang out in Gasoline Alley all day, cozying up to the team owners who had back-up cars that hadn't qualified yet and trying to talk themselves into a driving gig.

He was six foot tall and pretty studly looking, with a lot of tousled blond hair and the kind of piercing blue eyes that chicks fall in the drink over. He was wearing street clothes, with his shades pushed up on his forehead and his shirt open around his pecs. I guess he'd decided to take a break from shmoozing car owners to chat with a car owner's daughter.

It looked like he was in the middle of telling Evelyn a story. He was holding his hands out like he was trying to describe the shape of something, and she was smiling up at him the way a woman just doesn't smile unless she's attracted to a man. Don Preel probably got smiled at a lot like that.

I kept gofering my tire cart. I didn't really want them to see me anymore.

Don Preel must have got to the end of his story. Evelyn laughed. She threw her head back, and Don Preel grinned, and then he made a big show of stepping in close and putting his hand on her waist and holding out the other hand so she could take it like they was ballroom dancers or something. And she did. I guess it was part of the joke he was telling. I watched her smile at him.

I ducked down low, so maybe she wouldn't see me while I gofered the tire cart past.

.   .   .

For about two hours after that I was in bad enough shape that Eldrich asked me what was wrong. I told him I thought it was food poisoning. Which was almost true, in a way. I'd finally been force fed a meal I'd needed to eat for a long time, of exactly where Hank the rube gofer stood with the great Mr. C's daughter.

Even though they'd just been fooling around. Still. She was the king's daughter in an all-man's sport. She had her pick of men. Maybe she'd felt sorry for poor little Hank at Hardy's with his baling wire 'Cuda and his drunk mom, and got me a trip of the lifetime to the Indy 500. Maybe she thought she could go off in some precious doll house with poor sick homo Logos, and coo and stroke his hair, and I could sit in there with them like a pet dog, until a *real* man showed up. Maybe a millionaire team owner. Maybe an A list driver. Then she'd pat her toys goodbye, and walk down the wedding aisle with someone on her level. And leave us there.

Well, it was a good thing I'd got straightened out. She'd given me something real, and maybe now I'd have the sense to concentrate on making something out of it. Maybe there was hundreds of know-nothing weekend warriors at the track who'd do heavy lifting jobs like me and Caspar did for nothing, but Evelyn had still got me signed on an A-list team, and Luke liked me, and maybe he'd give me advice on how to parlay it all into something after the race. It really was my big second chance in life, just like I'd figured on the way East. It just didn't have Evelyn in it. It never had.

She could go ahead off in her precious doll house with sick little Logos if she wanted. I wasn't going in there with them. My faggot friend could take care of himself.

CHAPTER NINETEEN

But that night I was about to peel off my team shirt and call it a day when I heard a light shave-and-a-haircut knock on the door of my room. I went over to see what Mrs. Henderson wanted. Maybe I'd forgot to put the seat down again.

It wasn't Mrs. Henderson. It was Logos.

He looked up at me in a shy, friendly way, like we was still as good buddies as ever, like he hadn't noticed that I'd as much as pretended he wasn't there when I'd been walking with Luke.

I blinked at him, in the fuzzy way I looked at everything after a day at the track. It was pushing ten p.m., and I'd been at the track since six in the morning, and I'd have to be there to plug in the Valkyrie's oil warmer by seven the next day. About all I did at that house was conk out, take care of the three Ss and try not to watch the milk bead on Mrs. Henderson's moustache during breakfast. We didn't do a lot of visiting there.

"Can I come in?"

I mumbled something and stepped back. Logos shut the door behind him. He looked around for a minute, like he was tallying up the differences between our rooms. Then he helped himself to a seat on the carpet, with his shoulders against the wall and his legs crossed Indian-style in front of him.

I sat on the bed and waited. I was already starting to feel weird. I knew it had to be something important. He knew the hours I was putting in at the track. Just the same: here we was alone in my bedroom, and he'd shut the door. What would Mrs. Henderson think if she heard us in there together?

Logos got right to it:

"I'm a man on a mission, Hank. A third party well known to us both has delegated me to tell the rest of the story of a certain mysterious artifact. She feels unready to tell the story herself, but thinks you deserve to hear it."

Logos looked at me like he was ready to launch into one of his college tutor lectures. I tried to blink the fuzz out of my brain. For sure I was interested now.

Logos nodded, like I'd just told him to go ahead.

"Join me, please, frère Hankus, in recalling the famous photo of the cup at the Bonneville Salt Flats." Logos held up his hands, like he wanted me to look at a invisible photo in his fingers. "There is the streamliner, in the background. A young Mr. C at left. The thirty something financier of the streamliner, Perry Mclendon, at photo right. And in the center a bedraggled Indian hitchhiker of questionable origin, holding the notorious cup.

"This we know. We also have been led to believe that the Indian insisted her cup possessed supernatural power, that the powers could be unleashed by drinking from the cup, that this drinking was taboo in all but extraordinary circumstances, and that Perry McLendon taunted her by drinking from the cup anyway. He then supposedly strolled to the highway, thumbed a ride and disappeared from terra firma.

"Are we on the same page so far, Hank?"

"Sure. I mean, come on, Logos. We both read that story a hundred times."

Logos gave me a long, careful look. He turned his head and looked at the door, like he wanted to check that it was closed. When he went on his voice was a little lower, and I finally stopped worrying about what Caspar or Mrs. Henderson might think of me being alone in the room with him. He had something big to lay on me.

"Perry McLendon never drank from the cup, Hank, and he never left Bonneville. His bones lie beneath the bare hills surrounding the flats. He was killed there."

Logos sat with his back to the wall and watched me, and let what he'd said sink in. Somewhere far off toward Georgetown Road I heard a bunch of party-hardy types rolling by, tooting their horn. Good old Speedway, Indiana seemed to be getting a little busier every day. May 25 was coming up fast.

"How much do you know about Perry McLendon?" Logos asked.

I shrugged. "His name. And he was bucks up enough to bankroll a streamliner. That's all anybody knew about him."

Logos shook his head.

"Perry McLendon was a rapist. Two prior convictions. Claude didn't know that. I think a teenage speed enthusiast can be forgiven for not running a background check on a potential sponsor. Perry's predilections wouldn't have made a difference, either, if they hadn't picked up a female hitchhiker. They were two men traveling alone to the middle of nowhere to wring out a race car, and planning to return alone afterward.

"But they did pick up a female hitchhiker. Misty. She was quite drunk and practically homeless, and prattled incessantly about her Sioux heritage and grievances accumulated in her life on the reservation, and a cup that she insisted on dragging out of her back pack to show them, that she believed to be imbued with supernatural power.

"Still, she was young enough to awaken Perry's dark side, and he lobbied seriously for pulling off the highway to take turns with her. Claude refused. Indignantly. Real men didn't take advantage of women in such a state, he said. Not where he came from."

Logos shut his eyes and sat still for a minute, with his runty chest going up and down, up and down steady and slow under his t-shirt. It was like the hurt that Evelyn must have felt telling the story had rubbed off on him.

I didn't rush him. Finally he opened his eyes and went on.

"They reached the flats. It was too late to make a run, but they set up the camera on the tripod and took photos of the car, and then went to a spot near the hills to camp for the night.

"Claude awakened abruptly several hours later. Misty was screaming. Perry was trying to rape her. Claude intervened. The half-naked Perry lunged at him with a switchblade, but was shot from behind by Misty before he could end the living legend's career. Misty had a pistol in her backpack. She killed Perry Mc-Lendon."

Logos shut his eyes again, but kept on talking with them closed. "Claude wanted to go to the police. But Misty was hysterical. She had too many priors to think she would get a fair shake in a caucasian judicial system. She wanted Claude to help her cover it up. He agreed. He knew she was innocent. He'd seen it.

"They never found the cup, which Perry had cruelly hurled off far into the hills as his assault on Misty had gotten underway. But they did bury the body thoroughly and well, and Claude got away with his tale that Perry had abandoned them at the flats for a ride to parts unknown. Nobody missed Perry enough to pester the police to do more, and the police certainly didn't miss Perry on their own account. Case closed."

Logos opened his eyes. "So that, Hank, is how Perry 'disappeared,' and how Evelyn's ill-fated late husband knew where to go hunting for the cup. But there is still a large riddle to be accounted for. Why does Evelyn care so passionately for the thing? Why did she so adamantly resist all our efforts to make the cup public?"

I didn't say anything. Logos pressed his shoulders on the wall and slid up to his feet. He walked past me to the window and looked out it for a minute, at Mrs. Henderson's crab grass floral arrangements and the night shadows of the giant honking maple trees they've got all over the place back east, that I'd never seen much of in California.

Finally he looked back at me. He looked embarrassed.

"Claude and Misty did not go their separate ways after disposing of Perry. They sired a child. Misty was Evelyn's mother." Logos smiled. "A drunken floozy who cadged hand-outs from strangers, who probably would have slept with Perry McLendon willingly had he offered a pint of gin, and who was as shameful a testimony to the decline of a proud tribe and the withering effects of reservation life as could be found on the continent. She died when Evelyn was five. Evelyn remembers wondering why Mommy took naps on the floor when she was pre-school age. It is as raw and purple a part of her past as you can imagine, Hank. She can't talk about Misty without becoming hysterical, which is why I have been delegated to tell you the story in her stead.

"Misty was the last in the line of the Broken Stick Sioux. Now Evelyn is. Red Cloud was a Bad Face Sioux. But all Sioux revered generosity, and when Red Cloud returned with the cup from Washington, he bestowed it upon the clan of a warrior who had died in battle under his leadership. They were the Broken Stick. There is no account for how the cup got to Palo Duro or Walker Lake, but what Misty said, and what Evelyn believes, is that it was handed down among the Broken Stick, from generation to generation. Now she is the last one."

Logos looked apologetic. "Add to this the fact that the cup was the last thing given to her by her husband before his suicide. She has no intention at all of offering it up to the museum system of the Sioux's conquerors. The door shall remain firmly closed.

Not even Claude knows that she has the cup now. Only you and I and Evelyn know.

"And I," Logos sighed, "will do nothing to spread the word. Even if I betray the very spirit of scholarship by remaining silent. I feel indebted to Evelyn." Logos squinted at me. "And unless my many years of Hank Kruzenski observation have misled me, you will remain mum about the cup, too. You are far too chivalrous.

"That's the crop."

Logos shuffled back to the wall and sat on the floor again. He crossed his legs and rested his hands on his knees, like he was going to meditate, and then sat with his head against the wall and his eyes shut. We didn't say anything for awhile.

So that was the big scoop about the cup. I nodded to myself as I mulled over what he'd said. No wonder she was so defensive about it, and didn't want to give it to a museum. It was all she had from her mom and her suicide husband both. And she was part Sioux, too. Everything clicked.

I tried to picture her having a big weepy tell-all with Logos about it. Sometimes she'd just walk out of the garage for one of their buddy sessions, even when Luke and Eldrich and Nash was busting their hump on the Valkyrie. She could do it, 'cause she was the C's daughter. And she didn't give a tinker's damn how good her dad did in the race.

Well, I cared how he did. I got a little tight in the jaw thinking about it. Everyone on the team was pouring their hearts into that car. Maybe she had a gripe against her dad, but he was footing the bill for us to be there. Maybe it seemed a little wrong for her to go off fussing with Logos with the most glamorous race in the world coming up. Especially when she had the team shirt on.

So I chewed my cud on that for awhile, and then from the other end of the house I heard a floor board creak. That damn brontosaurus Caspar must have got up for a trip to the john. Pretty soon I heard the water pipes hum, and then a toilet flush.

Then it hit me: what if Caspar came tromping down to this end of the house to raid the fridge? He'd see the light under my door. He'd hear Logos talking, in my bedroom with me with the door closed. Logos and me alone.

I started to lunge up to get the door open. I felt almost panicky. Like a freeze frame from my worst nightmare I could just picture that ox-necked hulk leaning on a tool chest the next day and telling the crew what he'd heard from my room. With a nice, cruel glint in his beady eyes. And the way Luke and Eldridge would treat me after.

But then I realized that I didn't have any reason to open the door. So I froze, and glanced at Logos, and then I went to acting like something had taken a pinch at me from under the corner of the bed. Like that was the reason I'd stood up so fast.

After a few seconds more I heard the floor board creak again from the far end of the house. Then nothing.

"I swear this thing's got a busted spring in it," I said.

I picked up the corner of the mattress and looked under it, and sat back down and gave it a couple of pushes, like I was feeling for a spring sticking up. But it wasn't any good. As soon as I looked at Logos, I knew. He sat against the wall and watched me with a tired, sympathetic smile, like he could see all the way through me, and there wasn't any point in pretending he couldn't, and he wasn't even going to make a joke about what I'd just done, 'cause that might embarrass me. He was still too good a friend to put me on the hot seat, even if all I cared about after all my years of knowing him was that Caspar didn't think I was hanging out alone in my room with a fag.

"I haven't had a chance to catch up with you this past week, Hank," he said softly. "It looks like you've done well for yourself."

I shrugged. "Well, I'm on the crew now. They keep me busy."

I tried to say it casual, like nothing had happened, but my voice didn't come out right. I went to scratching a big imaginary itch on the back of my neck.

"Do you think it could turn into more? After the race?"

"Well, I don't know." Boy, did that imaginary itch need scratching. "Maybe. I hope so. Boss says I'm a good worker. If they need anybody after the race. That would be kind of a dream come true for me."

"It could happen, Hank. It could happen." Logos hesitated. "You know, it might be better if we keep a certain distance from each other in the days ahead. I'm not the most popular fellow at the Speedway, with Caspar and some other members of the crew. Rumors about my sexual identity issues seem to have spread. I don't want to jeopardize your chances."

"Come on, Logos. I've known you more than half my life. We don't have to play games like that."

But I didn't look at him while I said it, and now my voice sounded like when I'd complimented Mrs. Henderson on how Caspar had turned out. I stared at the floor. I could feel Logos watching me.

"I think it would be prudent, Hank. In fact, I don't think it would hurt if you were to pretend to ... dislike me a little. I wouldn't mind. Really. I'd understand."

"Come on, Logos. Don't say stuff like that."

I shook my head, and held up my hands like I didn't want to hear another word about it. But I still couldn't meet his eye, and I knew the relief showed in my face. He knew. If he just hadn't seen through me, I wouldn't have felt so ashamed. But he did.

• • •

This time it was Logos who looked at the door.

"Past my bedtime." He pushed himself to his feet. "And certainly past yours. You're the first to the track, aren't you, Hank?"

I said yeah, and he asked me about that, and that gave me a chance to yak about how I got there early to plug in the oil warmer, and the other stuff I did in the a.m. Logos nodded. He didn't care what I did at the garage. He'd just asked so I'd feel better while I explained it.

I finished, and he started to go, but then he stopped as he was about to turn the door knob.

"Hank, may I ask an unusually personal question?"

I didn't answer right away. An unusually personal question. But he didn't look like he had anything up his sleeve. He just looked curious.

"Well, sure. I mean, what am I going to say, Logos? No? How'm I going to tell you not to ask me something?"

Logos leaned his shoulder on the wall. He looked curious. That was all. Curious.

"Before I ask it, I want you to know that your answer will never leave this room. This is strictly between the two of us."

"Come on, Logos. Just ask me what you want to know."

"Are you attracted to Evelyn?"

. . .

Well, that floored me. I felt like Gorilla Monsoon had whizzed a medicine ball at my gut. My deepest hope and most private thought, and he'd shone a big flashlight on it. 'Cause he was curious.

I felt my face get all hot, and my jaw flap around like a sea bass. Then my inner Sir Laurence Olivier came out. I remember seeing Marlon Brando yak on the tube once about how everybody was an actor, even if they hadn't got to go to the big Stella Adler Acting Academy like him. Well, old Marlon would've loved to see me that night at Mrs. Henderson's. Totally proved his point.

I coughed up a fake-a-loo laugh, and tacked a grin on my mug, and tried to act like Logos had tried to hitch me with the Abominable Snowman.

"What?! Come on, Logos! Get your brain out of the microwave. She's a hippy. She don't shave her legs. Why do you want to say something that nutty?"

Logos nodded at me, friendly enough. But not like he believed me.

"Of course, I could always be mistaken. I apologize if that's so." He gave me a friendly, stubborn look. "You do act very differently when she's around, Hank. I'm sorry if I'm being more observant than you'd like me to be, but we've only known each other since elementary school. I haven't seen you so flummoxed in a female's company since your third grade crush on Karen Scheckter."

"Schlacker. Karen Schlacker. You can't even get her name right." I shook my head. Just a big har de har. "I don't know what you've been drinking or smoking, but you keep this up, you're going to be seeing Indianapolis from inside the local mental hospital. I mean, she's the C's daughter. I wipe the toilets around here. I'd have to be out of my gourd to get a crush on someone like that."

Logos nodded, but not like I'd convinced him. He promised again not to tell anyone, and said I might not want to be so sure of my assumptions about Evelyn. Then he went for the door again, and this time he followed through, and I was alone.

CHAPTER TWENTY

The next morning I made a big point of yakking it up with Logos at the breakfast table. I kept asking him if he wanted more juice, and practically knocked over the pitcher handing it to him. Logos looked startled. Caspar hadn't come out to eat yet, but he threw nervous looks at Mrs. Henderson, like maybe she'd fry me up like leftover hash browns for daring to be nice to him.

Fortunately, Mrs. Henderson was too distracted to notice. She'd got a bug up her fanny that I ought to be able to get her *Let's Make a Deal* tickets 'cause I lived in California. Like every state resident got Monty Hall's home phone number. She kept blowing Kool 100 smoke at me and gabbing about how Jesus would tell her what curtain to pick, and how Monte had given away an inflatable pool she'd wanted for her back yard.

At the track I plugged in the oil warmer and got the coffee going, and thought about what I'd say to Boss and Luke and Eldrich when they came in. Even if I had to stand on a stack of tires to do it. Logos was my friend. Everybody in Prado Diablo knew how generous and charitable he was, and treated him with respect. Maybe he had a disease now. People got diseases, didn't they? All he needed was a good psychiatrist, and he'd be slobbering over Miss Hurst Golden Shifter like the rest of us.

But a garage at Gasoline Alley isn't the best place for that kind of speech making, at least when the Indy 500 is just days away and the guy who wants to talk is head floor sweeper. Boss and Luke and Eldrich was already yakking about the Valkyrie before they shut the horse stall doors behind them. The rule change a couple of years earlier had cut way down on the size of the rear wing, but Boss thought they could still jigger the wing they had to make the rear end more stable. So they got right to work on that, and bustled around the Valkyrie like bees over a flower bed. Nobody was interested in the floor sweeper's opinions on Logos. Boss didn't even say Hi to me until he gave me the latest list of stuff to pick up in town in the C van.

•   •   •

And maybe it had just been fated to be that way. Things might have shook out a lot different if I'd made my little speech, and stood up for Logos. But I didn't. I got sent out before I could have my say, and while I was running those errands I saw something that checked me into the boards on whether I wanted to make that speech at all.

It happened while I was stuck in line at the drive thru at the Rancher Pete's over on Lafayette. Eldrich liked the steak fries there. Maybe one of Rancher's hired hands had called in sick, or maybe the biddy in the Rambler ahead of me thought she was ordering onion rings flambé from the Chateaubriand, for all the time she took.

One way or the other, I was stuck in line. I spun the tuner knob on the dash radio, and hitched my boot up on the van engine cover, and over the roofs of the cars ahead of me in the drive-thru line admired the scrumptious scenery of beautiful Lafayette Road, which is poised to be a major tourist destination by the next Ice Age. And maybe it was because I had time and was bored that I got to noticing a clapped-out Falcon parked by itself on the vacant lot next to the drive-thru, and the three guys sitting inside it.

They were about my age. They looked like HM&F workers. Maybe there was a factory out there somewhere, and they was on break. I tried to read the company logo on the driver's baseball cap. He was slouched low in the Falcon, with his dirty blond hair pulled back from his ears and fanned over his t-shirt. He was grinning about something, and then I saw his buddy's hand come over from the back seat with the smoking roach in it, and the driver take the joint and toke up. A minute later I saw the glint of a bottle and a whiskey label.

Just like HM&F. Exactly like HM&F, and Tyler. Getting stoned on break.

The biddy in the Rambler finally got her onion rings flambé. I put the van in gear and rolled forward, but I still had two cars ahead of me. By then I had some serious bad memories coming up and was ready to hop the retainer to get out of there, but I couldn't. I didn't have to look at those guys, but I knew I was going to.

They had the Falcon facing toward Lafayette. That's just how Tyler would have parked it. So they could keep an eye out for the law. If a cop car rolled by they'd hold the bottle and the roach under dash level and sit like statues, and then when it was gone they'd snicker and rib each other like they was these oh so cool rakehell playboy stoners, and living the fast lane life in Indy 'cause they knew how to put one over on the man, and wasn't just three stone cold loser loadies, which was what everybody outside that Falcon sized them up as in two seconds, the cops included. They were still young enough to put on the big act to themselves. Maybe in a few more years their guts would hang over their biker belt buckles, and all the booze they'd drunk would've parched the young look out of their faces, and then they'd look like losers even to themselves. Tyler had been headed that way. I had, too.

It was ten more long minutes that I was stuck in that line watching those guys before my turn came up. By the time I met Miss Rancher Pete and paid for my order, something in me had changed.

Maybe it doesn't seem like any big deal to you. Maybe you've handled your life better than I had, and never got that far behind the curve. But I'd as good as sat in the car with those three, and lived that life. If the Man Upstairs had wanted to take me by the scruff of the neck and get me to look at something hard, and slosh it around a little before I swallowed, He'd done a real good job.

This was my big second chance in life. I'd better know it for what it was, and keep my eye on looking good to the C Team.

Palling around with Logos wasn't going to help my cause any. He'd just have to row his own canoe for awhile.

•   •   •

That night at eight I was cleaning up by myself in front of the horse stall doors, and wondering why everybody on the team had split earlier than usual, when I spotted a trim-looking dude strolling up on Gasoline Alley. I didn't ID who it was until he came up into the pool of light from our garage.

The man. He was wearing jeans and a brown leather bomber jacket, like he was fixing to hit the Speedway saloons. I'd got more used to seeing him around, being on the team and all, but I still felt a little spark of awe.

I put down my broom and got ready to give him my best guess about where Boss was. I figured that was who he wanted to see.

But what the C said was, "Just the man I was looking for, Kruiser" like he'd expected me to be exactly where I was. "Time to lock up this barn and hit the road. We got things to do and people to see."

Ten minutes later, I was hustling to catch up with the living legend on the way to the C Team van. He'd given me time to wash off the worst of the grit and lock things up for the night. I was still wearing my work duds.

I asked him if we was going to meet someone.

"In due time, Kruiser, in due time. Mysteries await." He snapped his fingers and held out his palm. "The keys, señor."

I handed over the van keys. The C climbed into the cockpit and latched up his seat belt, and looked at me dirty until I put mine on too. I felt weird. I'd never rid shotgun in the C van before. I wasn't used to getting chauffeured around by famous race car drivers. Maybe tomorrow Bobby Unser would be waiting in front of Mrs. Henderson's to give me a lift to the track.

The C shot me a look. "Are you comfortable with me driving, Kruiser?"

I said sure.

"If you're not 100% comfortable and secure, we can let you take the wheel. I don't know if I can handle this kind of horsepower."

I said I'd take a chance. Then I just looked through the windshield in a daze, while the C motored the van through the maze inside the Speedway that let us out on Georgetown Road, and headed south to West 16th Street. Maybe I didn't have any idea where we was going or what we was doing, but I figured I could sit tight and find out. If he got us in serious trouble, at least it'd make the airwaves, and Mom would see it on TV.

•   •   •

The C spent the next two hours reminding Indianapolis that he was in town. Maybe he'd half intended to pick me up and drive somewhere straight off, but he wouldn't have been the C if he hadn't been a major extrovert. As far as he was concerned, the whole city was just another branch of his fan club. One thing led to another.

First up on West 38th we passed an auto parts store, and there was some innocent bystander lugging out a foreign brand muffler kit. Oh, no. That wouldn't do. Treason in progress. The C pulled the van into the strip mall lot and blocked the bystander's car, and jumped out and asked Bystander just what the hey he was trying to pull, and of course Bystander thought somebody must've dosed the Indy water supply and got him hallucinating, 'cause since when does a major celebrity interrupt your shopping trip 'cause you bought a made-in-Taiwan muffler? Come on. Then the C actually yanked the box out of Bystander's hands and tromped into the auto parts store to demand a refund, and pretty soon there was a big crowd gathering, 'cause even in Indianapolis in the month of May people don't expect to see one of the world's winningest racers kicking up a hullabaloo in a bohunk parts store.

After awhile the C jumped back in the van and with all these Hoosiers crowded around the front got on the CB radio. "Breaker, breaker, this is the tomcat, I've got Hank Kruzenski with me, the Hank Kruzenski who made a fool out of Hard Charging Harry. You want Kruiser's autograph, you'd better get out to the Denny's parking lot in ten minutes, or you'll lose out." Then he drove us out to the Denny's. We had a caravan by then, 'cause a bunch of the cars from the parts store followed, and some drivers who must've heard him on the CB, too.

We had close to fifty cars in the Denny's parking lot. The C was telling everybody to get Hank Kruzenski's autograph, and stomping around and BSing with them about their cars, and when some galoot said he could break a 13 second E.T. in his 'Stang on street tires the C said he wouldn't run that 'Stang against a Greyhound bus with a empty gas tank, and they could go right out to the drag strip on Sunday and race the 'Stang for pinks against the C-team van with no handicap, and maybe the C would pull half his spark plug wires to give the galoot a advantage. And the galooot said Suuuuure, and then a squad car pulled up, because by then nobody could get into Denny's to get a patty melt, and the C accused the cop of rooting for Johnny Rutherford. But the cop just grinned, and the C said we'd break it up, and as they piled out of there people clapped the man on the shoulder and said they was rooting for him, and I knew damn well they was now, too.

Even if they'd been rooting for someone else before. He did that to you. I'd only been on the streets with him for one evening, and look at all the folks he'd charmed, who'd go home and tell their buddies how they'd met the C, and who'd never forget that moment for the rest of their lives.

. . .

A little before 10:30, the C parked the van on a ranch-houses-and-mowed-lawns street that looked like it had got baked up in the same mold as Mrs. Henderson's block near the Speedway. It was quiet. We'd disbursed the big caravan. I could hear traffic droning on the main drag a half mile away, but that was all.

The C was done horsing around. He shut off the ignition and pushed the driver's seat back, like he was ready to put in a big P.I. stake-out. I looked through the windshield at the mostly dark windows of the houses ahead of us, and a streetlight glinting through the maple leaves a half block away.

"Is someone going to be meeting us here?" He still hadn't told me anything.

The C shook his head. He flicked his forefinger at a house about fifty yards away.

"You see that old green Nova in the driveway up yonder, Kruiser? With the light on in the window above it?"

I said I did. The Nova was a beater. Even with the mag wheels. Maybe $500 in the Recycler.

The C nodded. "Pretty soon, that light's going to go out. Everybody in the house'll have turned in by then. Then you're going to take this ..."

He fished something out of his bomber jacket and handed it to me. A car key.

"... this key, and walk over to that Nova, and Kruiser, you're going to steal that car, and follow me in this van out to a garage on West 10th Street. Got that? Then some of our C Team volunteers — including you, Kruiser; you just volunteered yourself, thank you — are going to slave on that Nova all night, and have it back here before the owner goes out to start it tomorrow morning. What do you think of them apples?"

The C was looking at me real serious. I was starting to wonder about that weed I'd smoked in my HM&F days. I'd never heard of marijuana causing flashbacks.

It didn't make any sense. He was a contender for the Indy 500. Now he wanted me to steal a dial-a-wreck for him. I didn't think A.J. Foyt or Bobby Unser was out stealing junker cars.

"You think I'm ready for the funny farm, don't you, Kruiser?"

He kept looking at me dead serious. I tried to smile.

The C nodded at the house.

"A high school junior name of Treat Scott lives in that house. That's his car. He's an Ask the Wizard subscriber, just like you. He's been on the gold medallion level since he was a pup. But Kruiser, that boy's got something else that you and me never had to deal with. You know what leukemia is?"

I nodded.

"It's a vicious bastard of a disease, Kruiser. It gets in your bones, and it eats at them, and it tries to kill you from the inside out. He's got the fight of his life ahead to whip that bastard, and there ain't a grunt in Pendleton who's ever fought a bigger one. But he's going to whip it, Kruiser. He Is Going To."

The C leaned in close and rapped out the words with his forefinger poking little taps on my arm. "He. Is. Going. To. He's going to have some tough days ahead when he thinks that leukemia's got him licked, but he's going to hold the line and not give that bastard one centimeter, and beat it, and when that leukemia's lying dead at his feet he'll be a bigger man than either of us put together.

"Now, I'm not a doctor. I can't help him chase that cancer out of his bloodstream. But I've got some friends who know a thing or three about cars, and I think I can give that Nova a nice unscheduled tune-up while he's catching his forty winks tonight. And you're going to help me."

The C scrunched lower in the driver's seat and propped his cowboy boot on the dash next to the radio. We was quiet for a minute. It felt like we was high school buddies who'd gone out cruising together. In the light from the street lamp I could see a crinkly line of scar tissue next to his nose, that I'd never been close enough to notice before. It looked like someone had smeared plaster over a drywall crack and forgot to sand it down.

The C cocked an eye at me. "You're looking at my beauty marks, Kruiser."

"Sorry."

The C tapped the scar with his fingernail.

"I got this one in the 1,000 Lakes Rally up in Finland. You ever heard of that one?

I shook my head. The C held out his arm and moved his hand up and down, like he had the shakes.

"The Rally of the Thousand Jumps. That's what they call it. I felt like I was racing a damn pogo stick. I went over one berm, maybe I had some brain fade from pulling woodies for those Scandinavian chicks. The next thing I know, I got about fifty tons of Finnish pine tree standing smack dab straight ahead. I yelled at that tree to get the hell out of the way of an American and go grow someplace else. I guess it didn't speak English."

The C yawned and started to stretch, but didn't make it all the way. He froze and winced and held his back for a second, and then settled slow on the seat again.

"That's what I get for telling tales about my sheet time. My creaky old back bones start acting up again. I got hurts on my hurts, Kruiser. This sport's hard on a man's body."

He scrunched around slow on the seat until he got a good bite on it that didn't bother his back, and propped his boot back up on the dash, and folded his hands across his stomach. We didn't talk for awhile. I looked out at the Nova and wondered about whoever Treat Scott was, and thought how tough it must be to have leukemia in high school. I knew the track had put on a big walkathon earlier for an ex-Indy driver who'd become a quadriplegic after an accident. Bob Hurt. I hadn't figured there'd be anything else like that.

After awhile the C said, "Kruiser, how was it you met my little girl again? I'm soft on the details."

I started to tell about the cup, but then remembered what Logos had said the night before: not even her dad knew. So I stuck to telling about the Vulcan of Speed cylinder heads, and how I'd met her at the swap meet next to the Fiesta.

The C chuckled. "'Cylinder halves.' Is that what she called them?"

"That's what she called them."

"Like she didn't know what they were. And she was the one hid them for me."

The C yawned and slid his boot around on the dash. I looked at the smear of dirt I'd get to wipe off the next day.

"That's one fine young lady I've got," he said drowsily. Like he was talking to himself. "Don't smoke, don't drink much. Don't respect her old man, but her old man don't deserve it. Now, she's going through this hippy phase. All her friends out in Peoples Republic of Berkeley look like they shacked up with Ho Chi Minh. But we're going to whup that, too." He squinted at me. "You're a decent start, Kruiser. You look all-American to me. I'm glad to see she's buddies with you."

"Thank you, sir."

"And we got plans for you. Don't you forget it." He yawned again. "After the race is over, you're coming back to HQ with us, win, place or show. You make a good impression on TV. Phil thinks we can make some money off you. This is a brand new start in life for you, Kruiser. You can bank on it."

He looked sleepily out at the Nova, like he hadn't said anything more special than what kind of weather they was having in Texas. I felt my heart pounding so bad I could hear my own pulse.

You're coming back to HQ with us. That's what he'd said. I'd heard him. As much as I'd hoped and dreamed and wondered since I'd got there. And now he'd put it into words. *He'd* called it a brand new start in life. *He'd* said so.

"'Course, we got a problem with your little fairy friend to take care of first."

•   •   •

Outside a little wind kicked up, like maybe a storm might be coming in. It made a wh-ooo sound that rattled my window and made the maple boughs sway in front of the street lamp, so the silvery light faded in and out of shadow on the C's face.

He was watching me. Real quiet and steady and serious, and with all his brains showing. Like he didn't want any doubt that he might be joking.

I felt my stomach twist around. I started to talk, 'cause I thought I should say something, but my mouth just opened and closed, and no words came out. I swallowed hard and looked at the dash away from him.

A brand new start in life. He'd said it himself. If I just did it his way. *A brand new start.*

After awhile the C went on:

"I run a business here, Kruiser. Maybe the public doesn't see it that way, and maybe I don't especially want them to, but it is. Phil's right about that. I can go gallivanting around the globe and play Santa Claus to people like Treat Scott all I want, but at the end of the day I've got to pay my bills, and that means the money's got to keep rolling in. You understand me?"

I moved my chin a half inch and looked down at the dash. All these good thoughts about Logos was popping into my brain, but I didn't say any of them. I thought of the three loadies I'd seen that morning next to the drive thru. *A brand new start in life.* Like the C team was holding me high up on a bridge, and if I just went with the program I'd get to stay on the bridge and never have to hang with anybody like Tyler again.

"Luke and Eldrich don't like having him around. Maybe they're too professional to say anything about it, but they don't. It's bad enough they have to put up with my daughter. Now Kruiser, I can take this van and pick up about two dozen guys who know as much as you and Caspar before I drive a block on West 16th, but I can't pick up mechanics like Luke and Eldrich. They don't grow on trees, and I need them to win. If they're not happy, maybe next season they sign up with my competition. I wish Bobby and A.J. and Johnny and Mario all the second place finishes in the world. But I want the checkered flag for me. I don't want my best talent pulling a wrench for them. That's one reason."

The C leaned toward me and held out his hand with one finger down. Damn if he didn't have a big scar on his hand, too. I didn't know where he'd got that one.

He held down a second finger.

"Number two: I've got a public image to protect. Maybe you think it's as casual and natural as can be, but Phil knows it's not, and I do, too. A Indy 500 victory means at least three times as much in endorsement money to me as it does to anybody else. We're just way smarter on the promotion side than they are. It's a fact. And just what do you think it's going to do to that public image if some fairy newspaper on Fire Island tells the world that Mr. C's got a pansy on the race team? You tell me.

"D Day's coming up on this, Kruiser. That boy's not sticking around much longer. Get ready for it."

He gave me a chance to answer. I can't pretend he didn't. For at least a half minute more we just sat there quiet in the front seat, with the feel of his eyes steady on my face while I looked at the cowhide tip of his boot on the dashboard. I thought of things I could say to defend Logos, things that was respectful and true and that he couldn't have held it against me for saying. But I couldn't make myself talk. I kept picturing those three losers in the parking lot. It was like if I fell off the bridge, I'd have to hunt up my HM&F timecard and get in the Falcon with them.

And then the light in the window over the Nova went out, and the C told me it was time to get to business.

•   •   •

I guess he'd got some car dealer insider to order up a key for that Nova. I didn't think you could call up the dealership when you wanted to steal a car, but I wasn't on a first name basis with auto corporation VPs, either.

The key slid right in the door lock. I climbed in quiet-like and wiggled the key in the ignition, and that funky old inline six fired right up.

The lights in the house stayed off. By the time I rolled out of the driveway, the C had the van turned around. I followed.

•   •   •

The garage was way out on West 10th, almost to Chapel Glen. Nick's Auto Service. I don't know who Nick was, but he'd donated his shop and his crew. The shop lights were on, and the roller doors was up. Luke and Eldrich were there, sipping the late night coffee right alongside the crew from Nick's. They'd never mentioned a word about going out. I knew any Indy team had to be ready to pull an all-nighter, but I'd sure never heard of doing it to spruce up a high school kid's car. Even if the kid had cancer.

They motioned me onto the lift, and then for the next six solid hours they humped it on that car. Like they was all on the engineering staff at General Motors, like they knew every bolt and mount and nut in that Nova as good as the socks and shorts in their dressers. They gutted it. New engine, new tranny, new front and rear end, new brakes. What I'd rolled in with couldn't have chased a Checker cab in a car wash. By the time the sun cleared the tree line and Luke gave me thumbs up to back out of the garage, that Nova was ready to take on a rally Corvette on a SCCA race course. A night of team work and totally transformed, and the only clue on the outside was the narrowed rear end.

Treat Scott came out carrying his school books under the arm of his windbreaker, and wearing a Cincinnati Reds cap to cover the chemo work. A couple of TV crews were out there to meet him, and so was yours truly. The C wanted me on TV again.

Treat looked a little taken aback to see a big media fest in front of his house. One of the reporters walked up with the microphone cord tangled around his leg, and asked Treat about being an Ask the Wizard subscriber, and what he wanted to improve in his Nova. Which gave them an excuse to keep the cameras on him while he got in and turned the key.

Well, that loaded-for-bear small block didn't fire up like the inline six he'd shut down the night before. You should've seen that kid's face. Like a rhino had charged out of the dash at him.

They got it on tape, and I knew it'd be all over the news that night, and I knew while I was catching a lift out to the track in that news van that I'd find Luke and Eldrich hard at work on the Valkyrie when I got there, 'cause the 500 was around the corner and they'd just have to make do without sleep. That was what pro race teams did. They was a great bunch of guys, and it was a privilege to work with them.

But every time I thought of my old friend Logos I felt sick and ashamed, and couldn't make the thoughts lie still. D Day was coming up, all right, just like the C had said.

CHAPTER TWENTY-ONE

D Day wound up hitting on Tuesday, May 20 at the big Knights of Corydon banquet. For a couple of days after we finished that Nova, I almost convinced myself it didn't have to happen. The crew might not have been nuts about Logos, but he didn't come around that much. Maybe everything would stay on a low ugly simmer til race day, and afterward they could shoot one last, frosty look at the weird little queer from the land of fruits and nuts, and exchange some awkward handshakes, and we'd go our separate ways. I'd march on to my great new life as a C Team member. I wouldn't have to betray my friend.

But that wasn't what Zeus had in store for us. I guess he'd got bored with floating in his slingshot dragster over Indy all day, listening to the C mutter about Logos and watching Caspar stare dagger-eyed meanies into the back of Logos' head, and waiting for a knock-down-drag-out that hadn't happened. Maybe sometimes those crotchety old Greek gods of yore like to see the donkey dung really slam into the fan blades.

So maybe the big bearded one leaned in and spritzed a nice gob of lighter fluid on the coals, to make the flames shoot up and dance through the grill, and get that barbecue ready to cook up the D Day T-Bone he wanted.

Maybe that's why the Valkyrie hit the wall on Bump Day.

•   •   •

Bump Day was the last day for the fifty odd entrants who'd paid their team admission fee to try to qualify for the starting field. May 10 Pole Day, May 11, May 17 and then Bump Day, May 18: those were the four days for qualifying. If Rick Muther ran a 181.726 four lap average to make the last row on the 17th, and Tom Bigelow aced him out with a 181.86 on Bump Day, old Rick got to pack up the trailer and head back to SoCal.

The C had qualified. He didn't have to run. But the Valkyrie still wasn't handling. It was a bear in turn 3, 'cause that's where the wind was bad, and a bear in turn 2, 'cause that's where the track humped over the pedestrian tunnel. Really, though, it was bad on every corner. Over and over they'd changed the stagger and the corner weights and the caster and camber and toe-in, and jiggered the wing angle, and talked it up with the Goodyear reps, and over and over every change had made something else go wrong.

They had that Valkyrie out on the track every day of the second practice week. Everybody kept on his game face, and talked how they was going to get it whipped, even if they didn't figure out the problem til the last minute.

• • •

Bump Day was wild and hairy, with a whole slew of drivers trying to get into the field. But by mid-day it was pushing eighty degrees, and nobody wanted to try to qualify with the asphalt that hot. After Eldon Rasmussen got flagged off, they opened up the track for awhile for regular practice.

The C team took the Valkyrie right out there. By now every race fan in Indianapolis knew what an ordeal they were going through with that car, but the team was hanging in there, and so was the C Faithful. The C and Boss was like the dynamic duo. They'd pull it off.

Well, if you were in the stands that day, or saw the clips on the tube, you know what happened in turn 3. The C said later it had felt like somebody had ripped the whole track out from under the back end like a piece of carpet. WHAM: a mini Fort Knox worth of race car slammed bang into the wall, with the whole right side of the Valkyrie sprayed over the track like pieces a kid dropped out of a Mattel model, and a nice oily spin out into the grass. It took clean-up almost an hour to wipe up the mess and open up the track.

• • •

The man was fine. Not a scratch. He got his mandatory ambulance ride over to the med services building, and had his one liners ready for the TV crews when he walked out. But I knew from the faces of everyone on the team what that crash meant when they hauled the busted-up Valkyrie back to Gasoline Alley.

It was over.

Not technically. The C was fine. They still had their spot on the starting grid on race day; a crash in practice didn't change that. They could put the Valkyrie back together again. They could still take the checkered flag.

But even their dumb gofer Hank knew it wasn't going to go down that way.

Because the track was closed now, see. Bump Day was over. No more qualification runs. No more practice runs. No more anything. The teams would get two hours, that was all, two sixty minute hours on Carb Day on Thursday, May 22 to do a little show for the fans and make a last check of the equipment. That wasn't a fraction of enough time. They'd had two solid weeks to wring out that Valkyrie, and still hadn't fixed the handling problems. How was they supposed to rebuild half the damn car and get it right now, with only two hours to test out the damn thing before the May 25 race?

They wasn't going to, was the answer. Unless they fell into a nice, fat Luck Puddle, and found the problem while they put the Valkyrie back together that they'd missed for two weeks straight. Which wasn't going to happen, either. Maybe the Cinderella team can come from behind if they're down three touchdowns in the third quarter. They can't if they're zip-to-forty-nine in the fourth. It was over.

•　　•　　•

About four hours after the crash, Logos swung by looking for Evelyn.

The team had the Valkyrie up on the set up pad by then. Or what was left of the Valkyrie. The C was hunched over the car right alongside Luke and Eldrich and Nash, talking about the parts they could salvage while they hacked and pried and unbolted the pieces off the mangled frame. Maybe he wanted to inspire them. He'd nailed the wall at 180 plus, and he'd still pull a wrench with his crew.

Logos had to let himself in. It was hot as a bastard in there, but no way they wanted to prop open the doors for a breeze and have to deal with looky-loos. Not now, not with their race day chances fresh shot to hell. I could see the sweat beading on the back of Luke's neck while he slaved over that car. We all knew we was pulling another all-nighter. Boss and the C didn't have to tell us.

Logos shut the door behind him, and looked around, and said he'd come in search of Evelyn.

That was all. Just something light and halfway joking-sounding. But it didn't come out right in that hot garage, with everybody sweating over that car, and knowing that they'd be there all night. It sounded like he was asking some other triple PhD college professor to stop playing around with the sewer workers and skip off to the opera with him.

Nobody said anything for a few seconds. Eldrich blinked at Logos with the sweat dripping off his nose. The C wouldn't look at him.

Finally I told Logos that Evelyn had already split for the day. Logos left.

"Must be an art gallery opening he wants her to go to," Luke said.

He wiped the matted hair off his forehead and tried to grin like he thought it was funny. But he didn't, and nobody else did, either.

I knew then. If I didn't know it from what Luke had said, then I knew it from how Eldrich had stared at Logos, and how the C wouldn't even look at him, and how Caspar was still glaring at the space Logos had been standing in, like Fidel Castro himself had dropped by to burn an American flag on the garage floor. The C had been right. We wouldn't make it to the race without a blow-up. Not after the crash, not with tempers as frayed as they was. D Day was coming up, and the fork in the road with it. I'd have to choose.

CHAPTER TWENTY-TWO

The Knights of the Corydon banquet where D Day hit was named after the Battle of Corydon, when 400 Indiana legionnaires duked it out with about 2,500 Confederate cavalry during the Civil War. The legionnaires lost — and you probably would, too, if there was six of them for every one of you — but it was the only battle ever fought in Indiana, so the Knights made a big deal out of it. First, they'd honored the surviving legionnaires. Then they'd honored the sons of the survivors, when all the original legionnaires had keeled over. Then the grandsons of the survivors. And so on.

Now the big annual dinner was mostly an excuse for a bunch of old geezers to get drunk. But they had lots of money and owned a humongous lodge in the old Northside district, and they'd hosted their yearly Month of May banquet there for as long as anybody could remember. At least half a dozen racers turned out for it. There'd be eight million courses of food, and waiters dashing around in tuxedos, and sexpot Damsels of Corydon who handed out awards and flirted with the geezers, and all the tables in the lodge banquet hall full up. Then the Knights would hunt up the big time racers like the C during the meal, and ask them for autographs between courses of rubber chicken.

The C had promised a long way back that he'd show in '75, 'cause he'd missed the last two banquets, and Evelyn had promised a long way back that she'd put on a dress and go with him, and got Logos to promise that he'd come, too. It was all set up. Like somebody had painted a fat bulls eye on the side of the lodge hall, and told Zeus where to stage his D-day.

•   •   •

At 6:30 p.m. there we were, at our own C Team round table near the stage and the podium, one big unhappy family. The C was close to the main walkway, so the Knights wouldn't push the other diners into their roquefort dressing when they came over for autographs. The Boss was on his right and Evelyn was on his left, mostly looking bored, and then Luke and Eldrich and Logos, in the Monkey Wards suit I'd been sent out to buy for him that morning.

Logos didn't wear the suit real good. I'd had to shop in the boy's department to find one near his size. His shoulders was ready to bust out of the jacket, and the cuffs rode up practically to his elbows, and his neck looked like a chunk of PVC pipe with a bump for his Adam's apple. He'd tried to comb his hair formal, but it had come out looking like two hunks of Brillo dunked in a lacquer tank. He looked like a mixed race Howdy Doody

They'd told me to get a suit for myself, too. I barely knew how to tie a necktie, but there I sat, with my coat cuffs practically dragging in the butter plate, and that tie like a noose around my neck.

Like a noose literally. I didn't have a real positive feeling about how the night was going to turn out. I could practically see Zeus up above, clicking his barbecue tongs and knotting a 'Don't shoot the cook' apron over his flowing Greek robes, and getting ready to make the sparks fly when he flipped the T-Bone on the grill. Or maybe he'd just flip Hank on the grill and fry up some Kruzenski Kabobs instead, and my second-chance-in-life dreams along with them.

I didn't like how Caspar was looking at Logos. At all.

Maybe he was like a big savage Doberman that craves to rip the jugular out of every stranger on the sidewalk, but knows he'll get put to sleep if he doesn't get the okay first. The uglier the team's mood had gotten, the uglier Caspar had acted toward Logos. Like now he knew he could get away with it.

At least I hadn't had to buy him a suit. Even if the one he had was too small. He sat across the table with that massive Big Ten defensive tackle neck bulging over the top of his collar, and his shoulders and chest ready to rip through the coat, chomping on his steak so I could see his meaty jaw muscles going, like I was watching a grizzly bear eat.

He was staring at Logos. Just glaring at him openly now, like the banquet had fired up his Hoosier pride, and it made him sick to see some tree hugging homo sitting in the same room with portraits of Bill Vukovich and Mauri Rose and the other great racers of yesteryear. Like it was such a outrage he wondered how he'd stood it as long as he had, and maybe now they'd take the leash off, and let him do something about it.

And he had his friends with him. The whole table behind Caspar was football players. I didn't know if they was teammates of his or if some other college varsity team had signed up for the big banquet, but they was all extra large-sized young guys who didn't fit their suits good and maybe heaved around farm tractors for work-outs instead of medicine balls, and looked like they was more interested in slobbering over the Damsels than in anything else at the dinner. I'd already seen Caspar leaning back in his chair to socialize with a couple of them, and what I'd spotted then had worried me plenty.

While Caspar talked to them, two of the guys had turned to stare at Logos. Not in a friendly way. Like they was sizing up a doe before they tucked their rifle butts on their shoulders and lined it up in their sights.

And then real quick from that table, almost drowned out in the clinking of silverware and the chatting and chuckling and the scraping of chairs on the hundred year old lodge floor, I heard somebody say:

"Fag."

•   •   •

"Knights of the Corydon. Knights and guests. Your attention, please."

At the podium a salesman-of-the-month looking Knight in a wide tie and a paisley suit was leaning over the microphone and clinking a knife on a drinking glass. The conversation died down. Evelyn swung her chair around. The three race fans hovering by the C dropped to one knee, so they wouldn't block anybody's view while the C finished autographing their banquet programs.

The Damsels stopped fluttering their fake eyelashes at the randy old Knights and came up to the stage. I thought maybe we'd have to sit through a Can Can dance, but all they did was sit in a line behind the podium. They were wearing medieval type costumes, with a lot more leg than King Arthur ever saw and at least as much cleavage.

Salesman glanced at a index card, and then he leaned over the podium and swept his eyes over the crowd the way preachers do when they want to make sure everybody ponies up for the collection box.

"The Indianapolis 500," he said, "is a spectacle. The Indianapolis 500 is a performance, and a pageant, and a show. But it is also a tradition. The thirty-three brave men who will take the green flag only five days hence shall race among the ghosts of the giants who raced before them. And what giants they were!"

The C finished up one autograph, and the fan whispered thanks and shook his hand and almost tripped into Boss while he crab-walked back to his table. Boss didn't notice. He kept frowning over a sketch he was making on the back of his placemat, like maybe he'd finally get the Valkyrie's chassis sorted out before they brought out dessert.

But Luke and Eldrich wasn't interested in the sketch. If George Bignotti had seen the C Team's mechanics look the other way while the great Boss Maryland did a chassis sketch, he might have told his drivers not to worry about the big green car come race day. A bad sign. Luke and Eldrich was talking quiet to each other and looking around the lodge hall, like the banquet was a big job fair, and they could check out the teams that might hire them next.

"Louis Meyer. Wilbur Shaw. Mauri Rose. From its earliest days, the Speedway attracted some of our country's most daring and colorful sportsmen. Tonight, our first speaker will share a few memories of a racer still personally remembered by some of the competitors in our audience tonight: that great Indianapolis champion of 1958, Jimmy Bryan."

"Jimmy Bryan!" the C snorted. He nudged Boss. "Lordie, am I glad I don't have to fight for no checkered flags with that big bastard anymore."

Evelyn whispered "shush" at him. Salesman started telling us about Jimmy Bryan, whoever he was. Then from the corner of my eye I noticed a goofy old Knight picking his way toward our table.

The Knight whispered in Evelyn's ear. Evelyn's eyes opened wide, and then she let out a groan and shook her head. Goofy waddled away from us.

"The name of Abner Keen," Salesman was saying, "may not be a household word. But he is one of our very own Knights, and had the privilege of working closely with Jimmy Bryan during two of his championship seasons."

"I have to take a phone call from Berkeley," Evelyn whispered. She pushed her chair back. "Our basement is flooding. Just what I need." She looked at her dad. "Where's the office here?"

The C flicked a forefinger at the ceiling.

"Straight up."

"I might be awhile," Evelyn said.

She left. I watched the hem of her special occasion dress waving around her knees, and Knights pushing their chairs in so she could ease past them. Something twisted in my gut while I watched her go. It took me a second to figure out why.

Caspar. Caspar and Logos. Evelyn wasn't in Caspar's way anymore.

"Let's give a warm welcome to our own Abner Keen," Salesman said. Then I clapped because that's what everybody around me was doing.

•   •   •

Abner Keen turned out to be a lanky hillbilly type with a lantern jaw and about a half a tube of Brylcreem on his gray Elvis 'do. It looked like he'd borrowed a suit coat two sizes too big for him. Then he got closer to the podium, and I saw better. He didn't have any right arm in there. He was holding his notes in the hand he had left, and waved them at us while he waited for Salesman to adjust the mike up.

Abner gave a fake dirty old man look at the Damsels behind him, which got some of the audience snickering. He stepped up to the podium.

"I'd blow you all a kiss," Abner said, "but I don't have much to blow it with." He swung the empty coat sleeve at us. "I got this puppy ripped off at the socket up in Puke Hollow at Langhorne. Anybody here miss Langhorne Speedway?"

He leaned across the podium and leered. I guess he knew his audience. Half the Knights groaned. The C rolled his eyes at the ceiling.

"Langhorne! Oh, God, Langhorne. Come on, Abner, I got to digest my food. Don't say Langhorne to me while I got dinner on my stomach."

Abner slapped his empty coat sleeve. "I hit one of those ruts broadsliding into turn one, and the next thing I knew I was airborne. We didn't have any roll cages then." He wiggled his coat sleeve at us. "Guess what I landed on."

The Knights did some sympathetic clucking. Behind Abner the Damsels glanced at each other, then figured they'd better cluck, too. The C looked at Luke and Eldrich and swung his arm in a wide loop over the table, like he was cranking a handle.

"Used to broadslide all the way around that bastard course," the C said. "And you couldn't see. Most dangerous track on the circuit."

Abner flashed a crooked grin. "'Course, I didn't need my right arm anyway. All I ever did with it was write checks and abuse myself. It saved me money and got me in good with my preacher."

The Knights snickered. The C patted the front of his blazer.

"We used to stuff cardboard in there," the C said. "Under our race suits. You'd get beat to death if you didn't because of all the rocks zinging around. And tape our hands. You wrestled your car around those turns for a hundred miles, you ripped all the bark off your palms."

This time it was Boss who told the C to shush. The C made his eyes bulge and put his fingertips on his lips. Boss went back to his sketch.

Then Caspar said:

"You're not eating your steak."

He said it to Logos. He was hunched over his plate with his beefy forearms dug onto the table cloth, like any second he was going to drop into a four point stance and charge across the table. His face was so full of hate it looked frozen. Like all the hate had backed up and got clotted and constipated, and made his face muscles stiff.

Logos went on scooping up his string beans. He didn't know Caspar was talking to him. Up above I saw Zeus strolling to the smoky grill, swinging that D Day T-Bone.

I shut my eyes. If Caspar just didn't push it. That was all. If this just blew over and Caspar didn't push it. Please.

"Hey," Caspar said. He rapped his knuckles on the table. "Yoo hoo. Honeybunch."

"Now," said Abner, "the man I'm going to talk to you about tonight thrived at Langhorne. As terrible as it was. You had to be built like Hercules to wrestle a car around that track in those days before power steering, and Jimmy Bryan was as big and strong as they came. He won at Langhorne twice, and he came out of retirement to race there again, and that's when Langhorne killed him."

The audience murmured. I guessed they'd heard of this Jimmy Bryan. Abner looked down to see the notes he was spreading out on the podium.

"Hey, Lucy." Caspar said.

He said it a lot louder. A couple of his football player buddies looked around. Caspar kept glaring, with the hate froze in his eyes and his beefy stub fingers flexing in and out.

Logos looked up. Caspar nodded at Logos' plate.

"You're not eating your steak."

Logos had cleared out a little island around his rib eye. He put his fork down slow and sat back and looked at Caspar in a sad, friendly way, like Caspar had got upset with another guest at a party Logos was hosting.

"Excuse me?"

"Your steak. You're not eating it. Don't you like it?"

"I've got plenty of food," Logos said.

"That's not what I asked you."

"He only likes tube steak," one of the football players at the next table said.

He was freckled and red-headed and lankier than Caspar, but still plenty big. Maybe he played defensive end. Not a day over nineteen. I couldn't picture him in college. He looked like he still thought it was a laugh riot to stick a whoopee cushion on the prof's chair.

The other footballers thought the tube steak line was a nice Har de Har. Logos smiled in a sad sort of way and picked up his fork and lowered his eyes to his plate.

Luke grimaced. He flashed Redhead a irritated look and pushed his chair back hard and stood up.

"Very mature," he said to Caspar. "Championship team behavior. We're ready for Monaco." He looked at Boss. "I'll be back before the ceremonies start."

He put his napkin next to the plate and gave Caspar another irritated look, and then the Knights at the nearby tables pushed in their chairs again to let him through. Then Eldrich got up. He looked more amused than disgusted. He said something to Boss and followed Luke through the lobby.

•　　•　　•

"In the 1954 race here," Abner was saying, "Jimmy Bryan's rear suspension blew out on the 135th lap." He snapped his fingers, like he was snapping a twig. "The rear shocks buckled, and then the whole back end went to hell in a hand basket. Wheel bearings, everything."

Boss seemed too wrapped up in his place mat scribbling to notice that his mechanics had left. The C wasn't paying attention to Abner anymore. He sat watching Caspar and the redhead and Logos with a quiet, poker-faced look I'd never seen on him before. Like for once in his big fabled life he just wanted to be a spectator.

"You don't like your steak, we better get you a new one," Caspar said. "Why aren't you eating it?"

"He was saving his piece for me," I said. My voice sounded froggy. I started to slide my plate across. "Toss that sucker over here, Logos."

But a hand stopped me before I'd moved it three inches.

"You're not in the trailer park, Kruiser. We don't toss our grub around at a banquet."

The C. He frowned at me until I moved the plate back. Then he settled back in his seat again with that same close-lipped, poker-faced expression, like Caspar and Redhead and Logos was playing out a scene in a movie he'd been waiting to see.

"I want you to visualize this," Abner was saying. "Jimmy Bryan was driving over bricks at 130 miles an hour. Not asphalt. Bricks. With no rear suspension to protect his body from the

❊ 299 ❊

hammering. With around 160 miles to go. So what do you think he did?"

Caspar leaned back and put his hand in front of his mouth so we couldn't see his lips, and said something to his football buddies, and then looked at Logos again. Redhead got up. He looked like he could hardly keep from laughing. Like he'd been out cruising with his buddies and they'd spotted somebody with a white cane or crutches, and his buddies had scripted him on a swell practical joke he could pull.

Redhead stepped to our table and pulled out the chair Eldrich had left, and sat in it, like Logos was an old buddy. But he was twice as big as Eldrich. He crowded in Logos so bad that Logos had to hunch his shoulders to make room for him.

"He kept driving," Abner said. He slapped his good hand on the podium. "That's what he did. Jimmy Bryan simply wouldn't stop."

Another one of the football players stood up. Damn if he didn't have a flat top. I hadn't seen anybody with a flat top since grammar school. He was bigger than Caspar, even.

He swung his big weightlifter leg over the chair on the other side of Logos, and hitched the chair in and sat staring at Logos next to him with his mouth open and his eyes blank and dead looking, like a shark. He looked stupid like a shark. Maybe the other linemen joked about how dumb he was and the coach didn't expect him to know the playbook too good, but if you needed somebody to bust through the line and cripple the quarterback, he was your boy.

"He kept driving." Abner sounded like he was talking about George Washington crossing the Potomac. "Any sane driver would have gotten off the track. But not the big man from Arizona."

Logos put down his fork. He was so smushed in he couldn't move his arm to eat. I guess he'd decided there wasn't any point in pretending that they wasn't doing it on purpose. He looked at Caspar with that sad little half smile of his.

"You don't mind if my friends sit with you," Caspar said. He nodded at the redhead. "Andy, why don't you cut up his rib eye for him?"

Andy picked up Logos' knife and fork and went to carving up Logos' steak. Except he kept hitting Logos' arm while he was doing it. Like it was an accident.

Logos shut his eyes for a second. He looked at Caspar again.

"I'm not going to eat the meat. I'm a vegetarian."

"A what?"

"A vegetarian. I don't eat meat."

Caspar tried to look surprised. Like we hadn't both heard his damn mom bitch about how Logos wouldn't eat sausage or bacon.

"Well, that's a shame," Caspar said. "These Knights went to a lot of trouble to prepare this dinner for us. I think it's a little bit rude not to eat what they serve to us. Don't you think you could make an exception, to be polite and show some respect?"

"The skin," Walter was saying, "was torn from his buttocks. His body was black and blue from the hammering he'd taken. But Jimmy Bryan hadn't quit. He finished the race."

Andy went back to carving up Logos' rib-eye. Logos didn't say anything. He watched the meat getting cut with that sad half smile, like this was about what he'd expected and it was a shame people had to be locked into the roles they played.

I kept looking at the main entrance. Evelyn. How much longer was her phone call going to take? With the C's daughter there they'd lay off of him.

Time had started to stretch out for me. Aways up yonder Zeus had slapped the D-Day beef on the grill. I could hear the sizzle and smell the meat, and knew that what I'd feared had come to pass and that the fork in the road was looming in front of me, even as I kept staring at that entrance and hoping that the C's daughter would come back and bail me out and not make me choose, while I knew deep down that she'd never come back *until* I chose, 'cause that was what the moment was about. It was like something had gathered up all the milliseconds and spread them out on a string, shiny and bright with the chandeliers in the banquet hall to light them up, so the C with his poker face watching and Andy bumping Logos' shoulder and Caspar practically leaking 140 proof hate down his cheeks and my sad-smiling old friend was like glittery glistening beads hung on a silvery thread, that I could see clearer than I'd ever seen anything.

And my hoping that Evelyn came back was hung up on that string, too. How I was waiting for the C's female girl daughter to come stick up for the friend I'd known ten times longer than she had, so Hank Kruzenski could keep wearing his plastic C Team ID card, and make believe he belonged in the same league as Luke and Eldrich 'cause he wore the same shirt, and not punch a timecard as a glue worker no more.

"By 1960," Abner was saying, "Jimmy Bryan had won it all." Abner bent close to the podium and squinted at his note cards. "Three times national driving champion. A champion at Indy. Victory in the Race of Two Worlds in Monza. He even told a *Sports Illustrated* interviewer that he hoped to retire.

"But Jimmy Bryan didn't take his own good advice."

•   •   •

"I keep asking you these questions, and you're not answering me," Caspar said.

Caspar glanced at the stage. He started to turn back to Logos, but something must have caught his eye up there, 'cause he stopped and looked at the stage longer. Then I felt something curdle in my gut, because I could see the light bulb going on in that wedge-shaped skull as clear as the mashed potatoes on my plate. He'd thought of something.

"Well, please do beg my pardon." Caspar said it almost dainty, like a mugger walking on tip toes before he swings the blackjack. "I see what the problem is. You've been too busy sneaking peeks at our woman folk to hear half of what I've said to you."

Behind the podium the Damsels was sitting in a row, staring at the back of Abner's head with the blank looks you see on security guards and doormen when they have to listen to a speaker as part of their jobs. Maybe for the rest of the week they were cocktail waitresses at some VIP executive club off Monument Circle, and carried highballs and martinis around on a tray and stuffed tips into their cleavage, and then once a year they got to rake in a few hundred extra for wiggling into Renaissance Fair get-ups and acting like something Lancelot would've chased around the moat. One was chewing gum. They looked bored.

"And you've got a better view on your side of the table, too. No wonder you're distracted. Sure beats sneaking peeks into the womens' shower, don't it?"

Caspar dropped his voice a notch, like he wanted to share a secret. "Now, fess up to me, Logos. Man to man. Looking at those chicks is making your underwear feel kinda tight. Isn't that right? You want to go up there and rip off one of those skimpy little skirts and dig in."

Next to Logos Andy was making a real project out of cutting up the steak. He'd bump Logos accidentally on purpose and dig the fork into another part of the meat and lower the knife to saw off another chunk of rib eye, like he'd volunteered to cut up the food for some great-grand mom in an old fogey home.

Logos sat and watched the hands cutting up the meat he wouldn't eat and didn't answer. He was still smiling that polite, sad half-smile of his, but it had frayed around the edges. His cheeks looked flushed.

"Which one's steaming up your little collar the most, Logos?" Caspar's voice had gone oily. "You look like a leg man to me. You must like that blonde on the end."

Andy nudged Logos, like he wanted Logos to point out his favorite. Logos tried to keep his smile up. But Caspar was getting to him. It was like they was boxers, and Caspar had figured out that Logos had a cracked rib, and all Caspar had to do was keep slinging punches at the same spot. They both knew damn well why he was asking about the Damsels. I'd never seen anything in a conversation really get under Logos' skin.

But this was different. There just happened to be this one ultra top secret that he'd held inside for all these years, and never told anybody until he wrote about it to Evelyn, and then Evelyn had messed up and told it to her dad, and now Caspar knew about it. It was raw and purple and bled if you touched it, and the reason Caspar's livery-looking lip was curled back over his ugly teeth was because he'd figured out how much it hurt.

"In 1960," Abner was saying, "Jimmy Bryan came out of retirement. At Langhorne. He took the seat of Rodger Ward in the Leader Card Special. Rodger Ward had refused to run another lap at Langhorne. It was too dangerous."

"You know, Logos, I think we're going to have to buy you a hearing aid. I keep asking you these questions, and you won't say anything. I just know one of those girls has got you all steamed up. Which one is it?"

"I think they all look very attractive."

Like he was trying to be some suave visiting diplomat. But that just wasn't how a man talked to another man about good-looking women, and his voice hiccupped when he said it, and Caspar practically snickered at him out loud. Like the other boxer had thrown a wild bolo punch and practically fell through the ropes. Logos' face flushed darker.

Then Logos' eyes met mine. Maybe for just one of those stretched-on-a-string milliseconds, because I was so worked up that I was radiating agitation like heat waves coming off the hood of a hot car, and he could read my mind. He looked at me and gave his head the tiniest shake, and looked at the plate again. So I knew. He was telling me to stay out of it. Like he'd said the other night. He wanted Hank Kruzenski to have his big second chance dream, too.

But that only made me feel worse.

From the podium, Abner said: "Rodger Ward personally tried to talk Jimmy Bryan out of the comeback. Langhorne was too dangerous for a driver just returning to action. But Jimmy Bryan wouldn't listen. Perhaps he knew he was destined to die at Langhorne. Perhaps he felt he had an appointment there."

Across the table Boss erased something on his placemat drawing, and bent low to pencil something else in. The C kept watching us with that same quiet, poker-faced look. Like he was some big crooked politico, and Caspar and Logos were lawyers in a trial he'd paid to fix, and he wanted to lie low in the back row of the courthouse, and watch, and make sure he got his money's worth.

And that was when I finally knew what was going down, as sure as if somebody had held up a neon sign.

The C had set this up. Maybe not this particular scene at this particular moment, but it was still the C who'd given Caspar the go ahead. His lucky rabbit's foot daughter would've ripped him a new one if he'd ragged on little Logos, but Evelyn wouldn't be able to say much if Caspar did the ragging for him. Especially if the C'd had a nice, private, man-to-man with Caspar beforehand, and told him to wait until his best girl wasn't around.

"'They all look very attractive.'" Caspar leered at Andy and Flat Top. "Well, that's right gentlemanly of you, Logos. Maybe you're studying to be a preacher."

Then he must've decided it was time to bust open that cracked rib for good. He leaned farther over the table, and when he went on his voice was almost sugary.

"'Course, maybe it's not the lady folk who really ring your chimes, Logos. What I heard is you don't even like the ladies very much. What gets you hot are the men."

"One of the last to see Jimmy Bryan alive that fateful morning at Langhorne," Abner was saying, "was the great Clint Brawner, his mechanic."

Flat Top's shark mouth twitched, like he'd just sniffed blood. Andy sat up and threw Logos a disgusted look.

Then time slowed down all the way for me, and stopped, stopped completely, because I'd reached the fork. I could sit and let them tear up my friend and not do anything, which was what Logos had as much as given me permission to do, and keep my C-team plastic ID and team shirt. But for the rest of my life I'd know how low I'd stooped to hold onto them. He couldn't fend for himself now. I could see it in his face. Maybe he was smarter than the rest of the table put together, except maybe Boss, but he couldn't deal with what Caspar was rubbing his nose in. He needed help.

And of all the damn things, what I started to think about was where we was from. Prado Diablo, California. Basically a bunch of tract houses and shopping malls with a lot of asphalt thoroughfare wrapped up around it. Maybe old Don Fernando Somebody had got a land grant there once and the old biddy tour guides at City Hall had more Saga of Prado Diablo type history they could tell visitors, but it was still basically Sprawl City, USA. It was like living inside a developer's real estate portfolio. That was how Logos had put it once.

But I was from there. It was where I'd been born, and where I'd learned to walk and count and spell, and out of those rows of all-the-same looking tract houses and all-the-same looking streets we'd managed to make Logos De Mello. Who everyone in Prado had known was special.

Someone from Prado would have stuck up for him now. Rosenfeld would have, and Maria would have, too, even if they'd made fun of her for being fat, and for sure people from our high school class would have. But they wasn't around now. The only representative of Prado Diablo who could stick up for Logos was Hank Kruzenski, and Hank was too worried about his sorry ass job.

"Is that *true*, Logos?" Caspar asked. "I don't think I ever met a real fairy before. I thought all the fags lived in New York. Maybe you don't like those girls on stage at all. You'd rather crawl under the table and have some fun with us."

"I think we'd better give him some of this rib eye," Andy said. "Next best thing to tube steak."

Andy speared a chunk of the meat and held it up to Logos and pushed it on Logos' mouth.

That was as far as it got, though. Fortunately. Because then somebody new showed up at the table. He wasn't big like Caspar or Andy, but he was brave and strong and wasn't scared of his own shadow, and he wasn't going to sit on his hands while a fine person got picked on, and I sure as hell wished he'd shown up a lot earlier.

"Why don't you concentrate on your own plate?" the new guy said to Andy, and nicked the fork out of Andy's hand.

Caspar's mouth got dark and ugly. Andy just blinked. He had at least fifty pounds weight advantage. Maybe he hadn't thought anybody could be that stupid.

"This isn't any of your affair," the C said.

The C sounded almost indignant. Like he'd paid his money to fix the trial, and now here's this surprise witness who's going to foul up the whole thing. But the new guy said it damn well was his affair. He'd known Logos more than half his life, and Logos was as kind and decent as anybody in the banquet hall, and it was flat out wrong to pick on him because he had some personal problems. And the C said "I guess I need a new errand boy," like a warning, and the new guy said hey, fine, go ahead and hire one, and by then their talk was loud enough that Knights was turning to look, and old Abner had broke off his Jimmy Bryan story to look toward the commotion.

Caspar looked stunned. "Maybe you're a fag, too," he said, like he was trying to regroup, but the new guy answered, "Call me whatever you want, you're not bothering my friend anymore," and then Andy snickered. But Andy looked like someone who'd snicker while he watched a gang rape. "Let's see you stop me," Andy said, and stood up. He had to weigh at least 260. Like he chucked barbells around the gym like javelins. It wouldn't be any kind of contest.

But that didn't bother the new guy. Or the new old guy, because I guess I'd had that brave, strong person inside me a long time. I sure wished I'd known earlier. It would have saved me a lot of trouble. I stood up, too.

CHAPTER TWENTY-THREE

Well, I got cremated something terrible. There's no sense mincing words. This is the third fight you've seen me get into in this book, and I got clobbered in every one, without so much as laying a pinkie finger on the guy I was doing battle with. Just for the sake of my masculine pride I'd like to write up a slug fest where I came out on top, but I'd have to go AWOL of the story. You're just going to have to take my word for it that I wasn't really so bad with my mitts.

Free tip from Hank: don't duke it out with a Big Ten college lineman who's got over seventy pounds on you when all his Big Ten buddies are at the table with him. And free tip #2: don't do it at a big race fan banquet dinner when you've got the living legend of auto racing at the same table, and people watching the fight might think you're taking a poke at him.

At least it was over practically before it started. Andy hit me first, and while I was watching the banquet hall do a lazy 360 spin one of the other gridiron greats slugged me, and then someone got the idea I was going after Mr. C. Well, I was innocent. All I was doing was standing still and getting punched out a few feet away from him. Maybe I would've fell and bled on Boss' sketches.

Somewhere in there I felt Logos trying to pull people away from me, but there were a lot of them and only one of him. The one really brilliant idea I had was to fall down and stay there.

· · ·

Three bruised and bloody minutes later, I was on my hands and knees on the parking lot outside the fire exit they'd just chucked us out of, with the brick walls of the lodge looming up toward the moon on one side, and the front bumpers of Caddies and Lincolns lined up on the other. Sidewalk street lamps was throwing off yellowy light under the maple boughs, but that was at least fifty feet away. It was pretty dark.

I was leaking. It was too dark to tell how much, but I could make out blood drops on the asphalt under my nose. If my nose was still in the same place it had been before. My jaw felt like I'd gone on a Caribbean cruise with a bunch of dentists. I might not be my beautiful self for awhile.

"They locked us out," Logos said.

Behind me I heard him rattle the fire exit door. Abner had gone back to holding forth in there, but the sound was too muffled for me to make out the words.

About five feet ahead of me was a gray metal trash can. That looked like a worthwhile goal in life. I crawled over and pulled myself up so my elbows was on the lid. Maybe I'd think of standing up next year sometime. I could do it for the Centennial.

"Are you okay?"

Logos' footsteps scrunched on the gravel, and then he was standing next to me. His blazer and shirt and tie was all messed up. He'd been in the thick of things more than I'd thought.

"Wonderful," I croaked. "Let's go hit the bars."

"Do you want me to call an ambulance? If you think they broke something we'll have to find a hospital."

I tried to shoot him a classic don't-be-ridiculous look, but my eye was too swole up to make it look right. I felt around my ribs and face.

"I think I'm just bleeding a little."

Logos stepped back toward the fire exit. A drop of my blood went *clink!* on the trash can lid. I looked out at the big fluttery maple leaves backlit by the street lamps. That was one big plus for Hoosier country: maple trees. Maybe I'd pull up a fifty ton granddaddy maple by the roots and lug it back to California.

"So much for your career with C Enterprises," Logos said.

Something in his tone rubbed me wrong. Damn if he didn't look all upset. Like the whole thing had been his fault.

"I don't have a job for you, Hank! Didn't you see me shake my head? You could have stayed out of it. Where are you going to get another job like that?"

For some reason that ticked me off as much as anything that had happened inside. I pushed myself up on two feet and turned to face him.

"Why, you little SOB," I said, and I meant it. "I did that for you, and you know it. If you don't apologize I'm never going to talk to you again."

Then the parking lot started to do a slow 360 too, and I figured I'd better go back to kneeling with my buddy the trash can lid for awhile longer.

Logos didn't answer right away. I held onto the lid like I was a damn dog up on its hind legs, and admired the maples some more. Then Logos sighed, and the gravel scrunched as he stepped up behind me.

"Hank, you are … quite correct. You made a tremendous sacrifice on my behalf, and it was insensitive of me to have spoken as I just did. Thank you. I am honored, and touched. Please forgive me for what I said."

I felt something light on my shoulders, like a kindergartner's fingers. The little gerbil was trying to give me an apologetic hug. That wasn't a very Prado thing to do, and he did it real light, like I might think he was going to spread his homosexual cooties on me if he hugged any harder.

•   •   •

Inside the banquet hall some kind of commotion had kicked up. I heard a muffled hullabaloo, like another fight had broke out and all the Knights was jabbering about it. The voice on the loudspeaker sounded like it was trying to settle everybody down.

"Our Evelyn hath returned," Logos said.

I took hold of the sides of the can and did a nice push up, and sat back on the lid facing Logos and the doorway.

Logos stood staring at the door with a real serious expression, while the ruckus went on inside and the emcee kept squawking "Knights, please!" and clinking his knife on the microphone. He looked like he was thinking hard on something, like the bedlam inside was hooked up with some big decision and he had to come down on one side or another, whether he was ready to or not.

Finally he turned back to me. He looked all sad and determinated, like some old school doc who'd decided he had to stick a big, fat needle into a squealing little kid.

"Hank, that is probably Evelyn. If it isn't, she'll undoubtedly be out here shortly. We are no longer welcome here, and she may be contractually obligated to remain with her father until the race is over. If there is anything you wish to say to her, this is likely your last opportunity."

"Say what to her? That I'm sorry I bled on the tablecloth?"

Logos shut his eyes for a second and looked pained, like I'd told a dirty limerick at the Ford inauguration. Something told me to get my guard up in a hurry, as woozy as I felt. I didn't know why he looked like that old school doc, but I had a good suspicion who the needle was for.

"Hank, we no longer have time for this. I know that you have already claimed to have no special feeling for Evelyn. There is nothing I would like better than to let this ludicrous fiction stand for the sake of your masculine pride, and instead trust nature to take her course as you get to know Evelyn better as a member of the C Team. But you aren't a member of the C Team anymore. Nature has run out of time. We have been 86'd, and your courageous defense of me is the reason why. It is time to be direct."

"I don't know what you're talking ..."

"But of course, you do know," Logos interrupted. The damn little gerbil stood staring at my busted-up mug like he was Cal the College Coach, giving a grim speech at halftime. "I have known you since third grade. Your ardor may be less obvious to strangers. To me you're about as subtle as a lovesick Basset. I don't enjoy embarrassing you in this fashion, but it's the truth. You look ready to chew on Evelyn's sneakers and howl at the door whenever she's within eyeshot. It is time to put your feelings into words."

It was Evelyn in there, all right. Even through the fire exit I could hear her yelling, and then her dad's hoarse yelling on top of it. It sounded like he was trying to explain about the fight, and she wasn't buying it. Then their voices was drowned out by a fresh "Knights, please!" from the emcee, and hundreds of old Knights all squawking and gobbling 'cause a fight had broke out during their big banquet.

I tried to give Logos a 'don't be ridiculous' look, but my lips was too busted-up to sneer proper, and the parking lot was still waltzing around beneath us. So I looked away, and shrugged, and held onto my trusty garbage can so it wouldn't start waltzing too. Most of the big speech he'd just fed me hadn't exactly cleared the Kruzenski coin slot. Maybe I wouldn't try to BS him anymore about how I felt, but he wasn't *really*, wasn't *actually* going to call my action in front of her. Dudes just didn't do that.

The fire door swung open. Out came the woman of the hour, with the same goofy Knight holding the door open after her. Evelyn looked at us like we was in an apartment someone had just ransacked.

"*Look* at you! What did they do ..." She swiveled toward Logos. "What happened?! Are you ..."

Logos headed her off. "I'm fine. Hank needs a first aid kit. They wouldn't give me one. Could you please get us one?"

Evelyn gawked at us a second longer, then spun around and stamped back inside the hall. Goofy kept holding the door. If you'd ever told me a seventy something could look like a dog with its tail between its legs, I wouldn't have believed you, but that's how he looked to me.

"She's not going to be long," Logos said.

He stared at me for another few seconds in that sad, mind-made-up way, like he was giving one more hunt for a reason to hold off on what he was about to do, and couldn't find one. He took a step closer. I'd only seen him get tough once in all our years in Prado, when he'd told some big biker he was too drunk to wobble home from the bar on his panhead. But damn if Logos hadn't stood off that biker and three of his friends when he'd done it.

"Hank, I am very sorry, but I am not going to have this on my head. I simply would never forgive myself if I thought your defense of me had cost you a chance with Evelyn. If you don't declare your feelings for her now, I will have to declare them for you."

"Why don't you brush my teeth for me, while you're at it? I mean, *man*, but you have your gall ..."

Logos held out his hand. He looked like a pint-size J. Edgar Hoover.

"I'm sorry, Hank. I'm going to have to insist."

Evelyn rushed back out. She asked Goofy to push the door open farther, so she could get more light from the banquet hall on my face. Then she propped open the first aid kit on the garbage can next to me and went to rooting around among the band aids and gauze and ointment. She looked close to tears.

"Those bastards," she said. "Those filthy, no good ..." She looked at Logos. "What happened?"

Logos cleared his throat. "Caspar and his chums were having some fun at my expense, and it got out of hand. Hank quite chivalrously stepped in to defend me."

Evelyn fished out one of those wet wipe things. She bit her lip and looked at my face.

"Is anything broken?"

I told her I didn't think so. She tore open the package and pulled out the little damp cloth and went to dabbing under my eyes, all the while biting her lip like it hurt to see my cuts. And then even through the wooze and fur clogging up my brain, it hit me just how right Logos was. She'd never touched my face before. I would've gone out and got beat up every night just to feel her fingers on my bare skin, and to have her stand that close to me.

Maybe Logos read my mind. He cleared his throat.

"Evelyn, Hank has something he'd like to say to you."

"HANK DOES NOT."

That was me. I bugged out my good eye and gave him my best Mr. Menace stare over her shoulder, like a second string hit man from *Godfather*. Evelyn stopped dabbing and stared at me. Logos just dug in his heels.

"Yes, Hank does," Logos said firmly.

"What's he talking about?"

I shook off Evelyn's question, and shot Logos another death ray stare. I was starting to panic. The little gerbil actually meant it. My face looked like leftover take-out pizza, and he wanted me to play Valentino.

"Somebody brained him in there. That's all. He's not talking about nothing."

"But I am." Logos rocked on his heels. "Evelyn, Hank has a few very important words that he needs to share with you."

"Go somewhere and die!"

"What's he *talking* about?!" Evelyn stopped dabbing my face and glanced between us. "Tell me what?"

"Would you like to tell them to her, Hank, or do you want me to say them for you?"

"Go crawl under a rock! I swear! Go buy a muscle magazine and lock yourself in a closet with it!"

Evelyn frowned. "That's not a nice thing to say to Logos."

"If you knew what he wanted me to say, you'd be mad, too!"

Logos shot me a Prado kind of leer. "I'm not the muscle magazine type, Hank. Also, it's rather chilly for that sort of thing." He harrumphed and rocked on his heels, with his thumbs hooked through his belt. He looked like a know-it-all penguin. "Hank, I shall not be dissuaded, no matter how you insult me. Evelyn, there are many time-honored ways of expressing the sentiments Hank wishes to convey, but all invariably include a simple transitive verb. Would you like me to say the verb, Hank, or will you?"

"I told you to *get lost*! Split!"

"What is this *about*?! What are you two *talking* about?!"

"I ..." Logos mouthed the word 'love' over Evelyn's shoulder. "You don't want me to say it for you, Hank. But I'm about to. Come, come. I ..."

"What is this *about*?!"

"By the count of ten, Hank. One. Two. Three ..."

And then I knew I was licked. No matter how ticked off I was with his gall and with him trying to run my romantic life. I was still cornered. If you'd ever, I mean *ever* told me I'd make my big play with a swole eye and bloody lips I would've told you what you'd been smoking, but there he was counting off like a ref in a prizefight, and I knew I was going through that door whether I wanted to or not.

And I'll tell you something else: you should've seen how beautiful she looked, standing so close I could smell her skin through my busted up nose, with her hair all fluffed out pretty around her neck. What Logos wanted me to say was the honest truth.

I shrugged. Once I was in, I was in.

"Will you marry me?" I said.

"*What?!*"

"I love you. Will you marry me?"

Logos nodded approvingly. "Very good, Hank." He looked a little worried, though. "A marriage proposal is a bit premature, however."

Evelyn looked like we'd just said old Goofy was an extraterrestrial. She stared at Logos, and at me. Not in a real romantic way, either. She thought we was nuts.

"Okay. I'll wait til I get a ring." I looked at her like I'd spilled blood on her dress. "I mean, I'm sorry if it's a shock, but that's what he wanted me to say, and it's a fact. I can't help it. Since back in Prado."

Logos gave his hands a little clap, like I was a kid who'd got a word right in the spelling bee. I looked at Evelyn, and for the first time I could let everything that had been pent up in me show in my face.

But Evelyn mostly looked worried. She said we'd both been hurt in the banquet hall, and that I'd obviously taken a beating, and wasn't thinking clearly. It was time to get to a hospital. We could talk about what I'd wanted to say to her later.

• • •

The sawbones who patched me up in the emergency ward had a nose you could've hooked a muskie with. Not a looker. He thought me getting pasted at the Knights banquet was a laugh riot. You know: boys will be boys, and the manly men racers had to let off a little steam, and likely the C and A.J. and Bobby and Johnny all went around bashing and bloodying each other up every day after practice to take the edge off. He was actually enough of a dip to ask me who I thought would win. I told him I didn't especially care anymore, as long as it wasn't the people who'd just hit me.

The doc thought that was another laugh riot. But he still patched me up good, and it turned out my schnoz and Grecian profile had survived the big dust-up in one piece. I'd frighten school kids and grandmothers for another few weeks, but after that I'd be as good as new.

A couple of hours later, the three of us was camped out at the bus station downtown, waiting for the 12:20 a.m. Greyhound to Denver. I hadn't thought we'd be able to get back into Mrs. Henderson's to pack our stuff, but Evelyn was still the C's daughter. She'd been a regular storm trooper about it. Caspar hadn't been there. Maybe some of the Knights had took him out to a bar to celebrate getting rid of the fag. Plus the fag's friend.

Logos had been wrong to think Evelyn might not come with us. No way she was sticking with her dad after the fight. But that didn't mean my big Romeo pitch had hit the jackpot, either. I was worried, and I was embarrassed.

The three of us had kind of clammed up after the big outburst in the parking lot. Logos looked happy to flutter around on the sidelines, checking out the bus schedules on the wall and figuring out how we'd transfer in Denver to the next westbound bus. I sat next to the shopping bags I'd loaded up with my gear at Mrs. Henderson's, and made an awkward joke every now and then, and probably looked as bashful as I felt. Evelyn kept sneaking worried looks at me, like Caspar had slugged me harder than the doc knew, and I'd got brain damage.

I kept thinking of a 7-11 cashier I'd known back in Prado who'd had a crush on Liz Taylor. He'd gone to all her movies, and had a photo album of magazine cut-outs about her. But if she'd come into his 7-11, and a buddy had twisted his arm to tell her how he felt, well, that didn't mean old Liz was going to jump over the counter and cover him with smooches and drag him off to the nearest altar. I mean, sorry. You needed two people for that.

Evelyn and me wasn't talking much. Once in awhile she'd ask how I was, and I'd catch that worried look, like now she didn't know how to act around me. I'd almost resigned myself to losing out. She wouldn't have looked that way if she was interested, would she?

But maybe it was still better that it had come out, one way or the other.

·   ·   ·

The bus pulled in twenty minutes late. Some of the passengers stepped out of the line to haul their suitcases to the cargo bays. The rest of us queued up at the stairs going in.

Then that damn runty Logos stepped in front of Evelyn so he could lead the way down the aisle. Like he'd planned this out too. He marched right in, past all the rows of riders who'd already got on in Cincinnati or Columbus or wherever the hey they was from, who looked sleepy and irritated like you would be at close to 1:00 in the morning, and like they just wanted the Indy riders to get on so the bus would start rolling again.

Old Logos found the first row with two free side-by-side seats, and waited for us.

"These two are for you," he announced.

That's the right word: *announced*. No discussion, no argument.

"I shall sit in the back. I think you two have some things to discuss."

The little communist fetched the carry-on out of Evelyn's hand, and shoved it in the overhead. What total gall. He made a little bow at us — while completely blocking the aisle, so we couldn't have snuck past him — and swung his arm at the seats like a doorman motioning someone into a cab.

Or like a cop motioning someone into a squad car. We was sitting together. He meant it.

I sat by the window, and Evelyn sat next to me. Logos didn't go to the back until he was sure we'd stay put.

•   •   •

Evelyn and me didn't talk much until the bus was out of Indianapolis. It was pushing 2:00 a.m. by then. A couple of night owls had the lamps on over their seats, but the bus was mostly dark. We was on the 70 heading toward St. Louis, passing miles and miles of flat farmland, with the seats vibrating beneath us and the drone of the bus engine all around.

Our overhead light was out, but I could see her good enough. All I could think about was her. Even in the dark I could see her lips and her eyes, and the soft skin of her cheek when she turned to me.

"Hank," she said finally. "Why did you say that to me in the parking lot?"

She looked nervous. Like I was this sorry nut job she knew, and it was time to talk about what had got me put in the strait-jacket at Bellevue.

"You were joking, weren't you? It was something you made up with Logos."

I didn't answer right away. I felt the seat back jangling against my bruised-up head, and listened to the drone of the big diesel out back, and looked at the outline of her eyes watching me in the dark.

It was nice of her to give me a chance to get out of it. Wasn't it? Sure, I could say; it was a joke. You don't think I'm nutty enough to think a joker like me would have a prayer with you?

I wet my busted-up lips, and squinted my one good eye at her. But what I said was:

No. No, I sure hadn't been joking. Maybe Logos had pushed me into it. But I'd meant what I said.

·   ·   ·

And then it was like I was up on a cliff with the high divers in Acapulco. Maybe I never should have gone up with them, but there I was, and now somebody's pushed me, and I'm over the edge. The sky's above and the water's coming up fast, and whether I'm ready or not doesn't matter anymore, 'cause there's no turning back. I'm committed. I've got to arch my back and stretch out my arms and try to hit the water right.

So I told her. With my one good eye locked on her, and my busted-up lips rasping on the words, and my cuts stinging under the bandages while I talked. Without feeling afraid, 'cause I was diving, wasn't I? There wasn't no point in feeling scared. I had to make my pitch.

I told her how it had started the night we'd buried Ruby. I'd never known a woman who could talk intimate the way she did, or look at me with her heart showing through her eyes, and give me goose bumps just by touching my wrist. I told her about Cupid and even about the dream I'd had, and I said I wasn't ashamed of it, 'cause love was all I'd felt when I'd had it. Maybe she was too good for me. Maybe I should've kept it to myself. But Logos had guessed, Logos had known, Logos had seen through me, Logos had known me too good not to see what I was trying to cover up. I loved her.

In the dark I saw her eyes open wide, and her collar bone moving under the open collar of her shirt as she breathed. Then the water was coming up fast, and I was about to hit it, and I just had to do my best.

I raised my fingers and touched her hair. So many times I'd dreamed of doing that, just that, so many times when I'd been covered with grit and glue and sawdust at HM&F and had tried to lock my mind on something in life I could hope for. I lowered my fingers and touched her cheek. Time was slowing down for me again. God had stretched out the seconds and laid them end to end so I could see myself inside them, and get the dive just right. My diving hands hit the water. The surf burst up around me. I sat up, and I looked into her eyes, and cupped my fingers on the nape of her neck behind her ear.

We kissed. I kissed her. We kissed.

• • •

And she let me. She didn't turn away.

But that wasn't the romantic part.

That wasn't the romantic part. It wasn't. It just wasn't.

There's going to be one. I'll tell you that much. But we had to lose something important to both of us first, and by the time it happened we'd almost become two different people.

There's going to be one, but you'll have to wait for it. I had to. I had to wait over ten years.

PART II

Chapter Twenty-Four

Bobby Unser won the 1975 Indianapolis 500. He took the lead on the 165th lap, and held off Johnny Rutherford until a thunder shower ended the race early on lap 174. Evelyn had thought he might get it. Maybe that shows how much she knew about racing in spite of herself.

The Valkyrie threw a connecting rod on the tenth lap. After all that hand-wringing they'd done about the chassis, it was the engine that did them in. The worldwide television viewing audience got to watch the C rip off his helmet and chuck it at the pit wall. He didn't even stick around for the what-went-wrong interview with Chris Economaki.

I watched the broadcast mostly by myself in the living room back at Evelyn's place in Berkeley. Or maybe I should say at our place: by then Logos, Evelyn and me were all camped out together in Evelyn's bedroom.

Every once in awhile, Logos sat on the couch with me so he could listen to old Hank help out Keith Jackson and Jackie Stewart with the color commentary. Nobody else came in. The Indy 500 wasn't a major viewing priority in Berkeley.

Then the rain fell back east, and Pat Vidan waved the checkered flag, and it was over. Bobby Unser stood in Victory Lane with the festival queen and the big Borg-Warner trophy, and told Chris Economaki why they'd risked the final pit stop, and Dan Gurney thanked their team sponsor. Then ABC switched the broadcast up to Chris Schenkel. Less than a week before I'd walked among those big time racers I'd just seen on TV, but the race was over now and my silver badge wasn't good anymore, and USAC sure wasn't going to send me a new one for 1976. I'd seen my last of the Indianapolis Speedway.

•   •   •

Our big problem now that we were back on the West Coast was money. Evelyn wasn't about to work for her dad anymore, and Logos had been getting by on Evelyn's dime, and I'd chewed through most of the bankroll that the C had sent out with the Kydra. Logos wasn't ready to go back to Prado, and no way we were moving in with Mom and her Old Arkansas bottles. We didn't have enough for a penthouse suite at the Hilton. That left Evelyn's place. The commune. And the only free space there was on Evelyn's floor.

It was pretty cramped. Logos insisted that Evelyn and me share the bed, even though Evelyn and me hadn't got close to doing anything that would've needed a bed to get done on, and that he nuzzle up with the insect life on the carpet. He was real shy about nudity, it turned out, so we had to go through this big ritual to keep him happy when we undressed for bed. I mean with blankets hung up on ropes, to block off parts of the room.

I was happy, though. I loved Evelyn and I loved Logos, too, though I was a long way from hanging the word 'love' on what I felt for him.

Evelyn had her cup out a lot. She didn't feel like she had to keep it hid away anymore, now that we were part of her inner circle. Sometimes she'd hold it close when we were sitting up gabbing, like a little kid holding a teddy bear. Or she'd stretch out on the bed and prop it on the mattress and lie looking at it, like she could see her drunk mom and suicide husband and Sioux heritage in there, all rolled into one.

One night she wanted us to do a meditation around the cup after Logos had gone off on one of his big orations. Evelyn liked to listen to him pontificate about stuff. One of his college science geek buddies had laid this trip on him that all time and space in the universe had started from a single point, so that Evelyn and me and the C and Bobby Unser and the weird De Mello family had all started out from this eentsy weensty speck of nothing, like the way the roots and bark and leaves of a tree all start from a single seed. Not just space; time, too. Sea jellies bobbing around in the Precambrian era and the first trees coming up in the Pennsylvania era, and Zeck and Meck the neanderthals chasing each other with clubs in the Pleistocene: all those eons of history class timeline stuff had come busting out of the same seed. So before the seed and the big bang, time and space hadn't existed, neither one. Just hadn't been there.

Logos was all hot and bothered about the idea. Evelyn asked if that meant that Ricky and her mom might still be around, and then while Logos was trying to answer she said she wanted us to do the meditation together. She was shaking a little. She put the cup on the nightstand and lit a candle next to it and pushed the bed back, and asked in an almost pleading voice if we could meditate with her, because it would be better if we all joined in.

It was windy that night. The rickety old house creaked in the wind, and the casement windows rattled, and enough air came under the sash to make the candle flame flicker in the dark and the orange light waver and dance on the Sioux and Incan symbols on the cup, that didn't have any business being on a carving that was supposed to be Aztec, but were there anyway.

And I don't mind telling you, I felt something inside that thing. Maybe Logos thought it was all myth. I didn't. The stories that had been told about it. The way the forehead symbols didn't add up. The way her gallivanting around with the thing in her damn purse and never getting a scratch on it didn't add up, either. There was something inside it, and I knew it, and it knew *I* knew, and while we meditated I felt it watching me. Not in a mean way. Not in a friendly way. Just watching, like it could see into the future, and knew what was in store for us.

•   •   •

Logos signed up for a stack of tutoring jobs to help us Three Musketeers pay the rent. Evelyn wanted him to go to the newcomer's center, but Logos was too busy chasing buses and BART from UCB to Stanford and explaining math to undergrads to think much about his romantic life. Or that's what he said, anyway. Evelyn thought he was stalling.

Evelyn got a waitressing gig at an organic food cafe on Shattuck. Owsley's. Best smoothies in Berkeley. Sure they were. The manager only hired her for two shifts a week, but one of the pothead waiters was always calling in sick, so she wound up working almost every day. She felt a little old to be serving avocado sandwiches to college kids, but the tips were decent, and at least it didn't have anything to do with mechanics.

I went through two jobs in two months. The Springer Spaniel looking guy in the room next to the kitchen downstairs got me hired as a bike messenger in the Financial District. My thigh muscles didn't like that gig much, but the rest of me did, and

I probably would've stuck it out if it hadn't been for a serious near miss with a trucker-in-a-hurry on Commercial Street. So I decided to take up cab driving, but that didn't last long, either. I swear, every old lady who wanted to tip a nickel for a three block ride to visit Aunt Mabel in the Outer Sunset got dispatch to put her request out for me. My hourly take home pay was worse than a paper route.

By then I was desperate enough to lean on Mom for a job referral. Even though she was still stuck in the cashier's window at the gas station. She basically told me to shove it. She'd been giving me the cold shoulder ever since I'd moved to Berkeley. No Hank = no rent from Hank = no bucks for Old Arkansas. What kind of son was that? But then just as I was thinking I'd have to sell my 'Cuda, a college kid four doors down asked how much I'd charge to fix his radiator. I gave him a quote, and it turned out he had a friend who needed his jalopy patched up, too, and a career was born.

It wouldn't have impressed the C Team much. I laid out my tools on the dirt driveway next to the Shack, which was what we called the commune, and then when I went big time I paid an extra $10 a month to take over the house garage. I wasn't any great shakes as a wrench, but I still had plenty of work. I'd let my hair grow out more then, so I looked like my college kid customers, and I lived close by. Plus I had Evelyn as a secret weapon to help me when I got stuck, even though she griped a lot when I had to ask her.

Time passed. In winter I spread a big tarp over the garage roof so I wouldn't have to work in the rain, and used some professional mechanic grade rocks and two-by-fours to hold the tarp in place. In spring the Berkeley insect community cruised in to watch me work and see how I tasted, and in summer the sweat soaked through my clothes and dripped off my forehead onto the weeds next to the car and whatever engine I was working on. At mid-day from spring through fall a nice fat shimmery patch of pure-D sunlight beamed down between the sycamore branches to keep me company, and except when it really cooked in September I always tried to maneuver my work inside that patch while it was there. You would have, too, if you'd felt what it was like to be inside it.

Mostly, I was happy. Some of my customers didn't pay me and a lot of others didn't pay as much as they owed, but I was making enough to pull my own weight and buy a round of drinks for Logos and Evelyn when we went out. I kept thinking about what Logos had said about everything beginning in one point. Time had started there, too, if I understood him right, and I could feel myself inside time, and time unfolding around me. I was twenty-six now. The sports reporters had just finished getting all excited about the 1976 Indy 500. The 1975 race was ancient history. I'd sure never thought I'd move to Berkeley, but I had, and it was working out. I had my friend Logos, and I had Evelyn. Or in a way I did.

●　　●　　●

By this time I'd accepted that Evelyn loved Logos more than she'd ever love me.

Not romantically. She knew he was gay. He was the one who kept wondering if he ought to see a therapist. He got a book by this shrink Irving Bieber that he wrapped a big book cover on, so nobody on BART would know what he was reading, and started quoting all this Bieber stuff to us about family dynamics and crippled heterosexuality. Evelyn just wanted him to go over to the newcomer's center while gorilla sweater was still there.

But love isn't just who you call your girlfriend and who you sleep with. Even a yahoo like me knew that.

I'd slept with Evelyn by then. I'd seen the birthmark on the inside of her thigh, and told her how I loved her as I lay with her arms around me and her heels crossed at the small of my back and her black hair spread out on the sheets. She hadn't said no. She'd been a little reluctant the first time, but not after that. She liked sex. It beat watching TV.

But it was only me making love. Do you understand? I'd climb into the saddle and give it my all, but what I was really driving for wasn't her getting her jollies or me getting them either, but for her to look back at me just once with a third of the feeling I had for her. She'd wrap her legs around me. She'd kiss me. She'd come. But with her eyes closed, and her chin on my shoulder so she couldn't see me. Almost like a robot she could make believe with, because she couldn't have the one she really wanted.

She loved Logos. She loved him because she'd spent all those years swapping those letters with him, because she'd almost lost him and had got him back. She loved his mind. It was like his mind was a lamp that had shone to her in all those years of letter writing, when sometimes all she'd had was her damn dad and car racing, and reading a Logos letter had given her permission to feel what he wrote about.

She was the one who'd prod him to keep talking, when he got off on one of his history tangents, or something he'd picked up from his geek buddies at UCB. She'd twist around on the bed with her feet next to my head and her elbows propped up on the foot of it, so she could look down at him bundled up in his sleeping bag, and watch him yak with the candle flickering next to him.

I knew Logos knew what I was thinking. Sometimes he'd stop in mid-gab and shoot me a guilty look, like he'd done something wrong, even if he'd just been answering one of her questions. Or he'd find some way to work me into the conversation. I knew he wanted it to work between us worse than anyone.

•   •   •

The C wasn't doing that great. The Valkyrie hadn't nabbed a single checkered flag for the rest of the '75 season. Some sports writers were wondering if the living legend had lost his touch.

That winter we were hit with a rash of hang-up calls. One of the extensions would ring, and whoever picked up would get a couple of seconds of silence before the line went dead. Two of our roommates figured the FBI had tapped the line.

Well, it wasn't the FBI. One night the phone upstairs finally rang just as Evelyn was tromping up the stairs from her latest double shift at Owsley's. I'd already come into the hall to get it, but she waved me away, and as soon as I saw her expression with the receiver at her ear I guessed who it was.

They talked for about five minutes. I heard her say, "Then why don't you just quit?!" about three times through the bedroom door, and then a lot of loud "No!"s and angry, muffled stuff about

Logos and public apologies, with about five times more swear words than she ever used with me. Finally she hung up on him. She didn't want to talk about it. She was so ticked off she kept cussing him on the pillow.

But the hang-up calls stopped, and he called pretty regularly after that. If Logos or me picked up he just asked to speak to Evelyn, like he didn't recognize our voices. She was always real tough with him. It was like she was more his mom than his daughter.

•　•　•

One morning I was lying on my back setting the valve lash on a Volkswagen when I spotted a pair of shoes by the front bumper. Hammering Hank had a visitor. I slid out to see who it was.

At first I thought some Telegraph Avenue wing nut had hiked over to give me a flier about the Pleiadians. He was wearing a dirty old man type overcoat, and a doofusey golf bucket hat that flopped practically to his eyebrows. Celebrities have to have their disguises, see. When I finally recognized him I was so shocked I almost dropped my feeler gauges.

The C tried to be nonchalant about it. "What's up, Kruiser?" he said, like we'd talked at some track a week before. It almost got messy. I didn't see how I could lead him to Owsley's if she wasn't expecting him, even if he was her dad. But then Logos spotted us through the window. The C really tightened up when he came out, but Logos was his usual U.N. ambassador self.

To make a long story short, Logos insisted that we escort the man to the restaurant, and then said he could go in first to get an all-clear from Evelyn. For awhile it looked like she wasn't going to give it to him. The C and I were waiting on that sidewalk in front of Owsley's for a long time, and as rich as the man's life had been I still felt sorry for him as he stood with the whole tie-died People's Republic of Berkeley population flowing around us, just to see if the queer he'd tried to ride out of Indy could talk his daughter into sitting face-to-face with him.

But finally Logos came out and invited us inside.

❈ 329 ❈

The reunion got off to a dicey start. Practically the first thing out of Evelyn's mouth was that she knew her dad only wanted to see her because he thought she was good luck. The C said that wasn't so, and Evelyn straight up called him a liar. She sat at the table with her waist apron crumpled on her lap, glowering like she was ready to throw him out if he pulled anything. Logos tried to make small talk, but it didn't go anywhere. The table was quiet for almost two minutes, until the C looked at Logos and me with an embarrassed expression and said he'd like to speak to his daughter in private.

"No," Evelyn said. "These are my friends. I'm not going to throw them out of the restaurant for you."

But Logos pushed his chair back and said that was a perfectly understandable request, and kicked my chair leg til I got the hint and stood up, too.

•   •   •

The C hung around for the rest of the day. Evelyn stayed pretty cool with him. She had a lifetime of memories of Daddy not coming to meet the teacher, Daddy not remembering her birthday, Daddy hardly even noticing if she had the flu, and then Daddy running the same old apology routine when she got sick of his B.S. She was positive he'd only come around because he wasn't winning races, and thought he needed his daughter's good luck. She said that to Logos and me at least five times. Like we just hadn't caught on to him yet.

But Logos said he thought there was more to it than that. He kept bending over backwards to help the C feel welcome, and even tried to loosen him up with racing questions, which I knew Logos was about as interested in as big game hunting. The C said he wasn't ready to retire, which got Evelyn mad all over again. His eyesight was still 20/15, and if Fangio could run the best race of his life at age forty-seven, well, maybe he could too. He'd just had a bad season, that was all.

•   •   •

About a week after he left, Logos showed me a letter that had come in the afternoon's mail:

> *Hello, Logos,*
> *I am writing to apologize for how I treated you in Indianapolis.*
> *Many years ago, I protected a young man with a cleft palate from bullies and teasers in Fresno. He became Boss Maryland, the greatest race car mechanic who ever lived, and the real reason for my success. I believe I should have remembered that experience when Evelyn brought you to Indianapolis.*
> *I do not believe in "gay rights." I think you should see a psychiatrist about your homosexual problem. But the strong can still protect the weak.*
> *During my visit, I learned why my girl speaks of you so highly. I hope you meet a woman who can straighten you out. She will have to be one of the best in California, to deserve you.*
> *Yours sincerely,*
> *C*

•   •   •

It took Logos more than a year to go to any kind of gay meeting. For the first three months after we got back from Indianapolis, he was too busy shuttling back and forth between tutoring gigs. Then he found out that the newcomer's center had closed, and that gave him the perfect excuse to blow the whole thing off. But Evelyn got on the horn and found out about a gay student union meeting that met twice a week in the city, and nagged Logos until one Friday he finally said okay, he'd go. He acted like he was on his way to meet an IRS auditor.

Well, he didn't get home til three in the morning. I think I was having a nightmare about working at HM&F when I felt something go Clump on the mattress, and when I woke up there was Logos, sitting on the edge of the bed and jabbering a mile a minute to Evelyn. Talk about excited. On and on and on (and between you and me, on and on and *on* and on and on) about what the meeting had been like and who said what and how the all-wise and all-knowing meeting facilitator had run things, and a pudgy grad student Logos recognized from Stanford and a black Southerner who thought he was going to hell for liking men, and awkward silences at the coffee pot, and when Logos had finally talked and what he'd said and so on.

I mean, sheesh. Frankly. When was he going to shut up? I had a new clutch I had to put into a Fiat first thing the next a.m. But Evelyn wanted to hear every detail. It had been one of the biggest nights of Logos' life. She understood that.

•　　•　　•

After that Logos was gone more than he was around. I don't know if you've heard what San Francisco was like for gays in the 1970s. Basically, you had thousands of people who'd gotten picked on for being queer or had felt ashamed for being queer or had never let on to anybody that they were queer who finally had a place to go where they could act like themselves. And it was a nice place, too. San Francisco beats Bakersfield and Barstow cold in a beauty contest.

So, they made parts of the city into a non-stop carnival. There were gay bars and gay bookstores and gay parades, and men kissing and walking arm in arm in the Castro and parts of Polk, and so much for Irving Bieber. Logos wasn't the only one who'd been in a closet. He was meeting people who'd been in the closet longer than he'd been alive, and talking about stuff he'd only shared with Evelyn and me. And it wasn't illegal in the Castro to look at a man the way he'd looked at gorilla sweater. He had plenty of company.

•　　•　　•

After a month of sleeping at the house only a couple of times a week, Logos met a biology professor who ran a kind of gay rooming house in a Victorian near Twin Peaks. He had a free room, and Logos grabbed it. By this time he was starting to work out a little and wear t-shirts with the sleeves rolled up. The rest of the household had figured out what was going on, but it was still a secret in Prado.

Evelyn got all teary-eyed while he packed up. I didn't see what the fuss was about. S.F. was twenty minutes away on the damn BART. It wasn't like he was moving to Borneo.

Evelyn lasted all of two weeks before she wanted to get on the damn BART for a visit. After that we went over almost every weekend. We'd transfer to Muni and get off at Castro Street, and either meet him there or at Corona Heights Park a couple of blocks away. Sometimes we'd just walk and yak. Other times Logos would drag us up to Golden Gate Park to see some new exhibit at the de Young I didn't care about, or we'd go way the hey up to Fort Mason and walk around there. Stuff like that.

By this time we could already see that Logos and the Castro weren't going to be a perfect match. He'd ditched the rolled-up shirt sleeves, and gone back to his off-the-rack-at-the-strip-mall duds. He said he was gay now, though, with no hedging. Bieber had been wrong; his biology prof landlord thought it was genetic, and Logos did, too, even though there wasn't any proof yet. He wasn't going to go back to pretending to be something he wasn't, even if he wasn't ready to come out in Prado.

But he'd never fit in in Prado, and he didn't fit in in the Castro, either. There was one bookstore-cafe he'd go to if we wanted to eat near his home, but the rest of the time he wanted to get out of the neighborhood.

One time we were walking near the Castro Theatre, and up waltzes this joker who could've played left tackle for the Niners, if the Niners line dressed like Tom of Finland cartoons. Leather hot pants, rings on his nipples, black leather cap, muscles out to here. Evelyn nudged me and I did a double take and Muscles leered at us, like he was a tourist attraction we were getting to gawk at for free.

But Logos wouldn't smile or look at the guy, and walked along frowning at the sidewalk. We'd been on our way to the bookstore-cafe, but after we saw that guy Logos changed his mind and said he wanted to get out of the Castro, and eat in the Haight instead.

• • •

One afternoon after we'd scratched our chins over all the de Young artwork I didn't care about, we hoofed it into the Richmond and caught a bus out to Sutro Heights Park. Logos liked to go up there, partly for the views and partly because of what a cool dude Adolph Sutro had been.

It was warm and sunny. Evelyn said San Francisco didn't get as many days like that as other places, because it was already so pretty and God thought She should even things up. We got off and walked into the park, and as soon as we passed the two lion sculptures at the entrance Logos started yakking about how everything there had once been Sutro's estate, but that even while he hung his hat there Sutro had opened the grounds so working stiffs could come out and enjoy the views.

We hiked up to the promontory next to old Adolph's digs. Logos and Evelyn sat on the grass next to a platoon of wild poppies, and Evelyn took the cup out and held it in her lap, the way she did when we were alone in our room at the Shack.

I walked across the plateau and hitched my foot up on the parapet wall and just dug on the mild sea breeze blowing my hair back while I gazed across the Pacific.

I must've gotten lost in my thoughts, or maybe in all the free air space floating around between my ears, because when I walked back I saw that Evelyn and Logos were in the middle of a big serious conversation. Logos was talking. He was sitting with his legs crossed and his head down, and staring at his hands as he twisted green weed stalks between his fingers.

I sat down with them and didn't say anything.

It turned out that Logos was talking about a man he'd spent the night with. It was like fate had set things up so I'd hear the kind of intimate stuff he talked about with Evelyn. He never would have started a conversation about that with me.

Miles. That was the man's name. They'd met at a party in Noe Valley, at the house of a friend of the gay biology professor. Miles had been standing with his drink in front of a print by an artist Logos recognized, and they'd got to talking about it.

The artist was Ludwig Meidner. It turned out that Miles was from Germany, where Meidner was from, and had dreamed of becoming a painter, too, but had decided that architecture was more practical. He'd come to the U.S. to study. He knew more about Meidner than Logos did, and as he talked Logos noticed how crisp and self-assured Miles' voice was, and his strong jaw and brilliant eyes, and the way he had of scanning the room like a hawk before letting his gaze swing back to Logos.

And Logos hadn't been able to not think: Maybe. Maybe. Finally. This time. He'd tried so hard, ever since the gay student union meeting, and nothing had come close to working out. He knew he wasn't handsome and that looks mattered, even when you were looking for someone for the long haul. He knew he'd only just met Miles and it was too early to get his hopes up, but still. Maybe.

The party wound down. Logos invited Miles back to his room. They walked up Diamond Street and it was cool and Miles said, 'You look chilly,' and slid his arm around Logos' waist in a self-assured way, like they were already an item. And Logos kept thinking, finally, finally, finally.

But all Miles had wanted was sex.

Logos stopped talking for a few seconds. He stared at the ground and watched his fingers curling around the weed stalks, like maybe he thought he could turn them into poppies if he touched them enough. He gave me a self-conscious glance, and then he went on.

It had just been a one night stand to Miles. He'd started closing in on the score as soon as Logos' bedroom door was closed. That hadn't been what Logos had wanted at all, not at all, but he'd been afraid he'd lose Miles if he didn't go along. But all the while thinking, Why won't you kiss me? Why won't you let me slide my fingers in your hair? Why are you acting like we just met in a bar?

Logos had asked afterward if he could see him again. Miles had snickered. Like that. Snickered.

"I don't understand what I'm doing wrong," Logos said.

He pulled at the weeds, and didn't look at Evelyn. Evelyn kept kneading the cup in her lap, pressing her fingers on the rim like it could fix everything if she touched it the right way. I stayed quiet. Maybe it was better that he didn't usually talk to me like this. He was my friend, and I wanted to help, but I just didn't understand. The poor dude. His jaw was trembling. Man, he looked like he was ready to cry.

.   .   .

Owsley's went through three managers in a year. The last one thought that food couldn't make you sick unless you needed therapy on your solar plexus chakra. The tack holding up the "All employees must wash hands" sign in the john fell off, and he didn't bother to put the sign back, and if the head cook walked straight from the crapper to the brown rice and kale entree he was fixing up, well, hey: who had to worry about salmonella if your chakras were aligned?

You can guess the rest. A UCB prof brought some of his star undergrads to Owsley's to celebrate, and they all spent the night with the heaves. Evelyn walked out.

After that she temped for a local employment agency for awhile, until she landed at a carpet warehouse long enough to impress the manager, and got a full-time gig out of it. She'd decided she wanted to go back to school by then. She'd just turned twenty-seven. She didn't feel *old* old, but she didn't feel like she was nineteen, either.

.   .   .

Hammering Hank's Auto Repair lasted another year. Then I did a brake job for a pre-law student who thought the pedal felt different after I finished, and when he rear-ended a hippy Volkswagen he blamed it on me.

Well, that put the fear of Lady Justice into me. I had to see a lawyer, and man, did that guy ever read me the riot act on Small Business 101. What do you *mean*, you don't have a business license?! What do you *mean*, you don't have insurance?!

To make a long, ugly story short: the lawyer got his fee, the pre-law student got his money back — and I still hope the S.O.B. lost it in Vegas, considering he didn't deserve it — and Hammering Hank hammered no longer.

Evelyn was taking college accounting courses by then, and not working anymore than she had to, so I couldn't spend much time savoring my new life of leisure. Fortunately, one of Hammering Hank's former customers told me about a dealer mechanic trainee program opening up on beautiful auto row in downtown Oakland. That wasn't the choicest part of the Bay Area to work in, and I felt a little weird applying to a Japanese dealer, but man, everybody was buying Japanese cars by then.

So I went in and interviewed, and started a week later. And that changed things for me. Just like Logos moving to S.F. had changed me, and Evelyn going back to school. I started shaving again every weekday morning, and I bought a windbreaker, to cover up my service uniform shirt and name patch when I took BART to work. Once my boss gave me the evil eye when I clocked in five minutes late to work, and that told me I had to watch my Ps and Qs again, like when I'd worked at Hardy's.

After a month the sales manager cut a trade-in deal for me on my 'Cuda. I knew that was the end of an era, but I wasn't driving or wrenching on it much anymore, and I felt pretty silly tooling around in a kid's muscle car. Frankly. I mean, I was an automotive professional now. And I was twenty-eight.

•　　•　　•

One night after one of her college courses Evelyn brought home a big article about the side effects of birth control pills. She'd had problems with bloating and headaches, and one of her CPA study buddies played amateur Marcus Welby and lent her the magazine. Half the ads in that rag were for stuff like milk thistle and grape seed extract, but Evelyn still got all hot and bothered about it.

"How would you feel if I stopped taking the Pill?" she wanted to know.

It was close to midnight, and we were huddled up under the sheets after giving the Pill its big nightly workout. I thought the little things were working just fine, but she was serious.

"I don't think that's my call. I can't tell you what to put in your body."

"I could get pregnant."

In the dark I felt her looking at me. So we yakked about it for awhile, about spermicidal foam and diaphragms, and me buying my first box of safes in almost five years. I didn't take it all that seriously.

We decided to switch to foam and diaphragms. If she got pregnant, Evelyn said, she'd just have to get an abortion.

Well, you can guess the rest.

Three months passed. Spermicide. Diaphragm. Whoops! We got a little careless. Maybe we got away with it. Morning sickness. Pregnancy test. No, we didn't get away it. She's expecting. And of course now that little Junior has set up shop in there: oh, no, no, she could never get an abortion, that's unimaginable, I don't know what I was thinking, maybe you misheard me, did I say that?, I couldn't have said that. It's unthinkable.

·   ·   ·

She kept getting morning sickness for awhile and got weepy a couple of times, and practically kneaded her cup to death, from all the time she spent huddled up on the bed and worrying that thing in her lap. Once when she was weepy she said I was *pressuring* her to get an abortion, which had to be the most whack patrol thing she'd ever said to me. She said she was sorry the next day, but by then I was doing some freaking out on my own account. A baby. We were baking up one of those little bald nudists that cry all the time. I had a steady gig at the dealership, but we lived in a Berkeley commune. Come on. Half our roommates looked like they'd been airlifted out of the last set at Woodstock.

Mom was exactly zero help. "Now you'll know how it feels," she said. Practically crowed it at me. And hung up.

But I had a good talk with Dixie, who was master tenant on the lease, and she said we could go Catholic and have a dozen kids, for all she cared. Plus it turned out that Casey next to us upstairs was about to join some ashram in Oregon, and if we covered his rent and pried out the 2 x 4s nailed over the connecting door, well, our budding family could have a regular hippy house suite. I said that was fine. One less thing to think about. By then I was up to my eyebrows in parent-to-be books I'd picked up at Moe's. I figured if I crammed up enough on trimesters and fetal stages and false labors during my lunch breaks, well, maybe I'd make that transcontinental flight, and not leave my toothbrush behind when I ran out to get the cab.

And I had another idea. Maybe things would be different now between Evelyn and me. Maybe she'd love me now, really love me, love me the all-the-way-from-the-inside-out way I loved her, if I showed her what a good dad I could be. We were going to have a child together. It didn't seem right that I should still be someone she'd just said 'Okay' to because I'd wanted her so bad, and because the real man of her dreams hadn't been available.

In her seventh month we had the big conversation about baby names. She was camped out in this big La-Z-Boy rig I'd set for her in Casey's old room, with pillows stuffed in to help out her back and a tray next to it for the liquids I kept nagging her to drink, and the vitamins I'd bought.

I went through the list of names I'd been working on, and watched her camped out in that recliner staring at the wallpaper with a stubborn, secret look in her eyes, and already knew deep down how it was going to turn out. I wanted her to at least suggest "Hank Jr." so bad I would've slit my wrists and bled to death on the carpet to hear her say it, but I knew she never would.

"How would you feel about naming him after Logos?" she said.

• • •

And it was like I was getting beat up by a friend who never wanted to throw a punch at me. Do you understand? I couldn't let my hair down with Logos. He would have died to hear what I was going through.

At the dealership my boss transferred out, and HQ sent hell's own shop chief to replace him. This guy made Dirk look like Mother Teresa. He tried to hustle us out of our lunch breaks, and wrote off our overtime hours so we didn't get paid, and bawled us out in front of customers when it wasn't our fault. Two mechanics walked out, and any other time in my life I would've been the third, but not with the big trip to the maternity ward coming up.

I kissed that SOB's fanny so good he didn't need to buy toilet paper. I had a bad boss, and the mother of my son wasn't all that keen on me. That was the hand I'd been dealt. I had responsibilities now. I had to suck it up.

．　．　．

Two was born a couple of days after California voted in Prop 13 in the big '78 election. That must be why the *Chronicle* didn't plaster his baby photos all over the front page. "Logos Kruzenski" was on his birth certificate, but we already knew a Logos, and Two was easier. As soon as I laid eyes on him with Evelyn on that hospital bed, I knew it didn't much matter what he was called. There'd never be anything else so important to me. My whole life would be different from that moment on.

Grown-up Logos stayed over a lot to help out in the first months. Two was a pretty mellow little dude, but there isn't a baby worth his diaper who doesn't wake up Mommy and Daddy for a good three in the a.m. holler sometimes. I got to be pretty good at settling him down. He liked it when I paced a little Indy Speedway circuit around his crib, while I cradled him and hummed a lullaby in his ear.

I'd whisper to him sometimes, even though he was too little to know what I was saying. I told him he was the most precious thing that had come into my life, and I wasn't going to forget it, and that someday I was going to win his mother's heart, really win it, so Mommy and Daddy would love each other like Mommy and Daddy loved him. So it wouldn't be half a marriage.

．　．　．

One afternoon I found out when I got back from the shop that Evelyn had booked us for a big dinner date in the city. She was all excited. Logos had a boyfriend. Finally; a real one. Two was old enough for a stroller by then, and Logos had picked out a family-friendly Mex restaurant in the Mission.

Mr. Right turned out to be a grad student who looked like he spent his whole life tracking down footnotes. Logos introduced us in front of the restaurant, real formal. Hank, Evelyn, I'd like you to meet Stephen.

Stephen managed a smile. A shy type. Maybe twenty-seven, with a brainy forehead and a set of horn rims that probably weren't even legal to wear if you weren't in Mensa. Logos had found a fellow egghead.

The waiter sized up our wallets before setting out the free chips, and leaned over the stroller to kitchy-koo Two, and flashed us a big *Buenas Noches* while he doled out the menus, which must have been all the *español* he thought we could handle. We yakked about how underrated the Mission was, and other places you could get good Mexican food, and how hard it was to eat out with a baby, and weren't the summers in San Francisco colder than almost anywhere else? Small talk. Stephen stayed shy. He'd open up a little about seismology, which was what he was doing his grad work in, but the rest of the time it was Yes, No, I'm not sure, and he'd flush if he thought you were staring at him.

The waiter brought our food. Evelyn fussed over Two a lot. Logos sat close to Stephen and sometimes got in whispery little side talks with him. Like he was checking to be sure he felt okay.

Once I saw they were holding hands. Just sitting quietly side by side, like they were married, with Logos' little paw resting on the webs between Stephen's fingers.

• • •

A couple of months later, Logos and Stephen moved into an apartment on Nob Hill. Logos was the only one on the lease because Stephen had maxed out his credit card, but Logos said they'd split the rent after Stephen got caught up.

Logos thought it was time to come out with his family. But he was scared of starting the conversation, and guess who Evelyn thought would be the perfect person to get the ball rolling?

So I got Greg on the horn, and wound up meeting him at good old Pilgrim's. He'd changed. If I'd just had a glimpse of that big wheel I was on, I would've seen how that was part of the picture: meeting someone you've lost track of, and seeing how Father Time put him on the potter's wheel and molded and re-shaped him, and guessing that maybe, just maybe, the person on the other side of the table can see the same kinds of changes in you.

Greg had joined Alcoholics Anonymous. He hadn't touched a drink in two years, and showed me a special gold coin he'd gotten for his sobriety anniversary. I laid out the deal about Logos' secret love life. Greg didn't care. Two alkies in his AA home group were queer. He'd break the news to his family.

But he thought I should know that things had changed at the De Mello household. Frank had got way too old to go out in the truck anymore. It was mostly Greg running All American House Painters now. Believe it or not.

•   •   •

Greg and Logos set up a date for the big family reunion on Nob Hill a couple of weeks later. Consuela couldn't walk very far and you practically needed a full clip in an M16 to get a parking space out there, but Greg figured he could double park long enough to let her out, and then Barry and Ronald could look after her while Greg hunted up a spot out near Crissy Field, or Sausalito, or however far he had to go.

It wasn't perfect. Apparently Frank hadn't taken the news too well. Even with me Greg didn't want to go into the details, which was a bad sign. He just said we could scratch the old man from the invitee list, period. But everybody else was on board.

The big day came. Evelyn wore a dress, and I managed to get a tie on without suffocating myself. I wanted to go over early so we'd have plenty of time to get a cab from the BART, because no way we were carting Two over on one of those packed cable cars, but Evelyn said Logos was already stressed out, and didn't need guests coming in stages. He'd scrubbed the place from top to bottom, and asked everybody he knew for advice on take-out food, and shelled out for a big Macys raid for silverware and dishes and place settings and a tablecloth. The little gerbil actually took his nutty family seriously. He'd called Evelyn twice, just out of nervousness.

Logos' apartment was close to Grace Cathedral. Evelyn and Two and me made it right on time. There was Consuela, leaning on Barry and Ronald so she wouldn't keel over, and the five of us chit-chatted until Greg got back from docking the car out in the Farallones, or wherever he'd put it. Then we rang the bell.

Well, that was some night. Logos was a brave host. The grub smelled great and the place was laid out like the Fairmont, and Logos kept his smile tacked up even though we all saw right away that one of the star guests was MIA. I made Daddy faces at Two, and Logos did the serving with Evelyn, who kept watching him to make sure he was okay, and then over French roast and pastries Logos cleared his throat for his 'Mom, I am a homosexual' speech. The De Mellos all nodded in the right places. Consuela said she just wanted Logos to be happy.

But I didn't think she was going to get her wish, at least not that night. Logos was playing host on his own, see. Mr. Right hadn't been so right after all. Stephen had moved out that morning.

· · · ·

Logos paid a small fortune to break the lease, and moved back into his room at the biology professor's. He didn't try to date anymore, even though Evelyn nagged him to. It was like he was a martyr. He'd gone through all this misery of trying to come out, but he didn't feel at home in the Castro anymore than he'd felt in Prado, and maybe God was trying to show him something. If there was a God. He'd stopped looking after wounded birds like Rosenfeld and Maria. He'd become selfish, hadn't he? Maybe this was what he'd got for it.

He started donating half his free time with a gung-ho eco transit group, and tutoring for free at a halfway house, and doing other volunteer stuff. Evelyn didn't think it was healthy. Sometimes I overheard her getting all exercised with him on the phone, about how he had to go out and date, and she'd even pay for a personals ad if he'd run it in a queer newspaper, and she hadn't held his hand through that first gay student union meeting to see him lock himself in a see-through closet.

But Logos wouldn't. Maybe he was like Frank Buchman, he said, who'd started Moral Re-Armament. Buchman thought God had made him ugly for a reason. And Evelyn practically yelled at him when he said that, but it didn't change anything, even though she fretted and stewed about him after they got off the phone.

· · · ·

Maybe a year after that, Charles and Pete packed up a U-Haul and moved out of the Shack to Portland. Dixie said she'd take care of rassling up some new housemates.

Well, she sure did. I don't know if she just turned over the house keys to the first panhandlers she met on Telegraph, or picked them out of a show-up at Berkeley P.D. Two obvious druggies. They made Tyler and his HM&F buddies look like Pat Boone.

First, there was the syringe plunger in the bathroom waste-basket. I don't know about you, but I don't usually use a hypo-dermic when I brush my teeth. Next, Evelyn couldn't find a gold bracelet Boss had given her once for her birthday. Then some of my tools went missing. Just a coincidence, right?

Well, no thanks. Not with a toddler to look out for. Another bookkeeper told Evelyn about a cottage out in Fairview Park that her mom wanted to rent, as long as the tenants promised to keep the garden watered. It wasn't the Ritz, but it was about ten times more than we were used to at the Shack.

And see, that was another change. I didn't get the big picture yet of the wheel I was on, of the cosmic game I was in. Maybe if you're pushing fifty you've got a better outline of that wheel than I had, of how the little changes stack up and make the big changes from your twenties to thirties and forties. You think it's just another blip in your life, but it's not. You can't see the picture yet because you're inside it.

A few months later we had a housewarming party. Dixie and a bunch of other people we'd known from the Shack came out, and parked their battered-up beetles and vans by the late-model Audis and Volvos of our new neighbors, and ooh'd and aah'd over the garden, and how the sun looked through the fluttery leaves of the willow trees. Logos couldn't make it, because one of his old S.F. roommates had dropped about thirty pounds and come down with some kind of weird pneumonia, and Logos wanted to stick around the city to take care of him. But everybody else came. I handed out beers and Evelyn showed off the backyard patio and the washer and drier we had all to ourselves, and every-body said they'd visit, that nothing had really changed, and they believed it when they said it, and Evelyn and I did, too.

But none of them ever came back.

After awhile I noticed how neat most of our neighbors dressed, and how they kept their houses up. Nobody slipped a Fairview Park dress code in my mailbox, but I felt funny hanging out there in my Hammering Hank duds, with a lot of junk stacked on the porch. So I spruced up the yard, and dressed better.

I thought that was just another little change that didn't mean anything. I didn't see the big picture.

• • •

For awhile the gung-ho eco transit group looked like it'd be damn near as big as the Sierra Club. Logos and some other zealots stood out in the rain at night to run line checks on Muni buses, and they organized a protest against these godawful trains Muni was about to buy, that had broke down and derailed in Boston. A local columnist wrote a big spread about them, and then a family foundation dumped a windfall grant in their laps. Major leagues, here we come, right?

But then the executive director started yakking about how "money is energy," and tripled his own salary, and took cabs everywhere. Four months later, the windfall is gone. Then these slick blow-dried dudes started hanging out at the office, and man, they looked like they wouldn't have been daught dead on the Muni. But they got the E.D. a sweetheart deal on a Pantera and comped him to a kilo of Hawaiian weed, and pretty soon when he wasn't toking his way through that kilo in his new car the E.D. was hogging board meetings with sincereamundo speeches about how they had to broaden their organizational mission and help the city prosper, and join his new blow-dried buddies in taking a public stand against the misguided anti-real estate development forces who wanted San Francisco to be a little fishing village forever, and never grow up and compete with Manhattan.

Two guesses what business the blow-dried buddies were in.

Logos quit. Evelyn said he was being defeatist. The Bay Area had plenty of sincere nonprofits. Why couldn't he join one of those? Or get the E.D. fired? Or start a group of his own?

But Logos said he felt worn out. You could zero in on a problem and work to patch it up, he said, but human badness would hatch three new problems while you had your back turned. It was like trying to rake leaves in a typhoon. We homo sapiens were doing our best, but we'd descended from quarrelsome apes, and could expect a lot more of the seven deadly sins from ourselves until we did some more evolving. If we made it that far.

And besides, these days all his time was booked playing Florence Nightingale in the Castro. The old roommate had died, and now another buddy had come down with some kind of freak skin cancer that had spackled these purple-red blotches all over his chest. Kaposi's Sarcoma. That's what the cancer was called. The poor dude was all of twenty-six, and he'd somehow picked up an oddball cancer that usually just went after old Italians and Jews.

Logos had heard of another guy who had the same thing. Maybe something was going around.

· · ·

Two had got potty training aced out by the morning that my shop chief called me off the floor for a phone call. Sergeant Greg Jenner, Prado Diablo P.D. Damn if I didn't remember him from high school.

Uh, Hank, we got your mom down here. She'd got all exercised when Grocery Baron wouldn't take a rubber check for a fifth of Old Arkansas, and slugged the manager. Now she couldn't make bail.

To make a long story short: adios Fairview Park. I burned the candle at both ends to get my wife and boy moved out of our home sweet home there, and back into the house I'd grown up in. Evelyn wasn't too keen on the idea, and neither was I, but it was either that or visit Mom in the drunk tank. She'd gone downhill fast since my last drop-by at Christmas. Both of the help-out-with-the-rent roommates she'd found in the *Recycler* had moved out, on account of her drinking, and she was damn close to losing her cashier job, too.

Our reunion got off to a rocky start. Mom promised to cut back on the sauce, but then almost crashed into Two's crib after she'd had three or four of what she'd promised to "cut back" on, and Evelyn put her foot down. Hard. She'd already lived with an alky. Mom either went cold turkey, or we moved out.

And damn if Mom didn't do it. I guess she knew her back was to the wall. Plus now she had a grandson to help take care of, and a couple of grumpy new housemates to talk to over breakfast. Pretty soon she looked better than she had since my grade school days.

We thought the move back to Prado was temporary. But that wasn't how things worked out. I still hadn't got a sense yet of that wheel I was on. I'd be out for a grocery run and glance at the guy lined up behind me, and the chimes would go off, and what do you know: it's none other than Kerry Matthews, who drew a moustache on my Mickey Mantle baseball card in fourth grade. Hey, Kerry, long time no see, how're things? Turned out that Kerry's an account representative for the phone company. Or here's the former big league sexpot Connie Dawson, with three kids in tow and pushing size twenty, and she pretends not to recognize me.

My hated boyhood foe Earl Howser was sales manager of a lease fleet out in Antioch. Dirk was supposed to be partner in a gun store. Tyler was still at HM&F, but Dean from our old car pool had sobered up and bounced back in a big way. He was running his dad's electronics business.

Everybody looked so damn old. They had hard lines in their faces where the puppy fat had been before, and some of the guys had lost hair, and others had gone paunchy. I'd almost felt like getting hitched and having Two were accidents that had only happened to me, but it sure looked like the same accidents had hit a lot of other people.

•　　•　　•

In late '81 Logos picked up a teaching assistant gig at Pacheco Community College. That's practically yodeling distance from Prado, so he rented our garage to have a crash pad near campus. His bank balance was running on fumes, but he still felt guilty for taking the job. He felt like he was walking out on the Castro at a bad time.

It looked like an epidemic was moving in. He knew of three other queers who had Kaposi's, and researchers had tied it in with the pneumonia that had killed his old roommate. It looked like it might be doing something to the immune system. That would explain why they got Kaposi's, and pneumocystis, and candida, and other weird infections that the body usually kicked out. Of course, maybe it *wasn't* an epidemic, and a bunch of unlucky queers had picked up a blood problem from a bad batch of drugs, but Logos didn't think so. It had hit the East Coast, too. The *New York Native* had run articles about it.

Logos had been on three dates since Stephen. Three. Evelyn didn't like it. He was only thirty-one. People were supposed to be with other people, weren't they? But Logos just said that wasn't his role. He felt something had made him what he was.

•   •   •

One Friday we were all watching the tube in the living room when this documentary came on about rare and precious objects of the ancient world. Here's the Rosetta Stone, here's the Dead Sea Scrolls, with a lot of tripey music and a Thor Heyerdahl type narrating the whole magoo. Mom would have made a flying lunge for the remote, but she was out at her AA meeting. It was just the three of us and the boy wonder, choo-chooing the play train Logos had got him around the living room.

At some point, the narrator wondered aloud what treasures would be unearthed by the archaeologists of tomorrow. Next to me I felt Evelyn tense up. Six years had passed since that bus ride home from Indy, and Logos had never once leaned on her to go public with the cup. It was like we'd sworn an oath to leave it up to her after we'd entered her inner circle.

The Heyerdahl type signed off, and the music swelled, and the commercials came on. None of us said anything. Evelyn looked embarrassed.

Then Logos started talking about it. Real matter-of-fact and calm, like he was picking up where he'd left off six years ago. Two would be ready for pre-school soon, and then grammar school. He'd go on field trips. Maybe the de Young didn't have a Rosetta Stone, but there were other amazing things he could see there, because the people who'd owned those things had been generous and shared them with the world.

He wasn't going to twist her arm. He just hoped she'd think about sharing it, so other people could get to see it, too.

Well, damn if Evelyn didn't say that she had. Freaked me out. Her voice got ratchety, but she went ahead. She said she'd thought of giving it to the Sioux. She could fly to South Dakota and maybe call a press conference, and present it to the Oglala Lakota nation on behalf of Ricky. But she didn't know any Sioux, and she just wasn't sure. She wanted to think about it.

That night she talked about it with me after we got Two to sleep. Maybe Logos was right. What did I think? It would change our lives, if she turned over the cup. There'd be reporters and TV crews. But she didn't *know* any Sioux. Did I think she was being selfish?

I told her it was her call. She said she'd decide in the morning.

· · ·

That night I had a dream.

Not a lightweight, run of the mill dream. A strong one. Like somebody or something upstairs wants to put you in a hammerlock and crank up the flood lights, because there's something important to be said, and you'd better be paying attention.

I was an actor in the dream. An actor, standing behind the curtain backstage in some fancy pants New York or Paris theater I'd never go to in real life. The show's sold out. They've got a full house. On the other side of the curtain I can hear the blue bloods in the audience chattering away in their tuxedoes and gowns and jewelry, lined up in the crushed red velvet seats under the big chandeliers. I don't know what the play is, but I'm an important player in it.

I decide to pull open the curtain to take a look at the audience. But I pull it open too far. Much too far.

They all see me.

Everybody in the audience is quiet for a second. Then a big groan comes up. I've ruined something, see. I came out too early. I ruined the surprise.

· · ·

That dream was still clear as a bell for me when I woke up Saturday morning. I thought about it while I pulled on some duds, and was still thinking about it when I waddled out to the kitchen. Evelyn and Logos were already there. They looked preoccupied.

I helped myself to some of the hash browns on the stove. I figured I'd better liven things up. I shot Logos a fake dirty look.

"Man," I said, "I don't know what you slipped into that tea last night, but I'm sure not having any more of it. Did I ever have a weird dream."

And then it was like I just knew. From the way neither of them answered, from how they both stared at me while I stood at the toaster. So I knew even before Logos asked me in a tight voice what the weird dream had been.

It turned out that they'd both had practically the same dream I had.

The theater in Evelyn's dream had been more like Fillmore West than an opera house. But the other details were the same.

•　　•　　•

Logos gave a big speech about coincidences. They happened all the time, he said. Coincidences like our dream didn't prove that anything supernatural was afoot, anymore than a Vegas jackpot proved that God watched over slot machines. When something unusual happened, he tried to remember something he called Occam's razor, and lean toward the simplest and most reasonable explanation. The simplest and most reasonable explanation for the dream was that we'd all been thinking about the cup. Okay? Maybe we'd seen something on TV about a theater.

But Logos' voice was froggy, and it sounded like the main person he was trying to sell on the coincidences argument was Logos De Mello.

He never suggested going public with the cup again. Evelyn didn't take it out as often. When she did, she handled it a lot more carefully. Me, I gave it a wide berth. I wasn't a superbrain like Logos. There were smarter and more powerful things in life than me, and I accepted it, and either the cup or the mind behind the cup was one of them. And that thing had some business with me down the road, too. I'd felt that way since almost the first time I'd laid eyes on it at Fort Funston. It didn't like or dislike me. It was just hanging out and watching, and waiting for our appointment.

•   •   •

A couple of months later Mom got all hot and bothered about having her AA sponsor move in with her. Shirley was about her age, and had ten years of sobriety, and never complained if Mom called her at three in the morning to gripe about world affairs, or how her useless son Hank had forgot to put down the seat again. They'd hit it off. Plus she'd already raised a baby, thanks very much, and maybe she wasn't as maternal as some other grand-moms, but she'd just as soon not pick up after a pre-schooler in her golden years. Hint hint hint.

So Evelyn and I started thumbing through the classifieds, and pretty soon our eyes wandered over to an ad for condos for sale near the BART. I didn't see how we could swing it, but Evelyn got out her accounting class calculator and ran the numbers, and pretty soon we were prospective first home buyers. Which was another notch on that wheel I was on, but by now I'd finally got to where I could glimpse the wheel a little. I wasn't the same man who'd gone hunting for those cylinder heads at the Fiesta.

We found a two bedroom about fifteen minutes from BART on foot. It cost ten grand more than the other condos we looked at, but it had a den that could double as a guest bedroom, and Evelyn was hoping we'd have a more or less permanent visitor. She even wanted Logos to check it out before we signed the paperwork.

But Logos only wound up staying with us through the summer of 1982. By then things had gotten a lot worse in the Castro. It wasn't 'maybe' an epidemic anymore. The network news stations had finally run stories about it, and one poor SOB with KS had put up a flier in the window of Star Pharmacy, so other queers could see what the lesions looked like. Almost everybody knew or had heard about somebody who had the lesions, or who'd lost a lot of weight, or who had these horrible white sores in his mouth. They were all part of the same disease.

Acquired Immune Deficiency Syndrome. That's what the scientists were calling it now. Logos didn't want to teach teenagers at a J.C. in Contra Costa County with that going on. He was gay. He'd come out in San Francisco. Maybe he didn't take well to a lot of gay culture, but it was still time to stand on the front lines.

•　　•　　•

After he moved out Evelyn and I saw two TV reports on AIDS. The first was a little clip on the network news. Here's Tom Brokaw and some lab coat dude pouring blood in a test tube, and an interview with one of the first AIDS victims. Bobby Campbell. He was the one who'd put the flier up in Star Pharmacy, with the pictures of his KS lesions.

"Oh, look, that's who Logos told us about," Evelyn said. Like Logos lived in Beverly Hills, and Bobby Campbell was a big celeb in the mansion next door. Like she didn't register what was going on. And Bobby Campbell looked fine. Maybe a little underweight.

But the second TV news report was different. It showed a patient with way bad KS. His face was covered with those scabby purplish-red blotches, like a Halloween mask. The narrator said he'd lost fifty pounds. You *knew* he was going to die, looking at those bulged out eyes and sunken cheeks.

Then the broadcast showed a line of queers waiting to get into a bathhouse at Eighth and Howard. "Many speculate that promiscuity among homosexual males is a significant factor in the transmission of the disease," the voiceover said.

Evelyn didn't say anything during that second news report. When the guy with the bad KS came on she sat up straight with a grim, hurt look. Then when it was two-thirds through she went into the bedroom without saying anything.

•　　•　　•

Logos threw himself into AIDS volunteer work. Evelyn called him practically every night. He ran errands for AIDS victims, fetching their mail and their meds from nice old Jackie at Star Pharmacy and hauling big bags of groceries on the J line.

He helped raise money for emergency housing, and trained to be a lay support person, so he'd know how to listen to dying queers who just needed someone to talk to.

We mostly saw him when Evelyn dragged him out to visit. Not as much as before. Two had started pre-school, and Evelyn wanted to spend lots of time there, and she'd started her accounting classes again. But Logos seemed fine. He even made a joke about the shoulder muscles he was getting from lugging those grocery bags up Dolores Heights. All he talked about was his volunteering. It was pure, he said. Nobody could sell a sleazy real estate project on the back of somebody dying with AIDS. Sure, there were problems. He thought the bathhouses had to be closed right away. It didn't make any sense to license places that spread the disease at the same time they were trying to control it. He'd had ugly arguments with queers who wanted to stick their heads in the sand. But gays put those arguments aside when it was time to pitch in. A lot of people were turning out to help.

•　　•　　•

In late '83 Logos invited us over to the city for the day. Or Evelyn pried the invite out of him. He'd gone on and on about all the great people he'd met volunteering. "So when are you going to let us come meet one?" Evelyn said. Then she gave him a hard time about how we hardly saw him anymore.

Finally they set a date for the next Sunday. Evelyn told me we'd be meeting one of Logos' co-workers. Another volunteer. That's what we both thought.

The address we had was for a flat in a Victorian near Dolores Park. We rang the bell and the buzzer sounded, and Two lit up the stairs ahead of us. He loved Uncle Logos.

But it wasn't Uncle Logos who was up there waiting.

The poor bastard had needed a cane just to make it to the door to meet us. He had an eye patch, and the skin was sucked up tight like dried leather on his forehead, so the vein popped out. The KS lesions were all over his arms. Maybe he hadn't thought anybody would be stone loco enough to bring a kid to see him, or he would've worn a coat. And there he was wavering on his cane and trying to put on a sociable smile for the little boy who'd dashed up the stairs, and you can guess how Two was standing and gawking at him. Like any five year old would.

"Oh, you brought your son!" the guy said. "Logos didn't tell me!"

From the rear of the flat a toilet flushed. Logos stepped into the hall. He spotted Two and stopped dead and looked sick. Evelyn and I had made it to the top of the stairs by then. Two rushed up to Mommy and stood next to her gaping at the guy, and Evelyn put her arm around him in an automatic protective way, like the poor dude was going to swing his cane at us, and Logos was looking miserable and making pantomime gestures behind the guy's back. Miscommunication. Major, major miscommunication, about who we were going to meet.

It lasted about twenty minutes. The guy's name was Paul. He gave his cane a work-out just to make it to the living room couch. Logos almost had to help him. Then he wanted us to sit down and feel at home, and did we want something to drink?, or to eat? Logos could help him be a decent host. Logos had been such a godsend. He had heard so much about Evelyn and Hank, and he was *delighted* to make the acquaintance of *this* young gentleman, too.

And here the poor bastard was sitting on the edge of the couch and leaning on that cane and smiling his sociable best at Two, and in the man's own apartment Two was looking back like he was the creature from the black lagoon dripping slime on the floor. And Evelyn was frozen, and I was my usual stupid self, and Logos was so discombobulated over the misunderstanding that he wasn't any good either. So the poor guy had to do all the social work in the conversation even though he was the one about to croak. Jesus.

Finally Evelyn stood up. All of a sudden, in the middle of one of Paul's sentences. She was trembling.

"I'm sorry," she said. "I think this is too much for my son."

"Oh, of course, of course," Paul said. Trying to smooth it over. "I know how I must look!"

Evelyn told me a restaurant where I could meet them later, and took Two and left.

Well, my inner orator doesn't come out very often, but it did then. We owed that man an apology, and I gave it to him. We'd had a miscommunication with Logos about who we were visiting, pure and simple. I know you've got enough to concern you now without my son staring at you like that. You didn't need us to come visit and make things harder for you than they are already.

But Paul said that was okay. He knew how he must look.

· · ·

Two looked like he'd gotten over seeing Paul. He was mad at his mom, though. She'd made him walk too fast on their way from the skinny man's home. He'd had to run to keep up. And in the restaurant bathroom she'd made him wash his hands three times in a row, even though he hadn't been playing.

· · ·

That night on the phone Evelyn got in a royal argument with Logos. The start of it was about all his volunteering, but when it heated up she dragged the long extension cord into the bedroom and shut the door, so I couldn't hear. When she finally came out Two asked why her eyes were all red.

She changed. She started clipping all the articles she could find about AIDS. She usually didn't smile or look up from making breakfast anymore when I came out to the kitchen. She still called Logos a lot, but these days if he didn't answer she'd sometimes sit by the phone like a robot for a half hour before trying again. Like she was so afraid something terrible was going to happen.

One afternoon I noticed she'd given the den a big cleaning. Then she asked if we could spring for some new furniture in there.

I said sure. But why? If she didn't mind telling me.

She said she wanted it to be a surprise.

Three nights later she had a writing desk in there, and a new bed, and some drapes for the little window. I knew what she was trying to pull then. She might as well have flushed the cash down the john. He wasn't coming back.

She didn't want to talk about it. Like I couldn't figure out who the desk was for.

She cooked up some excuse to drag him out the next weekend.

Logos looked a little irritated. Paul had just checked into the AIDS ward at S.F. General. Logos didn't actually say we were keeping him away from his volunteer work, but I could tell that's what he thought. But Two was as happy as ever to see old Uncle Logos, and beat the tar out of him at checkers. Logos said he just couldn't get the hang of that game. Little Two always seemed to win.

After lunch, Evelyn brought us into the den and showed Logos the big surprise.

"I just think you'll be better off here," she said.

She sat on the new bed and tapped the headboard and tried to smile at him in a nonchalant way, like Logos was Two's age and she was switching rooms on him. Except she was nervous, and the smile was all twitchy, and her eyes were wet. Like a part of her knew that the Evelyn in Central Control had lost it.

Two was watching cartoons in the living room.

Logos just stood at the door and stared at her.

Evelyn went on. She'd thought about it a lot. He was over-extending himself in San Francisco. He was sacrificing his life for a problem he hadn't made, and he might not be able to get that life back if he didn't stop now. She had put her foot down years ago about the newcomer's center, so she felt responsible. He needed to meet an intelligent, stable gay man who was appropriate for him.

But her mouth kept trembling while she talked.

Finally, Logos said, "Evelyn, you know I have commitments in San Francisco. I can't leave."

Evelyn nodded, and looked at the floor, and then she looked back with her jaw set. Like now it was time to pull out the heavy ammo.

"Well, maybe you'll do it for the sake of historical research," she said, in a clipped voice.

Then she dropped the bombshell: she'd go public with the cup if he'd agree to move in. He could call up some of his friends at Berkeley or Stanford and choose the museum he wanted it donated to. She'd as much as give it to him.

She sat on the bed and brushed the hair back from her eyes and tried to look like she was making a sober business proposal. Except her mouth kept jerking.

But Logos told her quietly that he couldn't make that kind of bargain.

Then it got ugly. You're throwing your life away on a bunch of degenerates, she said, and then when Logos tried to break in she raised her voice. They're so sex addicted that they won't stop going to the bathhouses even though it's spreading the disease. Didn't you, didn't you yourself tell me that they spit, actually *spit* on a gay reporter who said the baths should be closed? They're sick and disgusting, and you don't have anything in common with them, and maybe if he wouldn't move in, well, she might just *destroy* the cup, smash it, so no one would see it.

Finally she stopped, and sat with her chest heaving and her mouth all haywire. Logos gave it about the count of three. He looked sad. He stepped up to the bed, and gave her a little hug, and told her he loved her. He'd better go now. He'd talk to her again when she was more herself.

So instead after he left *I* got to argue with her. Not that it did any good. She wasn't going to apologize. I was the one who didn't understand. Logos might die.

•   •   •

In 1984 the death toll went way up. Bobby Campbell died. The AIDS poster boy. Paul barely made it to February. The obituary count in the big gay newspaper skyrocketed. Camera crews turned up regularly in the Castro, filming interviews with gays about how they were coping. You saw more sick people in the Castro now, Logos said: young dudes with canes, or men who'd been jocks and work-out buffs in '83 who could hardly get around in wheelchairs. The AIDS ward at S.F. General was going to have to expand. They didn't have enough beds.

One afternoon he saw a skin-and-bones queer with KS parade up and down Castro with his shirt off. Like he just wanted to show everybody the lesions on his torso and how much weight he'd lost, like he was so angry to be handed a death sentence in his twenties that he was going to make everybody at Elephant

Walk and Toad Hall look at his KS and his ribs sticking out instead of their vodka tonics.

Evelyn had finished up her classes by then, and got a part-time job with the city planning department. Two had a longer school day now that he was in first grade, but she still wanted to be around in the afternoons until he was older.

She talked to Logos a few times a week. She would've called a lot more, but he'd said they should keep their distance for awhile. He thought she was too worried. He was right; she was. She never smiled like she used to. Two even asked why Mommy always looked upset. She'd sit with her cup a lot, staring into space. Or she'd hunt through magazines for stuff about AIDS, and send Logos the articles she found. Sometimes clips for dingaling quack therapies, like DMSO. Like Logos didn't get enough of that from the desperate queers he was working with.

Maybe women do have a sixth sense. It was like she could see what was coming.

•   •   •

The C rang us up about once a month. He'd call me Kruiser, and talk trash about the latest flagship model at the dealership, and shoot the breeze with little Two about grade school. But his best girl was who he really wanted to talk to. If she got to the phone first, I could always tell when her dad was on the line by how tough she sounded.

She said he didn't have any business racing anymore. Boss had retired. He hadn't won a big race since 1978.

In spring the Dallas P.D. chucked him in the jug for plowing a rented Vette into a string of parked cars next to a shopping center. The story was all over the news the next day. Some sixteen year old had challenged him to a street race. I'm serious. Over fifty years old, trophies and world championships up the kazoo, and he gets in a hundred mile an hour stoplight duel with a high school kid. For sure he would've sent anyone in those parked cars to the hospital.

Well, that was the last straw. Maybe she had a short fuse because of all the worrying about Logos. First, she wouldn't come to the phone. Then she stood next to me and yelled at the receiver that she'd see a lawyer about a restraining order if he called again. Her son wasn't going to have a grandfather who put innocent people at risk. She might change her name. She might disown him.

So maybe that set the stage for what happened next.

•   •   •

About two weeks later we were camped out in the living room watching the Giants battle the Astros when the color commentator interrupted the play-by-play with a news announcement. Racing legend Claude Winters, better known to his fans at Mr. C., was in critical condition at Black Point Medical Center after a crash at Shale Mesa Raceway.

I don't remember the rest. He used the word "critical" twice. Then back to the ball game.

If she would have screamed, or knocked over the set, or busted out crying, or sat there and cursed her dad for five minutes. Any of that would have felt better than to watch her sit and shut her eyes the way she did.

By then the phone was ringing. Everything started to happen fast. I was getting directions from the hospital on the phone, and Evelyn was telling Two that Granddad had been in an accident, and as I was hunting up the car keys and wondering if we should bring a game for Two to play in the back seat everything seemed so unreal to me, like the C had us roped in as actors in this end of life movie he wanted to star in. Of all the race tracks in the world for him to pull his fatal. Shale Mesa was practically next door. It was like he'd planned it so he'd run that last lap next to his daughter.

He managed to stay alive until Evelyn got there. The shrapnel from the crash had ripped out chunks of his lungs and shot his heart and his liver full of metal. They had a mask on him and tubes sticking out everywhere and he was white as a ghost, but he still managed to crinkle his eye corners as we walked up.

Evelyn finally fell apart. Her face got twisted like plastic melting under a torch, and then she just stood there trembling and blubbering, because it was all over and there wasn't any point in calling him names.

The C crinkled his eyes over the mask, and nodded his head a little. He'd stayed alive until his best girl had got there. He'd won that last big race after all.

*   •   •   •

Evelyn's friends called or sent cards. I figured for sure Logos would come out, but it turned out he'd come down with some god-awful bug, and couldn't leave the flat.

Evelyn bought a box of gold picture frames and put up photos of her dad in the living room. She got out her middle school calligraphy set and made up captions for the shots, and mounted the captions under the photos. So anyone visiting could see that so-and-so shot had been taken at the Targa Florio, or at the 12 Hours of Sebring.

Nobody came over to look at the pictures. She wasn't bouncing back real good. She never went out with her old accounting class girlfriends anymore. I tried to explain that the C had dug his own hole in life, but when I brought it up she'd roll to her side of the bed and say she didn't want to talk about it.

She pulled her old C Team shirt out of the storage bin in the carport, and washed it and ironed it with lots of starch, and started wearing it around the condo. It looked like a mechanic's shop shirt. I felt like I was chowing down at the dealership. She told Two that the shirt reminded her of Granddad. Man, she was shut down. She got up and went to work like she was checking off stuff on a 'to do' list, until she could crawl back in bed and pull the covers over her head.

Logos sent Evelyn a nice letter, and a book about unfinished business with a difficult parent. He was in the same boat, in a way. Old Frank hadn't said one word to him since he'd come out.

But he still wouldn't set aside a day for a visit. The whatever-it-was bug had kept him home for two weeks, and then after that he was either too busy seeing AIDS patients, or too busy helping out with some other AIDS project, or too tired to be decent company. Evelyn got his message machine more often. Sometimes after she called he'd ring up the dealership the next day and leave a message for me that he couldn't make it. Which was weird. It would've been easier to call the condo.

That went on for about three months. Then one night an-other 'Coping with AIDS' type story came on TV, and when the camera showed the first guy with KS I saw something cold and distant come over Evelyn, like a black curtain falling. She went to the phone and called Logos. This time she didn't let him off the hook until he gave her a definite date.

Maybe we both knew by then. Or a part of us did.

• • •

Logos had told Evelyn we could meet that Saturday at some new vegetarian restaurant near the Panhandle. Then the day before he called me at the dealership and asked if we could push the time back to 7:30. We hadn't gotten together with him at night once since the big family pow-wow on Nob Hill. But Logos said he had a lot on his plate that day.

I leaned on Mom to babysit. Then Evelyn said she didn't want to have to deal with the crappy Muni at night that far west, so I got to drive over.

The Harvest. It looked like another hippy-dippy storefront restaurant tucked in among all the creaky Victorians they've got over there, with a smiley Buddha face on the awning and a cluster of clubby-looking twenty somethings milling on the sidewalk. Logos wasn't out front. I checked my watch and the address, but then Evelyn opened the door for a look inside and spotted him. He was sitting by himself behind a table stuck off in the corner.

We went in. Man, it was dark. He'd picked a place to eat that was dark like a bar.

Logos smiled and stood up, and then I guess he decided he'd better slide out in front of the table to greet us. He'd got a new jacket. This big down mountain man thing, that made him look about four sizes heavier.

We hugged. Through the jacket I could feel his ribs.

"Thanks a lot for making us hunt for you, you little gerbil. Why weren't you out front?"

"I'm sorry if I've deviated from my usual pattern, Hank. I wouldn't want to give you a headache."

He flashed me a friendly leer. We were still standing close and it was a little lighter on that side of the table and for those few seconds even in the dark I could see him decent.

He'd lost a lot of weight. A lot. The mountain man jacket couldn't cover it up. The skin at his eyes and mouth looked tight. He'd lost close to twenty pounds.

My face must have given me away. Logos looked nervous. He bumped into a chair backing up to the spot he'd picked out in the dark behind the table. His hair looked sweaty. On his cheek he had some kind of salve smeared. A half-dollar sized patch, like to cover something up.

Then we sat down, and even just a few extra feet away across the table I couldn't see him so good anymore.

"It's been too long, Hank, Evelyn. You must tell me all."

But Evelyn didn't say anything.

A waitress came with menus and water. Logos sat back to let her open the menu on his plate. His cheeks looked sunken. He'd never had any kind of jaw line before, but I could see it now, because of how tight his skin was.

"They don't believe in putting much strain on the PG&E tab here, do they?" I looked around. "I'll bet they've got some wino out back pedaling a bike to make the generators go."

I tried to smile but my lips wouldn't hold. I looked away. Logos acted like he didn't notice.

Evelyn still didn't say anything. She sat up stiff and straight and stared at him.

"Perhaps they don't want us to see anything crawling out of the quinoa," Logos said.

I tried to laugh. My voice came out way too high. My gut was churning around. I looked at the menu, but I could hardly see the letters.

"You must tell me how my little namesake is getting along."

He said it to Evelyn, but she wasn't going to answer him. I cleared my throat.

"Fine, man." I stopped and swallowed and pretended the water had gone down wrong. "Little math whiz. He's even got some of his times tables aced out. You ask him what's 3 x 3, he'll fire it right back at you."

Logos reached under his seat and pulled out a couple of kiddie books. "I spotted these at a garage sale," he said. "Does he have these yet?"

I spread them out on the tablecloth so Evelyn could see. *The Lorax* and *The Giving Tree.*

"No, he doesn't. If he knows Uncle Logos gave them to him, he'll scarf them right up. Thanks, Logos. Seriously."

The waitress came back. I ordered some falafel tahini thing. Just the first dish my eyes focused on. Evelyn said she'd have what I had.

"Man, why can't you be a T-Bone-atarian? I feel like I'm ordering hay and bird seed in these places."

"We're just trying to preserve your Mr. Olympia figure, Hank. You're going to have your own float in the Gay Pride parade next year."

Then Evelyn asked why he'd called to change the time of the meal.

Quiet and point blank, like she didn't care if the question was rude. She sat stiff and straight, with her mouth like the mouth of a mask and her eyes like when she'd watched her dad kick off at the hospital.

Logos took a sip of the water. He didn't look at her.

"I'm sorry about that. I had a lot of errands to run today."

"What were you doing?"

"Just a lot of little things."

The waitress came back with some bread. I reached for the bowl and missed because my hand shook, but got the side of it the second time. I broke off a hunk of bread and passed the bowl around.

"You have something on your cheek," Evelyn said.

Logos coughed and looked at the bread between his fingers. The goop was in a patch between his left ear and cheekbone. She must have been staring at it.

"Just some ointment."

"Did you hurt yourself?"

"No." He looked at me. "Hank, you must tell us what's new at work."

I talked about a new factory recall that we all had to get trained on. I hardly knew what I was saying and my voice was way off, but Logos acted interested.

The waitress brought our food. Logos asked about my boss and co-workers and the condo. He didn't look at Evelyn. She hardly touched her food. She just stared and stared at him.

The Castro had changed, he said. There were more dry social clubs now, and AA meetings. But a significant minority of gays were still in denial. The bathhouses were deadly. He'd heard of one French-Canadian steward who'd infected dozens, who knew he had AIDS and was *still* going to the baths, who was as much as murdering his partners, and no legal mechanism could keep him away. And the bathhouse owners weren't any help. They were too worried about the bottom line to look at how many thousands of people they were helping to kill.

And on like that. Picking at his food and looking at me most of the time, because Evelyn kept staring at him.

Finally he said he had to use the head. He pushed his chair back and stepped past Evelyn's chair and then around a table full of furry college kids into the one bright-lit spot in the restaurant: the entrance to the little hall that led to the bathrooms.

I watched the crown of his head come into the bright light there, and his shoulders in that big down jacket that bulked him up like a football player, and then under the jacket his pants sagging limp around his legs because of the weight he'd lost.

Evelyn was watching him, too.

The light shone on Logos' hair. He turned out of sight.

Evelyn stared down at her plate.

I touched her hand.

She stood up.

"Evelyn."

She wouldn't look at me. She walked around the college kids to the bright-lit hall. She stood under the bright light and stared down the hall at the door Logos had gone into. Waiting for him. Her eyes looked wild. One of the college kids gave her the once over.

I felt sick. I heard my pulse in my ears.

Logos came out.

For maybe a half second he looked at her, and then quick he turned his head away and tried to slide past her.

She blocked him. He tried to slide past.

She grabbed his shoulders.

"No!" she said.

She yelled it. The college kids stared. I got up.

"Why won't you let me see you?!"

Real loud. Everyone in the restaurant stared. She grabbed his shoulders and shoved him against the wall.

"*Let me look at it,*" she shouted.

I pushed past the college kids. Logos was trying to get away. He looked shocked. She blocked him off and scraped at the salve on his cheek.

"*Let me see it!*"

I got between them. I had to push her off like I was breaking up a fight in a bar. Logos looked shocked. I caught one good glimpse of him in the bright light, of his hollowed out cheeks from the weight he'd lost, and the purple-red KS mark on his cheeks that she'd scraped the salve off.

He brought himself up quick and stiff and headed to the door. While I was still holding Evelyn I spotted him on the sidewalk outside, rushing away down Haight Street.

Evelyn started to cry. I swung my eyes over the heads of all the people staring at us until I spotted the waitress. I mumbled an apology and shoved a wad of bills at her and went back to the table to get the books Logos had brought for Two. Evelyn stood under the light blubbering. I hooked my arm through hers and got her out of there.

That was how we found out that Logos had AIDS.

•　　•　　•

Logos told me later that night that he thought he might have been infected in 1976. He'd so wanted to fit in, in those first months after coming out. Other gay men met partners in gay singles bars. He knew he wasn't attractive. Even meeting that one special someone would be harder for him.

He'd hated the bars. He'd always had to get drunk to sit in them for more than a half hour, but a few times he had, and had gone home with a stranger. He'd given all that up after a few months, but not soon enough, apparently. He'd picked a bad time to experiment. You only had to get infected once.

Months ago he'd noticed that he was losing weight and felt tired a lot, and that his lymph glands were swollen. He'd suspected AIDS then, but hadn't known for sure until he saw a doctor about the first KS lesion. He was sorry for the stunt he'd tried to pull with the dark restaurant at night. He hadn't been thinking clearly. He'd felt afraid of seeing Evelyn. He'd known how she'd take it.

·   ·   ·

I went back to see him after I'd dropped off Evelyn and told Mom to keep an eye on her. At first he didn't answer when I knocked on his door in the biology prof's rooming house, but then he did after I said through the door that I was alone. He'd taken off that big jacket he'd tried to fake us out with, and washed off the salve. I could see how much weight he'd lost. The lesion on his cheek was about the size of a nickel.

He didn't look mad, or hurt. Just a little ruffled. He wasn't the type who got shoved around in restaurants.

I told him that Evelyn was going to wind up in a mental ward if he didn't call. He nodded, like I'd pointed out a broken light bulb that needed to be replaced, and I followed him to the phone in the hall. While I stood next to him I heard Evelyn sobbing through the mouthpiece.

"I should have told you earlier," Logos said to her, at least three times. And "I'm not mad." He said that a bunch of times, too. Then real gentle he told her that he didn't think they should stay on the phone.

Afterward we talked for awhile in his room.

He wasn't going to stick around for the bitter end. Science might offer a treatment for AIDS someday, but it didn't have one now. It was fatal, period, and he'd seen too many people die in Ward 5B to want to be one of them. He had some things he wanted to do before he died, but then he'd pick his place and time. He hoped I'd respect his decision.

I asked if there was anything he needed help with.

. . .

About a week later Logos moved into a little house way the hey down in the Excelsior with a guy with terminal cancer. He'd told his family by then, but he didn't want them or anyone else looking after him. It felt different if his roomie was terminally ill, too. Logos figured they could take turns being sick.

The new roommate's name was Mark. I think the hospital matched them up. He turned out to be this real conservative, Pentecostal kind of guy, which was weird enough in S.F. and weirder still in the same house with Logos.

Mark thought he'd gotten leukemia from a big church relief project he'd volunteered for in the Southern Urals. The Russkies produced nuclear fuel out there. Nobody at the hospital thought he'd be around for the next inauguration, but he still ironed up a fresh button-down shirt and set of twills every day, like he had an appointment at the Officers' Club. Sometimes the pain in his joints was so bad he had to hobble around the house on crutches.

Damn if those two didn't start their own mutual admiration society. Mark had done church relief work in Guatemala and India, besides the stint in Russia, and if Logos was impressed by that, well, Mark was plenty impressed by all the volunteering Logos had done with AIDS patients. And Mark understood how the eco transit group had gone bad. Exactly how. He'd seen the same thing happen to do-gooder evangelical groups.

Mark was super courteous, like Logos, and another big brain, even if he saw everything through a King James kind of lens. The one time I visited them together, they were so caught up in a big philosophical discussion that they'd practically forgot they were sick. It was funny how things had worked out. Logos had been about as unlucky in the romance department as a human could get, but at the end of his life he'd finally found a boyfriend. Or a brother. That's what Mark said they were.

. . .

The last time I saw Logos was a couple of weeks after Rock Hudson kicked off. Usually S.F. gets an Indian summer that time of year, but a cold front had come in, and I shivered all the way up from the 14 stop. I had a couple of mementos with me, and one special one. Logos had said he was going to pull the plug the next day.

"It's open," Logos said, when I knocked. He was sitting by himself on the living room couch, all bundled up, with the heat blasting away. He said Mark had a hospital appointment.

"You're neglecting to tell me how good I look, Hank."

With some of the old leer in his voice. I pulled up a chair, and apologized for leaving his GQ magazine modeling contract behind on the Muni.

He looked pretty horrendous. He was under a hundred pounds, and the KS on his face was real bad, so the big purple blotches were the main thing you saw when you looked at him. He still had all his wits, though. He'd sworn he wouldn't stick around long enough to get fuzzy headed.

I showed him the stuff I'd brought. I'd found some photos of us on Ripper's Hill in high school. Plus I had our senior yearbook. Then I brought out a giant mini-poster thing that almost everybody who'd known Logos in high school had signed. It had taken a week of toodling around Prado after work to line everybody up, but they'd all said yes. Logos had a fan club.

Logos made a fuss over everything. His fingernails were all bunged up from a fungus infection. Another AIDS gift. He looked real weak. I noticed a walker parked next to the couch.

"She'd just as soon you read this in private," I said, and gave him a thick letter from Evelyn. And then the special thing I'd brought.

We talked about AIDS for awhile. He'd thought that some right wing group might have started it, but he didn't think so anymore. Some gays at the bathhouses had been getting it on with three thousand new partners a year, with no condoms. That had made for a real choice petri dish for an epidemic. Even in the seventies, some of the MDs had been jumping up and down about how far up the creek they'd be if something lethal kicked in.

Well, something lethal had. That was all. Maybe Patient Zero had deserved to die, for spreading AIDS right and left after he was infected. But Logos hadn't. Innocent people died in earthquakes and floods and hurricanes all the time. That was life.

He asked about Two, and Evelyn. I pulled a lot of punches on what a mess she was. He'd tried seeing her one more time after the scene at the Harvest, but she'd lost it again. She hadn't been much better on the phone.

I leaned close and asked if he had all the pills he needed. Whispering, like SFPD was about to bust in. Logos said he did.

Then old Hank started to cry. Not a very Prado thing to do.

"Now, now, Hank," Logos said, and shot me a shady leer. I had to look on the bright side. Pretty soon he'd be able to look up the C in the afterlife, and put in a good word for me. I might finally get those cylinder heads.

·   ·   ·

I helped Greg set up a memorial service on Mount Diablo. He only sent out a few invitations, but so many people came out that we backed up Gate Road for two miles, and the cops had to come. Greg and some of our old high school buddies took turns reading stuff about him. Two read a poem that I'd helped him with.

Evelyn stood stiff in the ugly black dress she'd bought, and as soon as it was over she grabbed Two's hand and marched him back to the car. She'd been wearing nothing but black for the past month. If she ran out of fresh clothes, she'd put on the same thing for two days in a row. Sometimes now I caught her talking to herself in the kitchen. Real angry, like the thing that had killed Logos and her dad was standing at the counter with her.

We hardly talked anymore. I knew that Logos' death had pulled the cover off something between us and that we had problems ahead, but I wasn't in any shape to hash it out with her. She hadn't married some shrink on the Donohue show. I was just an auto mechanic. I hadn't expected to lose my best friend when I wasn't even thirty-five yet. I felt like all the color had drained out of life, like I was riding BART to work and bolting in shock absorbers in a washed out, black and white world.

·   ·   ·

But then about two weeks after Logos' death, we got hit with a weird customer epidemic at the dealership.

I don't mean garden variety weird. I mean the stone cold record busting dings came out, that you usually only get once every five years and tell stories to other mechanics about. Like some invisible force was combing every curb and garage and parking spot from San Leandro to El Cerrito, and sending every whack who might need a tune-up or a brake job anytime in the next decade to rush up to Oakland to consult with old Hank. Because I got assigned to every one of them.

The first had about a dozen books on colonic irrigation stacked on his back seat. Okay, fine. That's none of my business. You want to leave your library at the shop with your vehicle, suit yourself. But I get the hood up and, sheesh, there's oil spattered all over his engine bay. It turns out he's been deliberately leaving the oil fill cap loose so the engine can rid itself of toxic fumes. Like an enema.

He came in to pick up his car wearing a t-shirt with a big drawing of the intestine on it. This colon stuff is a big deal to him. So I tried to explain, sir, cars and people are different, and from now on I'd like you to keep that cap screwed on tight.

Well, no soap. We're standing there next to his hood, and he's munching some kind of take-out Chinese goulash with chopsticks, and shaking his head at every other thing I said, like I just wasn't enlightened enough to *get* it about enemas and high colonics, okay?, and then, I swear, this Hiram hauls out a hunk of broccoli with the chopsticks and flicks it into the oil fill cap. Into his engine. Like: musn't forget to give *you* a little treat and clean out your colon while we're here, can I?

So I had to go to the office to get my boss, because no way we're standing behind dealer warranty if this idiot's going to stick human food in his engine. He can go buy a Subaru.

And while I hunted up Roy, I could just swear: from somewhere far, far off in the wild blue yonder, past the mountains and the clouds and the sun, I could make out the shadow of someone I'd loved and thought I'd lost, beaming down at old Hank and chuckling.

Two days later I got this People's Park Earth Mother type who thought I'd sabotaged her radio so she couldn't get KPFA.

I'm serious. Ms. Melissa Kroner-Heebly. She'd come in for a clutch job. A clutch job, and that's supposed to bung up her radio reception.

I put the car on the lift for her. I'd seen our training video about customer service. "Many drivers are intimidated by mechanics." Okay, fine. I don't want to be intimidating. I showed her where the bell housing was and explained about pressure plates and friction disks, and how they've got nothing, I mean *nothing at all* to do with her radio. Okay? I hadn't touched her radio. You don't need to for a clutch job. I hadn't even looked to see if she had a radio.

Well, I might as well have not bothered. "All I hear from you is a lot of hot air," says Ms. Kroner-Heebly. Then point blank she asks if I voted for Reagan, and then she drops her big thesis on me, which is that all the multi-national car corporations are wiring this secret FBI signal-jamming gizmo into the receiver anytime a car comes in for service, and that's why she can't listen to Michael Parenti on KPFA anymore. "I know you're just a pawn in all this."

And I'm watching her foam at the mouth and wondering how many kittens I must've accidentally kicked to rate getting two screwball customers in a row, and then behind her, I swear, there's Logos. Or he's there and he's not there. He doesn't have AIDS anymore. He looks like when he hung out at Rosenfeld's, before life got so complicated.

"Hank," he says, looking at me over her shoulder, smiling and shaking his head, "I wish you the best of luck in extricating yourself from this misunderstanding. You may need it."

After that a whole swarm of nuts came in. One dude wanted us to bolt wings on his compact so it could fly over traffic jams on the 580, like a Cessna. Another thought that rotating his tires had made his paint turn darker. They were all once-every-five-years cranks, and we were getting them all at once, and every single damn one was coming to me.

I knew what it was, then. You can say what you want about coincidences, but sometimes a person just knows. In my heart I looked up at Logos and said "Ver-ree funny, pal," and after that the weirdsville customer wave ended. I didn't feel so bad about him being dead anymore. Because maybe he wasn't, really. He'd gone to all that trouble just to show me he was still around.

.   .   .

Evelyn gained about fifteen pounds. Sometimes when it was her turn to cook she'd just stop at a burger joint and bring home junk food. I had to pick up after her in the condo. She didn't care whose turn it was to clean, or what the place looked like.

She didn't want to gab with me anymore. If I started a conversation she'd give one or two word answers, and if I pushed it she'd say she didn't feel up for conversation. She never wanted to make love. She didn't even want to feel my skin on hers in the bed. Sometimes when I woke up I saw that she'd dragged blankets out to the living room and slept on the couch.

If anything came on TV about AIDS she'd change the channel without asking. If I had the remote, she'd walk out of the room.

Once when we were out driving something came on the radio about how high the death toll was. The gay papers were full of obituaries. The epidemic kept getting worse.

"Maybe they'll all just die and rot," Evelyn said.

She looked at least five years older. It was like everything hopeful inside her had been snuffed out, and without the light from the hope all that was left was an empty mask, cold and hard like stone. Sometimes I hardly recognized her.

.   .   .

One afternoon I came home from work at six, and Two didn't run out to give me his usual 'Hi, Daddy' hug. It was just Evelyn, watching the tube on the living room couch.

"Where's Two?"

"He wanted to sleep over at Toby's," Evelyn said.

I walked up to her. She was still all duded up in her 8 to 5 accountant get up, except she'd slipped her sensible heels off.

"I thought we were both going to decide together before he did any sleepovers," I said.

"He's already stayed there three times."

On the TV the narrator was blabbing about the legacy of the Berlin Wall. Evelyn still hadn't looked at me.

"Well ... yeah, okay. But didn't we decide? He's only in second grade. It's a big deal staying over."

"I know what grade he's in."

She shot me an irritated glance and turned back to the TV. I looked at her hair fluffed out on her shoulders. She had some gray in it now. It was funny how age had snuck up on us. We'd be forty in a few more years. Forty years old.

"Well, okay," I said. "It's done. He's at Toby's. I hope we can talk about it next time."

She didn't say anything.

I was starting to feel sick. Something told me that this was it. I couldn't keep on living like my wife's enemy in the same home with her.

I stepped closer and sat on the armrest on the other side of the couch and stared at the TV. Evelyn didn't look at me.

Almost five minutes passed. I looked at the cold, angry set of her jaw and pawed around for a way to start the big conversation. Evelyn, I think we need to talk. Evelyn, I know that since your dad died, and Logos. Evelyn.

But I couldn't make myself start. I wasn't going to have a marriage left. It was like she practically hated me.

"Well, I guess it's just the two of us, then," I said. "What do you want for dinner? I'll be the chef."

"I already ate. Make anything you want."

Rapping it out like I was a panhandler she was getting rid of. I knit my fingers together and gave my hands a squeeze and looked at the thin black lines under my thumbnails. No matter how I scrubbed, those lines were always there. Mechanic's hands. That's all I was.

"Well, maybe I'll watch the tube with you for awhile."

"You don't have to."

"Well, maybe I'd like to. Sit with my wife and watch television. What're you watching?"

She shook her head. "It's just something on PBS. You wouldn't like it."

"Why wouldn't I like it because it's on PBS?"

She sat up without looking at me and turned the set off. Her jaw was trembling. She stood up and walked past me out of the living room.

"Evelyn," I said.

I got up to follow her. She went into the bedroom and closed the door hard. I heard the lock click, but I tried the knob anyway.

"Evelyn." I rattled the knob. "Could you open the door, please?"

Nothing. I raised my hand to knock, but caught myself. Knocking on the bedroom door in my own condo.

"Please. I want to talk to you. It's important."

Nothing.

I started to talk. I sure hadn't planned it like this, but this was it now for sure. I didn't have anything to lose. I stood close to the door and talked to the frame. At first I tried to keep my voice steady, like some marriage counselor on TV, but it busted up real fast. Pretty soon I was sobbing as much as I was talking.

I knew I wasn't what she'd expected in life, I said. She hadn't wanted her first husband to die and she hadn't especially wanted me, to be real blunt about it, and we'd both always known that she loved Logos more. That wasn't my fault and it wasn't hers and it sure hadn't been Logos'. Things had just shook out that way. But Logos was gone now. I couldn't take back the AIDS or bring him back, or bring back her dad. We'd both gotten old and gray and now it was just the two of us and our boy, and I couldn't offer her more than myself, as much as I wanted to. I was sorry I couldn't, but that didn't change anything.

I rattled the knob again. My vision had blurred up. The knob had all this wet drippy crap on it. It was on my face, too.

I was going, I said. You can write your own ticket. I'm not going to be a boat anchor dragging you down when I can't be the man you want. You can tell Two that Daddy took a trip, and I'll call you in a couple of days and we can work something out. You want a lawyer, you can get one, but I'll do any kind of child support you want. Please just let me see my little boy again. Please.

And I grabbed some stuff and headed out to the car.

•   •   •

I drove out to the freeway and tooled along in the slow lane for awhile, with traffic booming past and one green freeway sign after another looming up and then disappearing past my roofline. It was getting dark. Hank, old boy, you better get off the road, if you don't even know which way you're driving. So I took the next exit and followed some thoroughfares that looked half-way familiar, and then spotted a shopping center.

Just pull off the road til you get your brain back. I turned into the shopping center and found a parking spot and shut off the engine. I draped my hand over the steering wheel and tried to blink the shock out of my brain, and watched the shoppers hoofing it in and out of the electric doors. Some of them were wearing ties or pants suits like Evelyn's, so you knew they'd just come from some downtown skyscraper job and wanted to pick up some grub now that they'd made it through the Bay Bridge gridlock.

Then the light bulb clicked and I knew I *really* wasn't thinking straight, because it had taken me that long to figure out where I'd driven myself to.

It wasn't called Hardy's anymore. They'd sold out to some chi-chi grocery chain at least five years ago; they had an olive bar in there now. Plus there was a big new condo development across the street, and they'd put in street lights to handle the extra traffic.

But I still should've recognized where I was. Damn if I hadn't driven back to where I used to work.

•   •   •

About a dozen parking spaces away from me a bagger was doing empty cart round-up. He looked about twenty-two. Maybe the same age as me when I'd started at Hardy's. Except twenty-two must've gotten a lot younger since I'd worked there.

But, there he was, and as I watched him pushing the first cart into the back of the second I wondered how many he'd rack before he wheeled the cart locomotive back to the store. I'd racked as many as ten carts at one time. It had felt like pushing a Harley.

He settled for just three. The kids these days. Dirk would've reamed me out royal for pushing three carts. Did they still take

❦ 375 ❧

breaks on the loading dock out back? That was where Evelyn had pulled up all those years ago, in the hippy Ghia that hadn't run like a hippy Ghia, with Ruby in the back. And damn if this wasn't practically the same place in the lot where Evelyn had hugged me goodbye, and I'd smelled her hair and skin from the shower, and Cupid had run a final pre-assault check on that seventy pound draw weight bow he'd been lugging around. Because I'd never forget the dream I'd had a few hours later. No, I sure wouldn't.

Well.

I drummed my fingers on the wheel and turned the radio on and listened to the traffic report for awhile, until I started to feel all depressed. Then a crew cut linebacker type pulled into a space near me, and gave me a dirty look and double checked his door before heading into the market, and I figured maybe I'd worn out my thumb-twiddling welcome in this particular lot.

So I started the engine and drove. At least I knew where I was now. Old Prado hadn't changed that much.

It was beginning to dawn on me that I hadn't planned the big walk out too well. About all I had was my wallet. Nothing to brush my teeth or wash up with. They'd probably appreciate it at work if I kept doing those things. I'd have to go to a mall and pick up some stuff. And then see about a motel room. It was dark now.

Maybe I'd call when she was at work tomorrow to leave a message on the machine. About telling Two that Daddy was on a trip, and what we'd do about the mortgage. You can have my whole paycheck, for all I care. Just please let me see my little boy.

•   •   •

I drove to another shopping center and bought a toothbrush and other getting-up-and-going-to-bed stuff, and found the pay phones so I could ring up a motel and book a room. By this time my mood had gone into a serious nose dive, so I started to do this self-talk thing I'd heard on the radio. Look on the bright side. I'd just never been her Mr. Right. That was all. Maybe now I could be a big Bay Area swinging single. Get me a John Travolta disco shirt. Show off my pecs. And I tried to picture myself waltzing into some Union Street bar with June Cochran on one arm and Linda Hurst on the other, and them having a hissy fit about which one got to ravish me first, and while I was trying to make myself smile at that I heard a big VRROOOOM from the gas station next to the far end of the parking lot.

I looked over. A Chevelle with mag wheels was parked on the tarmac over there, with about a half dozen rodder types milling around the open hood. One guy with a Z28 t-shirt was leaning over the engine. Blipping the throttle.

I walked over. Without really wanting to. It was like my feet made the decision for me. I was on my own now, wasn't I? I had to get a social life.

The rodders noticed me coming up when I was about twenty yards away. They were just kids. Teenagers. I hadn't seen that before. I looked for something else at the gas station that I could pretend I'd been walking to instead, but there wasn't anything.

So I said, "That looks like a '68, isn't it?"

I stepped over the dinky chain link rope thing onto the gas station tarmac.

"A '70," one of the kids said.

It was full night by then, but we were close to the shopping center lights, so I could see him okay. He wasn't even old enough to buy beer. He had peach fuzz on his cheeks. His girlfriend looked like she was all of a year out of high school.

They were all about that age. I walked up to the front bumper. It was too late to turn back. The guy who'd been blipping the throttle straightened up. He was a blond kid with a mullet hair do.

I nodded at him. "You having trouble with it?"

"Sort of." He shook the hair back from his ears. "It keeps bogging on me."

He leaned in to tug the accelerator again. It sounded like it was cutting out around three grand.

By then the whole group was eyeballing me the cautious way twenty year olds do when some middle-aged dude wants to be pals. What's the old guy trying to pull? I wished to God I'd never come over there.

But there I was. I asked about the bogging. I guess they could tell from my questions that I knew how to change my own oil. Mullet stood straight and gave me the big deferential treatment. The others gawked at me. Like I was a J.C. shop teacher.

Chapter Twenty-Four

"I think it's these vacuum secondaries," Mullet said.

But I said no, you want to think twice before you run mechanical secondaries in a street car, unless you want to run a lot more cam than he was running now. What he ought to do was study up on tuning the rig he already had. And I could tell that impressed him, and he nodded like I was this wonderful mature friend-of-his-Dad's type who'd come to help with his problem, even though the others were still giving me the wary eye, because why did a middle-aged dude want to be buddy-buddy with a bunch of kids?

"Do you mind trying it out," Mullet asked, "to see how it feels to you?"

I leaned in and hooked my finger around the throttle. Basically the same thing I'd done all day at work for two hundred fifty odd days every year for the past ten years, except I wasn't up to speed on big block Chevys.

I revved the engine a few times. It was just a typical scotch tape and baling wire teenage hot rod, like my 'Cuda had been and Earl Howser's Charger had been, and ninety percent of the rods I'd taken so seriously when I was their age. I didn't care if he had a lawn mower engine in there. I wished to God I'd never come over.

"If I were you, I'd take it back to shop class and work on what you've got now," I said. "You don't need any new equipment."

Mullet wanted to shake my hand. A couple of the kids nodded at me. They were glad I was leaving, though. Now they could act like themselves, without an old guy around.

I stepped back over the dinky fence and headed back to my car. Some thunderheads had come in, and in the dark I looked at their black shadow shape on the horizon, over the thin red line where the sun had set. The neon of the chain drug store sign looked bright. Green neon.

I remember all the details because those minutes of looking at that kid's car had been about the worst of my entire life up to that point. Worse even than when Logos had died. Maybe this was all I had to look forward to.

*   *   *

I headed back to the freeway. I drove toward the motel, but man, I felt so bad I could hardly see the road. So I took an off ramp and spotted a dark little strip mall, and thought I'd take a little breather there. I didn't want to get in a wreck driving to my new bedroom.

I parked the car. By then my head felt like somebody had poured a pound of buck shot in it. I lowered the seat back and looked up at the headliner and let my eyes close. I told myself to wait til I got to the damn motel before I took a siesta, wasn't that what I was paying for a bed for?, but my temples were throbbing and that bummed-out feeling poured in on me like a monsoon. I fell asleep.

Damned if I didn't have a dream about Logos. He was bobbing around in the afterlife with his angel's wings strapped on, and giving me a look like I'd forgot something. In the dream I tried to explain, look, Logos, Evelyn and I broke up, but he just flapped his wings and shook his head at me. You forgot something. He didn't look like he even cared about the break-up. He leered at me in the old way, and shook his head when I tried to interrupt, and said, Hank, please indulge an old friend and take one more trip by the homestead. I'm confident that you'll see what you've forgotten once you're there.

I woke up.

The dash clock said 8:30 p.m. I'd konked out for about thirty minutes.

I got the seat up straight and started to drive the rest of the way to the motel. But I kept thinking about that dream. I felt silly thinking about it, but still. With Logos shaking his head and not looking at all concerned about the split, just so long as I went back to see what I'd forgotten.

Finally I decided I might as well head east to see if there was anything to it.

·　　·　　·

By the time I got home it was close to nine. Maybe half the lights were out. It was a typical Kondo Kommunity type of block, with landscaping and all the buildings put up by the same developer, and the damn BART maybe fifteen minutes away if I walked fast.

I pulled to the curb and looked up at our place. The living room light was still on. Well, so much for that idea. I'd thought maybe Evelyn had taken off to spend the night with a girlfriend, and I could go in and pack a suitcase. I'd figured that was what Logos had been trying to tell me. Served me right, for listening to dreams.

So I pulled away from the curb and started to motor on my merry way. I was puzzling over the fastest route to the motel when I spotted a car coming up in my rearview mirror.

The driver started honking at me.

Jeez, buddy, can't you hold your water? I looked at the lights in the rear view mirror. Right on my back bumper. Maybe there was some neighborhood nut who only went driving at night.

I pulled over to let the ding pass, but the car pulled in right behind me and went to honking louder than ever. Like a lunatic.

In the condos around us now lights were flicking on. I shut off the engine and got out. Maybe it would've been more sensible to run for cover, but I was too bummed to care much if the nut hit the gas and rammed me. I walked right back into the headlights. It wasn't until I got to the fender that I saw who was driving.

I'd never seen her that hysterical, not even at the hospital when the C died. Even when I walked up she kept crying and honking that horn. And I'd thought I was a mess. I had to open the door and shut off the engine for her.

• • •

Well, that was the start of the romantic part. I told you there was going to be one and that you'd have to wait for it, and you have, and so did I, and now here it is. I'm sorry it took Logos dying and an argument to show us both how bad we needed each other.

We didn't sleep at all. If you think I'm going to do a blow-by-blow you can go hunt yourself up another kind of book, but we spent the night in the bedroom, and we weren't resting up in there. Figure the rest out for yourself. Those hours had been a lot rougher for her than for me, and remember, I'd had the worst minutes of my life in there. She'd thought she'd lost me for good.

She was still plenty upset. She cried a lot before, during, and after, if you know what I mean, and in the second before, during and after, and the third, and she didn't want to let go of me. Like I was going to duck out and go missing if she even let me lay on the far side of the bed.

She didn't even want to let me go to the john. I told her, look, when you gotta go, you gotta go, but she kept her legs locked like a vice around me and told me to take her with me.

So that's what I did. And I'm sure glad this happened before the age of dinky video cameras everywhere, because that had to have been the most ridiculous scene in the Bay Area that night, and I'm glad there's no record of it. She was a pretty good sized girl, and I wasn't any Arnold Schwarzenegger. Here I am staggering to the john with her legs and arms locked around me, and now I've got to take a whiz without being able to see the floor. I got about a quarter of it on the tiles and wiped out a towel rack.

And think what you want, that was about the happiest time of my life for me. Trying to feel the side of the john with my shins, and hearing the towel rack go crash, and wondering how long my back would hold up with her draped around me. Even more than when Two was born. Because now I knew Two had a real Mommy and Daddy.

•   •   •

Six months later, I set up a top secret surprise party for Evelyn's birthday. I was in tight with the manager of a buffet restaurant close to the Walnut Creek BART station, and got his okay on the surprise I had in mind. Then I played Hank Kruzenski P.I. hunting up old friends from the Shack days.

Jules was easy to locate, on account of his size. He owned a computer store in Hayward. The IBM PC had come out, and people were buying Apples and Ataris and Commodores and floppy disks to stick in them, and 1200 baud modems to hook up to their phone lines and log onto BBSs. Jules helped me track down Jimi, who had about as much fur up top now as Yul Brynner and did gang intervention work for Oakland P.D., and then

I located five more friends who'd rented a room at the Shack or crashed at the Shack or just bummed food at the Shack, but who I knew Evelyn would want to see again.

Time hadn't stood still for any of us. We were all in our late thirties, and looked it. Evelyn wouldn't ID them right away.

I swore them to secrecy, and filled them in on the plan.

Along came the big night. The buffet place looked like it always did, except for this new crew of middle-aged servers behind the counter. We picked up our trays and Evelyn nagged Two not to grab so many napkins, and our turn came up. Evelyn held up her plate to the first server and asked for some salad.

'Coming right up,' the server said. I thought Evelyn looked at him a little longer than usual. He wasn't too swift with the serving tongs, for one thing. And maybe he looked a little familiar.

Off she went to the next station. 'I'd like some casserole.' 'Of course,' the server said, but this server wasn't much good with the ladle, either. And there was the Looking Familiar part. Evelyn tilted her head and squinted like somebody was trying to slip a fly into her food, and I had to bite my lip so I wouldn't laugh. But she still didn't catch on.

I'd put Jules at the end, because I'd known he'd be a stone giveaway. She almost made it that far. Then she caught on all at once and damn near dropped her tray, and threw her hands up to her mouth. I started 'Happy Birthday,' and the others joined in singing it with me, and so did Two, and then they turned over their aprons to the regular servers, and joined us at the big table the manager had set up for us by the window.

The whole thing got to Evelyn a lot more than I'd expected. Her birthdays growing up hadn't been that great. Sometimes the C had just forgotten the date, and then other times he'd sent these giant expensive presents, but hadn't been there to help her blow out the candles. Or maybe it got to her because of however she'd felt that day crunching numbers at work, or because of the change between us, and knowing she didn't have to wear that hard protective shell around me anymore.

We all sat around her at the table and the manager brought a cake, and poor Evelyn was blubbering so bad she couldn't blow out the candles. She'd start to talk and then get weepy and have to stop to get a grip, until Two actually gave her grief about it, because he was a kid and even he didn't cry like that. We talked about who was doing what, and wasn't it funny how time passed?, and would you believe that Charles worked with the D.A.'s office now?, and the great deal that Karen had gotten on her house, and how maybe Howard would throw a surprise like this for his wife, because they had their fifth year anniversary coming up.

"But *you* have the best husband," Dixie said.

She'd meant it half as a joke, but Evelyn didn't take it that way. "I do!" she said. Then she got weepier than ever, and started to laugh and cry at the same time. "I do, I do! I have the absolute best husband."

"Mom!" Two said, but she couldn't stop crying. The tears ran down her cheeks and messed up her 8 - 5 make-up, and she was pushing forty and looked it, and so did I, and that was fine with me. Linda and June could pull all the hissy fits they wanted. They'd never get me.

CHAPTER TWENTY-FIVE

Evelyn and Two were killed in a traffic accident in 1990. She was driving him out to meet his junior high astronomy club for a camp-out at the Observatory. Not even a race car driver's daughter can do much if the other guy barrels around a blind curve on the mountain at eighty miles per hour, and in your traffic lane to boot.

Don Dale Dancourt. Kind of a catchy name for a drunk driver. .15 blood alcohol level, and five prior DUIs. Evelyn and Two helped him get to big number six.

.   .   .

That wasn't exactly the best news I'd ever had in my life. I stopped going in to work for awhile, and had to see a therapist so I wouldn't go out of my mind, basically, and for maybe four solid years afterward old Hank didn't have many bright smiles or one-liners to offer the world. Friday nights you'd find me sitting up with the photo albums, looking at the pictures of the wife and son I didn't have any more. Which the therapist said was about the worst thing I could do.

But I pulled out of it eventually. I could almost feel Evelyn talking to me from the great blue yonder, just as I'd imagined Logos had. "You're not going to ruin the rest of your life over something that wasn't your fault." That's just how she would have put it to me.

I started dating again. The whole Internet thing had kicked off, and when I could get my modem and my commie port to stop fighting long enough to get online I hooked up with a web dating service, and that's how I met Karen. We've been together close to fifteen years now. One of these days I'm going to buy a cell phone jammer to keep her from squawking on the horn so much, but I don't always remember to pick up my t-shirts or put in a fresh roll, so I've got my weak points, too. We'll probably stick it out for the long haul.

.   .   .

And damn if that hasn't been most of my life, more or less. I'm sixty-three now. I pay attention to all the Social Security and Medicare stuff I used to chuck in the circular file, and maybe in a few more years I'm going to put in for retirement and hang the ratchet wrench on the wall for the last time. 'Course, I still feel like I look like a cross between Brad Pitt and Paul Newman, but I can't seem to latch onto any photos that do me justice. In photos I always look like some old guy. It must be the cheap digital cameras people use these days.

Most of my life has passed. I never thought it would shake out like that. One day got stacked up on top of the one underneath it, and when the pile of used up days got big enough, well, there I was: an old guy. Just be careful it doesn't happen to you. And I'm likely to keep on getting older from here on in, unless I get the hang of time travel. Eventually Hammering Hank's going to follow Evelyn and Two and Logos and the C off into the sunset. My time here will be over.

And that brings me to something I'll bet you thought I clean forgot, even though it's why I got to know Evelyn, and what Logos and me chased after for the first third of this book. That's right. You know just what I'm talking about. I don't even need to say it.

After the crash the sheriff turned over everything in the car worth salvaging. That included Two's sleeping bag, and Evelyn's purse, and a cup tucked inside the purse that Two might have made in a pottery class, except for the symbols on the forehead. The crash hadn't even chipped it.

It's mine now. I keep it in a hiding place in the bedroom closet, behind my photo albums. I've never told Karen about it. She knows it's something personal and important to me, but that's all.

Nobody knows about it but me. Or I guess the history buff college eggheads know, but they don't know that Logos ever turned it up, and that I have it now.

I just took it out and put it on the table next to the keyboard.

·   ·   ·

I've told you a lot in this book, so maybe it's my turn to ask you a question: what do you think I should do with it? I've given it a pretty wide berth since that backstage-in-the-theatre dream. I wouldn't use the word 'afraid.' If you work at a refinery, you don't have to be afraid of all those millions of gallons stacked up in tanks around you. But you don't play with matches there, either.

Should I ring up the Sioux Indian tribe out in South Dakota, and give it to them? Or maybe to a museum. If they put it in at the de Young and the press gets wind of it, man, I'll bet the crowds would back up clear to the Tea Gardens for three months straight. Six months.

But maybe I'm not supposed to do anything with it, until I have another dream like the last one. Maybe the spirits that watch over it want it to be exactly where it is.

Sometimes when Karen's out I take it out and sit with it, just like Evelyn used to do. I'm positive it's real now. I didn't tell you before, but Evelyn wanted Logos to drink from it before he died. That's when all the heavy supernatural stuff is supposed to happen. She had me take it over and leave it with him along with the big letter she'd written, so he could drink from it right before he took the pills.

He *knew* it was real then. He wrote about what it helped him see. He left a letter for us:

·   ·   ·

I WAS ALIVE. ALIVE. I wasn't a rock or
a candy wrapper or a rusty bottle top, even
though vast, vast, capricious Life could as
easily have herded into these unthinking forms
the lucky molecules that instead became me.
The sperm pierced the egg; the zygote snug-
gled into the uterine wall; my neural tube
emerged, reproducing a <u>quarter million cells a
minute</u> that became sight, smell, touch, that
revealed my spit-slickened toddler fingers on
a linoleum orphanage floor, the basso profon-
do of my adoptive dad, my reflection in a mirror; that endowed me with consciousness to
know and love you both utterly, utterly, far

more than I ever knew myself capable of love.
I swung a giddy third grade foot at a tumbling
dodge ball on a Prado playground, held Stephen's hand in a Mission restaurant, learned
in a Castro clinic scant years later and a
few blocks west that the biopsy was positive
and that I was as good as dead. And for every
cadenced tickety-tock cellular nutrient ex-
changing second of that life, a mega trillion
unintelligent and lifeless molecules in the
yawing mega trillion miles of space might have
<u>seethed with envy</u> for me, or would have, had
they minds to know what they missed.

Because I was ALIVE, baby. ALIVE. 1950 to
1984. Respiring. Sentient. Conscious. ALIVE!

END

AFTERWORD

The book you have just read began life as a commercial novel I finished but didn't sell in 1991.

From late 2011 to early 2013, I rewrote the novel from scratch.

I was thirty-five in 1991, and fifty-six in early 2013.

People change in twenty-one years. "Tim Adams" may have written this story, but not a Tim Adams existing in any one chronological space. The author wafts about somewhere in the fourth dimensional ether between 1991 and 2013: a trick multiple exposure shot, simultaneously brunette and clean shaven, mustachioed and gray-haired. Both younger and older Tims are confident that the book couldn't have been written without them.

Both are right. I think I did a much better job with the novel this time around, but what I have rewritten in middle age is still fundamentally a young man's story.

· · ·

The commercial novel evolved (or metastasized, if you haven't liked it much) from a 1989 nonfiction article I intended to write about street racing in the Bay Area suburbs. I traveled to Concord for research, questioned my sanity while riding shotgun in a pick-up race on Ygnacio Valley Road, and collected quotes from a half dozen Concord car enthusiasts. I then wrote several drafts, never finished one, tried not to think of how I had wasted my interview subjects' time, and instead contemplated a more ambitious article about street racing for bigger jackpots in South Central Los Angeles.

Off to Los Angeles I went, tape recorder in tow. This time I wasted a whole weekend of my subjects' time, and struggled afterward to pry a serviceable draft out of my word processor. My conscience was bothering me. The Ygnacio Valley Road race would have happened with or without me, but a late night race I had observed in Los Angeles seemed to have been staged for my benefit. What if someone had tried to cross Main while one of those 1,000+ horsepower racers had thundered past? What if my story encouraged more of the same? Someone might get killed or hurt. Wouldn't I be at least partly responsible?

Sabotaged by conscience or not, the article I wrote was pretty dreadful, and I wasn't surprised to see it rejected. Soon I felt grateful for its failure for other reasons. A conservation-minded friend had imbued me with her concerns about the environment. I never thrilled to the trails as she did, but the earth sciences balance sheet argument rang true to my inner accountant. Stockholders would make short work of a management team that plundered an irreplaceable corporate asset as recklessly as we humans plunder the earth.

I contemplated *Sierra Club* membership, socialized with green sympathizers, read environmentalist manifestos. I felt convinced, but also amused in a fatalistic sort of way, like the scion of a cattle trading family listening to starry-eyed talk at a vegan luncheon. The street-racing-in-the-suburbs article idea had sprouted from my own hobbyist career as an amateur mechanic. I had swapped plenty of car talk with auto buffs in shop classes. I could predict the stupefied expression I might elicit in a hot rodder if I seriously suggested he leave his prize steed in the garage and help save the planet by riding the bus to work.

Thus was begotten the first iteration of this novel, with Logos as the environmentalist and Hank as the proud 'Cuda owner. I liked the story for its own sake, but thought of it as 'commercial' because I had outfitted it with plot elements that might help it sell. Publishers who had rejected my more literary efforts might take me seriously if I submitted a manuscript with a mystery, a coveted object, suspense, a romantic interest.

Well, no soap, as Hank might say. They didn't. Or perhaps I didn't try that hard.

I put the novel on the shelf and contemplated a move to Los Angeles. Perhaps I could find work as a teacher there.

· · ·

Nearly twenty years passed.

I did become a teacher, and an environmentalist teacher to boot. In 1999 I founded TransitPeople, a more-quixotic-than-I-had-intended-it-to-be nonprofit that conducted field trips for elementary schoolers aboard the much-maligned Los Angeles transit system. TransitPeople has completed trips for more than forty thousand children all told, including students in the upper elementary class I then taught near the central city.

A few reporters — a very few — paid attention, and I believe that one from a public access station played a small, harmless joke during an interview. As I sat beside her in the studio, I could watch her interrupt our Q&A to introduce announcements that would be included in the final broadcast. I couldn't see the announcements myself until I received a tape of the show later.

It turned out that one was a PSA from a police agency, darkly warning car-crazed Southern California teenagers of how tough it would be to wrangle a date aboard a public bus, if they drove badly enough to lose their provisional licenses. I suspect that this PSA was included intentionally. The juxtaposition of this real-world message with the off-in-his-own-world tree hugging interview subject was supposed to be funny.

And it *was* funny. I felt I couldn't say how much I thought so, because I represented TransitPeople as a director. But it was funny just the same. Wistfully I remembered that long-ago commercial novel, and wished I had tried harder to publish it. It did a far better job than anything else I had written of presenting the comical and not easily resolved conflict between environmental ideals and car nut culture.

•   •   •

In 2011 I retired from teaching and returned to my native San Francisco. I was still an environmentalist, of sorts, even if my TransitPeople years hadn't left me with a dewy-eyed view of many nominally green Democrats or the Los Angeles transit bureaucracy. This was my time in life to either finish up long-unfinished projects, or set them aside for good. I thought of that long-ago TV interview, fetched my now twenty year old commercial novel from the shelf, and gave it a re-read.

I decided that I still liked the story. Perhaps now I could re-write it for its own sake: without any hope of fanfare or a fat advance check, simply because it was something I had cared about that I regarded as incomplete.

Often while rewriting, I felt like a parent curling a disapproving lip at the inadequately self-censored prose of a footloose son. People often become more conservative as they age, and certainly can be changed by their jobs. As a volunteer TransitPeople trip leader, I had spent ten years cringing every time a reckless driver roared past a class I chaperoned on the sidewalk. I simply would not dream now of writing anything that glamorized irresponsible driving, let alone street racing.

Other conflicts arose between my past and present selves. Hank the shade tree mechanic would be an unwelcome neighbor for any homeowner concerned about property values. The vagabond Ruby didn't seem so whimsical and harmless; stray dogs breed, bite, crap on lawns, are run over by cars. An altruistic Logos might pay a high long-term price for abandoning a gifted class to return to regular ed, and neither Hank nor Logos had any business traveling with the worrisome Dwayne of chapter 7. I also thought it a bit unfair to typecast football players as bullies in chapter 22.

Yet the plot depended on these elements, and I acknowledged that maturity and the teaching life had made me too straight-laced for my own story. I would ruin the novel if I tried to clean it up too much. It simply was a young man's story, intrinsically, fundamentally. I either accepted its youth or left it alone.

My older and younger selves worked out a compromise. Some scenes were left to stand; others disappeared; still others remained only on the condition that Tim the elder could voice misgivings and concerns in an afterword.

The afterword is what you're reading now.

My main misgivings and concerns are:

· · ·

I don't want to glamorize cars or racing. With reservations, I am on the side of the environmentalists.

1975 Indianapolis 500 winner Bobby Unser was a much more thoughtful man than I had ever guessed from watching him on TV, and I am still impressed by his generosity in fielding research questions from an unknown on the telephone. Veteran racer Bob Harkey met with me several times when I traveled to Indianapolis for research. He is polite, self-effacing, funny, the grandfather you wish you had, the one you'd look forward to visiting. And I was reminded of how much like the sacrifices of an artist were the career decisions of Johnny Parsons, who walked away from the security and pension of a police officer's career to follow his passion on the tracks.

All of these men are products of a different age and culture than mine. Bobby Unser grew up in a racing family, and spent part of his childhood in a cabin without electricity or plumbing. Harkey started racing in the 1950s. Parson's father, John Sr., won the race in 1950.

I came of age across the Golden Gate from San Francisco during the heyday of the 1960s counterculture. I am old enough to understand how much my world view owes to my upbringing, to the Zeitgeist of my era.

Still: my sympathies must remain with the tree huggers. I will be happiest if you think of the pomp and pageantry, the legends and lore of the '75 Indy as romantic artifacts of an age gone by, like river boating scenes from a Mark Twain novel. The Foyts and the Unsers enriched American popular culture of yesteryear, but I think of them as folk heroes of an imagined world of unlimited resources, without an environmental balance sheet. Many transit riders and cyclists eschew the comforts of a private car partly because they want to help preserve the world for their offspring. I must stand beside them.

At the same time, I don't want to outfit the transit lobby with white hats that they don't deserve. In Los Angeles, Democratic politicians talked a green game to promote transit tax increases, but consistently funneled those tax dollars into rail and real estate development projects that would benefit well-heeled developers and contractors. The working poor who depended on bus lines in unglamorous regions could ride on the roof or rot on the curb, for all the politicos cared about them. A 2007 *Los Angeles Weekly* article exposed how unlikely the L.A. politicians were to live in the transit oriented development they encouraged. They hung their hats in neighborhoods where you needed a car to get around.

But still, bottom line:

I hope this novel doesn't encourage an interest in racing or old muscle cars. I do own a car now, after a decade without one in Los Angeles, but it's a cheap compact, and I take several transit trips for every one behind the wheel. I don't want a 'Cuda. I hope the Kydra never exists outside the pages of this book.

. . .

I don't want to put any one group on a pedestal.

I lived in the Bay Area in the era when AIDS decimated the gay male population there. Before AIDS, I watched as classmates in my nominally progressive high school made an absolute leper out a youth trusting enough to admit his attraction to other males. No one needs to show me a research study on anti-gay prejudice in the 1970s. I was alive and of age then. Fag jokes were safe almost everywhere.

AIDS, especially, made me think of some gays as martyrs, and this influenced the development of Logos as a character. But Logos is noble because he is Logos. His preference for men is only one thing to be known about him, like his height and hair color.

If you watch the documentary *We Were Here*, you will learn about the selfless volunteer work during the epidemic by the real life Ed Wolf, who was kind enough to sit for an interview with me in his San Francisco home. Ed is gay. But so was the sexually profligate AIDS patient zero Gaetan Dugas, who infected scores of new victims long after he knew he was as much as killing his victims with his semen. So were many of the bathhouse owners who lobbied to keep the baths open, as obvious as was the role of the baths in spreading the disease.

My fifty plus years here have convinced me that nature does not divide the virtuous and the despicable by skin color, gender, ethnicity, income, nationality or sexual preference. I generally judge people as individuals, not because it's the PC thing to do but because it's the only accurate way to take their measure. I humbly recommend this practice to others.

. . .

No novel should be taken too seriously.

Some of my friends know that I haven't owned a television for more than thirty years, and almost never go to movies. Few know why.

In high school, I devoured most of the titles in the IMDB database of most popular movies of the early 1970s. I now wish that I'd watched a fraction as many, and that I'd taken them a lot less seriously. I didn't suspect it at the time, but I now regard most of the films as carefully packaged products to extract discretionary income from a young adult demographic. They told a teenager with money in his wallet what he would be foolish enough to pay to get told, rather than the much less appealing truths it might have helped him to hear.

I don't think I was alone in putting too much stock in the make believe. In Los Angeles, I used to regularly board a bus near a city welfare office. I didn't think it was an accident that so many of those I saw in line there wore *Star Wars* and *Spiderman* t-shirts.

Characters in this and other novels are exemplars, reifications of traits that are generally too muddy and dilute in real-life people to make for good story material. Hank wavers in his support for his childhood friend, but never enough to disgust us. The Evelyn of the next to last chapter seems to dislike gays, but we understand how stricken she feels by the loss of Logos, and forgive her trespasses. Logos is angered once by a substitute high school teacher, but is otherwise saint-like throughout.

What if these three were as messy, flawed, inconsistent, and only occasionally noble as you, me, and the real life most everyone else? What if, say, Hank had faked a stomach problem to duck out of the Knights dinner just as the bullying of Logos intensified? What if Evelyn had been a hypochondriac who coldly cut off all ties with Logos as soon as the AIDS epidemic began? And what if a more carnal Logos had infected new partners in bathhouses after he knew he had the disease?

They'd be less appealing people. They'd be much more like the imperfect, annoying, sometimes wearisome, petty and selfish real people who surround us at work, cut us off in traffic, shove into us on the bus, and write snide comments on news web sites. We see enough of such folk already. I don't want to be reminded of them in a novel, and especially don't want to be reminded that I can be imperfect, annoying, wearisome, petty and selfish, too.

Events in this story also work out far better than they do in messy real life. Hank's HM&F months are pathetic, but only last for a few chapters. He catches that inside straight when he needs it.

What if he hadn't? What if Logos hadn't found Evelyn in Berkeley? What if Evelyn hadn't invited Hank to Indy? He was an unskilled, freshly unemployed twenty-five year old with a bad work history. He might have had to summon up a lot more long-term courage to get back on his feet than anyone had to show in this novel, or he might simply have let go of the figurative boot straps and failed, as real life people fail regularly. He could have drifted back to Tyler, suffered a nervous breakdown, fallen apart.

Please don't get me wrong. Maybe it takes an idealized and unrealistic Atticus Finch to motivate an undergrad into a career in poverty law. Maybe she's still glad she chose that tough career twenty years later, long after she's stopped expecting to meet anyone like Atticus Finch in real life. Maybe the story can still make her cry. Where would we be as Americans, as humans, without novels like *To Kill a Mockingbird* to show us what we care about, why we breathe?

I never gave up novels, as I gave up television and movies. But I hold them at a certain distance now, and suggest you do as well. Even if I hope you care about the imaginary Hank, Evelyn and Logos, as I have cared about them.

It's still just a made-up story.

Some of my former elementary school students are now young adults, fending for themselves in the real world. If any were to seek me out for advice, I would suggest that they can best navigate life's pitfalls by seeing life just as it is.

As I write this afterword, the now eighty-seven year old author of *To Kill a Mockingbird* faces a legal struggle to regain copyright in her own book. I am afraid that one can learn more of practical value by studying this real life conflict than one can ever learn from the novel itself, no matter how beautiful it is. I can't tell you how passionately I wish this weren't so.

FACT AND FICTION

The vast majority of this novel's people and places are entirely imaginary. The significant exceptions are noted below:

Red Cloud was very real. He was a legendary Sioux warrior, as Hank writes, and did visit Washington D.C. and Manhattan in a peace delegation. However, he never dreamed of the fictional Tom Samson, and was never invited to a séance conducted by a Henry Towpfer at a Maximillian Lodge. Samson, Towpfer, the séance, the Lodge and everything related to them are made up. The Cuauhtémoc cup is also fictional, and so necessarily are the photos, writings and sightings of it.

Red Cloud's real-life wife was Pretty Owl, but she certainly had nothing to say about the cup. Neither did Crazy Horse, another legendary real-life Sioux warrior.

In chapters fifteen through twenty-three, I superimposed fictional characters onto the real-life practice weeks preceding the 1975 Indianapolis 500. Everyone in or connected to the C Team — the C himself, Boss Maryland, Phil Shay, Luke, Eldrich, Caspar, Hank, Logos and Evelyn — has been conjured up out of thin air. So were Don Preel, Rosabel Henderson, Cole Donohue, Donohue Engineering, Harry Hicks, Treat Scott and the track worker uncharitably referred to by Hank as Combover. There are no Knights of the Corydon; no Abner Keen spoke at a Knights banquet, and no football players bullied Logos there.

These characters are entirely imaginary. I have never been tempted to include thinly camouflaged real people in my stories. Readers wondering who inspired the C or Phil Shay will wonder fruitlessly; I made them up.

The closest I come to attributing fictional behavior to a real person is the scene in chapter 18 in which Hank imagines that the real life Bob Harkey is smiling at him. Bob Harkey did race at the 1975 Indianapolis 500 for the Dayton Walther team. I asked if I could give him a cameo appearance in my novel, as he so graciously fielded my hours of research questions. But he certainly didn't smile at Hank in 1975, unless endowed with psychic powers far more covetable than anything to be won in a car race.

A few odds and ends:

Some elderly San Francisco transit buffs will remember that the 18 line didn't circle Lake Merced in the middle 1970s. Likewise, some Indianapolis race fans will scratch their heads over a 1975 track entrance on Georgetown Road, or a credentialing office near the yet-to-open new museum.

I sent the 18 on its present route and materialized the entrance and credentialing office by dint of a supernatural power novelists call "literary license." I also employed this redoubtable power to create the MAVTA transit agency, and the Freeway Flier in chapter 7.

What Hank describes as Logos' "gung-ho eco transit group" and its corrupt executive director are entirely fictional, although one needn't look far in real life to find modern nonprofits suborned by unethical leaders.

DEDICATION AND THANKS

I will permit myself two dedications.

First, I feel sheepishly obligated to dedicate this story to the car nuts whose time I so scandalously wasted in the late eighties, when I researched two non-fiction stories I either didn't write or wrote badly: one set in Concord, and the other in Los Angeles. They probably will be happier if I don't name them, given what I have said about street racing in my afterword. Courtesy extended. They've grown middle-aged, like me, if they've lasted long enough to read this. I doubt they do it anymore, or approve of it.

Second, I dedicate this novel to the memory of Lee Joseph, another man I interviewed but never published an article on as I limped along as a non-fiction writer in the 1980s. Lee's story was too much like that of other gay hustlers felled by AIDS. He fled a violently abusive father at age twelve, eked out a living as an underage male prostitute as the epidemic-to-be was gaining steam, and was dead before his twenty-second birthday. You can find his obituary at <u>obit.glbthistory.org</u>.

• • •

Several former race car drivers and mechanics were kind enough to answer my research questions on the phone and in person. Bob Harkey gave me the most time. I met with him three times while in Indianapolis, and am still grateful to him for patiently fielding my often tedious questions about differences between the Speedway I visited in 2012 and the place where he raced in the sixties and seventies.

I also must have taxed the patience of veteran mechanic Laurie Gerrish, who crewed for Bobby Unser when Unser joined the Penske racing team, and has been involved professionally in motorsports for decades. Mr. Gerrish was unfailingly gracious, even though I kept him on the phone for hours with my questions about the Gasoline Alley of the 1970s.

1975 Indy 500 victor Bobby Unser certainly was the best known person I interviewed. The impression I had formed of him as a television-watching teenager turned out to be far from accurate; he is thoughtful, intelligent and considerate, and struck me as determined to always make time for his fans. I'm not a motor-sports fan, but still felt a little star struck to hear that so-familiar voice on my telephone ear piece.

Fred Carrillo, Jim Dilamarter, Johnny Parsons and Jack Martin also gave me time as an interviewer, on the phone or in person. And I'm sure Indianapolis 500 fans are already wondering if I could possibly have researched a novel about the speedway without interviewing Donald Davidson. Well, I didn't! Mr. Davidson was too busy to speak to me when I visited for the race, but answered my questions later in a phone interview.

I told all of these people that I was at work on a novel that included scenes at the 1975 Indianapolis 500, and little else. I never mentioned Hank or Evelyn, or Logos, or Logos' environmentalist leanings, or Logos' struggle with his sexuality. I have no idea how any of the people just named might feel about such characters.

I also did not ask what sentiments they might have expected in Indianapolis in 1975 toward a suspected gay male. I didn't want to risk alienating an interviewee, and felt confident that I didn't have to ask. I'm an old guy. I remember U.S. culture in 1975.

• • •

I felt I could rely more on memory when writing the AIDS-related scenes in the novel. Still, I knew I had to speak to Ed Wolf after watching his interview in the documentary *The Way We Were*. My tape recorder and I spent about an hour with him in his San Francisco home. You might expect a kind and generous character from one who volunteered so extensively on the front lines in the worst years of the crisis, and you would be quite correct if you expected that of Ed.

Much of this novel is set in the fictional Prado Diablo, which could exist in Contra Costa county somewhere east of Orinda and west of Pittsburg. My Marin County stomping grounds were only forty or fifty miles away, but I still wanted to talk to some real life folk who had their feet on Contra Costa soil when Hank and Logos attended high school there. For this, I turned to the Ygnacio Valley High School class of 1969, and interviewed

Dedication and Thanks

JoAnn Hansen, Guy Gettie, Gail Sangenitto, Pam Daly and John Marin at an alumni meeting in Concord. I thought it was exceptionally generous of them to spend so much time with an unknown writer. Thanks to all of you!

I doubt anyone will leave this novel thinking that the eccentric De Mellos were typical Contra Costans of the 1960s and 1970s, but just to be on the safe side, I'll say aloud that a family of eccentrics could be found anywhere: certainly in Marin as easily as in Contra Costa.

Lastly, I must include special thanks for San Francisco attorney Laura Drossman. She was referred to me by California Lawyers for the Arts, and was kind enough to answer many questions for me as this novel neared completion.